Autumn

D1455561

Also by Vina Jackson

Eighty Days Yellow
Eighty Days Blue
Eighty Days Red
Eighty Days Amber
Eighty Days White
Mistress of Night and Dawn

Autumn
The Pleasure Quartet

VINA JACKSON

OPEN ROAD

INTEGRATED MEDIA

NEW YORK

Cover design by Simon & Schuster UK Art Department

978-1-4976-8406-5

Published in 2015 by Open Road Integrated Media, Inc.
345 Hudson Street
New York, NY 10014
www.openroadmedia.com

Autumn

1

The Song of the Missing

I always knew I was different from other women.

An eminent psychiatrist has established there are five stages of grief: denial, anger, bargaining, depression and acceptance.

When Dominik died, I initially experienced none of these.

So, exclude me from the ranks of humanity if you will.

At first, there was only shock. And then all I could do was miss him, miss him and miss him all over again.

Today was Valentine's Day. It was the first time I had left the house in a fortnight, and as I shrugged my way into my winter coat and made my way down to the local High Street to pick up some fresh coffee beans and bread from the Tesco Local down the way from the Everyman cinema, I wondered at what kind of skewed logic had made me choose today of all days to venture out of the comfort of the sprawling

Hampstead home overlooking the Heath that we had shared together for the past three years.

I paused and stared into the window display of a stationery store at racks of cheap and cheerful greeting cards and the fat gold cupid that stood alongside them holding his bow string taut and aiming at a bunch of red balloons that floated overhead. 'Forgotten something, Mr?' was printed in a calligraphic black font onto a white speech bubble protruding from his heavy-lipped mouth.

Dominik would have made a joke of it all, particularly the notion that it might be him who had forgotten any romantic occasion rather than me.

Just two months had passed by since the last day that I had spent with him.

It was the morning before Christmas and we were lying in bed together, side-by-side. Dominik's breath was hot against my ear as he pressed his lips to my earlobe. I held my eyes shut tightly and pretended to be still asleep, although I knew that he knew I was awake. The pattern of my breathing was different when I slept. As was his. The sort of thing that came naturally to lovers and couples.

A sudden current of cool air swept across my back as he lifted the covers and slipped out of the far side of the bed, before turning back again and tucking the duvet up around my shoulders. He smoothed a lock of my hair back from my face as he did so and then he was gone. I stretched out my limbs like a starfish and then curled up into a ball again, as if the smaller I became, the longer I could fight off morning.

Downstairs, I could hear the hum of the coffee machine as it warmed up, and the bang-bang sound of Dominik knocking the filter against the sink to dislodge the used grounds from the previous brew. He was always careful to wash the machine and wipe down all the parts each time he used it. Getting a coffee machine was one of the concessions that he had made when we moved in together. He had always railed against it, complaining that the sleek silver beasts that squatted on bench tops all over North London were bourgeois and a waste of money, when a teaspoon of instant or a cafetiere did the job just as well. But he had quickly succumbed to my ingrained caffeine habit.

The deep, rich scent of freshly ground coffee beans wafted into the room and the door squeaked closed. He padded quietly across to the bed, slid my cup onto the bedside dresser and then crawled across me to his side, careful to hold his weight an inch or two above me. He had slipped on a loose pair of cotton pyjama pants and socks to keep the chill off as he braved the journey across our cold wooden floors to the kitchen, and he struggled to pull them off with one hand as he wriggled back into bed. Now naked again, he pulled me into his arms. He brushed my mess of hair behind the nape of my neck and nipped my earlobe. His lips mapped a trail of kisses along the line of my jaw. I nestled against him and murmured a low moan, a sound of sleepy approval.

His left arm was snaked beneath my throat like a pillow and his right arm hooked over my body. He held my breasts in his open palms and squeezed them gently, as if he was getting to know the shape and weight of them for the very first time. We were like two S's lying next to each other, the full length of his body tracing a path around mine. My back against his torso, our thighs clamped together, the front of his knees locked into the back of mine, the soles of my feet resting on the top of his. If I could choose only one position for us to lie entwined for the rest of our lives, in the same way that people are asked to name one food or piece of music that they would take to a desert island, then this would probably have been it. Dominik often remarked on the uncanny way that we fitted together so well despite the difference in our height. It was as if our bodies had been carved from the same piece of stone.

The soft, silky helmet of his cock began to press against the small of my spine as his erection grew, but I kept my eyes closed. Of course, I wanted him inside me. I always did. But I was not a morning person, and invariably, on this morning like every other, my arousal warred with my desire to keep snoozing as I struggled against the arrival of a new day, still too lazy to move or to caress him. I stirred, made a purring noise in the back of my throat and let him continue to stroke my breasts. I wriggled my hips from side to side, arched my back and pushed my arse against him, burying myself into the V shape that his torso and hips made on the bed. That was the sign that I always gave him, to indicate that I was awake enough for sex. He always seemed to want a sign that I wanted him, no matter how often I told him that he could fuck me even if I was asleep, or at least appeared to be. No matter my state of mind, health or the time of day, I was always in the mood for sex. It was only the type of sex that I was in the mood for that changed, depending on my energy levels and temperament.

His hand dipped down lower and cupped the mound of my mons. By the time he lightly separated my pussy lips with his finger I was moaning softly and I knew that I was wet. He raised his forefinger as if shushing me and ran the moisture that I had left there over my bottom lip so that I could taste the sweet-salt tang of it. Dominik had never stopped insisting how much he loved the taste of me, and he had never stopped trying to prove it, either. His knuckles scraped across my spine as he grasped his cock and began to guide it inside me after all our wriggling had failed to connect us.

The moment that his cock head broke through the tightness of my entrance always made me gasp. Dominik didn't have the biggest cock in the world. His was just on the right side of average. Perfect, for me. It was not his size that made me lose my breath. It was the moment that our physical connection became complete. Maybe I was a simple woman, different in some way from other women. It wasn't that I didn't love all the other caresses that we shared, or that I didn't value the intimacy of cuddling him, spooning him, the touches that we exchanged whenever we were together. But I lived and died for the sensation of his cock sliding inside my cunt, and nothing ever felt as good as the moment of his first stroke. We rocked back and forth like that until he came, and then he cradled my body in his arms until he shrank and slipped out of me.

'Thank you,' I said to him, stretching my arms over my head and reaching for my coffee. I wasn't talking about the drink that he had made for me which was now cold and had developed a thin layer of film that broke apart as I sipped. 'It's my favourite way to wake up.'

'I know it is,' he replied, with an infuriating, knowing smile spread across his face. Then it had bugged me, how he knew me so well already. I liked to imagine that I was a closed book. An enigma. A contrary mess of psychological intricacies where the bad me and the mad me hid behind a clever veil of contradictions. But I was none of that to Dominik. From the very first time we had met on that day in St Katherine Docks after he had contacted me following the brawl on the tube when my old violin had been damaged, he had intuitively learned how to press my most secret buttons and bring out the best and worst of me. He had immediately mastered the mixed-up mess that made me who I was. But none of that mattered to Dominik. The way he looked at me made me feel as though I was transparent.

We had that exact conversation after every time we had morning sex. It was one of our rituals. I hadn't realised until he was gone how many rituals we had together. How deeply entwined in the fabric of my life he was. I didn't have a life without Dominik. He was my life. All of the little moments like that, they were my life.

Why had I ever imagined that anything else mattered?

I'd agreed to be involved later that afternoon in a small charity event at a church in nearby Highgate. Lauralynn's string quartet was also performing, and I would be joining them for a single section, one of Paganini's '24 Caprices'. I often played the short Paganini pieces as part of my practice exercises, having been thoroughly schooled in them during the course of my turbulent teens by my music teacher, Mr Van der Vliet, back in New Zealand. They were all technically awkward to master, but then that was the point and we had all rushed through a quick rehearsal the previous weekend.

Dominik and I had both kept the morning free for some last minute shopping. This was the first year that I would be cooking for him on Christmas Day, as on previous occasions we had always eaten out as we'd been travelling. We had revisited New Orleans where after a late dinner at Tujague's, off Jackson Square, Dominik had endeavoured to find the secret club where under his instructions I had once danced nude in full public view, still under the spell of the strange primal ties that had brought us together and the influence of the dazzling Russian dancer we watched performing. However, the local where the club had been was now closed, and no one knew where it had moved to. Much later during the course of our sometimes tempestuous relationship he had flown me to Reykjavik, where we had hired an SUV and hunted the Northern Lights over the eerie darkness of the black lava plain by a deserted glacier on the stroke of midnight and his kiss had melted away the sub-zero cold from my lips and inflamed my heart.

The turkey we had ordered online had been delivered two days before and had now defrosted. Following a recipe book we'd been obliged to buy, as despite the fact that the house was a refuge for thousands of books, none of them pertained to food, I'd prepared a herby stuffing and squeezed it down the bird's cavity and, dutifully basting it with sugar and further spices, had fitted the succulent animal, just, into the oven where it was now roasting away. It was enormous and I was more nervous at the prospect of cooking it correctly than tackling any new piece of music or confronting one of Dominik's now occasional, but always welcome, sexual kinks.

'It's huge,' I said. 'And with my luck, will likely end up either dry or raw.' I was dizzy with apprehension. 'We'll have food left over for weeks ...'

All Dominik did was smile back at me and remain silent. His eyes glittered and a sheen of mischief trailed across the pattern of his lips.

He walked down the store's central aisle, picking up a bottle there and random boxes of chocolates and premium biscuits, examining them closely before settling on a choice.

We had friends and acquaintances invited for drinks on Boxing Day and we'd decided to get them some post-Xmas gifts to celebrate the occasion.

It all felt curiously domestic.

Which is when I realised that I hadn't prepped the vegetables. I had planned to do so straight after breakfast, but the dreamy state of our lovemaking had left me aimless and disoriented, despite the fact that we had cut our morning sex session short so we could get the day started. On occasions where we both had time, after spooning led to sleepy sideways sex, he would tip me onto my back, kiss a path between my breasts and down my torso to my mound and then lap at my clitoris until I came. Pleasuring me like this aroused him so much that he was inevitably hard again when he raised his head proudly and began to crawl up my body to kiss me, and that usually led to more sex. It had become a routine, one of a whole palate of sexual regularities that was now a sequence

I knew by heart, but it never felt rote. More like learning a string of musical notes – no matter how many times I played a song I loved, I never grew tired of hearing the same notes in the same order.

'Damn,' I said. 'I didn't put the potatoes on. And I have to play at the recital soon ...' I told him. 'I'd better get back home.'

He looked up at me, his dark eyes catching the reflection of the shop's elongated neon lighting strips.

'No problem. I'll keep on doing the shops. Maybe find a surprise for you? You go, and I'll be home in an hour or so.'

I pointed out that I would just have time to ready the vegetables and pick up my instrument and travel to Highgate for the charity do, so there was no need for him to hurry. The oven was on a timer, and I would be back in late afternoon with leisure enough to get everything ready for the dinner we had planned.

I walked away with a perfunctory wave.

I didn't even think of kissing him.

Fuck.

The aromatic smell of the turkey roasting slowly in the oven reached me as I opened the front door and made my mouth water. Maybe I would turn out to be a cook after all! I quickly washed, peeled and cut the vegetables and wrapped them in foil. They would go in the oven when I returned. I rushed up to the study, hesitated a brief moment as to which of my violins I would play today and settled on the Bailly. It was an instinctive, irrational decision, seeing I hadn't played or practised with it much recently.

I pulled a delicate, lightweight silk dress from the wardrobe, short-sleeved, smooth to the touch, just one from my arsenal of little black dresses for public functions and performances. Almost a uniform. Checked it for stains and slipped it on, then foraged in the drawers for a pair of tights and matching black shoes and ran out of the house, grasping my heavy winter coat under my arms next to the violin case as I entered the right combination on the bicycle lock and pedalled off up the hill towards Jack Straw's Castle where I would take the Spaniards Inn road towards Highgate past Kenwood House.

I arrived at the church 15 minutes later, just as a black cab was drawing up outside and Lauralynn stepped out from it, seemingly taller than ever in a sleek grey tailored pinstriped suit, pulling her battered cello case from the carriage onto the pavement before paying the driver.

'How quaint,' she remarked, as she watched me seeking a railing which I could attach the bike to.

'The advantages of playing a somewhat lighter instrument,' I replied, winking at her. Despite her past relationship with Dominik, we had become the best of friends since I had begun living with him again in earnest.

The other members of Lauralynn's ensemble were already

waiting for us inside, and the elderly charity organiser running the show effusively greeted us as we joined them in the narrow gift shop which had been transformed into a rudimentary green room for the performers. The quartet were playing an improvisation on a theme by Philip Glass before my turn came, and I sat down in a rickety chair, with the door open to the nave, so I could listen to them playing in the area that had been cleared for the musicians close to the lectern. The jug of coffee prepared for us was weak and insipid, and a single sip was enough for me and I switched to tap water. The dark, sensuous tone of Lauralynn's cello skirted around the repetitive melody like a bird in flight, domineering, regal, elegant, masculine in its forcefulness. Her fellow players were highly competent and professional but to me it felt like she was leading them through a merry gavotte, the comforting warmth of her strings gliding across the music like a lion set loose in a jungle of church-like resonance and occasional coughs from the invisible audience.

There was a smatter of applause and I grabbed hold of my trusty Bailly and stepped into the nave, after the organiser had announced me.

The audience was a blur of pastel-coloured coats, sweaters and scarves, a jumble of faces. I never truly saw the spectators attentively watching me when I played. From the moment the violin settled on my shoulder and I raised my bow, all my normal senses automatically switched off and I was in a world of my own.

Alone in my body, living for the cascade of notes, the waves of exquisite sound I invoked from my instrument, the pizzicati I plucked out of the silence and ordered into a pattern of beauty.

It was, as ever, as if the whole world retreated into the distance and I was alone with my emotions, my soul burning with a gentle fire which spread through my body as the tempo increased and I became a servant of the instrument and no longer its player, its mistress.

The music turned the blood in my veins into arrows of light and pleasure. I tingled, from head to toe, a creature of the senses, wanton, liberated, alive again. The nearest I could come to expressing my emotions fully, just like in the throes of sex and its dark and sometimes contradictory desires when I craved, yearned, begged to become whore, victim, conqueror, lover and all those dangerous undercurrents that were the foundations of my soul that only Dominik had managed to tame. Even when they lay dormant, I knew they were lurking around the corner of my mind, diseased, predatory, waiting for any sign of weakness on my part.

Ahhhh ... the music and Dominik: the harbours of my sanity.

When I had walked into the nave, it had felt chilly. Now

an unseen warmth caressed me, all over, as the leather of the violin's chin guard softly rubbed against my skin to the rhythm of the Paganini melody and my eyes closed and I allowed myself to wander and get lost inside the meandering and labyrinthine folds of the song until it felt as if it was playing me and not the other way around.

My mind drifted.

Tonight, I decided as I unleashed another waterfall of quicksilver notes, I would ask Dominik to take me hard. I wanted to scream, cry out, to find my core again in sweat and tears.

I wanted this Christmas to be different.

How little I knew.

I awoke from my trance. The grey faces in the audience were applauding politely, some watching me with concern, sensing how unsteady I was on my feet, the echo of the Caprice still floating through the nave. I turned round and saw Lauralynn sitting there, with a wry smile on her face as if she could read my mind like a book, clapping along with the crowd and the other musicians. She rose to her feet, leaving her large cello leaning against her chair and gave me a peck on the cheek.

'That was ... hot, darling,' she whispered in my ear. 'Good girl.'

There was such a look of complicity on her face that I felt naked and almost blushed.

'It's a piece I often practise,' I defended myself. A lie.

Her lips twisted, unbelieving and her eyes sparkled. I acknowledged the public's applause, retreated to the green room and seized my overcoat and walked out of the small church as Lauralynn's ensemble began playing Schubert's String Quartet in G Major, not my favourite piece of music by a long stretch. I knew she wouldn't be offended by my sudden departure.

I liberated my bike from the railing. Glanced at my watch.

Dominik would be home by now.

We could fuck.

For all I cared, the damn turkey waiting for us in the oven could roast a little longer. It would keep the salmonella at bay . . .

A late afternoon cold was falling.

I turned the key in the lock, half-opened the door and a fragrant wave of warm and reassuring cooking aromas swept over me. There was music coming from the study where Dominik worked. He always wrote accompanied by the sound of rock music playing loud. I set my violin case down by the door and was careful not to slam it shut and alert Dominik to my presence. I hurriedly checked the kitchen oven and moved the vegetables I had prepared earlier onto one of its lower shelves, below the now darkly-braised turkey, and changed the setting, still faithfully following the instructions from the cookery book I had acquired a few weeks earlier.

I tiptoed up the stairs to our bedroom, slipped out of my coat, unzipped the little black dress and stepped out of it, treading on stockinged feet to the wardrobe to hang it up and pondering what I should now wear.

Echoes of the music Dominik was playing as he typed resonated from the floor below. I recognised a Lana Del Rey song and all its lush orchestration. The record came to an end and I stood there uncertain as to the outfit I should present myself to him in, torn between thoughts of simplicity and ostentatious excess, a familiar fever dream spreading through my veins as memories of games and embraces past swirled through my mind. I waited for a while for the next album to start so that I might perhaps select something that would effectively accompany the music, materials, colours, looseness or tightness that would prove perfectly complementary to the tune he would choose to spur on his imagination. He'd been working on a new novel for some time now but the details he had been willing to provide me about it were still sparse.

I waited.

The thin grey pencil skirt that emphasised my small waist, with a white cotton blouse, if he chose Arcade Fire?

The pleated trouser suit, if he opted for country music?

I stood facing the wardrobe mirror, standing in my underwear, matching Victoria's Secret opaque panties and bra, with just the right balance of sexiness and propriety, and a pair of open crotched tights.

Still no music.

Possibly he was deeply absorbed in the section he was writing and didn't wish to be distracted by having to hunt for the right music to play next?

Or maybe I should walk into his study just naked?

No, I concluded. Nudity had its codes, its rituals. Sometimes it even became a uniform. Something I had learned from experience with both Dominik and other men.

The silence spreading across the house was beginning to puzzle me. So unlike him.

I took a final glance at myself in the mirror. I looked nothing like a lingerie model. Let alone a porn star. My hair was a tangled mess of red uneven curls falling down to my shoulders, my breasts were far from voluptuous, my painted lips a comic parody of come hither-ness and my skin was deathly pale.

But I knew this was also the way Dominik liked me.

I stepped back.

Horny woman in underwear. It would have to do.

I slowly made my way down the stairs.

At the study door, I couldn't hear any sound of typing. Nor any movement inside.

I knocked. Not that Dominik ever appeared annoyed when I interrupted his writing.

There was no answer.

I reckoned he hadn't heard me, lost in the pathways of his writing imagination. As I was so often when I allowed the music to take me over.

My hand reached for the doorknob.

Turned it.

I pushed the door open with my toes.

The room was in part darkness, just illuminated by the standing lamp by the desktop computer. The deep black leather chair in which he sat faced the screen and I could see the tip of his head. He was motionless.

'Dominik? Do you mind if . . .'

There was an uncanny stillness in the air.

Hesitantly I walked towards the desk.

Dominik still didn't move.

My mouth felt dry.

I reached the chair.

He was still wearing the same clothes from when we had shopped a few hours earlier.

He sat immobile in his chair, facing the shining screen. Seemingly lost in thought.

My eyes were absurdly drawn to the flickering cursor left abandoned there in the middle of a word *penumb* . . .

It would have been penumbra, I knew. A wave of guilt rushed across my mind, as if I had been found spying on him, his thoughts. Betraying his confidence. Cheating. Reading his words before they were ready for public or private consumption.

My movement at his side did not catch his attention.

I looked down.

He was pale as chalk, his features frozen into a mask of indifference.

I knew in an instant he was dead.

I remained calm even if inside of me a storm was brewing, frantic, confused, waves of despair and fear grappling in close combat. I clenched my fists and tried to remember the little I had learned about mouth to mouth techniques at school in New Zealand, although a voice deep inside kept on telling me it would prove useless.

It was useless.

There was no magic in my breath, and unlike in a bad movie he didn't come to with a spluttering cough and a look of surprise.

I didn't cry.

I called for emergency services.

A heart attack they said later. Sudden and destructive. There was nothing I could have done, I was told, even if I had been present.

But I knew I should have been there. At least held his hand, whispered final words in his ears, lullaby him away on that dreadful journey. Said something he would have heard, words to cushion his passing. Something.

'Just one of those things,' they said.

I knew Dominik's father had died of a heart attack, but had put that down to simple old age, and Dominik was still young. There had never been a sign of anything wrong with his health, at any rate in my presence. He still jogged around the Heath regularly and used some home gym equipment which he said kept him alert and able to concentrate on the screen for long periods of time, but I always suspected was down to a vanity he was unwilling to admit to.

The ambulance came. In a daze I opened the door to the green-and-yellow-suited paramedics. They went through the motions, nodded sympathetically. But it made no difference.

They took the body away and left me with a sheaf of papers I would have to fill in. Forms. Questions. Only then did I realise I had stood with them all that time in my under-wear, the way I had been dressed or rather undressed when I had walked down to Dominik's study. Not one of the ambulance staff had thought to bring it to my attention while they went about their business. Not even the older woman who appeared to be the vehicle's driver. I didn't care. So many strangers had seen my body that it no longer made any difference.

The ambulance drove away. To the Royal Free Hospital down the hill? To a morgue somewhere? A warehouse where the bodies of the dead were kept in cold storage until all the formalities were completed? I had no idea. The only thing I had asked them before they left was whether a post-mortem would be necessary in the circumstances and was told it was highly unlikely. It was a clear open and closed heart attack case.

Right then, I couldn't face the possibility of Dominik being cut open somehow.

Then realised with a shock that I didn't even know whether he would have wished to be buried or cremated. It was something we had never even thought of discussing.

I took my tights and bra off and went to bed in my Victoria's Secret panties. I wanted to cry but the tears just wouldn't come. I slept a long time.

Two days later, there was a call for me to visit the hospital with the completed paperwork and I was asked whether I wished to pick up the clothes he had been wearing at the time of his death and in which he had been carried away.

Shocked by the request, I choked, unable to provide an answer.

I was hanging up the coat that he had last worn and left folded over a stool in the kitchen when I came across the envelope, tucked into the inside pocket. It was addressed to me in Dominik's elegant script.

For Summer on a Winter's Day, I read.

An anxious spasm tore through my stomach as I

unceremoniously ripped the envelope open, hoping for lost words from beyond the one-way mirror behind which Dominik now rested.

There were none. Just a rough map.

At first it made no sense. It was rudimentary and stylised, like a child's sketch of a desert island, with a large X marking the location of a lost treasure. I turned the page around and some features became familiar.

I paused for breath.

Suddenly realising where all the thin string of little arrows led and the message the map conveyed.

When had Dominik drawn it?

When had he intended to let me come across it?

On January 1st, I guessed. He'd always had a pronounced sense of ritual, which sometimes bordered on the melodramatic albeit in an intensely romantic way. Was this some scheme to lead me like a fairy tale heroine towards a post-Christmas present?

Where had he planned to leave the envelope?

On the low bedside table on my side of the bed, where I would have found it on awakening while still fighting back the reefs of sleep, and Dominik had conveniently left the house so as not to spoil the surprise.

I grabbed the sheet of paper, and ran downstairs. Here I tightened my running trainers' laces and slipping on an old scuffed leather jacket I hadn't worn in ages walked out of the house. The snow that had fallen a few days earlier had mostly melted away, just small hillocks and clumps now, like muddy collars, circling the base of the trees that lined the other side of the road by the Heath.

The steep descent into the Vale of Health was just a hundred yards away from our house and the first tall tree below it was a peculiar shape and stood at an uncommon angle. I remembered Dominik once pointing it out to me.

And it clearly was marked on his crude map, next to a sketch of what appeared to be a guitar pick. An image indelibly carved into the back of my mind. I crossed the road, bent down by the tree's trunk and, gloveless, dug into the thin layer of snow and dirt with my fingers, closing my eyes and relying on my sense of touch explored the crumbling pocket of broken ice and disturbed soil until I found it.

A guitar pick.

I knew where the trail would lead.

From the last time a similar trail had been created.

By me. For Dominik.

As an affirmation.

I hurried down the hill. I knew that in my rush I was missing out on a score of further cheap guitar picks outlining the route, but I had no doubt in my mind where they would lead.

I pulled up the jacket's collar as an arctic breeze enveloped me when I walked out into the open space of the Heath, near the car park and continued down the dirt road by the ponds.

Then across the bridge and a narrower path to the left that led into a wooded part of high trees.

I could have made this journey with my eyes blindfolded.

And I involuntarily shuddered at the thought of the actual blindfold.

That first time in the crypt when I had played for him . . .

My breath was fogging as I quickened my pace and, finally, reached the clearing.

The hill of grass that led towards the metal bandstand.

I was panting by the time I reached the large gazebo.

Checked against the map he had left for me.

N for North. S for South and so on . . .

Got my bearings.

The large X dominating the sketchy map indicated the northern angle of the bandstand.

Once again I fell to my knees, and broke the thin layer of ice that covered the ground. My fingers could no longer feel the cold. I burrowed. My heart on hold.

Felt something hard. Dug around it. Took hold of the object between four fingers and pulled it out.

It was a small box.

Within the box was another box. Not an ordinary cardboard sort, like the outer layer, designed to protect the contents from the elements but a minuscule trunk, about two inches thick, square, and half the size of my palm, with tiny gold hinges at the back. It was covered with a fine layer of deep-blue velvet that was silky to the touch.

I clasped it tightly in my hand and sucked in a mouthful of cold air that burned my lungs. I had been holding my breath. My heart beat rapidly in my chest.

Oh, Dominik, what have you done? Surely not an engagement ring. We were both of the view that marriage was for other people, not for us. And maybe it was something of a resolutely old-fashioned pretension, this idea that we didn't need the trappings of tradition to bring us closer together. Neither of us had ever wanted children, either, so the legal and other benefits were not so important.

My knees began to ache on the cold ground. I pushed myself to my feet and brushed my hands off on my jeans.

No, I thought. Dominik would never buy me an engagement ring. He had far too much imagination and an ingrained taste for the unconventional for that.

My mouth turned up in a smile as memories of other creative and daring situations he had previously surprised me with flooded across my mind. Once, as I stood in front of him nude and about to play the final solo from Max Bruch's violin concerto he had asked for my lipstick and then used it to paint both my nipples and cunt lips a deep, vivid shade of red. I would never forget the feeling of shock, when I realised what he was planning, and the sensation of the cosmetic on my skin, waxy and arousing as he painted me. His lover, his whore.

I didn't count to ten, or take a deep breath. I just flipped the lid open. And there, resting on a bed of black silk lining was a delicate gold bracelet, so thin that it seemed as though it would break with the slightest force. I picked it up gently and studied it as it lay on my palm. It felt sturdier in my hand than it looked. Rather than a regular clasp, the closing mechanism was a tiny padlock – not even half the size of my pinky fingernail – that snapped over a loop with a gentle press and twist motion.

It fitted around my slim wrist as perfectly as if Dominik had taken a measurement while I slept. He did not have the option of checking my size against other similar items in my wardrobe as I did not own a watch and rarely wore jewellery.

Despite having been out in the cold for no doubt many days, the metal was not cool to touch. The gold had a warmth to it that I knew would suit the red of my hair and pale skin.

I only wished that it had been Dominik's hand securing it to my wrist and not my own.

Which made me think.

It was obvious to me what he meant by the padlock. He had never really approved of BDSM-style collars – thought them too obvious, and although he never said as much, I knew instinctively he would have felt that such an accessory would have added a pantomime rather than erotic element to our relationship.

So, this was another compromise. I would have dearly liked to wear Dominik's collar, but it just wasn't his style.

Even if the padlock's symbolism was obvious, it wasn't like him to not leave a note or a card, in place of any words he might have spoken in person. The written word was Dominik's expressive medium of choice. He often left little notes for me around the house. Sometimes just to say that he had popped out to run an errand and when he expected to be home, and sometimes with instructions of what he wanted me to be wearing or doing when he arrived back.

I picked up the box again and studied it more closely. There it was, tucked inside the protective case that I had nearly discarded. A sheet of white notepaper, folded in half and then again. Thicker than computer paper and sharp at the edges. It was a bright night, and light enough that I could still read the black font.

Dearest Summer,

A bracelet, and not a collar – because I only ever hope to own a part of you. That part I will keep locked in my heart forever. The rest, my dear, is yours. As I will always be.

Your Dominik.

I thrust the note and the bracelet's case into my jacket pocket and began to run, tripping and sliding on the Heath's soft earth as I negotiated my way over roots and stones too quickly in the fading light, wishing with every particle of my being that I could somehow summon him back so that he would be there when I returned home, triumphant, having solved all the clues in the puzzle he had set me.

But when I pushed open the door and walked inside there was nothing but empty rooms and the sound of my own breathing, still ragged.

I missed him. I missed his presence. I missed the rich timbre of his voice and the habit he had of calling me for no particular reason, even though he knew that I hated phone calls. I missed the sound of his fingers tapping on the keyboard late at night that sometimes kept me awake or permeated my dreams. I missed the way that we laughed about it. How I sat across the breakfast table from him on nights where he had been possessed with inspiration or was simply too terrified by the spectre of a deadline that he refused to come to bed and we would both be haggard, him from sleep deprivation and me from the strange visions that his keyboard created in my brain as I slept to images of tap dancers beating out a rhythm on a stage or the pitter patter of raindrops on a tin roof. He would forcibly argue that I couldn't possibly hear him from all the way up the stairs and I would jokingly say that, in the same way other couples were joined at the hip, we were joined at the brain.

I missed the woody, masculine smell of him that was never cologne or soap or hair gel, just Dominik. I missed the way that one corner of his mouth always lifted slightly higher than the other when he smiled. I missed the arrow that his hip bones made, pointing to his groin, and the way that he complained about his 'middle age spread' which left me with barely even an inch of fat to grab from his perpetually flat stomach. I missed the light dusting of hair on his chest and I missed lying half on top of him on the couch and running my fingers through it on the rare nights that we watched television together, catching up on past episodes of endless series or DVDs or just the world news.

I even missed the things he did that annoyed me. His occasional snore. The way he hung used towels from the bathroom doorknob instead of the rail so they were sure to always fall on the floor. How he refused to eat grapes unless they were seedless. His habit of following me around the house, switching off the lights that I had left on and tutting even though I knew all too well how much he was blissfully indifferent to environmental issues or money matters. The endless spoonfuls of sugar that he stirred into his coffee. The look on his face when I teased him about how much I wanted a cat, knowing how much he hated even the thought of us owning a pet.

Most of all though, I missed the familiar hard warmth of his body in the bed next to me when I awoke each morning and evoked all the ways he would make love to me and how I had opened myself to him and his desires like no other man before him. Nor could I imagine making love to any other man after him, though God knows I was aroused enough and had known many before we had finally come together after the heartbreak of our initial on and off relationship.

My grief took the form of desire, and my desire for Dominik was an ever-present longing. A white heat that filled every fibre of my being until I felt as though it might consume me like a flame that would keep on burning, ceaselessly.

Every day now, I relived waking up with him for the last time. Sometimes I imagined our last morning exactly as it was. Other times I pictured how it would have been if I had known it was the last time I would wake up with him. All the things that I would say. How I would tell him that I loved him and that he meant everything to me, and how I wouldn't care if he teased me for being soppy. Oh, how I longed for him to tease me. I imagined turning towards him as soon as I felt his hand caress my hair and how I would touch him back. I thought about how I would press my lips against his skin and trail a path of kisses down to his groin. How I would take his cock in my mouth and worship him. Run the blade of my tongue up his shaft and over and around every groove and crevice until I tasted him on my tongue.

When I lay awake at night restless and unable to sleep I

would summon him to my mind. The precise firmness of his touch, the press of his lips against mine. The way that he would act playful and provocative until I was ready to erupt and then pull away and laugh as though watching my rising desperation was the funniest thing in the world. I could even recall the way the pads of his fingertips felt trailing over my skin. The pattern of his fingerprints was etched into my memory like a map of pathways that I roamed like a lost soul in my dreams. I knew every single groove, every valley, every dip and every curve in his flesh. The broken byways of his lifeline.

Sometimes I felt as though I didn't exist at all any longer. I never had. I had been nothing before Dominik. The lodestone that had ever so briefly kept me grounded was gone. And the emptiness had returned.

2

Dance Macabre

Thinking of Dominik occupied the jagged jigsaw of my dreams and the deserts of my days.

At night, I wore my grief like a shroud. As if I had been enveloped by a heavy cloak and the tighter I wrapped myself in it, the closer I felt to him.

During my waking moments though, I got on with the business of death.

The funeral came and went, and my sister Fran and old friend Chris stayed for a short time, though they were no longer dating. I had never managed to quite put aside the feeling that neither of them had ever really completely understood or approved of the relationship between Dominik and me. So despite the fact that my heart felt as though it had been roughly torn into pieces, I somehow managed to locate the kink equipment that Dominik kept secreted away in various parts of the house, to make sure that neither of them accidentally stumbled upon a length of bondage rope or a flogger.

There wasn't much of it. He had never really been one for all the trappings of kink. Handcuffs and paddles were not Dominik's style. It was our natures that had each warred and surrendered to the other in the bedroom, and we had never needed any implements for that. He had collected a few things, either out of curiosity, a desire to treat, tease or torment me, or simply to sample new sensations, particularly when it was all so new to me and like a kid in a candy shop, I had wanted to try everything from candle wax to electro torture.

When my guests arrived I had hastily stuffed all of the things that I didn't want prying eyes to see into the deep, solid and lockable drawers in the low cabinet that functioned as a side table by our front door and then hidden the key. Then, until they had left again, I had behaved how I thought I ought to behave. How they expected me to behave.

With my face frozen into the rictus of a grieving widow I lay on the couch and let them bring me mugs of hot tea and answer the doorbell and call our utility providers and the car insurance company, pretending to be me and changing all of the accounts into my name.

Amending the insurance turned out to be impossible. 'We need to speak to the policy holder,' I overheard a loud, singsong voice saying at the other end of the line. 'You don't understand,' Fran hissed back. '*He's dead.*'

Letters addressed to Dominik continued to slip through the mail slot and land on the floor by the door just as gently as all the others, no matter how heavily the shock of seeing his name in print weighed on my heart. The paperwork of death was seemingly endless, and of all the banal ways that a person could linger on, junk mail and electricity bills were the worst.

At first, I only wore the bracelet with its tiny padlock charm that he had hidden at the bandstand when I was alone, though most nights I slept with it clutched in my hand. I wasn't ashamed of what it represented, or of publicly marking myself as Dominik's submissive. It just felt too personal and too perfect to share, or to sully with the ordinariness of everyday life.

In time, as soon as all my friends, family and various well-wishers gradually disappeared, I got up off the couch and drowned myself in activity.

The public Summer and the private Summer. It came so naturally to me, the dichotomy of my two sides. And the contrast made me realise how terribly lonely I had become without Dominik. He had been the only person I had fully shown my whole self to, complete with all of my flaws, strange yearnings, and mixed-up emotions.

For the first time since the day of his death, I walked in

to his study and contemplated the darkness of his computer screen, the uneven piles of papers, reference books and folders laid out across the desk. Noticed the faint red light on the face of his music player; it had been on all this time and I'd forgotten to switch it off.

There had been a request from his editor to ascertain how far Dominik had made progress with his new book. He'd always made it a rule not to discuss works in progress and I had no idea if the novel had gone as far as a first draft even.

I tried to make sense of which layer of print-outs actually formed part of this project I knew nothing about and distinguish between random notes, past drafts of academic lectures, household bills, statements and handwritten jottings, but it was useless.

Instead, I waved the mouse, watched the screen jump to life and ordered a house moving kit from Argos to be delivered that afternoon. Dominik would have railed against my impulsiveness, spending money on an expensive courier service when I could easily have waited a few days for free standard delivery. But right then, I couldn't face leaving the house.

The blue-uniformed delivery driver arrived two hours later, dwarfed by the large cardboard box he was carrying that contained a further nine boxes, packing tape and a marker pen set. I signed for the items wordlessly, shut the door and began fitting the boxes together and disposing of the remnants of Dominik's life.

My memories of Dominik were like pearls clutched tightly in my fists. I knew that the more time passed by, the more they would turn to smoke, blur at the edges and begin to drift away. But, right then, I was not particularly sentimental about his possessions. The whole house could have burned to the ground for all I could have cared. All of it was nothing without him.

I began with the easy stuff. The dress shoes and ties and cuff links, the things that he didn't wear unless an occasion demanded it so they didn't seem a part of him. In fact, I could imagine him grinning as he saw the evidence of business conferences, networking events and the odd acquaintance's wedding vanishing into the anonymous depths of brown cardboard containers and sealed with duct tape.

My flurry of activity came to an abrupt halt though, once I had rid the cupboards of meaningless items and came to the things that actually meant something to him, or that he used day-to-day. The things that still held his scent. Warm and masculine and comforting. He had worn so much black. Black jeans, black smart trousers, black cashmere sweaters, black scarves, black leather gloves. Dominik's living clothes were clothes for a corpse and so I left them in his wardrobe.

I moved to the items on our hallway shelves, planning to rearrange his books and put at least some of them into storage. He was a collector, and by the end, the sheer number of volumes that he had accrued had become quite unmanageable. We had even discussed building a loft to accommodate his ever-growing collection, since it was a hobby that I knew he would never abandon, and so much a part of him that I couldn't bring myself to try to change it, even if that had been possible (and I had always known that it hadn't).

I opened a volume at random, held it to my face and inhaled deeply. The peculiar smell of old books hit me like a punch to the gut. It was the very same scent that had assaulted my senses the first time that I had ever come to this house, and it reminded me so much of Dominik that if I closed my eyes and kept breathing in, his ghost appeared alongside me in such vivid, three-dimensional detail that he might have been really there.

One by one I pulled them out and tossed them from the shelves; pulp fiction thrillers and novels of the weird, cheap paperback detective stories and penny dreadfuls often with busty blondes on the covers and slogans like 'he took one look, and vowed to possess her'. There were heavy, gilt-edged, hardbacked literary tomes, thick fantasy novels, glossy photography collections and an uncommonly large section of books featuring antique maps, lightweight and loose-leafed poetry magazines and ponderous biographies of writers, explorers and musicians. One by one they fell to the floor with a thud or a flutter until I was surrounded, and then I dropped to my knees with them, curled up into a ball and began to sob.

'Who were you, Dominik?' I wanted to scream. Aside from the occasional magazine or thriller hurriedly purchased to pass time spent on aeroplanes and in airport lounges or hotel rooms when I was travelling, I barely ever read. Why had he surrounded himself with all of these other imaginary worlds? I knew that he kept them in some kind of order. But I had no idea what it was. Suddenly it seemed like the most important thing in the world, the way that he had kept his books. Why had I never asked him?

They were the first real tears that I had shed since his death, and they came thick and fast until I had no more tears to cry. Wrung out and exhausted, I laid my head down, pressed my cheek against the pages of a paperback, and drifted into a fitful slumber.

I had begun sleeping in different rooms of the house, or wherever I happened to be when I drifted off. Only ever once in Dominik's study, on the bed that he had lifted me onto the first time that we made love here, after I had performed for him, nude and alone in the isolated crypt where he had been so aroused by my music that he had first taken me against a stone wall before taking me home. My memories of his study had always been an equal measure of lust and homeliness. It wasn't just the room that we had first really made love in, it was the room that I most associated with Dominik, the room where he spent so many late and lonely nights typing the words that meant so much to him, the room that I instinctively felt was so much his territory. But now it was also the room in which he had died and I could not bear to be in it. The rest of the house just felt empty without him. But his study felt more than empty. It felt as though he had left a black hole behind him, a vast cavern of absence so great that if I stood near it too long I might be sucked inside.

My dreams were infrequent but acute in their pain. I wanted to say that I slept like the dead, but, even within the solitude of my own mind, that expression now made me wince. I slept as though stupefied, far more hours than any normal human needed and that despite all the coffee I drank and without any help from whale noises, pan pipes or narcotic sleeping aids. When I did dream, my dreams were either violent or fantastical, but always, I dreamed of Dominik. Of his hands around my throat as he rode me hard, or around my wrists as he pinned me down. Even the way that, in the depths of our hardest lovemaking sessions he would sometimes make me gag or spit in my face as I kneeled in front of him and tried my damnedest to swallow him right to the base of his cock. During the day, I recalled his gentle affection, the warmth of his body as we lay together and spooned, or the way that his hand fitted into mine as we walked. But at night, it was inevitably Dominik's dark side that fuelled my imagination, emphasising how much that part of him had proven indispensable to me.

I was roused by a faint noise outside. It was both cold and dark, as I had fallen asleep with the lighting and heating switched off. I opened the front door and peered out. The brisk, late evening air cut against my tear-stained, swollen face, as refreshing as a splash of cold water. A large wicker basket with tea towels draped over the top of the handle lay on the doorstep. Gingerly, I lifted back the cover. It contained muffins, and a still-warm bread and butter pudding. '*Thank god it's not a baby,*' I thought to myself, almost sniggering, as I lifted the basket and carried it into the kitchen, picking my way carefully over the books I had earlier scattered. I put the glass dish with the pudding in it on the bench next to the sink, where it would sit until the custard congealed and the crusts began to wilt and wither away from the dish, and then went back to the hall and returned all of the books to the shelves.

Immediately after Dominik's death I had been overwhelmed by flowers and cards, hot soup and casseroles with caramel-coloured breadcrumb crusts that Chris and my sister had either eaten, thrown away or neatly separated into single portions, labelled and placed into the freezer, where they still sat uneaten. Now the gifts were fewer and further between, but they still arrived, and I just left them in the kitchen, sometimes nibbling on the crusts of muffins or edges of biscuits as I drank another cup of coffee.

It wasn't that I didn't appreciate these small gestures of kindness. I knew that people were trying to show that they cared. They didn't know what to say to me, so instead they baked. But I could barely taste food in those first few weeks and I certainly couldn't be bothered to chew it. Mouthfuls of anything solid just lodged in my throat. I lived off caffeine and bags of sweets. I wasn't trying to starve myself. Food just didn't seem important. The effort of lifting my hand to my mouth was too much trouble.

Physical hunger came in fits and starts, like my bursts of cleaning. One morning I had spied a bag of bagels in the pantry, the sort that Dominik and I often ate on the weekend smeared with cream cheese and sometimes a little jam. They were stale, but not mouldy. There was still a pot of Philadelphia, unopened and just within its use by date hiding at the back of the fridge. I toasted a bagel, spread it thick with cheese, and gulped it down so quickly I barely tasted anything and burned my tongue on the hot crust and dough. I fixed another and ate that too. Then I opened the cupboard door and grabbed all the spreads that I could find. Dominik's favourite brand of plum jam, my jar of chocolate spread, the peanut butter. I didn't bother to toast the next. Just tore off hunks of bagel that I then dunked into a jar of something and pushed into my mouth. I did the same with the next, and the next, until suddenly I realised that I was standing in front of the toaster with an empty bag clutched in one hand, and one remaining bite of bread in the other. My tongue felt dry and my stomach distended. I threw the last chunk into the bin, rinsed my mouth and lay down on the couch with my arms wrapped around my belly until I fell asleep. When I woke, I was still full, and the day was gone. I pushed myself up, climbed the stairs to the bedroom, crawled on top of the bed and promptly fell asleep again.

Weeks passed like this. I knew that I was a wreck, inside and out. I didn't care. I only fully dressed when I went out, which wasn't often, and even then I just pulled on whatever clothing was nearest, tucked my hair into a tangled bun and didn't bother with make-up. Around the house I wore an old robe or a T-shirt and underwear, whatever was handy.

Sometimes I didn't bathe for days and other times I turned the tap up as hot as it would go, slid down the shower wall to the floor and let the water rain down on me until it turned cold.

And then, the morning of Valentine's Day, I woke up at an ordinary hour and out of nowhere, had a hankering for breakfast. Not sweets or bagels but a proper breakfast, the sort that I used to regularly eat at home in New Zealand. Eggs Benedict, perfectly poached so the yolks were still runny on the inside, served on sourdough bread with a glass of chilled pulpy orange juice and a flat white coffee. I showered, dressed, nipped down to the nearest small supermarket to pick up supplies and then set about preparing the first real meal that I'd eaten in the better part of two months.

Inspired by my early morning industry, I then resolved to pack away the last of Dominik's things, besides his books, which I had decided to keep on the shelves indefinitely.

Lauralynn arrived just as I was getting started.

'God, he had awful taste, didn't he? I tried to change him, you know.'

A bejewelled silver tie-pin that had found its way into his regular wardrobe slipped from my fingers and fell to the floor, broke into two pieces and clattered along the wooden floorboards before disappearing under the sofa.

'Christ, hun, can't you knock?'

'You left the door open,' she replied in a muffled voice. She was now on her hands and knees groping blindly beneath the furniture. 'I'm going to get Viggo to come over here and Hoover,' she added as she pushed herself up again and brushed off her now dusty palms on her trousers.

Viggo had become a permanent fixture in Lauralynn's life, and they now shared a house together in nearby Belsize Park. Their relationship bore many similarities to mine and Dominik's, albeit with the shoe worn on the other foot. Viggo was the lead singer of a band, and his public persona was that of the typical eccentric rock star, all shaggy dark hair and swagger, rake thin limbs and drainpipe jeans that sat low on his hip bones.

Behind closed doors though, I strongly suspected that Lauralynn took charge of their sexual as well as their domestic lives. She owned enough riding crops to furnish a stables, I knew. We had once even dominated a man together, and I had been both aroused and shocked by the feelings that had been evoked in me as I watched Lauralynn circling around him with a whip in hand and her long blonde hair falling like a sleek wave around her shoulders. I did not ordinarily desire women sexually, and I had never imagined that I possessed even the slightest domineering streak. But Lauralynn's charisma was like a siren song, and it was impossible to deny her anything.

She held her hand out to me with the two broken pieces resting on it.

'Sorry. I hope you weren't fond of this.'

'It's fine. Really. He hated all that stuff.'

She tossed the pieces unceremoniously into the bin and began unpacking the contents of her handbag into the kitchen cupboards. Coffee. Haribo sweets. A large bottle of gin.

A lump rose in my throat. Not for Dominik, this time, but for Lauralynn and her kindness. She, too, knew me well, and so hadn't sent flowers, casseroles, a sympathy card or any of the other stuff that had ended up in the trash. Trust her to bring the things that I actually wanted, even if they weren't good for me. She had developed a habit of turning up unexpectedly at times when I least wanted company, and therefore probably needed it. She had been a vigilant overseer, and keeping an eye on my well-being, I was sure.

Lauralynn still had a key, which she had never returned after the brief period that she and Dominik had platonically shared the house. She and Viggo had been kind enough to pop in and open a window when we travelled, or let us into the house on the one occasion we'd managed to lock ourselves out. So it could only have been her, or Viggo under her instruction who had let themselves in while I'd been out walking on the Heath and washed the pile of dirty dishes in the sink and disposed of the food going off in the fridge.

'You need a stiff drink, lady,' Lauralynn said, when she returned from the kitchen, holding a short glass full of ice, gin and a splash of tonic. 'And a hot bath.'

'I showered this morning,' I rebutted, like a petulant child.

'Your hair needs washing,' she said, wrinkling her nose as she eyed my limp ponytail. I would not have put it past her to lift me up and deposit me into a basin so she could wash it herself.

Lauralynn was no stranger to grief. Her brother had passed

away in recent years, and though we never really talked about it, I knew instinctively that she understood in many respects the way that I was feeling.

'But I didn't come over to nag you,' she added. 'Or to help you clean up. Though god knows this place needs it.'

I waited for her to continue.

'Actually,' she said, 'I need your help.' She turned her back to me and stretched across the bench top for the gin bottle and a glass and poured herself a shot, neat. Her black jeans were high-waisted and emphasised the extraordinary length of her legs and the round curve of her rump. Her blonde hair was held high in the centre of her head, making her seem even taller. It swished as she swung back around to face me again, awaiting my response.

'Sure,' I replied. 'Anything. Though I can't imagine what help I could possibly be to anyone at the moment.'

'You can still play, right?'

Her question caught me off guard. I hadn't actually touched a violin since Dominik had died.

'I haven't tried. Since then. But I can always play . . .'

Music was my refuge, and the simple act of running my bow over violin strings was like a soothing balm to my soul. It occurred to me then that I hadn't even thought to pick up any of my instruments since Dominik's passing. Perhaps, since my playing had been such an integral part of our meeting and eventually falling in love, it simply reminded me too much of him. But I knew that he would have wanted me to play.

'Good,' Lauralynn said, tossing her head back and gulping down the remainder of her gin. She put the glass back on the bench and wiped her mouth on the back of her hand.

'Viggo has a show next week. Just an intimate performance in a small theatre ... but some industry people will be there. And these people are ... Well, they're not the usual rock music types. He's been working on some solo stuff, reinventing himself, but it's not quite coming together. He needs something else, something different. You.'

'Me?'

'Yes. You've played rock on stage before. He said you were great.'

It felt like a lifetime ago now, but she was right. Chris's band, Groucho Nights, had opened for Viggo and the Holy Criminals at the Brixton Academy and Chris had called me on stage as a guest. I'd become a regular fixture on their European tour. Dominik and I were apart at the time and the excitement of those days had been overshadowed by how much I missed him.

'OK,' I agreed. 'I'll do it.'

'Good,' she said. 'Because Viggo's waiting in the studio for you now.' She checked her watch, a slim, plain silver affair with a small oval face. 'I told him you'd be there in 45 minutes, so you'd better hurry. I'll finish this.'

'And what if I had said no?' I protested.

'You are eternally predictable, Summer, even if you think that you aren't,' she replied.

I quickly changed into a clean pair of black leggings, ballet flats and a long-sleeved white shirt, pulled my cycling jacket over top, put my gloves and scarf on and headed out the door. There was no need to take an instrument. Viggo had dozens in every persuasion and would provide me with whatever best suited the tone he was trying to achieve. Most likely, it would be plugged in.

My legs spun quickly as I pedalled the short journey to Viggo's. It was the first time I'd ridden my bike since Christmas Eve, the afternoon of the recital and Dominik's death. The road was icy and even with gloves on my hands were stiff in the cold. But it felt good to be moving on two wheels.

Lauralynn had been right about Viggo. I had half suspected that he didn't need my help at all, and the whole thing was just a plan to distract me and get me out of the house but when he arrived at the door to let me in he looked even more dishevelled than usual and his eyes were red, as if he hadn't slept in days.

'Morning,' I said chirpily, realising as the word left my lips that it was probably the middle of the afternoon. Time held little meaning for me anyway, since I had never worked a typical 9 to 5 job. Of late, my weeks folded in on themselves like an accordion and the hours floated by without my noticing, or sped up and slowed down according to my emotional state. The worse I felt, the longer the days seemed.

'Summer, hi,' he replied, managing half a smile as he swept a hank of long dark hair back from his face. 'Come in.'

He didn't offer me a drink, or any of the usual social niceties. Just led me to the studio where he was practising his routine. I had to break into a jog to keep up with him as he strode through long passages to reach the basement room he was now using as a studio. His jeans were a deep shade of grape, a blur of colour against the white walls that surrounded us.

'When is the show?' I asked him, as he handed me an instrument. As I expected, he wanted me to play electric. It was a Bridge. I raised it into position and began to run through some warm-up exercises. The violin's tone was nice, but I hadn't played electric since my brief tour with Groucho Nights and it would take some getting used to. My fingers felt stiff and wooden on the strings.

'Next week,' he replied. 'Wednesday. Just a small affair, but I'm trying some of my own stuff and a couple of journos will be there ... God, I must sound so un-rock n' roll. But I really want it to go well.'

The public Viggo was a world away from the private one. I found it hard to believe now that I had ever been seduced by his stage character, the version of Viggo that had women across the world lining up and screaming outside concert venues when he played live. This man sitting in front of me staring at the floor and scuffing the toe of his boots against his chair leg as we discussed the line-up and my possible involvement now seemed like an entirely different person.

We agreed, in the end, that I would open with a riff on 'The Sorcerer's Apprentice'. A technically demanding piece with just the right degree of originality and well-suited to Viggo's typically phantasmagorical stagecraft, I felt.

'It's cool, Sum, don't worry,' Viggo insisted, as I tried again to master the electric. My hands were moving so stiffly I felt as though I was dragging my fingers through tar instead of air. 'It will come back to you.'

'I don't have my partition here ...' I explained, 'and it's a tricky piece to play from memory ...'

I pumped my legs furiously as I cycled uphill. My gloves were stuffed into my jacket pockets and I had accidentally left my scarf in Viggo's studio. It was now dark, and within minutes my hands were so cold that operating the gears was painful. The wind whipped against my bare throat. I had forgotten to bring my lights, and relied on memory to navigate the back streets and just my bike's small fixed reflector panels for safety. Dominik's image appeared unbidden in my mind, berating me for my recklessness. He had always worried about me cycling in London.

'Fuck you, Dominik,' I thought bitterly. Tears rolled down my face, making my cheeks even colder. My fingers were too frozen onto the handlebars to attempt to wipe them away, even if I could summon the energy to do so. As soon as the words entered my head I was assaulted by waves of guilt and grief, and wished that I could take them back, though I knew he couldn't hear me anyway. I had no truck with ghosts, or any kind of afterlife.

But had the grief, the shock affected my ability to play music?

Part of me knew that I was being melodramatic. I was out of practice, and for reasons unknown even to myself I had opted to play a virtuoso piece that would be challenging even on my best days. But right then, I didn't care. Emotions flew through me like a tornado, and I had no other way to express them. All I had ever had was Dominik, and my violin, and now I felt that both had abandoned me.

I dumped my bike against the side of the house without bothering to either lock it up or carry it inside. My Bailly was in its usual place, leaning against the wall in what was now my bedroom. Once it had been ours. The lights were all off. Lauralynn had evidently finished her work and left, but I didn't stop to check. I took the stairs two at a time, picked up my violin case and turned to leave again. As I did so, I caught my reflection in the mirror. My hair mussed from the wind, and pulled back into a hair band – a practical style, but one that always left me feeling not quite myself. Though cumbersome at times, my thick, red curly locks were one of the things that I associated totally with my identity, with me as me. I didn't typically wear trousers, either, unless occasion or practicalities demanded it. And my cycling coat was hi-vis and unfashionable. I didn't recognise myself.

My hands seemingly moved of their own accord. I tore the band from my ponytail and let my hair fall around my shoulders. Pulled off my ballet pumps and leggings, underwear, blouse, bra and jacket. I was naked. I picked up the case again and hugged it against my bare skin.

When I reached the front door, I paused, and picked up my long, hooded grey puffa coat from its hook. I could abandon it again when I reached my destination, but at least I wouldn't be stopped and arrested on the way for indecent exposure. Even in my most self-destructive moments, I still retained some sense. I stuffed my feet back into the trainers I had initially kicked off.

But I needn't have bothered, as not so much as a solitary walker stopped to glance at me as I made my way across the Heath to the bandstand, despite my dishevelled appearance and musical cargo, which might have passed for something more sinister in the dark.

The bandstand. It was the place that I had first played for Dominik. Where he had instructed me to stand, fully nude in bright daylight, as I performed for him –Vivaldi, the 'Four Seasons'. That had also been a challenging piece. It was the place that I had led him to, shortly after we had moved in together, where we had reaffirmed once and for all that unusual though our relationship might be, each of us fitted the other as perfectly as if nature had moulded us to form a pair. And it was where he had left the bracelet with the padlock for me to unearth. And now it was the place where I intended to find whatever part of me it was that had been buried when Dominik died. I wanted that part back.

I took my place in the bandstand's centre, dropped my coat, and began to play.

One by one the notes fell into place, and soon I had forgotten my surroundings entirely. Forgotten my scratched ankles, forgotten the icy wind that cut against my bare skin like the vicious claws of a frozen hand, forgotten my nudity and the strange picture that I would make to any passer-by.

The frenzied lullaby of my song enveloped me in the soothing balm of both presence and absence. With my focus on only the next infinitesimal movement of my fingers on the strings I was hyper aware and yet completely lost. My grief temporarily disappeared, from my conscious mind at least, and if my music had taken on a new dimension of yearning that had not previously been present, I was unaware of it. We can only ever be the sum of our parts.

I played on.

I caught my breath and my fingers moved away from the instrument's neck and strings where they had settled by the top nut and I slowly but triumphantly lifted the bow. I'd finally mastered the Dukas piece. There was a loose string dangling from the end of the bow which I hadn't noticed in the mad frenzy I had attacked the music with. I felt feverish and before I'd even batted an eyelid, the night cold assaulted me with full frontal wrath, enveloping my body in a glacial carpet, raising goosebumps all over my skin. I laid the violin on the bandstand's floor and reached for my puffa coat and wrapped myself inside it, shivering already. The fervour of the music had protected me while I was playing but its force field had as quickly evaporated.

I drew the material close over my nudity, reaching for the zipper to shield my body from the cold. I bent my knees to lower myself and retrieve the instrument and carefully placed it back in the safety of the case, rose to my feet and began the descent from the bandstand to the sketch of a walking path that unfurled a hundred yards below and which would return me to the ponds, and eventually home.

A cloud passed across the path of the moon and I found myself in pitch darkness.

Which was when a voice reached me.

'Bravo, bravo . . .'

It was a man's voice. Raspy, educated, BBC-like with just the hint of an estuary accent.

I looked ahead and squinted. The red dot of a cigarette consuming itself pierced the darkness.

I shivered.

Stopped in my tracks.

'I won't bite.'

I remained motionless, becoming increasingly conscious of my vulnerability out here in the wide open night.

The fear steadily beginning to flow through me paradoxically reminded me of some of the contradictory feelings I so often experienced in the first year following my initial encounter with Dominik. When I had recklessly but deliberately fallen into dangerous situations and the anxiety had been both a craving and a magnet for the broken part of me. A moth attracted to the flame.

Now, I could smell the smoke of the cigarette through the veil drawn by the London night. Acrid but fragrant, powerful and aromatic. A cigar maybe? Or some exotic form of tobacco?

The dot of red light piercing the darkness separating me from the stranger rose and fell in intensity with every successive puff the man took.

'Don't be afraid, move closer, music spirit . . .' he said.

Did I have any choice?

The moon above made a shy reappearance, a slice of distant light piercing the cloud cover as I reached him.

He was tall, heavily-bearded, stocky, wearing a thick woollen top in dark undistinguishable colours and jeans. His eyes glinted with mischief.

'That was quite a show, young lady.' His voice dripped with malevolent irony.

How much could he have actually seen properly from this distance?

Surely not.

'What are you doing here?'

'I could lie and say I was walking my dog, but I won't insult your intelligence,' he said.

I looked around. There was no sight or sound of a dog anywhere nearby. Giving the man and his menacing bulk another glance, I noted that if he did have a dog it would have to be an Alaskan Malamut, furry and massive. A random thought. My imagination already weaving the web of a story around him.

Noting my silence, he continued:

'I was curious . . .'

'Curious?'

'Did you know you've become something of an urban legend in these parts?'

'A legend?'

'Indeed. There have long been rumours of a beautiful

red-haired violin player who would perform concerts in the altogether. But no appearances had been reported recently, though ...To tell you the truth, I didn't believe them.'

'You saw me playing? Just now?'

'Couldn't see a damn thing. All the pity, by the looks of you now. But I could hear you loud and clear. I'm surprised the music didn't attract more of a crowd.'

I looked around, peered into the trees and what could be perceived of the clearing. There was no crowd. Just us.

'You liked the music?' I ventured.

'"The Sorcerer's Apprentice",' he said. 'A charmingly apt selection ... Do you enjoy playing with fire?'

There was an air of understated authority, of barely concealed brutality and self-assurance about the stranger now facing me. I was impressed by the fact he had recognised the music I had been performing. These days everyone was into rock and other more popular forms and the classics were known to fewer and fewer people. Even more so as the Dukas piece I had been playing was initially an orchestral one and not designed for violin and that I had been wildly improvising with its principal melody.

He intrigued me.

'I'm ...'

He interrupted me. 'I don't wish to know your name. I actually believe not knowing it adds some spice to the situation. And, conversely, why should I provide you with my own? Doesn't anonymity make our encounter more interesting?'

I nodded in understanding.

'But I can think for myself, and, if I may be just a touch presumptuous, have a quiet and intuitive understanding of women like you …'

He looked me up and down, his gaze unfailing, as if measuring me inch by inch, X-raying past the material of my long jacket and summarily taking possession of the landscape of my naked flesh.

'You're no ordinary flasher,' he continued. 'And neither do you come here to regale the masses with your music.'

I held my breath.

There was a flash of recognition. Even though we had barely spoken a few minutes, I realised this man illogically knew the real me. He perceived the core of darkness that I kept hidden inside. A prey always recognises its predators. It came with the shifting territory I had become accustomed to.

'You have your demons, young woman. That even the music you play so eloquently can't pacify. That's why you wander here … to purge them. But they can never be lost, you know. Only exorcised.'

His eyes were like dark negative flashlights, judging me. Sentencing me.

'Am I wrong?' he asked.

I took my time answering, weakness overtaking my limbs,

my mind in turmoil, not unlike the feelings I had been drowning in since Dominik's death.

His hand reached out towards me. He was gloveless. I took it. He seized my wrist. I did not resist. His fingers were calloused, hard, hot, holding me captive with a strength and authority that I immediately craved.

He came closer. I could feel the heat from his body surrounding me like a force field. Looked up to him. He was at least a foot taller than me. His neatly-trimmed beard a salt and pepper shaped forest of both intricate and intimate patterns, his full head of dark hair a crown of night. Normally I cultivated an intense dislike of beards.

'Let me see you properly. Open your coat.'

I obeyed.

'Hmm ...' the man said, taking in my nudity. Again I couldn't feel the ambient cold. Stood there. Nature morte. Summer morte. Girl in landscape. Summer nude. 'Absolutely stunning. Very tasty. Indeed, very,' he whispered, his voice an octave lower as he expressed his appreciation. His gaze steady and judgmental.

'What is it you want?' he asked.

'I don't know,' I replied hesitantly. 'I just don't know.'

'I can help you find it,' he said. 'Come with me, will you?'

Any other woman would have declined the invitation. I should have declined it.

But I didn't.

I stood rooted to the spot, fully exposed to a total stranger whose calm self-assurance spelt danger and attraction in equal ways.

'You may close the coat. Don't want you to catch cold, do we?'

I pulled the flaps together, clutching my violin case in front of me, the weakest of shields.

At the back of my mind, I somehow wished that Dominik could be here to advise me, suggest I take another road but the inevitable one. But I knew this would not happen. There is a comfort and a familiarity about well-known paths, even the wrong ones.

The stranger held out his arm, a gesture of gallantry in normal circumstances, although I was aware right now that it was just another subtle reminder that I was embarking on this of my own free will.

I took hold of it.

'Perfect,' he said. Was he referring to my docility or my weakness? Or both, more likely.

Arm in arm, we walked back towards the ponds and the adjacent car park where a single vehicle was stationed. It was a swarthy Audi, polished to perfection, intercepting the thin sliver of moonlight that shone down from the darkened sky across its metalwork.

He opened the passenger door for me and walked down the front of the car before unlocking his own with his finger on the fob and settled into the deep, buffed leather of the driver's seat. We had walked all the way to the car park in silence.

'Comfortable?'

'Yes.'

'Ready?'

'For what?' I asked, although I knew all along that it was a totally unnecessary question.

'A challenge. But you're aware of that. I can see that in your eyes, the way you walked here.'

'I suppose so.'

'You fear what might happen now, don't you? But at the same time, you are attracted to it, consumed by curiosity, you can't turn back without going through whatever I am planning for you ...'

Damn him, I thought. Why was I such an open book?

'You just came to the Heath with your coat and the violin?' he asked.

'Yes.'

'No clothes, handbag, money?'

'No. Is that a problem?'

'Not at all, you won't need anything where I am taking you.'

'OK.' I was ready. I was scared, a hard kernel of guilty need beginning to fester inside me, growing with every passing minute, my loins resisting a rising wave of wetness and excitement, both hoping and dreading for it all to happen. And wondering confusedly whether when I finally emerged at the other end I would have managed to draw a line under the pain that Dominik's loss had triggered.

The car strongly smelled of the same unusual tobacco I had caught a whiff of earlier.

He switched the car's engine on. I distractedly noticed that it was an automatic, whereas Dominik's BMW, 'our' BMW was a manual. Funny how such irrelevant matters spring unbidden to mind. While the Audi was warming up and a thin layer of condensation began melting away on the windshield, he spoke briefly on a cell phone he had pulled out of his glove compartment. He was making arrangements with someone for a certain room to be made available.

'. . . yes, I do have a volunteer,' he concluded.

I was watching his profile. His nose was hooked and there was something of the devil about him in his rugged handsomeness. Maybe it was the tidy beard and the even shine of his hair.

He placed a hand on the steering wheel and with the other moved the gear stick up and with a rich purr the car began to move. I glanced at his watch: it was just past midnight.

Empty North London streets whizzed by as we cruised at a fast but controlled pace through darkened side lanes and clumsily lit high roads with endless rows of shuttered stores and dull display windows flickering weakly in our wake.

I recognised Camden Town, now more like a ghost town, its weekend market stalls in hibernation and its pubs having long since disgorged the hordes of punters back into the bleakness of their lives. We took a turn left at the normally busy intersection by the Tube station and veered northwards towards Kentish Town. The urban landscape turned even more desolate and empty.

'No questions?' my driver asked me, as I persisted in my silence, my mind a blank slate as I tried to settle my nervousness.

'Not really.' I hoped my voice was steady and betrayed no fear.

The car slowed. Turned sharply into an improvised lot created by the recent demolition and pulling down of a no doubt derelict building. A scattering of other vehicles were already parked there. In the shadows, an attendant stood smoking, a necessary form of security I guessed. The stranger nodded at him as we left the car. I turned my back to him and bent over to pick up my violin case and felt his hand on my shoulder.

'You won't need it where I am taking you,' he said. 'I don't intend you to play, however exquisite your musical talents might be.'

I was about to protest but his grip on me hardened.

He gestured to me and I handed him the violin case and its treasured contents and he locked it in the boot.

'It will be safe there,' he concluded.

I followed him.

We walked down the empty high street. As we turned the corner and I caught sight of a sputtering neon sign outlining of all things a palm tree in shocking pink hues, my newly-acquired companion spoke again.

'You know what is going to happen to you?' he enquired.

'I suppose so.'

'You are going to be used.'

'Yes.'

'Hard. Rough. Repeatedly. There will be no turning back, you understand.'

'I do.'

'Good. So we both know there is no misunderstanding.'

'There isn't,' I assured him, with a tremor of expectation in my voice as I said so.

We reached the door over which the tacky neon sign presided. The stranger knocked and we were buzzed in. There was a plaque at eye-level which I managed to decipher in the darkness. Private sauna, entrance by invitation only.

We walked in. The atmosphere in the lobby was damp, with the smells of disinfectant, chlorine and sweat floating in the air like a permanent low-flying invisible cloud. There was just a desk, where the man who had brought me here signed us in under the bored gaze of an attendant clad in a white hospital-like smock. The muted sound of mass market muzak from remote speakers greeted us, which reminded me of a supermarket.

The uniformed attendant reached under his wooden desk and presented my escort with a couple of large dark towels. The stranger returned one of them.

'She will not be needing one,' he announced. I thought I saw a smirk on the younger man's face.

'Yes, sir.'

To me: 'The lockers are downstairs, as are the showers. I'll want you clean. You're then expected in the steam room.'

The basement area was lined with bruised metal lockers. Half were already closed while others were yawning open, a small key on a string awaiting in their locks. He indicated to me to remove my puffa, which I did, and he hung it in one of the available lockers. I stood there, naked again. This time he looked me over with forensic curiosity, the first time he'd had the opportunity to examine me in full light.

'Shoes,' he ordered. I looked down and realised that's all I was now wearing and kicked off the trainers.

'Turn round,' he continued. 'Let me see your arse.'

I did. His hand swept across my buttocks, gliding across

my skin, testing its suppleness and firmness. It was a part of my body I was inordinately proud of. There was a groan of approval. As he finally pulled his hand away, he suddenly extended a couple of fingers lower and dug them inside my delta and fingered me.

'Already wet, eh?' he said.

As much as I wanted to be detached from the whole episode, my body was betraying me in familiar ways.

I was beginning to sweat, a thin sheen appearing like dew across my stomach and thighs. The atmosphere inside the club was stifling and close, heat from the nearby sauna insidiously leaking towards the changing room where we were stationed.

His fingers disengaged from my cunt.

'Turn round again,' he ordered.

I turned and faced him again. He looked down. Frowned.

'You've been neglecting your hygiene,' he said.

I knew what he was referring to. Where once I had been attentive to keep my pudenda smooth when Dominik was around, I had been both forgetful and indifferent since his death. Couldn't be bothered as no one was likely to gaze on my intimacy or even care, I reckoned.

'The showers are over there.' He pointed in the direction of a narrow door to my right. I could hear the sound of water cascading down. 'You'll find disposable razors there. Clean yourself up. I want you fully shaved.' There was a hint of irritation in his expression as if he was already thinking of some exquisite form of punishment should I not return fully smooth and to his liking.

Half a dozen fixed shower heads controlled by metal taps sticking out from a grey concrete wall and a lengthy shallow trough in which to stand was what constituted the shower area. It was totally open, with no privacy. It felt like a pre-historic, less than basic version of a gym. As I walked in, two men soaping themselves at the other end, looked up at me. Both smiled.

I ignored the onlookers and turned the tap on. The water scorched me as it fell over my body like a heavy curtain and I was unable to control its heat and get it to run colder. I gritted my teeth and proceeded to scrub myself down as fast as I could. Further men entered the area and began watching me. I lowered my eyes in false modesty and ignored them.

As I finally walked out from under the hot stream, I noticed that the stranger had joined us in the shower area. He had stripped down and now wore a towel across his waist. He was surprisingly hairy and I was annoyed by a stray thought I was unable to repress as to how it would feel passing my fingers through his chest hairs; how it would compare with other men I had known.

For a brief moment I stood there nonplussed, almost lost in thought, somehow oblivious to my surroundings and the developing situation. Out of the corner of my eye, I saw some of the spectators were touching themselves, and others were already erect.

The bearded stranger handed me a plastic disposable razor. I began scraping the bristle of my renascent pubic hair away. I must have done an adequate enough job despite having no mirror to check on my progress as he nodded a silent approval once I had completed the task. He passed a hand across my mons to verify my smoothness, then with a firm push on my shoulders he forced me to squat down with my legs wide apart, in a somewhat undignified urinating position and inserted a hand between my legs, dragging it from cunt to anus, to check how thorough I had been.

He then extended his arm and helped me up.

I was still dripping wet but he wouldn't give me a towel to dry myself. I probably looked quite bedraggled, but that was the way he wanted me, it seemed.

We stepped out of the shower area and passed through the changing room again and I was led through a maze of narrow corridors until the heat and humidity in the air confirmed we were heading for the steam room. It lay behind a frosted glass door. We stopped and I heard a shuffle of steps behind us. The men who had watched me shower and shave earlier were following us. I caught my breath.

Standing in front of the steam room door, his guiding hand abandoned my elbow.

A pearl of water dripped from my forehead to the tip of my nose before kamikazeing down to the stone floor.

'Put your arms behind your back,' the stranger ordered.

He cuffed me.

And opened the door.

Heavy swirls of white steam rose to greet me and a forceful hand on my back pushed me past the threshold. I could see nothing and a note of acrid burning reached my nose and made me briefly cough. The tiles on which I was now stepping were slippery. It was impossible to know how large the room was, whether the size of a normal bathroom or a Tardis-like immensity. I was lost in clouds. Isolated between the hiss of steam rising from all quarters and the breath of an unknown number of perspiring bodies occupying the steam room. All men, I had no doubt. I could have been blindfolded for all it mattered. My lungs slowly grew accustomed to the sauna's insidious heat and my hearing to the imagined whispers now surrounding me.

The cuffs were removed. 'Get down on your knees.'

I lowered myself down where the swirling white clouds gathered even thicker.

'On all fours.'

My hands flat against the wet tiles.

'Open your legs,' he ordered me.

I felt the stranger's towel drop to the ground beside me, brushing against my flank as it fell.

A finger penetrated me. Gauging my wetness, my tightness.

Another finger tested my sphincter. Forcing its way through the ring, digging deep inside me.

Lost in the rising steam, buried under its successive layers, I tried to picture the scene, distance myself from it and see it from the point of view of a detached spectator.

Either way I looked at it, it proved obscene.

A hand held down my head. Tobacco breath drifting from my ear to my nose, skimming my cheek.

His cock breached me.

3

Don't Look Now

There was a contradictory dryness to the pervasive humidity of the sauna. It caught in my throat and lingered invisibly, hanging aloft among the swirls of thin, white, ever-shifting clouds filling the room. The stranger's rigid penis thrust its way into my body with an energy that took me by surprise, invasive, destructive, stretching me faster than I wanted so early in the ordeal. I was too dry. He was too large. I felt a painful stab against my cervix, like a blunt knife piercing me roughly in one expert, practised movement. As much as I had been expecting, even welcoming, his penetration, the sensation was so savage that I howled in protest. He had buried himself deep inside me so quickly, unhesitantly, that the outer skin of his cock felt like sandpaper against the fragile epidermis of my bruised sex lips and began to light an unwelcome match under my whole sexual parts.

The pain was like a brand, and surely, I thought, the dry-ness of my sex must have hurt him too, but if it did, he showed no signs of slowing his assault on me.

I should not have been surprised that my cry out only served as a spur for him to begin his mechanical thrusts in and out of me and in and out again with all the steady infernal rhythm of a piston. A lone teardrop formed in my left eye as further layers of pain began to superimpose themselves over and across the initial wave, not so much extinguishing the first nexus of fire but spreading mercilessly outward in con-centric circles until my whole body felt as if each nerve ending was being tortured, while I happened to be por-nographically displayed for the hungry gaze of god only knows how many other men standing further back in the floating white shadows of the sauna and watching the terrible spectacle. Waiting for their turn.

Ignoring the dreadful dryness of my loins, the stranger's cock with every repeated jut kept on burning me, invading me, opening me, gaping me, marking me as his sexual prop-erty, his chattel.

I also realised he was taking me raw, unprotected. I hadn't even thought to insist on condoms. Had taken it for granted that everyone wore them, these days. But it was too late for regrets now.

My throat was unbearably tight as I attempted to swallow, my prone body animated by his steady thrusts. Almost choked. Just another pitiful sound that I imagined brought a smile to his lips as he continued to plough me from behind.

My knees hurt, his heavy body pressing down on mine, his balls slapping against my rump.

The teardrop fell.

Dominik never stops looking up at me, even with his nose buried into the folds of my cunt, his tongue lapping studiously at me, his teeth gently teasing my clitoris, his lips biting my soft, engorged labia. The warmth and understanding in his brown eyes brings me peace. As his mouth orchestrates the parallel melodies of my heart-strings, playing in time with the primal sensations of arousal rising deep in the pit of my stomach, the clever, knowing way he has, his intuitive understanding of my body, makes me feel like both a woman in love and a slave to my cravings. The gentleness in the way he fills that void inside me and makes me feel whole and wanted, helps me reach that level when sex ventures beyond the physical realm of just cock, cunt, and entwined limbs. My lover, my master, my rock . . .

Time stopped, my body swaying this way and that under the physical blows of his lust, my opening on fire and unable to summon any relief, inner and outer skin bathed in the deep-seated chilli pepper-like burn of salt on open wounds. But I was beginning to relax into the pain. He violently slapped my buttocks and I pictured the shadow of his hand and all five fingers clearly delineated in shocking pink against the white skin of my pale arse, a graffiti pattern of possession. The slap brought me back to reality as every sound in the room was suddenly amplified, the staccato of his breath, the steady pizzicato of water dripping, the hissing of steam, the lustful agitation of the male spectators.

The bearded stranger's final thrust dug into me with furious intensity as he grunted and released a flow of added moisture, flooding me with his juices.

His movements ceased, but his cock stayed hard, impaled deep inside me. His breath steadied and the steam room settled into an eerie hush. A deep sense of anxiety weighed, leaden, on my mind. I knew all too well that this fuck was just the beginning.

'Is this what you wanted?' he asked, his voice slicing through the white mist enveloping us.

'Yes.'

'Yes what?' he insisted.

I panicked, searching for the hidden meaning of his question. Then it came to me.

'Yes, Sir ...' I bleated out, and a wave of shame swept across me as I realised that I had allowed myself to fall into this situation and that I probably deserved it. I was now paying for the brief months of peace I had managed to enjoy with Dominik. This was my punishment.

'That's better,' he said, and slapped my arse once more.

His wet hand vociferous against the white humidity of my flesh. It stung badly.

He pulled out of me.

I waited for the next stage of my ordeal. On all fours, fully exposed, the welcoming folds of my open cunt a mess of secretions and unnatural lubrication. He stepped back and turned to face me. His hand gripped my hair and forcibly raised my head and lips to his level.

'Here. Lick me clean.'

His erect cock pushed its way past my lips and invaded my mouth and throat. He tasted acrid, although I knew it was as much me as him, the blend of our juices somehow creating this strong flavour, betraying the fact that we did not truly fit together.

My tongue ran across his thick shaft, guided by the topography of his ridge and the veined landscape of his trunk until he filled me once again to the brim, his balls swinging against the barrier of my parched lips.

Pulling me by the hair towards his body, he kept on forcing his way down my throat. I almost bit down on him, an unwitting slave to my gag reflex and thirst for air.

He slapped my face in disapproval before pulling his penis from my mouth, disengaging.

'Hmmm . . .' he said. 'Out of practice, are we?'

I was.

★   ★   ★

Pain and pleasure arise in unison from my depths as Dominik's expert fingers slowly twist my nipples while he calmly observes the immediate reaction on my face. The blood flows from surrounding veins and passages to my areolas, the darker territory of pinkness at the tip of my breasts and my nipples begin to tighten in response, nubs of flesh imperceptibly growing harder under his ministration. The sensation is like a slow crescendo where the initial axis of hurt is washed over by a massive wave of merciful release vibrating across my whole being until I become the pain, inhabit it. And the pleasure. My limbs loosening their anchors, my heart floating in a sea of calm acceptance.

'More?' he asks, the pads of his fingers tightening their grip on the nipple, twisting just an infinitesimal thousandth of an inch anti-clockwise further.

I gasp.

'Yes . . . Please . . . More.'

I want to tell him to take me even further beyond the wall of pain until my thought processes are erased and I can melt under his touch, like a pool of water and become oblivion, just a mindless knot of sensations under his control.

He takes my chin in his other hand and raises my face so he can look into my eyes. There is an enigmatic smile on his face. Both observer and worshipper. A stab of excruciating agony births in my nipple as he squeezes it again between thumb and forefinger, drawing out the pain in slow motion like a magician pulling another phantasmagorical trick from his hat or sleeve. I am reaching the zone. Where nothing else exists.

I close my eyes, surrender to his wonderful torture, becoming the sum of all the unworldly sensations dancing across the delicate surface of my skin, my pleasure geography.

'More,' I whisper. 'More, more, more.'

My heart is beating faster and faster. It feels like I am approaching a frontier from which there is no turning back.

His fingers relax and the flow of blood returns to my breasts, my emotions in free fall as I gracefully return to the surface of this strange planet he has been exploring with me. This man of mine who can turn pain into gold.

Under the bearded stranger's instruction, two of the men present in the sauna picked me up from the floor and laid me out on a wooden bench over which they'd draped a large towel. Through it, the geometrical lattice pattern of the slats cut into my back.

The steam clouds were thinning and I could now see that there were half a dozen other men in the restricted space of the room. Some were naked while others had tightened towels around their midriffs in a futile attempt to conceal their erections.

Peering at their faces, sweaty, pasty, predatory, I absurdly thought of them as an audience, as if I was on a stage about to perform and couldn't help wondering what piece of music I should select for the occasion.

The man who had brought me here must have nodded in

approval as they all began approaching me and I was quickly surrounded.

Calloused hands began to knead my breasts with talentless greed, while someone slipped a couple of fingers inside my mouth and others directed their attention to my cunt, forcing my legs apart, beginning to frig me. Through a corner of my eye, I could see the stranger looking on, a taut expression stretching across his full mouth, as if relishing the spectacle and speculating as to what each new man would wish to do with me. Alien hands swarmed all over me, inside me and outside of me and although I couldn't summon any form of disgust faced by their eager clumsiness and roughness, neither could I evoke any atom of pleasure to trigger its familiar takeover of my mind and body to relieve the tension freezing me in place. I just felt like a spectator imprisoned in a stasis of supreme indifference, detached, faraway.

The sound of hissing steam and dripping water was now joined by shortness of breath and indistinct murmurs, a choir of want unleashed.

A nail scratched me as it busily foraged between my pussy lips, fingers grazed my nipples, a hand pushed its way between my legs in an attempt to reach my anus, mercilessly pinching the taut skin of my perineum. I shuddered.

One of the men in the sauna moved behind the bench over which I was unceremoniously laid out and squatted over my head. His heavy balls dangled above my face as he inserted his cock inside my mouth and began a series of rhythmic thrusts. I shifted so I could accommodate him better and not gag. My acquiescence to my situation appeared to encourage the other men, unless the whole scenario was actually being orchestrated from afar by the stranger in charge. A man positioned himself between my outspread legs and entered me.

'Yes . . .' I heard him whisper.

I was still so wet from the bodily releases of the earlier fuck that he sliced into me like a sharp knife into soft butter. Behind him, the others lined up.

I told myself it was only sex, but still my mind roamed out of control and I tried to repress the lust the situation was beginning to initiate. I did not want to enjoy this. I shouldn't find any of this gratifying.

The first man came quickly, and slumped momentarily across me, his breath reeking of cheap street food. He withdrew and was quickly replaced by another, with a shorter but undeniably thicker cock that bruised my lips as he pushed his way in.

One by one, the men used me, taking their appointed position between my legs and sating their lust. I lost count. Most came back for more, as I was repeatedly assisted up and turned, spread, opened from missionary to doggy style positions and variations in between so that they could all enjoy me to the full according to the scriptures of their limited imaginations.

I felt limp, tired, stretched beyond endurance.

Their faces blurred. Their cocks, moving from my cunt to my mouth and back again in an infernal chain of penetrations became a jumble of hard muscle and sinews until they all felt the same, an identikit penis throbbing away like a malevolent heart whose sole purpose was to impose its will on me.

When I felt it must all finally be over, hands seized me under my arms and pulled me up. I was arranged into yet more positions and the barrage continued as they now combined and I had to accept two cocks inside me, then three, a relentless march of dreadful improvisations.

Was this what I had craved for, the depravity that could wash away my sins, my memories?

His face a mask of blank ambiguity, Dominik takes hold of the flogger. I cringe in anticipation. Again he intends to make me walk that narrow goldbricked road between pain and pleasure, despair and hope. My hands are tied to the bedstead with short lengths of red, silk rope he had me publicly choose in a store in Islington in the full knowledge the sales assistants and other customers knew all too well for what purpose they were being acquired. The knots are tight. I am lying on my stomach. It's a summer evening and the windows are open to the breeze sweeping gently across the branches of nearby trees outside on the hill road that separates us from the Heath. A tongue of air travels slyly across my uncovered backside.

I grit my teeth.

He waits.

Does he want me to beg?

I can feel the wetness birthing between my thighs. Something I am unable to control. And Dominik knows it.

A faint smell reaches my nose. My nostrils unavoidably flutter in a futile attempt to detect its nature. Fragrance? Food? Breath? His? Mine? A green note like freshly mown grass, a hint of fruit, a sweet and far from unpleasant if astringent undercurrent of bitterness. But as soon as my brain captures an element in flight, it disappears to be replaced by another. Is it the confused smell of my lust, my feelings?

The flogger in Dominik's hands is made up of a handle and several straps which are attached to it. The hardwood is coloured warm burnished rust and matched with a fall of hair on cowhide. Depending on how he chooses to wield it, it can either sting or caress.

Now I wait.

Dominik's silence persists.

I realise it's become a battle between our wills, as to who will say something first.

I feel him move above me.

A strand of material grazes the delicate skin of my left buttock and I shiver, as if the flogger has miraculously been electrified, plugged in by some miracle of science. A river of desire is growing between my legs.

He pulls the strap across my skin, slowly, allows it to linger sensuously, almost tickling my aroused epidermis where every nerve ending is unbearably alive, keening for his touch.

He retreats.

Plunging me back into unfeeling silence.

He draws back, raises the flogger and allows its hanging straps to slide across the soles of my bare feet.

Words form in my mind, but I say nothing. I know he wants me to. I resist his wishes. Even though I can't see his face, I know there is a faint smile on his lips. A beautiful mask that affirms his desire. The way he loves me.

I hear him shift in the darkness.

The flogger's flowing hairs again linger against the small of my back, as if searching for a specific target. I am floating in my own juices.

My heartbeat slows and matches the rhythm of my breath. My tongue is dry. I want him so much. I crave the sting of the leather that will bring me to life, enhance my emotions, make me whole.

'Oh, Dominik . . .' I whisper.

He bends his head and breathes against my cheek.

'Yes?'

'Do it, do it, I beg you . . .'

He steps back and I hear the flogger swish in the air before it falls.

They came and went between my legs and inside my bruised mouth, mindless automatons, strangers, men. I'd become a rag doll. Manipulated, used, swaying like the branch of a tree between their attacks, their inhuman form of loving.

The steam had evaporated after someone had likely switched the sauna controls off, and everything was now starkly clear. The pocked wall tiles in dirty shades of white, the water dripping in fat globules from the ceiling, the tangled mess of soaked, abandoned towels littering the floor, the squat hairy legs of men circling me, the pale landscape of my body. I felt broken, trampled, I hurt everywhere, each single inch of my defences shattered, on edge.

There was a lull in the storm.

I heard the stranger's voice.

'How do you feel?' he asked me.

'I don't know. I'm ... confused ...'

'Confused?'

My lips were parched. There was a disconnect between my words and my brain.

Already, the memories of my ordeal were blurring and running beneath the undercurrents of pleasure and acute psychic and physical pain, there was a subterranean stratum of times past, better times. I struggled to understand.

'I can't explain,' I protested feebly.

What did he want me to say? That throughout the obscene theatre of my continuous sexual use I could not prevent my mind revelling in the actuality of my debauchery, that there were indeed moments of unpreventable highs? Because he knew that if I admitted to this, I was lost in more ways than one.

He pulled me to my feet.

The fire in my body was ebbing.

I must have looked pitiful. My hair was damp, lank, falling in wet strands to my shoulders. I looked down, there were random scratches scattered along my arms, my body, my freshly shaved mons was almost a shade of scarlet and was unnaturally swollen, bruises highlighted the unsteady length of my legs.

'I'll tell you then what you are unable to express,' he whispered in my ear. 'This is indeed what you wanted and you enjoyed it and every day to come you will think of this night and you will experience that thrill over and over again. You will feel both ashamed and aroused but as much as you try and resist somewhere inside you there will be an irrational, ingratiating voice encouraging you to let it all happen again. To become that wonderful whore one more time. And eventually you will break and pick up the phone and call me and I will make it happen.'

'I won't . . .'

'You will.'

His voice had the softness of the devil. Because I knew he was right. He had perceived my weakness in a flash and known just how to exploit it.

He waved the few remaining men in the steam room away

until there were just the two of us left in the now cooling down sauna. He looked me over, relishing the spectacle of my devastation.

'Get on your knees,' he ordered.

'I can't take any more,' I said. 'I just can't . . .'

I tried to squat but my calves were too weak and I settled on all fours.

I looked up at him.

He was holding his flaccid penis in one hand.

His jet of urine smacked me in the face. It was shockingly warm. Marking me. Like chattel.

I hurriedly closed my mouth and it streamed down my cheeks and chin as I passively accepted this further humiliation.

Once he had emptied himself he held his hand out to me and I rose.

'Next time you will keep your mouth open,' he proclaimed.

'No, I won't,' I muttered silently, inside the safety of my own brain. I did not have the courage to disobey him to his face.

He led me to the now deserted showers where I washed the night away, insofar as I could.

I retrieved my discarded puffa jacket and wrapped myself as tightly as I could within it before leaving the building in his company and, in the bleak light of dawn, walking with the stranger to where he had parked his car. He asked me whether I wished to be dropped off anywhere in particular. I turned his offer down and retrieved my violin case from the car's boot. I wanted to walk home, determined to clear my mind. And I did not want him to know precisely where I lived. Across the road, a grocery store was opening and setting out its outside display of fruit and vegetables. I hankered for an apple.

He handed me a business card. It had no name, just a telephone number. I swore to myself I would never call him but didn't have the guts to dispose of it as soon as his Audi turned the corner and headed south towards Camden Town.

I dug deep into my jacket pocket and found a pound coin and bought a shiny red apple from the store and began the lengthy walk back towards Hampstead.

'I like to see you tied,' Dominik says, with a glint of mischief in his dark brown eyes.

'I like to be tied,' I say.

'Do you enjoy feeling helpless?'

'Losing control.'

'Thrown to the wolves.'

'Ripe for plundering.'

He is inside me, moving with exquisite slowness, his velvet cock mapping every single contour of my inner walls, sentient, exploring me.

His tongue gently wets my lips. He raises himself slightly, his hands reach for my throat.

'You like danger,' he says.

'I do,' I say. 'It makes me feel alive.'

His expert fingers press against my throat.

'One day maybe we will go too far.'

'I don't care.'

My breath is shortening. I can feel him growing even thicker inside me. Will he ever tighten a rope around my neck?

The games we play.

I closed the front door behind me and hung my keys and coat on the hook in the hall. I was naked, besides my trainers, but not cold. It was as if the heat from the steam room had seeped into my bones, and even the long walk home hadn't been able to banish the lingering warmth. I imagined that I was the right temperature for bacteria to grow on. Like a perfect petri dish in a science experiment gone wrong.

I walked into the living room. The house looked the same as it had when I had left it, only minus the last few boxes of Dominik's things. Lauralynn had packed them all up and taken them away. She had left something on the kitchen counter, alongside a note. I stepped across to it, padding gingerly along the floor as if I was at a crime scene, trying not to disturb the evidence.

Thought you might want this,
Lx

It was Dominik's watch. The watch that I had bought for him, to celebrate our last 'anniversary'. We'd joked that it would be an impossible event for us to celebrate, since we'd had so many firsts. So I'd chosen the day, and bought him a gift. He'd worn it every day since. I picked it up and ran my thumb over the engraving on the back. Nothing fancy, just the date of our first meeting, in italic font, and our initials. D, S. It was our little in-joke, the coincidence of our first names beginning with letters that represented the style of our relationship, dominance and submission. I had revelled in that fact, and Dominik had rolled his eyes at me. He hated the acronym BDSM.

The metal was ice cold against the sheen of sweat that still coated my skin. It reminded me that I'd never been good at gifts, in the way that Dominik was. He always managed to choose something that was both surprising but also utterly me. Blissfully symbolic. Whereas my gifts to him had something of a catalogue buy about them. As if I'd never really known him the way I should have, not truly. He'd been the one who was good with words, good with romantic surprises. I showed my love for him the only way that I knew how. With my body.

★　　　★　　　★

'Shhh,' he says. 'Relax. Let go.'

He has me pinned to the bed, belly down, his body over my body, his torso against my back, his breath hot against my neck as he whispers into my ear. My pulse flutters as he gently brushes a lock of my hair away from my throat.

His erection presses against my anus. A solid, hard, unrelenting presence wedged between my buttocks, waiting for my initial resistance to subside, for me to welcome his cock's entrance to my arsehole.

My ever patient dominant Dominik, who never craves my subservience but rather my permission, not from the words I utter but from my flesh and bones, my muscles and sinews, the parts of me that are unable to lie, cannot be manipulated into giving away anything that I do not truly want to give. He does not want to take me, he wants me to open up to him.

So he lies prone, expertly holding his weight above my body, careful to push just far enough but not too far as millimetre by millimetre I let him in.

The hair on his arms tickles my skin as he lowers his head and plants a kiss on my cheek. My face is turned to one side. It's an affectionate kiss. I can't see him properly in this position, but I know he smiles, after he kisses me.

I go to that place in my mind. The safe place. The place that knows this is Dominik, and I want Dominik to have all of me, to own me. I want to give him everything.

I relax.

He groans.

His cock slides into me as if it was made to fit, even though when I am tense there, he feels unbearably large.

My body shifts to accommodate him.

My Dominik.

I put the watch down again. I'd been gripping it so tightly that the tiny knobs that moved the watch's hands had left two red indents embedded in the skin of my palm. I couldn't bear to touch anything of Dominik's when my flesh still bore the stink of the bearded stranger and the men from the sauna. I didn't even cry, when I thought of them. It felt too unreal. Like I'd had a bad dream.

I pressed the toe of one shoe against the back of the shoe on the other foot, sliding it off without undoing the laces. Then the same in reverse, my bare toenails scraping against my ankle. I hadn't thought to put on any socks and the journey home in just trainers had left my feet scratched and sore. Good, I thought. My feet throbbing as a result of something as banal as a sockless walk gave me something else to think about, something for my mind to hold on to, distracting me from the other parts of me that ached for reasons far worse.

The shower water, when I got in at last, was a soothing balm, and I turned the temperature up as hot as it would go and scrubbed myself with a body brush until I was red and tingling.

Autumn

I wrapped myself in a thick, white, soft dressing gown. In the mirror I looked blameless, my mass of ginger curls, now washed and dried, a shock of colour against my white skin. The only sign that I was a scarlet woman.

When I woke up it was almost a whole day later. I was lying on top of the bed still swaddled in the towelling robe, exactly where I had finally collapsed. It had been a sleep full of nightmares, images and unreal adventures combining with flashes of anonymous faces, tangled limbs, bodies known and unknown, and delicately etched portraits of pain.

My eyes landed on the slim gold chain of Dominik's final gift to me, the bracelet with the padlock attached. Thank god I hadn't been wearing it in the sauna, I realised. I scooped it up and deposited it in the security of my bedside drawer. So that it couldn't be tarnished, by touching my flesh.

In the kitchen, I found the loaf of thick white toast bread and the bags of sweets that Lauralynn had brought with her. It was an unlikely meal, but I was hungry, and I didn't care. I slathered slices of bread with butter, pressed jellied, sugar-coated candies into the middle and rolled them up like hot dogs, then wolfed down one after the other, barely chewing. Maybe, if I got fat enough, I wouldn't need to worry about men like the bearded stranger coming across me playing naked on the Heath and wanting me, pressing all of my sexual buttons. But I knew this wasn't true. Men like that want women like me for our minds and our desires, not just our bodies.

I picked up the bottle of gin and poured it down the sink. Giving myself an alcohol problem on top of everything else was the last thing I needed. The acrid smell of it burned my nostrils as I watched it disappearing down the plughole. I wished that I could disappear in the same way, and I cursed the part of me that wanted to live. Damn me, why couldn't I be suicidal? Death would have made everything easier. But at my heart, I remained resolutely pragmatic, and alive.

Music and work. That is where I would seek solace. Without Dominik, it was all I had.

Later, I rang my agent and asked her to set up a solo tour of small venues at short notice. She protested, explaining it would be a wrong career move and also gently suggested that I was not quite ready to embark on such a venture in the current circumstances. Meaning so soon after Dominik's death. But I insisted and eventually she agreed. It would be easier, she said, to select venues across Europe, as British concert halls were all booked up too far ahead.

In Brussels, I visited the Musical Instrument Museum which had been set up in an old department store and initiated a conversation with a middle-aged man in the strings room and fucked him in the men's toilets, before rushing off to my gig with his smell still lingering across the surface of my skin, and played to the small audience with his come still inside me.

Barely 48 hours later, in Amsterdam, I allowed myself to

be picked up by a swarthy Russian who could barely speak English as I lingered with intent in a red light district sex shop. He poured champagne over my cunt and drank from me in his luxurious room at the Kempinski, oblivious to the ensuing mess on his bedsheets. He was probably wealthy enough to buy the entire hotel. Once he mounted me, he came too quickly and was unable to regain his erection and, in frustration, threw me out of the room with my clothes following shortly thereafter into the hush of the softly-carpeted corridor.

In Berlin, I flirted outrageously with one of the venue's stagehands and, following the recital, had sex with him in the theatre's basement, among discarded furniture and coils of dusty rope which he refused to use on me.

The silver-haired aristocrat in Paris sent a lavish bouquet of flowers to my dressing room and I agreed to join him post-performance for a coffee. He had a certain elegance and was something of an expert on baroque music and could hold a conversation about the subject for hours on end. He liked to take photos and blindfold me. I spent a whole day with him, after which he gave me an amber brooch as a souvenir and asked me to become his mistress, which I declined, pre-texting another involvement in another country.

In Rome I was recognised by a restaurant head waiter. After the lunch service, he took me to the wine cellar and never stopped muttering obscenities under his breath as he took me anally with, I knew, half of the kitchen staff watching, the short floral skirt I had been wearing for my earlier morning rehearsal together with my abbreviated knickers bunched around my ankles.

South of Barcelona, I found an isolated nude beach on a late spring afternoon and two young local men walked down from the dunes. Not a word was ever spoken between us, not that I knew any Spanish. They leaned over me, momentarily obscuring my view of the sun, provocatively enjoying the display of my body. I purposely refrained from covering myself and they both disrobed and lay on either side of me in the sand. They had beautiful cocks and I took them in each of my hands. Later they spit roasted me in silence. Hot with sweat and laughing, we swam together until I was out of breath and stumbled back to the beach where we shared a six pack of beer from one of the boys' rucksacks. All too soon, my bladder filled and I had to pee. I indicated with a gesture that I had to relieve myself, pointing to the nearby dunes or the ocean, but they giggled, shook their heads and pointed to the sand. I squatted and allowed them to watch. I do think I even blushed as they observed this biological function in fascination. As I wiped myself clean with the back of my hand and made to rise to my feet, the two young men exchanged a look of complicity, and one of them moved behind me and took me by the shoulders while his friend bent over and picked me up by my feet and they carried me like a parcel to the shore and crying out *uno, dos, tres!,* dunked me into the water where they soon followed and pretended to wash me, their hands and fingers moving frantically all across and inside me while laughing hysterically. Back on the sand, the taller one stuffed his cock inside my mouth and I sucked him to hardness. Then they fucked me again. I never asked for their names.

In Montpellier, I met Jean-Jacques on a tram. Later he would steal my handbag from my room as I showered post-sex. I never carried much cash and was able to report and replace the credit cards as lost with no particular inconvenience, and my passport had been safely secured in the hotel room's safe using my date of birth for the combination as I and no doubt countless others always did.

In Nice, my lover for a night took me from behind as I stood by the window watching the sea lap the sandy shore beyond the promenade. As he did so, I heard a piece by Mussorgsky in my head. At my concert the following day, I hastily rearranged the running order of my repertoire and insisted to the promoter that I had to play it even though it wasn't listed on the programme he had printed for my recital.

Was it in Dubrovnik or Zagreb that I picked up a gypsy fiddler, thinking that maybe two musicians in bed together would create even sweeter music? The sex was uneventful and at the next day's concert I made a brief mistake whilst playing a Mendelssohn solo as my mind wandered. No one in the sparse audience noticed, I hope.

The tour came to an end and I returned to London. I didn't feel like doing so but had no other pressing plans and was, at any rate, getting tired of living from a suitcase and haunting hotel rooms and lobbies.

In outward appearance, I was still the same. Inside I knew I was broken. In the pocket of my grey jacket hanging on the hook in the hallway, that anonymous business card with just a telephone number sat, challenging me. Every day, alone, lost in my conflicting thoughts, I almost walked down the stairs to retrieve it. Then thought better of it. But I knew that eventually my resistance would crumble. It existed there like a red rag to a bull.

Dominik scoops me into his arms and we each curl up against the other in spooning position, as neatly and naturally as two bodies of water meeting and melting into the same sea.

He closes his arms around me tighter, gives me one last squeeze.

We've just fucked. Nothing out of the ordinary, but just right. Kissing in bed. A goodnight peck becoming passionate, open-mouthed, our tongues dancing and lips each pressing harder against the other's then Dominik pulling his body on top of mine, sighing with pleasure as he takes his hard cock in his hand and sweeps it gently between the folds of my cunt and finds me already wet and plunges straight into me and I wrap my arms around him and cling on to his shoulders like a desperate woman at sea, holding on to a lifeboat or an improvised raft, and we rock back and forward until he comes.

He lies on top of me until he goes soft, and the moment of desperate passion has passed. He knows his weight is heavy. I fidget beneath him.

Then this, the best moment of all. The calm after the storm. The quiet after all the noise. We are at peace together, with each other.

'I love the way you fit me so perfectly,' I say, drifting into slumber. And I mean fit me. Not fit into me, or against me. Fit me. Dominik fits me, and I know that I fit him.

'And I love you, Ms Zahova,' he says sleepily. 'You are perfect.'

'I love you too,' I reply.

But I'm not sure if he hears me. I think he's already fallen asleep.

4

The Vines! The Vines!

'I've heard rather racy rumours spreading about you, darling ...' Lauralynn said. 'What the fuck have you been up to while on the road? Look, I'm not one to judge and your private life is your own affair. But these sort of stories circulate pretty fast. If it gets any worse, it's going to get you into some serious trouble,' she insisted. 'All it needs is for someone to leak a tasty morsel to the tabloids and you'll be Page Three news. "Sex-crazed musician whores herself all across Europe" stuff, if not worse if one or other of your pick-ups provides any juicy details, and knowing you I'm sure they certainly would prove far from conventional!'

'What are you talking about?' I protested. Lauralynn had barged in past me the moment I had opened the front door to her. She was wearing a baggy tracksuit and a sheen of sweat coated her features. She must have jogged up the hill at a rapid pace. This was the nearest I'd ever seen her to angry. 'Anyway, I don't give a damn about my career. It means nothing to me.'

Lauralynn gave me a scornful look, like a teacher disappointed by my petulant, childish reaction. It seemed that my hopefully anonymous encounters in Europe had not been as discreet as I would have hoped and venue staff and others had become aware of my meaningless adventures and, somehow, word had even reached Simon, my erstwhile orchestra conductor lover for a while, who was back in South America, and he had thought it right to contact my London friends to ask them to try and intervene.

I'd been back in London for over two weeks and spent much of it wandering around the large, empty house clad in just pyjamas or an old fluffy dressing gown which had seen better days and ordering ethnic takeaways for bodily sustenance. I couldn't concentrate on anything, feeling unable to read or even watch movies on TV.

I had become a ghost in my own home. What had once been our home. His home.

The images of what I had been up to in Kentish Town and the blurry memories merging into each other of the sex I'd had in all the European cities of the past month bubbled in my mind like bad reminders of the damaged state I was in.

I felt no shame, just an intense awareness of being broken

inside and knowing all too well that the casual sex had done nothing to piece me back together again.

'Oh, come on, Summer,' Lauralynn unzipped her grey top and threw it onto one of the sofas in the study into which she'd followed me, giving a distasteful look in passing at the desk still littered with fast food containers I hadn't bothered to sweep away. 'Grow up. Please do.'

'So?' I stood my ground. Both touched and annoyed that my friend should feel so concerned about my well-being.

The silence that followed weighed on both of us as we looked at each other.

'Oh ... Summer ...' Lauralynn said and there was a genuine sadness in her voice.

She held out her arms to me, opened them as if to embrace me.

I ran towards her and wallowed in the warmth and softness of her body as I wrapped myself round her, chin on her shoulders, the herbal and autumnal fragrance of her hair enveloping me as it brushed against my cheeks.

We remained that way for a long time. Words had become superfluous.

In the kitchen, sipping coffee together, the conversation finally resumed.

'A mutual business acquaintance tells me you've suggested going on yet another tour, Summer.' We shared the same agent. 'I don't think it's a good idea,' Lauralynn continued.

'Playing keeps me sane,' I replied.

'And once you've stopped playing, you go batshit crazy again,' she said.

'So what's your solution?' I asked her.

'Listen: Viggo and I have been talking about it. We're taking charge. Pack up some things and come and stay with us, for a bit. You've become a danger to yourself and this large house is too big for you alone. You need a break. And most definitely a better sort of company.'

It felt like walking back into my past as I provisionally moved back to the Belsize Park mansion and its rock star accoutrements and cache of secret rooms and treasures.

Viggo would be busy for the initial fortnight working in an outside studio with pick-up musicians on his fusion project of rock and classical and I felt somewhat spurned when he did not even ask me to join in further. We had laid down tracks for the improvisation on the 'Sorcerer's Apprentice' theme before I had embarked on my tour but he insisted he wanted to use different participants for each individual track and refused to let me know who else he had chosen or what other pieces of music he had selected for the project.

I spent most of the time with Lauralynn and was grateful for her lack of questions and any attempt at psychoanalysing me, which I would have vehemently resisted anyway. We pottered around the house, cooking, cleaning and slobbing away to our heart's content, the conversation never veering away from safe banalities. Once Viggo had completed his sessions, the vague plan was to go away somewhere warm for a vacation in a sunny clime. A beach, maybe. But far away. I was happy to leave the details to them.

I was staying in what Lauralynn jokingly described as the penthouse suite, a medium-size bedroom on the last floor, carved out of what had once been a vast attic in a major conversion long before Viggo had acquired the property.

At night, through the flat roof window above my bed I could watch the stars swarming in the late spring sky and listen to the minute sounds of the dark, along with the noises of the house below, the imperceptible creaks and whispers and breath of wood and water as the building settled. I found sleep difficult, sometimes lying between the sheets for hours awaiting peace of mind, tiredness battling with the buried fears of what tonight's nightmares might bring.

A distant cloud obscured the sea of stars and the weight of night felt oppressive. I shifted uncomfortably, my feet tangled in the sheets, an invisible weight falling across my chest.

I threw the bed cover away and stepped out of the bed. All I could hear was the sound of my breath. Halting. Scared. I walked out onto the landing and made my way down the stairs, one cautious step at a time, careful not to make any noise.

Lauralynn and Viggo's bedroom was on the floor below. Their door was half open and, standing there wearing just the short T-shirt and cotton knickers I normally slept in, I gently pushed against it. The room was in total darkness, heavy curtains drawn across the bay window which looked onto the large garden at the back of the house.

I tiptoed towards their bed, guessing at their slumbering shapes beneath the quilt. As I approached I saw their naked shoulders peering out and listened for the irregular rhythm of their breath. Viggo snored ever so lightly, I recalled from the brief time I had been in a casual relationship with him.

My eyes were getting accustomed to the room's darkness and I could now make them out better.

It was a large bed and Viggo was on his stomach, splayed out, his body almost balancing on the left edge, a few toes sticking out between the sheets and quilt, his dark thatch of curls spreading like creeping ivy across the pillow. Lauralynn was on her back, statuesque, still as an odalisque, a faint smile separating her plump lips. I wondered briefly how Dominik and I must have looked when sleeping and a rush of emotions came swirling back and I felt tears welling up inside my eyes, as I realised that unlike the distance that lay between my two sleeping friends in the privacy of their bed, Dominik and I had always slept close to each other, bodies together, skin to skin, the barrier of intimacy shattered and how the steady beat of his heart had always lullabied me to sleep when I stayed awake longer than him.

He had died alone.

I hadn't been at his side.

The thought just annihilated me.

I slipped out of the T-shirt and pants as I attempted in vain to dam the tears and pulled the cover away from my friends' sleeping bodies and inserted myself between them and pulled the quilt back as I settled between their warmth.

They both stirred indistinctly as they became aware of my presence. Viggo turned round and shifted, moving closer to me, his haunch brushing against mine, and then kept on sleeping. Lauralynn opened her eyes and noticed me. There was no need for words of explanation; she knew clearly I hadn't entered their bed in search of sex. My now abundant tears staining the edges of the two pillows I was straddling was evidence enough.

'Shhh . . . .' Lauralynn said.

Her hand moved to my cheek and wiped away some of the tears. 'It'll all be OK. Just give it time . . .'

She rolled over to me, squeezing me tight between her naked body and Viggo's. He grunted slightly but didn't evade the contact.

Her arm draped itself across my shoulder and pulled the quilt up so that we were both cocooned in its growing warmth. I closed my eyes, allowing the comfort of their body heat to invade me.

'Sleep, darling,' Lauralynn whispered.

And I welcomed the night.

★　　　★　　　★

'We've made arrangements,' Lauralynn said the following morning, shortly after we'd all had breakfast together. I had woken with a start, briefly shocked to find myself wrapped around the nude bodies of my friends, both with eyes wide open and still, not having wanted to disturb me and waiting for me to wake. After I'd opened my eyes, both of them had leaned over me and kissed me on each cheek to greet the morning.

We'd all showered together as if it was the most natural thing to do. Through our complicated past involvements, we had long become accustomed to the spectacle of our naked bodies.

'Somewhere warm?' I asked her.

'Of course.'

'When?'

'Tomorrow.'

'Already?'

'No time like the present.'

Later, we would drive up to my house and pick up some clothes, although Lauralynn instructed I should not pack too many, as one of the sections of our journey would involve a small boat, so weight restrictions were inevitable.

I was intrigued, but she refused to give me any clues.

After I'd gathered a bunch of summer stuff and beachwear, I made my way to the study and opening the Chinese wood cabinet where I kept my violins, experienced a pang of guilt for the fact it had now been a few weeks, I had last done any practice scales, exercises of any kind. Lauralynn had stayed back in the kitchen, having volunteered to clean out the leftover food from fridge and cupboards so it didn't rot in my absence.

I was holding the Bailly in one hand and my other favoured violin in the other, a more modern but sleek Italian-made instrument whose warm tones were perfectly suited to the majority of my repertoire. Wondering which to bring along. Weighing the pros and cons. Both were heavily insured so their worth was not a problem, although the Bailly had of course considerable sentimental value. Surely, it would be foolish to take both along, I reflected. I wasn't going to have that much use for them, just an hour or so's practice every day at most.

'No.'

Lauralynn had walked in and seen me weighing the two violins.

'What?'

'You're not taking any instrument, Summer.'

'Why?'

'It's supposed to be a vacation. I don't want you to think of music. The whole idea is to take you away from all that.'

'But?'

'No if and buts, darling,' Lauralynn looked terribly severe.

'Neither am I taking my cello,' she added. I was about to remark that her own instrument was so much heavier than mine. 'I know you feel incomplete when you're not playing. But I've also seen the way the music consumes you, the way it warms your blood, brings you alive. It leads you to temptation . . .'

I was about to protest, argue that she was being melodramatic — surely there would be few temptations where we were going, just sand and sun and exotic cocktails — but part of me knew she was right.

I left my instruments behind.

That night, I slept with Lauralynn and Viggo again, sheltering inside their welcoming warmth. It seemed like the natural thing to do.

In the morning, a taxi drove us to the airport.

I'd seen more than enough airports those past few months, and become so tired of travelling that I simply followed along after Viggo and Lauralynn in a haze as we navigated through terminals and departure lounges, customs officials and security barriers. As soon as we settled into our seats, I took a sleeping pill, rousing only briefly to eat the plastic chicken dish, bread roll, anaemic salad and cupcake placed in front of me by an air stewardess who bore the expression of someone who has awoken to find herself in the middle of a bad dream, working in a job she despised. I ordered a Bloody Mary, my drink of choice when flying, although most often it could only be made with vodka and tomato juice, livened up by just a sachet of salt and cracked pepper, without all the other accoutrements.

'We're going to Rio?' I asked Lauralynn. My lips felt like two rubbery sausages and my mouth was dry. I pushed the call button, braving the grumpy flight attendant to request some water. The discomforts of drugs, alcohol and long haul flying.

'Yes, although we'll just be passing through. There's no actual airport where we're going. Not a lot else, either.'

I meant to ask her how long we would be staying and if she had been to our destination before but before the words could escape my lips another wave of fatigue had swept over me and I fell into a doze, my head uncomfortably propped up against Lauralynn's shoulder and my legs folded up like a grasshopper's to avoid pressing into the seat in front of me. Viggo was in another world altogether, large headphones sheltering his ears, listening to his iPod and its treasury of rock sounds.

We stayed two nights in Rio, just long enough to recover from the travelling and begin to relax.

'But I've barely been working,' I complained to Lauralynn, who insisted that I sleep in, breakfast late and do very little besides laze around.

On our second night, we had an early dinner on the

balcony at Zaza, raw tuna ceviche with a spicy coconut mayonnaise scattered with wasabi peas that lit a pleasant fire on my tongue with each mouthful. Lauralynn ordered one improbable cocktail after another; strawberry mixed with basil with a rim of black and white chocolate, star fruit and chilli, passionfruit and peppercorn. Viggo was a dedicated red steak and french fries sort of guy and left the exotica to us women.

Out front, hungry prospective diners milled, sipping drinks and waiting for a table. Night was beginning to fall and the beach was relinquishing its hold on the holidaymakers and locals; a river of scantily dressed men, women and children flowed up the street carrying cheap tennis rackets, volley balls and canvas chairs, the debris of a Sunday afternoon. Few had towels. They let the intense heat that still pervaded the air dry their bodies. Many were taut and tanned. Thick droplets of seawater clung to bare chests with abdominal muscles as clearly delineated as that on any underwear billboard. Full breasts, ineffectively restrained by bikini tops swayed a seductive rhythm in time with their owner's footsteps. Small swimwear was not just the preserve of the fit and young. Hairy, round paunches hung slack over the waistbands of the briefest of swimming briefs, thin legs with knobbled knees protruded below. Arses that were so high and firm they seemed unreasonable outside of a pop music video shared the street with buttocks that had long sunk past their prime, plump and dimpled or shrunken and saggy. A democracy of flesh on display.

The city was practically pulsing with sex. Lingerie stores lined the streets, half a dozen to a block. The heat made everything feel like it was heavy breathing. Even the air seemed to be gasping, sucking desperate breaths in and out against my skin.

Later that night I ignored the rules sternly outlined in the guide books and went down to the beach alone after dark. It was unseasonably warm and humid, and a bank of low clouds had gathered overhead. Thunder rumbled nearby, or was it the loud engines of the motorbikes that regularly whizzed past? Spots of rain fell and cooled my sandalled feet. The streetlights from the road adjacent to the shore lit the sand.

That afternoon, the Ipanema fields of golden sand had been crowded, a veritable bank of bodies and umbrellas. Now, they had all emptied to bars, homes and restaurants, and just a few stragglers remained behind, clustered by the picnic tables near a kiosk drinking bottles of beer and coconut water from large green shells. A crew of green T-shirted council workers equipped with rakes and wheelie bins were collecting the litter that visitors had discarded. It was like a kitchen the morning after a party, on a larger scale. The remains of an afternoon's large scale hedonism.

'Not like the seaside in New Zealand, huh?' said a voice,

beside me. My sneaking out had evidently not gone unnoticed. Lauralynn had followed me down to the shore.

Hot weather suited her. She had shed her winter persona as if she had been born to live in tropical climes and now wore a loose fitting pair of khaki short shorts, a slinky white silk top that made no secret of the fact her breasts were bare beneath, and a pair of gold sandals. Her toenails were painted tangerine and her hair was pulled up into a loose ponytail. Within a day of our arrival she had managed to gain an all over golden tan. I suspected that while I had been napping in my room, she had been lying naked on the beach baking her skin in the sun.

'No, it's not at all like home,' I replied. The beaches that I was used to were deserted by comparison.

'Have you ever seen a tropical storm?'

Bursts of forked lightning lit up the now violet-coloured sky, showing us brief flashes of the famed Sugar Loaf, Two Brothers, Pedra da Gavea and other mountains and rocky outcrops that our taxi driver had pointed out as we'd driven here from the busy airport but that I could not recall the names of.

'Just a couple,' I replied, 'on holiday in Australia.' I sniffed the air. 'It reminds me of that here, but without the smell of gum trees. Like I'm reliving only half of a memory.'

I felt the same way about being on holiday without Dominik. It was the first time in years that I had travelled without him, besides all the work-related touring. As much as I tried not to think about it, I couldn't help imagining what he would like and dislike and laugh at, or what games he would play. He would have enjoyed making me parade on the beach in the skimpiest Brazilian style bikini that he could find, I knew it, and I could imagine the expression that would have played across his lips as he watched the men watching me, and thought of how he might punish me later for teasing them.

Tears rose unbidden, and I swallowed them back.

Lauralynn took my hand and squeezed my palm tightly in a gesture of support, as if she knew what I was thinking and feeling, but if she did, she didn't mention it.

'I love storms,' she said. Her shoulders were jutted forward and her face held aloft into the wind, as if she was about to go running down from where we stood across the sand to dive into the water.

I turned and kissed her on the cheek.

'Me too,' I replied, breaking away. 'But we should head back.'

'Yes, we should,' she said. 'We're leaving tonight. There'll be a car coming in about an hour. That's why I came to get you.'

I didn't bother asking where we would be heading to next. She had already made it clear that our ultimate destination was to be a surprise, and letting Lauralynn boss me around made life a lot easier. Since Dominik had died so many decisions had been required of me, and there had been too much to organise. Having all of that taken away was a relief.

The journey began by car. An initial long, winding drive through brightly lit, busy streets and then morphing into darkness as we left the city behind us. Hours later we arrived at a ferry terminal, and travelled in a glass-encased cabin across the water to what I guessed was a small island. I was unable to even see a station sign pinpointing our location as another sleek vehicle pulled up immediately as we arrived, my bags were efficiently collected and stowed into the boot and the driver directed me to the back seat, shut the door and whisked us away. Lauralynn sat in the front seat and some papers exchanged hands. Passports? Money? I wondered, but could not make out their whispered conversation. Viggo sat next to me, apparently entirely nonplussed. He nodded off immediately and slept for the duration of the short journey, just his gentle snore and the heat emanating from his body the only signs of his existence.

From a white-painted, dilapidated pier we were lowered into a dinghy, no larger than the sort my father and I had fished from on occasional weekends spent by the sea near Te Aroha. Large enough for six people to sit, balanced precariously, but no more. I could understand now why Lauralynn had insisted I leave my suitcases at home. With just the three of us, and our bags, plus our so far unnamed companion who had helped us in and was busy furiously pulling the cord to start an engine which had seen far better days, we had precious little room to stretch out.

Once we had set off, the captain of our small ship grunted a brief greeting. His name was Tony, and unexpectedly, his accent was English. Essex, I guessed. I didn't ask him what he was doing sailing this tiny boat in a remote part of Brazil. Tony passed each of us a cold can of beer from an ice bucket, and a bag of salted peanuts. The bright white of his board shorts shone in the moonlight but his face was hidden by shadow and his tendency to avoid eye contact and stare either at the motor or at the floor of the boat. I could make out a thick jaw, and full mouth decorated with a thin black moustache, like a pirate version of Rhett Butler. His hands were unusually large and rough. He looked up, caught me staring at him and smiled widely, exposing a set of well-kept, white teeth. I turned away. Settling in for the ride, I imitated Viggo, and kicked my sandals off, then lay back on one of the metal benches that lined each side of the craft, propping my head up on my backpack. He was resting his head on Lauralynn's lap, who was running her hands through his hair.

We were silent, besides the noise of the motor and the sound of the sea against the boat. Initially, there was just the gentle lapping of choppy waves against the prow, but the further we travelled from land the more we picked up speed and the larger the waves became until we were crashing against the ocean and our captain signalled that I should shift from the side to the back of the boat to avoid being drenched by spray. The water was warm, and when I ran my tongue over my lips I was surprised to note that the droplets of water that had rained against my face were not salty, but sweet. I looked up, as if to find an answer to this unusual circumstance in the heavens, and saw that the sky was teeming with stars, so many that the horizon resembled a sheet of glittering sequins, enough to clothe an entire troupe of dancers at the Moulin Rouge and more to spare. As I stared in wonder, they appeared to shimmer and shift into an array of patterns, and none that I recalled from any of the basic astronomy that I could remember from high school science classes. I swore I saw the shape of a woman slowly twisting her hips and raising her arms overhead like a ballerina in a music box, but when I blinked, and looked again, this odd celestial configuration had disappeared and in its place, the sky now looked perfectly normal, if still festooned with glimmering stars.

I turned to Lauralynn and opened my mouth to speak, then closed it again, as words to explain what I thought I had briefly glimpsed escaped me, and besides which, she was gazing overboard into the water. The angle of the back of her head was fixed, as if she was looking at something in particular rather than staring into space, so I shifted my position and glanced in the same direction. The sea was aglow with a myriad of brightly coloured, luminous banks of fish, as if the stars that adorned the heavens had now fallen into the sea. They were either close to the surface, or an indeterminable distance below very clear water. The light they cast lit up the water beneath us, casting an eerie shimmer onto the waves that made it seem as if we were in fact floating through the air above the surface of the water rather than directly upon it.

Lauralynn turned back to face me, holding her hand aloft which she had evidently been trailing over the side. She grinned. Her fingers were covered with an unearthly sheen, as if she had dipped them in neon paint.

'What is this place?' I asked her.

'This is nothing,' she replied. 'You just wait until we arrive.' She bore an expression of insufferable smugness, until Tony, stationed at the helm, turned and scolded her in words that I did not understand, but presumed related to her leaning over the edge and risking tipping all of us into the ocean. Lauralynn snapped back at him and he responded by turning away from her and opening another can of beer, then passing an additional can just to me.

'I didn't know you spoke Portuguese,' I said to her, enjoying the refreshing taste of the cold lager but knowing that I would likely regret it later, and wondering if it might be better to stay sober, so I could be sure of what I had and hadn't seen.

'I don't,' Lauralynn replied. She did not elaborate any further and I did not question her. They both spoke English, and I was irritated by the linguistic exclusion, but not bothered enough to complain about it. Perhaps it was just the alcohol seeping into my bloodstream but I felt cloaked in a strong sense of peacefulness for the first time in as long as I could remember and I did not want to risk losing even a single moment of simple happiness for the sake of an explanation. It didn't matter, really, where we were going or why. For now, Lauralynn was my closest friend in the world, and I trusted her without doubt.

Buoyed by my good mood, and resolved to simply relax and enjoy whatever events were in store, I drifted into a kind of waking slumber until the engine died, and a change in the size and direction of the waves indicated that we were approaching land.

'You're swimming from here,' Tony advised me, indicating that I should jump over the side. I heard two loud splashes; Viggo and Lauralynn had both already disrobed and jumped in. There were other bodies in the water swimming towards us, perhaps to attend to our bags, or offering help to moor the boat. In any case, I did as instructed and pulled the light cotton dress that I was wearing over my head. I hesitated briefly but then also discarded my bra and knickers.

What did it matter if one more man, who I was unlikely to ever set eyes on again saw me naked? A quick glance in his direction confirmed that he had already turned back to the motor, anyway.

The water was cooler than I expected, and felt thicker than it ought to; more viscous, like milk. It was invigorating, and I emerged from my dive feeling far more vibrant than I ought to considering that I hadn't slept in – how long? It occurred to me that I had no idea what time it was or how long we had been travelling. I wasn't even sure if we were still in the same time zone.

My feet connected with the sand and I rose and scanned the shoreline for Viggo and Lauralynn, but they were nowhere to be seen.

That was when I heard the music.

At first, I thought that my ears were deceiving me. That the sound was no song, but the steady lapping of the waves, the wind whistling through trees, or even a set of bamboo chimes that might be hanging in a nearby guesthouse doorway. But it was unmistakable. Not one violin, but many.

The sound was so rich and thick it felt primal, like a cord connecting to something deep in my chest and pulling me relentlessly forward. I could not make out the melody precisely, but I was able to identify chords from the music I loved most, layered on top of one another. A truly eerie greeting, a fanfare of sorts. There was 'The Sorcerer's

Apprentice', and there, the beginning of the Spring movement from Vivaldi's 'Four Seasons'. A hint of Debussy, a
smidgeon of Grieg, a touch of Shearwater and Arcade Fire
and a teasing soupçon of Stravinsky. It was as if an unseen
Pied Piper was playing just for me.

There was nothing else for it, I still couldn't see Lauralynn
or Viggo, so I followed the music. Even if I hadn't mentally
decided that was the best thing to do, my feet would have
carried me in that direction anyway.

We had arrived at a bay, shaped like a crescent moon and
surrounded by mountains. A bed of golden sand led up to a
tropical jungle. Verdant, lush. A full moon shone like a spotlight over the island. The vegetation was almost lime green
with a ghostly white hue, like row upon row of tropical
Christmas trees. At any moment I expected to see Titania or
Puck stumble out of the shadows and carry me away. My
feet were now bare, but the ground was not uncomfortable
to walk on. As I began to pick my way through the gnarled
tangle of tree roots that lined the beach's edge I fervently
hoped that any snakes, insects or other dangerous creatures
were safe in their nests, far into the forest and not sneakily
lying in wait for me.

On I walked, aware that I was now entirely alone and
vulnerable, naked and without even my instrument to hide
behind as I had previously done in similar circumstances. I
was not afraid. The island was cocooning me in a strange

sense of blissful calm and relaxation, as if the whole place was a living creature and I was held safely within its core, like an infant bound tightly in a papoose.

A breeze brushed against my skin, thick, heavy, soft, the island's air currents massaging my flesh, carrying me along. Tendrils of gentle wind, like fingers, slid over my shoulders and caressed the curve of my breasts until I felt my nipples inevitably harden despite the humid temperature. Invisible hands crept further down the length of my body until they reached the tender skin of my thighs.

The response that this eminently strange sensation elicited in me was akin not to a sudden electrical spark, but rather the very gradual heating of a pot from cold to hot. Eventually the fire of arousal rising from deep within me caused me to stop dead and find my balance by resting one hand against an overhead branch.

'Lauralynn, Viggo?' I called out. There was no response. My words floated from my mouth like notes of a song and joined the chorus of strings that lullabied through the trees and continued to draw me deeper into the undergrowth.

It was not a tree branch, I realised, as I touched the low hanging coil, but rather a vine. The outer skin was vivid green and as smooth as a clean-shaven cheek. It was wonderfully cool and refreshing, and left the parts of me that made contact with it tingling. I dipped the end of my tongue against the plant and found that it tasted of peppermint. The music was louder here, I noticed, and more insistent. I stepped closer to the green coil and found another, and then a further length, each apparently longer and thicker than the last and equally as smooth.

No longer in motion, the air's caresses against my skin had stopped, but in its place, the tendrils that now surrounded me began to move.

At first, they simply swayed, seemingly pushed here and there by the wind, and as I allowed my weight to sink against them the plant held me until even my feet were lifted off the ground, and it seemed as though I was lying in a hammock. My whole body rubbed against the vine's strange peppermint fragrance and buzzed, as if its skin contained some kind of drug that was seeping through my epidermis into my bloodstream.

I closed my eyes, and as the rocking motion became more insistent, so too did the string lullaby that still reached my ears. I couldn't tell whether it was the plant's coils caressing me or the chords of all the tunes that had for almost my entire life fuelled my being, but something was connecting with my flesh that was at once totally impossible and yet seemed completely natural, normal, inevitable. I relaxed more, my mind entering the hypnotic state that I usually reached only when Dominik had found the perfect balance between pain and pleasure and then pushed me over the edge of it, beyond what I thought I could handle, or when I played so furiously that I lost myself entirely in the movement of my bow.

A soft moan escaped my lips. And on the music played, each note seeming ever closer to my ears and producing a new wave of pleasure inside me, each melody finding its way from my brain to my body until my flesh felt electric with desire.

I felt a gentle pressure as each of my ankles and wrists was encircled and my arms and thighs were spread apart as far as they could comfortably stretch. The refreshing coolness that had at first just soothed my skin now completely flooded my veins and I felt at once terribly alive but also thoroughly cleansed, as if I had bathed in the rivers of a baptism. And still the vine crept across and around me, trapping me in its spider web of coils.

With my eyes closed and my mind so relaxed, I could no longer discern one physical sensation from another. There was just the ever-present coolness that kept flowing through my body and more and more smooth caresses that felt something like an unending orchestra of hands and tongues playing across my flesh, stroking, licking and massaging every part of me from my cunt to my fingertips.

Images began to burst forth in my mind. Memories that matched each individual touch against my skin. Unable to identify what was actually happening in the present, I sought explanations in the past. There, that stroke, Dominik's index finger, trailing up my wrist and reaching my elbow, teasing me, knowing that soon he would reach my breasts and then begin to torture each of my nipples in that way that I so loved. Pulling, twisting, squeezing, turning each of them so hard that he would make me cry out.

A firm lick against my clitoris, that was the touch of an unnamed woman, one of the sparse handful that I had been with over the years. Then a too hard thrust, that belonged to an anonymous man, one of many who I had met in casual circumstances, his face now a blur but the peculiar size and shape of his cock and how it felt inside me remained unforgettable. I recognised a playful nibble on my earlobe that might have been Viggo, or even Lauralynn. A sudden, knowing, prying tongue against my arsehole that could only be Dominik, again. He who had known me so well and always pressed the right buttons.

Pictures continued to burst forth before my eyes like a cinemascope procession of sex, my memories and my fantasies all playing in time with the music that grew ever louder until my whole mind was overtaken with no room for anything besides sex and song. The visions were so life-like, so real that I wasn't sure whether my eyes were still closed or if I had opened them and these events were occurring all around me in the jungle.

The dreams grew darker at times. Not just the good experiences, but also the banal and the bad. There were the men from the sauna, and the terrible thrusting of the bearded man's too-long cock against my cervix. The pointed-tongue kisses of Victor, an acquaintance of Dominik's who I had known long ago and who had been the wrong sort of dominant. He had been a small, mean man, and at the time I was naïve and too consumed by lust and manipulated by the spell of his power to see the harm that he was doing me, until it was almost too late.

I saw the long, lean limbs of my old friend Charlotte, her tanned legs wrapped around Jasper, the man she had hired on a whim who had gone on to become her long-term lover. My swimming coach, who had witnessed me masturbating in the changing rooms. The way that his breath had smelled of old cigarettes when he had kissed me. I felt the soft, tender hands of Simon, the South American conductor who had been wonderfully kind and was terribly handsome but in the long run too gentle for me.

Every sexual thought and experience gone by flashed into my mind's eye like a video in fast forward and I not only felt the physical sensations over but I saw it all from afar, a bird's eye view, the expressions on the faces of all those that I had fucked and who had fucked me.

In the remembering there was a kind of forgetting. A realisation that all of it had been and was now past. That the more I tried to hold the pain at bay by pushing it out of reach, the heavier it became. The pleasures that I had enjoyed carried their own thorns, by virtue of them having been and gone, but I saw that I could let the memories stay with me, and not suffer any harm.

Dominik's lips pressed against mine in a final kiss and I did not try to pull away, to avoid the suffering that such a remembrance would bring, nor did I try to hold him fast as I so desperately wanted to. I just kissed the phantom Dominik back, until he was gone, and replaced by a whole new set of visions, these my sexual fantasies or perhaps future experiences, as yet unrealised.

I saw a group of long-haired women in a tangled circle, each with their head between another's legs as they writhed in unison. Another group; three men taking turns to lap at the cunt and arse of a woman who was standing up but so overcome by pleasure that her body was beginning to fail her and she eventually fell to the ground. A lone man with a cock as thick and large and heavy as any I had ever seen masturbating over the bare breasts of a young woman who knelt in front of him, until he exploded and white, hot juice flooded over her chest. He fell to his knees and sucked it up as it ran from her pink, hard nipples.

In another corner of my mind, or my peripheral vision, two men, each with close-cropped beards were passionately kissing. Their mouths remained locked in perpetual motion and they each had a hand on the other's cock, pulling and tugging in perfect rhythm as their tongues continued to dance. A young woman with flowing white-blonde hair stood fully nude, hand in hand with a red-haired man. He was staring at her, and she was staring at all of the events occurring around her, and me, with just the hint of a smile on her shocking crimson lips. She was covered in tattoos. Watching the crowd of people engaged in pleasure, listening to their moans of lust, witnessing a barrage of bodies in all shapes and sizes and ages each bringing to another simple joy and hedonistic release in wild and unashamed abandon.

A firm hand inexorably crept up from between my legs to my cunt. My lips were slick with moisture and the pressure upon them steadily grew, and then moved away to cup and pull apart my buttocks. I felt a firm pressure, like two or three fingers, against my anus. The sensation moved back again to my pussy. Forward and back, forward and back it swept, as if I were being invaded by the shaft of a large, hard cock that never actually breached my entrance, but instead kept sweeping the full length of my cunt and perineum, until I was ready to cry out, to beg for something to fill me and fuck me hard.

My hips moved like a metronome, the rhythm steadily increasing and increasing and the pressure rubbing against my clit faster and faster until suddenly I came in a burst of shuddering, my whole body pulsing in shock waves that seemed to emanate not from my cunt but my solar plexus, each stronger than the last until I reached a crescendo and straining against my bounds felt as if I would tear apart. Finally the waves retreated from their peak and like the ebbing of a tide I felt my desire gradually retract, the visions in my mind faded away and my tense limbs softened and stopped twitching.

The vines released their hold from my wrists and ankles but continued to support my weight. Either their texture had somehow softened or I had grown used to it as I now felt as though I were being borne along on a cloud. I flexed my muscles, mentally bringing my focus back to the present, trying to decipher whether I had been dreaming or had actually stumbled into an orgy but I was still in such a state of hypnotic, giddy relaxation I could not bring myself to try to move, or even to think or wonder where I was or where my friends were or what had happened. I drifted away into sleep.

I woke, still naked, on the sand. My clothes lay a short distance away from me, neatly folded up in a pile alongside my flimsy sandals. My head was resting on a clean, soft towel that I did not remember placing beneath me as a pillow or even having seen on the boat. I heard splashes, and sat up. Viggo and Lauralynn were a few feet away, swimming in the water.

'Come on, sleepyhead!' Lauralynn yelled. 'It's almost time to go. One last swim.'

I wiped my hand across my brow and struggled to recollect where I had been the previous night or how I had returned from the jungle to the beach, or what time or day it now was. The water beckoned. In daylight, it was as sharp and crystalline green as an emerald. I stood up, brushed some of the sand from my backside and then walked down to the sea and dived in.

'Ah!' I cried out, as the first wave hit me. It was an expression somewhere between shock and pleasure.

Lauralynn's body was invisible, as she dived repeatedly under the waves like a dolphin. I turned to Viggo, who was floating, spread-eagled on his back with his mountain of dark shaggy hair spread out like the dial of a clock around his face. He looked like a rock version of Poseidon, only skinnier.

'The water . . .' I said to him. 'It's like spearmint.'

'Tastes delicious too,' he replied. 'Open your mouth.'

I did as he suggested. It wasn't a strong taste, but a sweet, minty note and total absence of salt was clearly noticeable. My tongue tingled.

'What is this place, Viggo?' I asked him. 'Was I drunk last night?'

'Not last night,' he replied, drawing his knees up to his chest and flipping over in the water so that he was now facing me. 'We've been here three days.'

Lauralynn burst up to the surface between us, showering us both in green spray.

'It's like trying to explain music, Summer. Or sex. There's

no telling how some things work. You just have to enjoy them. And don't think about it too much.'

She was right, as bizarre as it all was. I nodded, wordlessly, and flopped over onto my back to float and watch the handful of seabirds that glided over the water and up into the sky.

Shortly thereafter, Tony and the boat arrived to collect us, and we returned to the mainland and a couple more weeks of relaxation in Rio, before heading back to the entirely different magic of London. On the endless flight home, Lauralynn repeatedly refused to answer any of my questions about the island and the bizarre events that had occurred there, or whether or not I had in fact dreamed it all.

Nonetheless, the break had blown my blues away, and I felt as if I was ready to start life again, anew.

5

Summer in the City

By the time I arrived back in London – Lauralynn and Viggo had arranged a stop-off in Los Angeles on the journey back for talks with his local-based record label about his new projects – it was summer.

Unlike places like Paris, and many others, which emptied at this turn of the season and transformed into impersonal ghost towns mostly populated by tourists and dull out of town visitors, it was a time of year when the city was truly effervescent, bubbling with activity and energy as if new blood had been pumped into it. On top of that, after the break or possibly due to the unexplainable events that had occurred on the island, I felt reborn, as if I had shed my former self and had become a brand new me and a fresh arrival in the big city. I picked up a listings magazine and was dazzled by the scores of unusual exhibitions which I felt compelled to see films I had read about beckoning to be watched, a multitude of plays and restaurants that had opened with menus strange and fantastic and combinations of ingredients and tastes that just begged to be savoured if the critics were to be believed. My sojourn on the island, it appeared, had distinctly awakened my other more prosaic appetites.

There was something in the air and it was dazzling. Rio de Janeiro and the island, despite their intoxicating atmosphere and hedonistic activities had turned into a haven of peace where my senses had been caressed, teased in subtle ways, the smooth tendrils of pleasure soothing my soul; but this was another life altogether, an explosion of possibilities that flattered the brain and not just the senses and it made me feel more alive than I had been for ages. London thrummed with excitement, it seemed to me. And I wanted to partake with greed and glee.

I took the tube from Hampstead to Borough, to breakfast at Borough Market before taking a stroll along the Thames Path, all the way to the South Bank. Unusually for me, I had woken early and I arrived at the market before the crowds had begun to gather. Red and white aproned vendors of cheese, meats and other various delicacies from the regions and abroad were still setting up their stalls. A handful of genuine, non-touristic shoppers, equipped with recycled canvas bags to carry their purchases home, were sorting through mountains of produce with steady hands and sharp eyes seeking only the juiciest, ripest fruits and vegetables with the best flavour.

Monmouth Coffee, the best in the area in my coffee-addicted opinion, would be open in 30 minutes or so, and not long after that the queue at the door would be so long it would reach up to the corner of the street and halfway to the next. I sat on one of the benches and waited. First my caffeine fix, and then I would seek food.

Shopping for sustenance at Borough Market was something of a ritual for me. For someone of my temperament, a slave to her appetites, the sheer number of choices on offer, each delectable in their own right and purveyed with such savage bias on the part of the sellers, was overwhelming. Would I start with a large punnet of fresh, new season strawberries, and walk through the other stands taking bite after succulent bite of the red fruits? Or go straight in for a hot option, a homemade beef or turkey burger, dripping with onion relish and hot sauce, or pulled pork with apple chutney stuffed into a warm, lightly-toasted bap? At the other end of the stalls I knew there would be grilled halloumi or boxes of exotic salads covered with a squeeze of lime, large wheels of cheese that I could sample on bite-sized pieces of baguettes, bowls of olive oil and spices to dip it all into, wooden bowls filled with handmade chocolates and Turkish Delight in flavours both ordinary and unimaginable and case upon case of sweet pastries, pies, tarts, cakes, meringues the size of cob loaves and custard squares double the width and breadth of my hand.

My mouth watered. Each one of my imaginary taste tests seemed more vivid than usual. I could almost feel the strawberries bursting in my mouth and the juice running down my chin. I felt as though I had accidentally wandered into Willy Wonka's chocolate factory and imbibed one of the food pills that turned the unsuspecting Veruca Salt into a blueberry.

'Opening soon?' I mouthed through the window to the barista who was wiping down the counter inside. He pointed to the sign on the door that I had somehow missed that indicated I had yet another 30 minutes to wait. I turned back, my eyes roving the nearby cafés and stalls for another option. Across the other side of the road, I saw a sign advertising Turkish coffee and two men serving someone at the counter.

Nearby, a woman was standing, waiting. There was something about her that marked her out, besides the heavy inked images that decorated her arms and calves, belying her otherwise conservative appearance. She didn't blend in with the rest of the morning shoppers or stall holders. Perhaps it was the fact that she lacked any sign of impatience and was not busily surfing the internet on a smart phone as most people did these days when not engaged in conversation or another activity. She seemed apart from the populace, somehow. I studied her more closely. There was something else. Something about her seemed familiar, as if I had seen her before, but couldn't place where.

Her dress had cap sleeves, a round neckline that covered her chest almost to her throat and was a pale lemon yellow. It flowed over her body like silk rather than cotton. Turquoise blue sandals encased her feet, tied with thin blue ribbons that wrapped around her ankles and her calves, just an inch or so below the hem of her dress. A thin green belt accentuated what there was of her waist. She was slender but had a long, lean straight figure, not an hourglass shape. A large floppy sun hat obscured her eyes and nose, but I could see that she had a wide mouth, and her lips were reddened with glossy rouge. Beneath her hat, ribbons of hair so blonde that it was almost white flowed over her shoulders and arms. The mixture of colours on anyone else might have seemed gaudy, but she carried each shade well so that her overall look maintained a sense of subtlety whilst still being irregular.

The man at the counter finished his transaction and walked across to her, holding two tiny polystyrene cups that were likely filled with espresso shots. She was transfixed, either by the sights and sounds of the market, or lost in her own thoughts, and did not respond to his presence until he touched his hand to her elbow. It was a lingering touch, a caress rather than a poke or prod to get her attention. Immediately her mouth turned upwards into a broad smile, as if just being near him brought her happiness. The coffees escaped her attention entirely until he placed one of the cups into her hand. She took hold of it, and brushed her fingertips over his jaw and lips, then kissed him briefly on the mouth. They both laughed as her large hat got in the way of their kiss, and when she pushed the brim back I saw the rest of her face. She was deathly pale, and did not seem to be wearing any make-up besides the red lipstick, which she was now wiping off her man's lips. I could not make out the colour of her eyes from this distance, but guessed they must be blue or grey. She seemed liked that sort. An ice-queen type. Beautiful in a sparse, elegant sort of way. I could not guess at her age. On the one hand she was free of the usual signs of age, but on the other, her fashion sense was not youthful, and a sense of maturity lingered over her. The tattoos seemed so much of a natural part of her they were barely noticeable once I registered their existence, despite their number and juxtaposition with her mannerisms.

I turned my attention to him. He was tall, by virtue of the fact that he was taller than her. Probably over six foot, I guessed. His hair was auburn. Perhaps red, but I couldn't quite tell in the light. Despite the heat that would likely come later in the day, he wore a white collared shirt rather than a T-shirt, and a pair of light brown chinos. His chest was broad, and he moved like someone who was fit, but not overly muscle-bound. His ankles were bare and he wore tan loafers on his feet. They fitted together easily as a couple. There was no need for words between them, for forced small talk or for one or the other to break away to check a phone or look at something. They simply stood, side by side, each basking in the physical presence of the other. When one moved, even just a turn of the foot or shifting weight from one leg to another then the other shifted with them, as if one was a wave and the other was the tide and they were each inevitably pulled by the direction of the other.

A knot rose in my throat. Dominik and I had been like that, I knew it. It would not have surprised me to learn that we breathed in time with each other, such was the fit of our bodies. Of course, since I had been alone following his death, I noticed other couples. Mostly, they didn't bother or upset me, because few couples seemed publicly happy together. Really happy. I had seen people sitting across from each other in restaurants for hours without exchanging a word. Others bickered, or seemed to just tolerate one another as their eyes roamed, checking out other men and women around them. Or they were engrossed by the pressures applied by young children, with little attention left over for anyone besides the toddlers who clung to their hands or pulled at their trouser legs. They might have been different, alone. But besides the hot lust of young, new couples or weekend lovers I rarely saw the easy affection displayed in the way that only two people who know each other in absolute detailed intimacy can display.

I noticed that neither of them carried any sort of bag or purse. They didn't look like shoppers or tourists. More like they were killing time, waiting for someone.

Then, to my surprise, the woman beckoned to me.

I looked around, thinking that she must have spotted a friend standing near me, but there was no one else on the street. She beckoned again. It was unmistakable.

I stood and walked over.

She removed her hat with one hand, and quickly ran the other through her hair before extending it to me. I was right, her eyes were blue. I shook her hand. Her skin was cool, and her hand was very light and slender but her grasp was firm and business-like.

'You're Summer,' she said. It was not a question, but an announcement. 'I'm Aurelia,' she added. 'Aurelia Carter.'

'Andrei,' interjected the auburn-haired man. His hands were large and smooth, and much warmer than hers. Of the two of them, Aurelia was the dominant one, I thought. Perhaps not in the way that they expressed their sexuality. Not like Lauralynn and Viggo. Nor like an employer and employee. Their relationship had layers that I could not yet identify.

'Please sit down,' said Aurelia, pointing to one of the

green plastic picnic tables that sat outside the coffee stand. It was no more a request than her greeting had been a question, and I did as she instructed. 'You don't remember us,' she added.

'Sorry,' I apologised, shaking my head. 'You do seem familiar, but I can't recall. Have we met before?' They must be acquaintances of someone I knew, I figured. Maybe old friends of Dominik's, or perhaps she was a musician. I became so lost in the music when I played that I regularly forgot to pay any attention at all to other members of the orchestra. I immediately glanced at her hands, although contrary to popular opinion, long, thin fingers were rarely a sign of anything. Hers were slim and delicate, but strong, I knew that from her handshake. She wore no rings. I turned to Andrei. He was staring at me with interest, in a manner that suggested that he was seeking something more than what I presented on the surface, but he was evidently waiting for Aurelia to speak.

'You recently visited a place where we sometimes hold events or use as a retreat. And where some of our performers go to ... to rest, or to train and plan new routines. It is a very special place ...'

'The island?' I asked. I leaned forward in my seat, eager to hear more about the mysterious activities that had occurred there. I hadn't seen much of Lauralynn and Viggo since my return as they had been busy working on Viggo's latest project, and when I had seen them, Lauralynn had been terribly vague. In the end I had passed it off as a dream, or maybe the results of a poisonous plant or a drug that had been dropped in my can of beer. Whatever had happened, the results certainly hadn't been harmful. Quite the contrary. I had still not lost that acute sense of peace and calm that I had experienced there and yet my days felt so much brighter. I still missed Dominik, of course, and experienced grief, but I had shaken the cloud of depression that had hung over me since he'd gone.

'Yes, the island. We were there too.' She held up her hand in response to the expression on my face, as if to reassure me that it wasn't a problem that my recollection of my time there was so shaky. 'It is difficult, even for those who have been in our employ for a long time to be certain of what is real and what is not, so please, don't be concerned. It is a place with its own kind of magic, but I promise, you were safe there. We have been watching you for some time.'

'Watching me?' A flash of alarm must have crossed my face and Andrei laughed. He was leaning back in his chair now, relaxed, and smiling, twisting his now empty espresso cup back and forth between his middle and index fingers. Whatever he had been looking for, he had apparently found it, or given up altogether. He turned back to the counter and motioned for another round of coffees, and within minutes, a cup was placed into my hands. I took a sip. It was wonderfully thick and strong.

'Because of the nature of the work that we do,' Aurelia explained, 'all of our performers must be very talented, and versatile in other ways.'

'The best in the world,' Andrei interrupted, nodding as he did so to emphasise his point.

'But they must have something else, as well. It's not just a matter of open-mindedness, or of high sexual drive. We require talented performers who possess a certain level of sexual power. Magick, some people would call it, but it isn't really that,' she continued.

'Depending on your point of view,' Andrei added, and they glanced at each other, sharing a complicit smile.

'What line of work, exactly, is it that you're engaged in?' I queried. I planned to direct them to my agent, who handled all negotiations for any performances, but my curiosity led me to question them further before I halted the conversation. Lauralynn had been right about the rumours, I thought with only a little misgiving. Evidently the nature of my encounters around Europe had not gone unnoticed, but I certainly did not expect to be offered work in – what – playing music in sex clubs perhaps? as a result.

'You must understand, there is only a certain amount that we can divulge at this stage.'

'Of course,' I replied, accustomed to the secrecy adopted by creative types that often masked a fear of failure, 'but you can't expect me to agree to anything without knowing at least a little more about it. Particularly since these events sound somewhat . . . alternative.'

Aurelia nodded, and continued to explain.

'We are connected with an organisation who run very high profile, erotic events. Typically quite small. Only for either the richest, the most discreet, the most persuasive or curious individuals who seek us out. We refer to ourselves as the Network, for want of a better name. Your anonymity, if you were to perform at any such event, would be absolutely assured. And the pay is very good. In fact you performed at one of our events some time back, although you were only allowed to see, how might I term it, the tip of the iceberg?'

I tried to recall which gig that might have been, and after thoroughly dredging through my memories vaguely recalled a set in a North London mansion, where the audience had all been unusually attired in risqué, scanty, or just plain weird outfits and afterwards I had been briskly ushered away and had wondered what was being hidden from me. It had stuck in my mind as usually the kind of crowds I played to were the cardigan and string-of-pearls wearing sort, or music students and a smaller contingent of hipsters wearing torn jeans or tweed suits picked up from charity shops in a bid to appear fashionably ironic. And a handful of city types in actual suits, straight from work. Not a whole roomful of swingers, goths, kinksters or any mixture of the three, that's for sure.

'I'm not in need of money,' I told her. I was beginning to bristle a little now, and becoming impatient.

'And the performances ... they are different. Not sleazy or vulgar in any way. Erotic art, of the highest calibre.'

I shrugged my shoulders.

'But that is not why we contacted you.'

'OK,' I said. I turned the coffee cup in my hands, as Andrei had done. The dark, bitter grounds had settled at the bottom and with some careful handling I knew I would be able to get a few more sips without taking a mouthful of sediment. 'Why did you really contact me?'

'We want you to perform at our Ball again, but this time you would be totally integrated into the spectacle, not just an opening act. It occurs more or less every two years. The next one is to take place in just under a year from now, in a somewhat unusual but fascinating area in America, in the desert. We would pay generously of course, and your travel expenses would be fully covered, and although the actual event is just one night, you would be expected to be involved fairly actively, both before and after. It would be a major commitment . . .'

'Would I be at liberty to play the music of my choice?' I asked.

'Yes of course,' she replied. 'That goes without saying. You would play solo if you wished. But then again, if you preferred some form of backing, we would also provide for that. And you'd have total control over every aspect of the performance.'

I felt my skin begin to tingle with excitement. Susan, my agent, would go nuts if she knew that I was even considering agreeing to even a one-off piece of work without consulting her and going through all of the proper contractual malarkey and paperwork. But for one night, and whatever they had vaguely referred to as 'involvement' before and after, I could probably disappear and call it a holiday. I had always wanted to visit the desert. Immediately images straight from the Arabian Nights burst into my mind in vivid, three-dimensional colour.

'What is this Ball?' I asked. 'You said it was related to the island? To what I experienced there? I thought that I was drunk, or dreaming ...'

'No, you weren't drunk,' she said. 'As for dreaming ... not entirely. When the mind is in that very relaxed state that you experienced, every thought and sensation is heightened, a hundred times over, at least ... May I?' she asked, indicating that she wanted to take my hand in hers.

'Of course,' I said, stretching my arm out across the table. This woman was like a witch. Enchanting. I could see why Andrei doted on her every word and movement. She could have hypnotised even the most hard-hearted womaniser.

Aurelia picked up my offered hand in one of hers, and turned it over. She ran the fingertips of her other hand very lightly over my wrist as she spoke. 'In your ordinary waking moments,' she explained, 'a gentle touch like this would feel like exactly that and no more.' I nodded. 'Now,' she said. 'Close your eyes. Let your body relax. Imagine that you're back there, swimming through the green water to the shore. Everything is calm. The sea is full of fish, but they won't hurt you. Now your feet are sinking into the sand, and you're walking into the jungle. You're totally alone, but you're safe, and your feet are stepping easily over the tree roots. You remember your way back to the vines, where you slept.'

I continued to nod, to indicate that I was listening, and mentally followed her directions. My back began to fill out against the chair that I was resting on, and my limbs relaxed. My mind started to wander, and Aurelia's voice took on a sonorous quality, like the intonation of a deep, heavy bell. I could hear music through the branches of the trees that had appeared in my mind, a mental lullaby that soothed my muscles into an even deeper state of relaxation.

'Now,' she said, 'concentrate on my touch.'

I did so, and suddenly, instead of a feather-light touch on my wrist I felt four hands travelling the length of my naked body; one slim, pale pair and the other thick and heavy, unmistakably belonging to Aurelia and Andrei respectively. The response of my body was immediate and unstoppable. I felt a familiar wetness gathering in my loins and a strong flood of desire sweeping through my veins, leaving me weak and breathless. I was sure that my face had reddened.

My eyelids opened immediately, partly in shock and partly in embarrassment.

I was still in the heart of Borough Market and its familiar environment. Aurelia was smiling at me. It might even have been a smirk.

'I did nothing more than touch your wrist,' she said, releasing me. Instinctively I cradled the wrist that she had been holding with the fingers of my other hand.

'And I haven't moved,' Andrei added.

It seemed that they both knew what I had been imagining.

'You see,' Aurelia explained. 'There's no trickery involved. Just a heightened sense of awareness possessed by only a very few individuals, and the readiness to accept that desire. That's what the Ball is all about. We work to preserve the joy and wildness of human sexuality, to remove the shame that clouds intimacy for so many people ... The Ball is a celebration of sex. And to make that happen, we stimulate the senses. The eyes, the flesh, the smell, of course, the hearing. We want you to arouse people, with your music. Just like what you experienced on the island, but on a much larger scale. It would be an unforgettable experience, for you and for all others present.'

They were both staring at me intensely.

I broke away from their gaze and looked down at my coffee cup, then glanced up again.

'It's an interesting proposition,' I said. 'But I'll need to think about it.'

I felt as if I was not being told everything about the Ball and the involvement they sought of me. Something was being held back. Or maybe it was just too weird to be believed.

'No problem,' Aurelia said. Her expression was relieved, as if to her mind I had accepted already. She slid her fingers down the front of her dress and pulled out a white card with a phone number handwritten across it in a neat font, in blue ink. 'Take as long as you like.'

I seized the card, which was still warm from the heat of her breast, and slipped it into my pocket, thinking immediately of the man from the Kentish Town sauna. What was it with me and strangers with cards?

They rose from their seats in unison, and I quickly stood up to bid them goodbye. My plastic seat clattered. We shook hands, and Aurelia tilted her chin towards me in a firm nod of acknowledgment.

I sat down again, and watched them walk away. They had linked hands within moments of leaving the table. It was an instinctive gesture. I could not have pinpointed who had extended a hand to the other first. A gust of wind caught Aurelia's dress and it briefly flew up at the bottom, displaying the meaty flesh of her calf muscles and the backs of her knees. I caught a brief glimpse of another large tattoo.

The waiter returned, and placed another cup of coffee in front of me, explaining that Andrei had ordered and paid for it earlier, although I hadn't noticed him do so.

My thoughts of the strange introduction and their offer were interrupted by the rumbling of my stomach. I had been so distracted by our conversation that I had entirely forgotten I had not yet eaten breakfast, and now my stomach was crying out for food. I took my coffee, stopped at the nearest food stand and ordered a beef burger with cheese and extra relish, then made my way home.

When I arrived, I stuck Aurelia's card to the fridge with a magnet. I would keep her offer in the back of my mind, I decided, and mull it over. Until then, I would get on with the business of enjoying London in summer, lazy days out, and even lazier mornings relaxing at home.

It was late in the morning and I was still in bed. No longer sleeping, but lazily half-awake, half-somnolent, on the fuzzy shores of indulgence. I was being distantly serenaded by small birds buzzing along the higher branches of the Heath's trees outside my window, and in the deepest recesses of my brain, was attempting to divine some sort of elusive pattern or tune in their random chants.

I stretched out like a snow angel across the thin white

sheet covering me. Extended my arm to pick up the bottle of mineral water I kept on the floor on my side of the bed and took a deep sip from it.

My phone rang.

I reluctantly shook off the cobwebs holding back my wakefulness.

'Hello?'

'Is that Miss Zahova?'

'Hmmm . . .'

'Summer Zahova?'

'Yes.'

The voice was male. English though accentless, with no regional traits. Deep and smooth. Seductive.

'Good. My name is Antony Torgerson. Antony without an H,' he spelled it out. 'I've been sending you e-mails but gather you've been overseas. Your agent's offices gave me your telephone number.'

He must be OK, I reflected, as they wouldn't have communicated my number to just anyone.

'OK.'

'Maybe you've heard of me,' he said. I hadn't. 'I'm a theatre director. I understand you've become the executor for the estate of Dominik . . .'

A dark cloud blanked out the rest of his words.

Something caught in my throat.

'Oh . . .'

'It's about his second novel. *The Violin Diaries*. I'm a great fan.'

I regained my composure. Pulled the bed cover up across my chest, covering my naked breasts, not that he could have been aware of my state of undress on the other end of the phone line.

'The book didn't do that well,' I pointed out. 'It was a commercial disappointment,' I added.

'I know,' the man said. 'All the more reason to help people become aware of it again.'

Dominik had blamed the novel's lack of success on timing and the vagaries of fashion in the minds of the reading public. The reviews had been sparse, although the storyline was original and if anything, Dominik had believed the quality of the writing had been better than his initial effort which despite its flaws had been a runaway success. Just one of those things.

'How?' I asked him.

'I think it would make for a great adaptation to the stage, I really do.'

I was intrigued, if dubious. The book's plot was all over the place and had few central characters. Unlike his first, outrageously romantic novel which I had unwittingly inspired, it had not even drawn any form of interest from the movies whatsoever.

'Do you think so?'

'Very much.'

'It's an interesting idea, Mr Torgerson,' I said. 'So what are you after? An option for the stage rights? In which case, I fear I'm not the person you should be speaking to. Maybe best if you contacted the publishers ...'

I certainly didn't want to become involved in any form of financial transaction. Just didn't wish for Dominik's memory and books to be dirtied by such considerations. As for me, I had money enough right now and was in no need of further funds, since the impromptu European tour had proven surprisingly lucrative.

'I have already spoken to them,' he answered. 'But I'd also rather obtain your blessing as Dominik's executor, some form of understanding and approval for what I'm hoping to achieve with the adaptation,' he concluded. 'It would be nice to have you on board before anything is signed off. I'd also like to put some of my ideas to you, casting and otherwise.'

He sounded genuinely concerned. I was still unsure whether to allow myself to become involved, wary that it might drag old ghosts back to the surface and disturb the fragile equilibrium the visit to the island had rebuilt. My silence spoke for itself.

'Maybe we could meet up? For a drink? So I can put you at ease and demonstrate that my intentions are quite honourable,' he said. 'It would be so much easier to explain in person.'

What was there to lose? He would just propose some ideas as to how Dominik's difficult second book could translate to a theatre stage. It might even prove interesting. Because of the subject matter of the cursed violin, maybe he had certain musical elements already in mind?

I agreed to see him.

I slipped back under the covers. The bird songs had ceased. I looked up at the ceiling, half guessing at shapes in the ever so uneven plaster as sharp rays of sunlight jutted their way through the open window and spread unevenly through the bedroom in a maze of geometric patterns.

I was casually hoping I would doze off again and briefly banish all thoughts of life and the reality I was still muddling my way through, but was unable to do so.

Reflecting on Aurelia and Andrei's strange offer and the telephone call about Dominik's book. A strange confluence: one road opening to a new future and the other leading back into the past, respective diversions that could either harm me or act as an exorcism. Which should I take? Or could I embark on both journeys and retain my sense of peace?

The phone rang again. I let it ring, unwilling to process yet more information. It stopped. Then began to ring again as if first time around the caller had decided he or she had been calling a wrong number and was determined to get through to the right one.

It was my sister Fran.

Tonight she wanted to take me dancing.

Oh yes, I would dance!

A decade or more of joyful sweat lined the subterranean walls of the club or dripped like candlewax in slow motion, down the outdated posters advertising long forgotten punk groups.

I was drunk.

Neither a merry or a sad sort of drunk, but a detached one, observing from afar how my steps were becoming increasingly uncoordinated and my gestures a touch too abrupt. The noise was unbearably loud and I kept my mouth shut, unlike all my companions blabbering away at high pitch with no one in our group able to hear a single word of what any other was saying. I felt like an observer in an aquarium watching the mouths of fish behind the protective glass distort into twisted shapes as they exhaled. It had been ages since I'd imbibed so much alcohol. I'd never been much of a drinker anyway, just the occasional glass of wine and rare half pints of beer in social circumstances, but Dominik had not indulged and I had found it easier to copy his habit in the time we were together.

The damage had been done by a series of cocktails in gaudy colours and a litter of miniature matchstick umbrellas was spread across our oval table, alongside the empty glasses. It was her birthday and Fran had sworn to sample her way through the entire list of cocktails on the card. Chris, still friends with us both but no longer her other half, appeared more in control, even though his gestures were growing broader by the minute and his laugh even more raucous.

A musician whose name I couldn't remember, a friend of Chris's, tapped me on the shoulder, indicating the swarming dance floor. Oh, why not?

I rose, unsteadily, although I was still half a dozen cocktails behind Fran, Chris and their other celebrating friends. I'd tried the emerald blue, scarlet pink, sickly green and sharp orange ones, but still had to face the deep purple, canary yellow and the turd brown liquid concoctions that lay on my side of the table, waiting for me to summon up the courage to continue this boozy road to meaningless damnation.

Using our elbows we made our way to a pocket of free space on the dance floor and within seconds we were submerged by a pack of bodies and separated, as the metal disco pounded out its relentless rhythms and the whole room swayed in its wake. The strobe lights flashed like robots on a rampage through a science fiction apocalypse, each shot of white lightning skimming across the forest canopy of shaking heads and crashing against the damp, sweat-laden walls in continuous waves.

Like a tide emerging from prehistoric depths the faint trace of a melody began to break through the din and my brain switched to a higher gear and instinctively focused on the underlying heart of the music. Through the heat haze I watched another dancer, a young girl with a distinctive dimple in her chin as she stretched her arms away from her seemingly convulsing body like a spider. She wore a tight black mini-dress and between the explosions of light I noticed how her under-arm hair was a bush of darkness until the next flash of strobe light blinded me and she vanished into the mass of heaving dancers, leaving that incongruous vision carved at the forefront of my muddled mind.

Another dancer, a man, all in black leather, shook like a puppet, his bulk stomping the floor like a mastodon. His companion, an ethereal blonde in a white T-shirt and skinny jeans with holes at the knees, towered over him, her spreading shadow enveloping him like a spectre and then they were gone in the blink of the beat and replaced by other couples, dancers, men, women, each one a whole world of particularities, each shaking, twisting, frozen in time, immobile for a nano second then gesticulating wildly like will o' the wisps on a frenzied rampage. I couldn't remember the last time I had been so drunk. I laughed.

I had never been great shakes as a dancer. The last time I had done so in earnest had been after New Year's in New Orleans when Dominik had ordered me to do so, naked, in that strange club. And my nudity had no doubt compensated for my distinct lack of grace. But ever since, my body had melted into music with uncommon ease, my violin forming an extension of my nerves through which all my feelings travelled. And dancing, right now, evoked similar emotions. My limbs felt loose. I hunted again for the deep-lying melody at the heart of the disco metal inferno unleashed around me until it finally began to communicate with me. And the world, the crowds, the other dancers all retreated and I was left, alone, in a bubble of my own making. My private space. In which I danced, disjointed, liberated, however clumsily I moved in a parody of elegance, in search of beauty and transcendence. I imagined I was playing the Bailly and the sharp dissonances of Stravinsky's 'Rite of Spring' were rushing from the depths and I was controlling them, conducting the shrieks of desolation about to be unleashed.

On and on I shook, swayed, turned, sang to myself, whispered, danced.

And danced.

And danced.

And became marginally aware that I was finally holding the darkness at bay and I had no need for anything else. Even sex.

There must have been a break between DJ sets and the music had ground to a shuddering halt, but I had kept on dancing and not even noticed. Eyes closed, gliding along the hard dance floor as if on wheels, an ice skater on a bed of clouds.

'Hey, Summer . . .' Fran had called out to me and I peered through the curtains of my own private world and realised I was almost the last one standing. I regained my composure and stepped back to our alcove table and, silently, considered the choice of purple, yellow or brown cocktail next. With accompanying umbrella, of course.

Prior to our meeting, I'd idly tried to picture what Antony Torgerson might look like from the sound of his voice. So when he walked into Patisserie Valerie on the corner of Charing Cross Road and Great Newport Street, I was not quite expecting the tall, slim dark blond man in navy blue corduroy jacket, open-necked white shirt and impeccably creased designer jeans who stepped past the door and cast an enquiring look at both rooms of the café until he spotted me.

A broad smile crossed his full lips as he noticed me and walked over. He wore light brown shoes, polished to a tee. I was nursing a creamy cappuccino and biting into a thin slice of cake dotted with wild berries. His handshake was firm.

'I have some of your albums,' he said. 'I must confess I'm more of a rock 'n' roll person, and not that knowledgeable about classical music, but the sounds you squeeze out of your violin are at times quite extraordinary.'

'Thank you.' I was unsure whether the compliment was meant as a bit of a backhanded one or not.

He hailed the waitress and ordered a double espresso and a croissant.

'I've been up working most of the night and just had a few hours' sleep, so this is breakfast time for me,' he explained. It was early afternoon.

He looked at me. His hair, cropped short at the sides but combed back with the mere hint of a nascent quiff at the front, sat on the frontier of dark blond and light brown. On anyone else the style would have appeared just a tad pretentious, but it completed his appearance to perfection, adding a necessary touch of foppiness to the carved hardness of his features. I held his gaze, captivated by the ebony black of his eyes, the darkness almost artificial and incandescent. Could he be wearing coloured lenses or was he one of those rare specimens, a genuinely dark-eyed blond? The effect was striking.

'You look different from the photographs on your CDs,' he said.

'They were taken a long time ago,' I pointed out. 'My hair was loose and free in the photos.' Today it was pulled back and unstyled.

'It's not the hair,' he said. 'Or time. Something else.' He continued.

'Oh, you know, the miracles of Photoshop . . .' I sketched a faint smile.

He downed his coffee in one hearty gulp and bit into the fluffy croissant.

'So, tell me what you had in mind. For Dominik's novel?' I asked.

'Of course.'

He swept the crumbs from the croissant off the table and onto the café floor with the cuff of his jacket, clearing space for a roll of pages he pulled out from his pocket.

He explained.

The book traced the history of a violin, from the time it had been carved out of wood, crafted, through a couple of centuries and outlined the way it had, seemingly in a super-natural manner, affected the lives of its successive owners. Sometimes it appeared to cast a curse on the characters, affecting their passions, ruining their relationships and destroying the course of their lives. It was almost like a ghost story in which the ghost happened to be a musical instrument rather than some fearful entity from the depths of hell.

As a result the book was episodic and as soon as you became captivated by a given protagonist, the storyline would move on to another, never allowing the reader to sympathise long enough or develop sufficient empathy with anyone. It was something that Dominik had been acutely aware of but couldn't find a way of addressing without undermining the whole concept behind the book.

And on a stage, such an episodic structure wouldn't pan out any better, Antony concluded.

'So why is the project of interest to you, then?' I asked him.

'Ah,' he waved his hands around to strengthen his point. 'That's just it.'

I must have looked puzzled.

'Apart from the violin, what's the main thread of the story?' Antony quizzed me, as if I was a schoolchild in a classroom.

I remained silent, unable to catch his drift, watching in fascination an unseen fire rise inside him, his features growing in animation.

'The music,' he said triumphantly.

'The music?'

'Yes. That's the whole rationale for the violin, isn't it?'

I nodded politely.

'So, instead of concentrating on one of the random characters who come across the violin along the tide of years and bringing them artificially to the forefront and slowing down the whole plot,' Antony pointed out, 'we make the music the main character. The thread that holds everything together. And the play becomes as much music as it is words ...'

He was beaming.

'Not quite an opera,' he said. 'Or a musical ...'

I was beginning to intuit what he was thinking of.

His enthusiasm was contagious. He unrolled some of the

loose sheets of paper and showed me a series of rough sketches for the possible sets. One for each historical period covered by the violin's story.

'And each era is represented by a different kind of music . . .'

It was a seductive concept.

I pondered over it.

'It could work well,' I admitted. 'But what music? Whichever classical pieces you happen to select it wouldn't be . . .' I struggled for the right words to translate my thoughts. 'Organic. That's it, organic enough. If the music is actually the play's main actor, it must have some unity from set to set, from character to character, the violin's successive owners, it can't be just a "Best Of" the classical canon.'

'Of course.' He was smiling. 'I knew you'd understand me.'

'Have I?'

'I read somewhere that the book was inspired by a violin you actually own, Summer. Is that true?'

'Partly,' I admitted. 'Dominik did some research into its history, but I must confess that when he wrote the book he improvised a lot, to make things more dramatic. That's what writers do.'

'I understand.'

'But I do like your concept,' I said.

'It's ambitious,' Antony conceded.

Silence fell. At the table next to us, two elderly German tourists were arguing between themselves as to which particular patisserie they should try before opting to share all three they had set their sights on between them.

Out of the blue, Antony took hold of my hand.

His was remarkably warm.

'Summer, would you be willing to become involved in the project?'

'Advising on the music?'

'No. More ... Only you could do it, I believe.'

'What?'

'Write the music for the play. I think you'd be perfect.'

His hand still gripped mine.

I could feel his hunger, his fire.

It had an edgy familiarity.

6

Two-Hearted Spider

Even though his heart belonged to the stage, Antony had directed a bunch of movies some years before. A play he had set up on the South Bank had proved a major hit with critics and public alike and he had been asked to adapt it for the big screen, which had led to a couple of further lucrative Hollywood assignments. The two movies that had then followed had performed adequately, but working on them he had found himself increasingly frustrated by the formulaic nature of the material he had a limited opportunity to shape to his liking and the countless interference by studio executives holding him back and restraining most of his more innovative ideas.

As a result, he had since been systematically turning down further movie opportunities, preferring to devote his time and energy to the theatre.

'Soon, they will learn to leave me in peace and stop offering me bad scripts and I will gladly become the cinema's forgotten man,' he explained.

But the money he had made had helped him acquire an expensive apartment on the penthouse floor of an imposing development on the Isle of Dogs, overlooking the Thames and much of London's most coveted horizons.

This was now our third meeting since his initial approach at Patisserie Valerie, but the first time I had been invited to where he lived and worked. The view through the vast bay windows was vertiginous and so unlike the vistas I'd once enjoyed over Hampstead Heath or, more recently, from my first floor maisonette overlooking Clapham Common into which I had moved after selling the Hampstead house as all my friends had advised me to. Much to my surprise, Dominik had actually made a will and left it to me, as well as most of his belongings. I had barely held on to a few cartons of his books as there was no way they would fit into my new flat, and at Viggo's recommendation, had donated the rest of his collections to a university library who had expressed interest in his papers.

It was a grey autumn day as I sipped coffee after coffee and faced Antony across the low glass table over which he had spread his notes, and sections of the script in progress.

Initially, I had thought my task would mainly consist of

choosing relevant pieces of music from the classical repertoire to suit the mood of the respective mini-plays set in specific historical eras through which the cursed violin in the story made an appearance. To my surprise and initial irritation, Antony had quickly dismissed the idea after listening to some of my choices.

'It's too predictable, Summer,' he had said. From the look in his eyes, I could see he was actually disappointed in me as if he had expected more. I was stung by his censure.

'I only play the music, you know. I'm an interpreter, that's all.'

He rose to his feet. He was wearing a loose white T-shirt and his usual jeans. He had visibly not shaved for a few days and stubble darkened his chin and cheeks. He looked thinner than the first time we had met. Rakish.

'You're more than that. I've heard you play. Actually seen you perform in concert once,' he confessed.

This was the first time he had revealed this.

'When?' I asked him.

'It doesn't matter where,' he answered. 'You were on fire, literally in a trance. It was an incredible thing to see ... Actually, very sexy ...'

'Oh ...'

'Although,' he added, 'terribly distracting and, to this day, I don't even recall what you were actually playing.' He flashed a wry smile.

'I'm glad you liked it.'

'That's the Summer Zahova I was hoping I could resurrect.'

'Maybe you expect too much of me?'

'I expect the best, no less.'

'So do you have any suggestions, perhaps?'

He handed me a few sheets of his papers. A scene where the violin's second owner comes across the instrument for the first time, together with various sketches about the set against which it might unfold.

'Take this and go home. Read it. Absorb it. Think about it. And call me when you have an idea.' He looked away from me and buried himself in his other notes. I was dismissed.

Summarily.

I hesitated a moment. What was this? Did he think I was at his beck and call?

I felt insulted.

I stood up. Leaving the proffered pages behind on the glass table, turned my back on him and walked out of the apartment. I was hoping he would call me back and apologise for his brusqueness. I think he never even looked my way as I departed and slammed the door. I was fuming.

I rushed down the corridor and called for the elevator. It took its time coming and as the doors opened, a short, curvy young woman with dark flowing hair in a flowery print dress with more cleavage than front, walked out of it. She glanced at me.

'Ah, you're his violin player,' she remarked, with a note of impertinence and superiority.

My mood was darkening. In as sarcastic a tone as I could manage, I responded 'And you are?'

She grinned. Her teeth were unnaturally white.

'Alissa.'

It meant nothing to me. 'Alissa who?'

The elevator doors behind her began to close and I rushed forward, blocking the sliding mechanism with my left foot.

'I'm an actress ... I might be playing you,' she shouted out as I took refuge inside.' The doors finally closed, before I could ask her any further questions.

I didn't press the 'down' button immediately, just stood there deep in thought.

I tried to control my anger. I was seething, not just in annoyance at Antony's conduct but also the presumption of the young actress who thought she could be me in the play, and seemed to find the possibility greatly amusing. Antony had sketched a part for a character based on me, the violin's final owner.

If Antony Torgerson wanted me to be involved in the production, I decided, he would have to treat me differently. It would have to be a collaboration. On my terms. But, in order to achieve that, I also knew I would have to impress him, come up with suitable concepts, the perfect music.

The elevator began its descent.

Weekend engineering works meant that I was unable to take the tube, and I couldn't face waiting for a likely over-crowded replacement bus service. It took me ages to find a cab and by the time I reached Clapham, I had calmed down. The weather had turned sunny and the Common was littered with folk hoping to catch what would possibly be the last manifestation of sunshine of the year. Small children galli-vanted between the trees, couples lounged on blankets, and an ice-cream van chimed further down the road beckoning for customers young and old, soothing images which all helped me restore some inner peace again.

Why had Antony's demands and the appearance of Alissa disturbed me so much?

I returned to the Isle of Dogs the following morning. Early. I'd rushed from bed to shower to my closet and slipped on the first pair of jeans that came to hand and a jogging sweat-shirt that probably should have gone in the wash before being worn next and I cycled all the way down to the river. Dawn was breaking lazily over London. At the door to Antony's building, an attaché-case wielding executive in a pinstriped suit was leaving just as I arrived, so I slipped in without having to call him on the intercom for admittance. The top floor corridor was a refuge of mute, carpeted silence and I walked over to his door and rang the bell. I had decided overnight to abdicate all involvement with the project and just wish him good luck. I wasn't right for the job, I had concluded. A mere, if talented interpreter, not a creator.

At first, there was no reaction from inside the apartment. I stood there, feeling out of place and thinking Antony might not be in and was about to raise my finger to the bell again when I heard stirrings inside. Steps approaching the door. It opened and there was Alissa, her hair in disarray, wearing a man's shirt that barely reached down to the top of her thighs. Despite her compact size, her shoeless legs appeared endless.

A triumphant smile crossed her lips.

'Ah, it's you,' she said. 'I didn't know you were expected.'

I stumbled over the words. 'I should have called before-hand,' I mumbled by way of apology. Did she live here with him or had she just spent the night?

'He's in the bathroom,' Alissa said. 'He wouldn't have heard the doorbell. I barely caught its sound in the bedroom,' she added, pointing to her state of undress, silently reproaching me for having visibly pulled her out of bed. 'Anyway, come on in.'

She turned on her heels and I followed her in, closing the door behind me. As we walked down the narrow corridor which led into the living areas of the loft-like apartment, she negligently raised her arms and pulled her fingers through her hair in a vain attempt at straightening her wandering curls, and the shirt she had slipped on pulled up, revealing the lower orbs of her arse. They were evenly tanned and a similar shade to her legs. I knew her flash of added flesh was quite intentional.

'Business, is it?' she asked me.

'Sort of . . .'

I thought she was leading me to the main room where Antony and I had previously tried to work, but we took a turn to the right and walked straight into the bedroom, behind a door that I had never seen opened before.

Unlike the rest of Antony's apartment which had functional clear and clean lines and almost brutalist and impersonal furniture, the bedroom was a jumble of untidiness, caused by the scattering of women's clothing, most of which Alissa had been wearing when I had spied her arriving the previous afternoon, and sheets and blankets hanging from the bed at curious angles. I could smell sex in the air, a musky odour underpinned by the fruity back note of Alissa's perfume. Her scent was overpowering, too rich and floral for my tastes.

She indicated a chair in one corner from which a thin pair of silk panties dangled and invited me to sit.

'He won't be long,' she said, and threw off the man's shirt she had been wearing. Her breasts stood impossibly high with a hint of unnaturalness and my eyes were inevitably drawn to her bush, which was dark and luxuriant and untamed.

She slipped between the remaining bed sheets which had not been shed across the floor.

We kept on gazing at each other in silence.

'He's shaving,' she finally pointed out, nodding at the door to my right leading to the en-suite bathroom.

'Oh.'

I was aching to ask a thousand questions. About the exact nature of their relationship, how long she had been with him, how and where they had met, even unhealthily about the way they liked to fuck, well, more precisely the way he liked to fuck, but of course remained quite mute.

Beyond the bathroom door, there was barely any sound reaching us, no buzzing of electric razor or even the faint splash of water in a sink.

We waited, an undeclared state of war now in operation between the two of us as to who would break the silence first. Provoking the other into saying something she might regret later.

Somehow they didn't seem a match. I had come across many unlikely couples and they were not that way, I just couldn't picture them together. Antony was undoubtedly a man of strong passions whereas Alissa had a brittle artificiality, as if she was always playing a role, faking emotions, manipulating. And I was increasingly convinced that her tits, teasing me, hard brown nipples on wanton display above the bed sheet negligently pulled up only so far as her waist, were not real. They seemed too round, too solid, gravity defying, somehow lacking in personality in their smooth, peachy perfection.

Finally, the bathroom door opened and Antony walked out. He wore just a white towel around his waist. Oblivious of me, he stepped briskly towards the bed and shed the towel as he was about to join Alissa then realised that I was present. His buttocks to me, hard, carved, muscles tight like a runner. He looked round with surprise, although he made no gesture to cover himself and I noticed his cock was long and thick and already at half mast.

'You should have warned me, Alissa,' he said, looking reproachfully at her, then at me.

He finally bent over and retrieved the shirt of his she had been wearing earlier and slipped it on. The purple pink of his glans could still be seen below it, but he appeared to be oblivious to its undeniable effect on me.

'I must apologise,' he said. 'I had no idea you were here.'

'I should have called,' I said.

'Maybe you should have.'

He was not circumcised. That was the only thought that came to my mind.

'She claims she's here on business,' Alissa said, with a gleeful look of mischief lighting up her delicate features. 'A bit early for that, don't you think?'

'I'm sorry,' I replied. I was probably blushing all over. What had come over me? I should never have come here unannounced this early in the day. Also realising I was jealous of Alissa. Madly imagining myself in that same bed with Antony. My mind was in a whirl.

'Was it something important?' Antony asked.

The careful speech I had rehearsed while cycling all the way here evaporated. All the talk about how the money was unimportant to me and how he should just leave me out of the equation and adapt the book with my noble blessing and that I felt unable to contribute to the project in the way he had hoped for.

'No,' I said.

His eyes drilled into mine.

Did he sense my confusion? Or my desire?

I felt I had to say something more.

Alissa intervened.

'Antony, don't you realise you're confusing the poor girl, with that lovely cock of yours on display? Maybe we should move on to another kind of business altogether and she could join us in bed? Might prove fun, the director, the actress and the fiddle player?' She made it sound like the beginning of a dirty joke.

He still didn't cover himself up.

I was rooted to the spot.

'Actually, I came along because I think I've come up with

a wizard solution to integrate the music into the play,' I somehow blurted out. It felt as if someone else entirely was speaking. I was even using words that wouldn't normally enter my head. Wizard? What the hell?

Almost ignoring me, he looked down at the young woman in his bed.

'I think it's time you should leave, Alissa. Didn't you mention you have an audition in Swiss Cottage later in the morning?'

Acknowledging her dismissal, she reluctantly rose out of the bed and petulantly stormed into the bathroom. Antony and I, left alone, wallowed in embarrassed silence. Having washed her face, she returned, still provoking us with her nudity and gathered the items of her clothing which she had dispersed across the bedroom floor and dressed.

So, she didn't live with him. If she had, she would have changed into other clothes from her own closet or another room, I decided.

I felt a surprising sense of relief.

She left, gratifying us both with a faint peck on the cheek.

'Enjoy yourselves, kids,' she said with a touch of departing bravado.

Her high-heeled steps click-clacking in the corridor faded in the distance. Antony looked at me.

'Whatever you wanted to discuss, maybe now is not the right time,' he said. 'I guess there will be a lot to say . . .'

'Yes,' I nodded.

'I have some appointments in town soon, with an impresario and a casting director whom I'm thinking of bringing on board.'

'I see.'

'Can you possibly make it tomorrow? As early as you wish. I'd love to hear your new concept.'

'That would be good.' He walked me to the door. It was an effort as we parted to shake his hand in a professional manner and not impulsively take hold of his dangling cock.

Now I had 24 hours to come up with an idea.

He was dressed when I arrived the following morning. Which was a good thing. Autumn had arrived overnight with a vengeance and London was cocooned in a curtain of greyness. The breeze had a cutting edge and I'd come by cab instead of my bike.

Despite the weather, I felt on fire, thoughts and tunes and unformed melodies and sketches of swirling images dictated by the music raging through my brain. I'd been up all night. My bow arm was aching and the wrist on my right arm felt as if it had been passed through a blender, my chin felt sore, my limbs barely holding me together against a sense of total physical and mental exhaustion.

As soon as I'd got home following yesterday's ambiguous confrontation at Antony's, I'd gathered all of my violins, a

pile of partitions and downloaded a whole selection of classical pieces to my iPod and had determined to come up with
some form of concept that would catch Antony's attention.
Charm him into acceptance or submission.

I'd attempted to match actual existing pieces to some of
the scenes he was hoping to stage in the play and had verbally
outlined to me but none of it truly worked. The analogies
I'd dreamed up in my restricted imagination were dull and
uninspired and all I could come up were clichés, even when
I ventured experimentally way beyond my own performing
repertoire. It was discouraging, but also a challenge.

Overdosing on caffeine as night fell and I had pulled the
curtains in my study closed, it came to me in a flash of understanding. I was trying to match images with mere sounds. It
was the wrong process altogether. What I had to summon
was the mood, emotions. It was so self-evident I could have
screamed.

I'd closed my eyes and recalled that night when, spooned
together in bed, Dominik had under cover of darkness
begun speaking of the section of the book he was then
working on in which one of the owners of the Bailly came
to realise that the instrument was cursed. The way he spoke,
his dark, mellifluous tones and the passion that visibly
gripped him as he did so had been hypnotic and touched
me so deep, held me locked in his spell. That was what I
had to recreate.

And, right then, images of wonders I imagined I had witnessed on the island surfaced in my mind, rising to the surface, the tenderness and the roughness of the embraces, the lazy copulations, the war-like battles of bodies, the untrammelled passion travelling between the couples, threesomes and every single wonderful combination of genders, sizes and shapes and electric fucks I had been privileged to watch in my waking dream. The music that seemed to rise from the mass of writhing flesh, the invisible warmth wrapping itself around the beach and the jungle. The fleshy caresses of the vines that had ensnared me, how desire had carved its brand into the landscape and the air. Although I no longer could distinguish between what I had experienced or imagined. Had I actually seen others, Lauralynn, Viggo, strangers at play?

A spark was born, deep inside me. Tentative at first, then furiously growing in intensity. I'd picked up the Bailly and begun playing the principal melody from 'The Sorcerer's Apprentice' but instead of slavishly following the partition, after a while, I began to improvise, doodle almost, surrender to the flow of the music until I had embarked on new shores, landed onto the solid sands of a completely new tune, which was part Dukas and part Summer Zahova, and it felt just right. Self-evident. I continued playing, improvising and in front of my eyes I began to picture the scene developing, the likely actors moving around the stage like dancers in a trance, the set itself spinning on its axis to the rhythm of my playing, the colours waltzing, the bodies floating on air, the beat hypnotic and exotic.

I disconnected from reality and reached the zone.

Played.

On and on.

A man's hand grazing my nipples.

Andante.

The slap of a palm against my rump, drawing exquisite and instant pain.

Allegro.

My earlobe pressured by the squeeze of teeth, quickly followed by a soothing tongue exploring its hollow.

Moderato.

Warm lips lingering, foraging between my thighs.

Furioso.

The welcome slow sting of an orgasm welling up inside me.

I drew my breath. Dropped down to the desk and picked up another page of Antony's notes; another scene. Instinctively drew the first notes of a Mussorgsky melody and as my imagination continued to flow freely, I veered sideways into a bridge borrowed from another Russian composer I couldn't quite identify on the spur of the moment and diverted to a new musical road. Glazunov, Glinka?

The room around me disappeared.

I was back on the island, my eyes and my senses overloaded by the emotions of pleasure, the unending portraits of desire.

Pizzicato.

That ineffable feeling of being penetrated after agonising foreplay, the sensation of being opened, filled.

I was in a bed and a man was holding me tight, controlling me, orchestrating with acute talent the patient rise of my lust from its infernal depths.

But in my unbalanced state, I could not distinguish who the man was.

Dominik?

Antony?

The devil stranger from the Kentish Town sauna?

A composite of all the men I had known, who had known me Biblically? Identikit lovers blurred by the winds of past times?

The final act of the play, in a contemporary setting, a theatre of war playing in the background and I set on my musical search with the vibrant echo of a Mahler symphony ringing in my ears, pastoral tones veering into war-like staccatos, or was it Shostakovich? The music painting battlefields, epic combats on fields of ice in broad, aggressive strokes.

Oh yes, it felt good. And it felt right. This is what the project should sound like. A different musical mood for every act. A parade of emotions that would bring it all to life.

By the time I'd conjured up the right emotion for each of the scenes and acts we had already talked about, I was sweating with excitement.

There was only one problem. Could I recreate all these sounds and aural moods again, record them in a studio? I didn't think so. In a recording setting I knew all too well I would be unable to evoke all those emotions with the same energy, the same fire.

There was only one way.

It was crazy.

Quite mad.

And an irresistible challenge.

I would volunteer to play the music, improvise equally, on the occasion of every performance.

It was unheard of.

All the more reason to propose such an aberrant solution.

Antony buzzed me in downstairs and his front door was already open when I emerged from the lift.

I walked in.

'This is what I want to do,' I said and set my violin case down, opened it and took out the instrument.

He watched me.

He was wearing his customary jeans and a white T-shirt that swam over his lean body, inviting stray hands to run up under the hem and over his chest ... Did he have a drawer full of identical tees?

I was so hot and feverish when I had left my Clapham flat that I had hurriedly pulled a thin summer dress from the closet, not taking the outside weather in consideration. I walked over to one end of the large room he led me to so that the meagre rays of sun breaching the bay windows would backlight me. And I played for him. Prefacing every piece with a brief verbal indication of the scene it should match. I knew that standing playing where I was, the dress was almost transparent. I hadn't memorised any of the improvisations I had come up with in the slightest, but it was no problem. I seized the original, inspirational melody and glided away unconcerned on the wings of song, twisting and turning as the music and my violin travelled in strange directions, one way streets and boulevards, oceans and landscapes.

Antony's smile broadened.

When I finally completed the ultimate piece and drew my bow away from the strings, my arm hanging limp by my side, Antony rose to his feet. He stepped forward and took the Bailly from my hands, laying it gently down on the padded leather chair behind us. I was still swaying back and forth in time to the rhythm of the now silent jumble of melodies that were still playing on in my imagination.

His mouth was on mine before I could speak. The hunger in my body responded instinctively to that in his, as if our flesh spoke a common language known only to a few. The well-matched, the lusty, the desirous few who ache, always to be touched, to fan the flames of a furnace that burns without pretext and without pause. I pulled up his T-shirt and gripped the smooth, bare, hard plank of his torso.

Immediately his hands tugged at my dress. His attempt to pull it over my head failed when the narrow cut of the waist intercepted with the barrier of my breasts. He fumbled with the buttons once, twice, then inserted his fingers into the gap between two of the buttonholes and ripped it open. Three hard tugs before a large enough tear was created for it to fall to the floor in a clatter of scattering cheap plastic fasteners. I wasn't wearing pants, or a bra, and had shaven my mound totally smooth in the shower the previous evening, a petty, angry response to the sight of Alissa's full thatch.

I jutted my chin out proudly. Expected him to take a step back, view me in all of my provocative nudity, make some comment or raise an ironic eyebrow acknowledging that I had arrived at his apartment without any underwear on and freshly shaved. But Antony was evidently a man of action, no voyeur. His hands were gripping my breasts, pulling my already hard nipples with the same violent impatience that he had applied to undressing me. I groaned and he tugged my nipples harder, pinched, twisted.

'You like that,' he said. There was no note of approval or otherwise in his tone, it was a simple statement of fact.

'Yes,' I replied, but could not master the same bland note. My voice was breathy, full of desire. Had I wanted, out of any sense of shame, to hide my desire I would have been unable to do so. My body made it impossible to be anything besides what I was. A woman of passion. Some might say a slut, and let them say it. Sex was woven into my make-up as deeply as the moon and stars make up the night sky, and I could have no more severed myself from my libido than from my own shadow.

I pulled him against me, hard, unbuttoned his jeans with one swift movement and grabbed his uncut cock. It was wonderfully long and thick and growing harder by the second. I closed my fingers around his shaft and ran my cupped palm along the full length of his dick, then pulled the skin backward and forward, revelling in his growing rigidity. A droplet of pre-come was gathering at his head.

But it was too soon for that. Far too soon. I wanted him inside me. We would fuck, before he came, even if it meant pushing him to the floor and straddling him in front of the bay windows, for anyone to see, if they happened to be holding a pair of binoculars at the window of a nearby tower block.

I did not yet know enough about Antony to conclude anything about his sexual proclivities, besides the fact that he was clearly ready to fuck, whether or not we would be working together and despite the fact that I'd walked in on him with another woman barely 24 hours earlier. I was sub-missive, in my sexual nature, but only with someone who I considered to be my dominant. With casual encounters, emotion-free fucks, I was as eager to find fulfilment on my own terms as my partner.

I caught the drop of his juices, withdrew my hand from his jeans and sucked him from my fingers. He was not wearing boxers, I registered. He was as nude beneath his clothing as I was.

He groaned.

'Summer,' he said, as I wrapped my hands around his neck and pulled him down to kiss me again. 'Your music ... it was perfect. Incredible.'

I stopped the flow of his speech with my mouth. I had never been one for talking during sex. It was too easy to ruin a perfect moment with the wrong words.

He cupped my arse with his hands and lifted me up and I wrapped my legs around his waist. It was a movement better suited to the perfection of sex scenes in Hollywood, I thought, as he stumbled backwards and we half crashed into the glass coffee table before tumbling over together onto the couch. I laughed, and before the sound had travelled the full length of my throat he had slipped his arm beneath my torso and flipped me over so that abruptly I had a face full of cushion.

I stopped, caught my breath, registering this new, fervent

exhibition of lust and he responded to my pause by lifting my leg at a higher right angle so that I was face down and none the wiser as to what he was planning next although I hoped and expected to feel the full length of his cock inside me. When he finally breached me the moment of his entrance felt sublime, his cock so thick and large against the tight circle of my hole that I gasped. He thrust into me and I pumped back against him, letting the peculiar angle of my body and the quickness of my thighs clenching around him be his guide. I was frantically eager for him. Desperate to feel full, brimming, to have the emptiness inside me pummelled away by the rigidity of his cock.

Antony fucked me until every thought in my head had disappeared and I was nothing but cock and cunt, and just as I began to feel as though I might come if the frantic thrusting against my cervix continued uninterrupted he pushed my leg up even higher, right up past my waist, so that my knee was close to my ear and then he drove his dick into me, hard, and then even harder. I could barely utter a breathless sound besides frantic panting as my regular exhalation was strangled in the cushion that my face was by necessity pushed into and he responded by wrapping his hands around my throat to choke me as each stroke of his penis hit the wall of my cunt.

By the time he came, finally, we were a mess of sweaty limbs and deep hiccups of breath, but instead of just rolling over and leaving it there he withdrew and in one swift motion hitched my hips up, moved back behind me and pressed his face against my pussy and the hot fluid that must have gathered there, my juices mixed with his, and lapped. The weight of his tongue pressed against my clitoris until I cried out and then he pulled away, waited not more than a moment or two and pressed his face again between my legs.

Antony, it would seem, liked to be in charge. Or at least, he liked to bring his partner pleasure, not necessarily before he found his own, but certainly before he ceased.

The sensation of his nose against my cunt was relentless. I twitched, jumped away, and he held me down so that I was unable to escape the intensity of his flesh pressed against the most sensitive parts of mine. I began to jump uncontrollably and he seemed pleased, and still more intent on his objective.

'Aah,' I moaned. The silent Summer was communicative. It was impossible not to be, with the tip of his tongue teasing my clit as it was. Though I knew that each lap of his tongue was nothing more than that, he had me in such a state of frenzy that every minute touch of his mouth to my cunt felt a million times more intense than it ordinarily would.

'Ohh, fuck,' I said. It felt good. It felt better than any mouth against my pussy had ever felt, as much as I might want to deny it. His tongue played a magical tune against my most sensitive parts, and I let him.

I was taken aback.

He lapped at me again.

Spread my legs even further apart and ran his tongue all the way from the base of my pussy to the apex of my arse-hole. Not just once, but again, and again. He cupped my cheeks and pulled my buttocks apart and then manoeuvred his tongue into one firm length and probed the fullness of my anus until his tongue felt as long and as firm as a finger.

My face was still directed into his sofa and my breath consequently interrupted by the fabric of the cushions that I sucked partly into my mouth with each in-breath. He was taking me right to the knife-edge that separated blissfulness from over-stimulation, eliciting sensations so extremely pleasurable they verged on pain. My limbs began to twitch and I scratched and bit at his innocent soft furnishings to try to stop myself from crying out. I wasn't sure how thin his walls were, or how conscious Antony was of the neighbours, but I didn't want to come off like the lead in a porn film on my first time with him.

It occurred to me then that I was already thinking there might be a second time.

Antony slid the flat of one of his hands beneath my hip and found the base of my mons, and then my clit, and he began to rub his fingers in circles while his tongue continued its exploration inside my cunt.

His fingers moved faster and faster and his tongue thrust in and out, in and out, until I could not hold back any longer. I began to grind my pussy against his face, a response which only made him bury his tongue even deeper inside me.

He continued to play clockwise laps around my clit despite the unlikely position that he must now find himself in. His jaw must be hurting, I mused, weakly, but my body was too much alight for my mind to hold on to any single thought for more than a fraction of a second and in the next moment I was moaning, tearing at the sofa with my nails and then coming in one enormous, roaring orgasm that felt as though it went on for minutes although it was probably only seconds.

With each spasm of my body he licked my clit, drawing out each shock wave to its maximum. I continued to shudder and jolt and stretched my arms out behind me, airplane style, to reach for his hands. Right then, I needed the intimacy of his touch, to ground me, to bring me back to earth again.

He responded by turning my arms up to right angles, threading his fingers through mine, and pulling himself back on top of me. As he did so his cock bounced against the inside of my leg; he was hard again. I pushed my arse up and tucked my pelvis under, to assist the angle of his entry. He brushed a hank of my hair aside, pressed his face against mine, squeezed my hands in his and in the same movement, thrust his cock inside me. He was so hard, and I was so tight, so slick and so sensitive from my orgasm that he felt even bigger than he had the first time he entered me, as if his cock inside me had knocked all the air out from my body.

I twisted my face up to meet his and we kissed. It was an awkward kiss - with my body trapped below his I could only meet him halfway – but that just made me more desperate to feel his lips against mine, and I wriggled beneath him to try to find a better angle. His cheeks and jaw were wet with my juices and he smelled of pussy, of me at my most primal. The scent and taste triggered another surge of desire in me and I bucked back against him with all the force that I could muster, once, twice, three times until he shuddered and collapsed onto my back.

He pressed his cheek to mine. Both our faces sweaty, sticky, a peculiar mix of my sex mixed with his and combined with saliva and perspiration. His hands remained threaded through mine and he kept them there. He showed no signs, as many of my other lovers had, of wanting to disentangle himself or seek his own space, now that the most physical part of our lovemaking had ended. He seemed to still want to feel my body held tightly against his, which was fine by me, although there was a little voice in my head that persistently reminded me that this kind of intimacy, his torso against my back, his now soft cock nestled in the dip of my buttocks, our fingers threaded, would inevitably pull my heart strings if it carried on.

★   ★   ★

When I woke, night had begun to fall. I had drifted off to sleep nestled against him, and at some point during the afternoon he had peeled himself away from me and replaced his body weight with a soft grey blanket.

I twisted, and produced that strange squeaking sound of bare skin moving against leather.

Antony sat in the armchair nearby, his face a picture of concentration. He was furiously writing notes onto A4 pieces of thick, unlined computer paper. When one sheet was filled, he dropped it over the arm of the chair onto the haphazard pile that was growing on the floor.

I recognised his mood. I'd seen it in Dominik, and often saw it in myself, in Viggo and in Lauralynn, in fact, in just about any creative person when they managed to tap into a rare vein of inspiration, unbidden, and the words, or the music, or images, or whatever it was that fuelled them rose seemingly without effort, as if they were simply a conduit for some kind of creative higher power, as if Antony had plugged into a theatrical surge conducting his hand by remote control to transform ideas to reality.

Nothing short of a fire or a tornado would have led me to rouse him from that state. I knew how precious and wonderful such moments were.

Instead I watched him work. He was naked, but sat with the demeanour of someone clothed, one leg draped over the other, like someone who would be entirely at home in a smoking jacket, with a pipe. One elbow leaned on the chair's arm rest, the other grasped his pen, an ordinary black Biro, and scrawled in large, cursive strokes on the sheet of paper that rested on top of the book that served as his writing table, balanced on his knee.

I could not make out the title of the book. Nor was I sure if he was a reader. Besides the mess that I had seen in his bedroom which I believed had been entirely Alissa's work, his apartment was neat. Spartan. Beyond minimalist. I hadn't seen any piles of books, or even a bookshelf. Perhaps he kept it all on some electronic device. I guessed that his tidiness was due not to personal taste but rather a lack of interest in anything besides his work. He evidently did not have much love for 'things'.

My eyes roamed over his body. He was lean to the point of thinness. His legs were long and the lack of fat on them made his muscles even more pronounced. The curve of one side of his buttocks was visible, as was the dimple that delineated his glutes. When he moved his arm, he revealed the slight bulge of his bicep. He was not a gymgoer, I guessed, or a rower or swimmer. A runner for sure, maybe a skier as well, though he seemed like too much of a workaholic to ever take a vacation. His body hair was blond and fine and just a dusting of darker hairs decorated his chest. He was left-handed.

His face avoided gauntness, but only just. Instead he

displayed the sort of high cheekbones that would make a cat jealous. His lips were neither thin nor full, but merely average, however they were unusually deep red in colour, like a plum begging to be bit into, and his mouth was wide and slightly upturned at the ends in a permanent smile that made him look as though he always had sex on his mind.

At least, every time I looked at him, I could not help but think of kissing him, or more. His nose was long, narrow in the middle and flared at the base with a pointed tip. I wondered if that anatomical characteristic had contributed to his skill at cunnilingus. It occurred to me that Antony's face was perfectly suited to sitting on, and I nearly laughed aloud at the obscenity of my own thought, which caused a pang of desire to twist in my groin.

Antony was an interesting man, I decided. Different in some way from the other men that I had fucked over the past few months. I felt as though I hadn't entirely worked him out yet. But, I would fuck him again, of that much I was sure.

I raised my arms over my head and stretched. The sofa creaked beneath me. Antony raised his head and gave me a lopsided smile. His eyes held the same expression as his mouth. Affectionate, approving, mischievous.

'You have the most appalling bed hair that I have ever seen,' he said.

'Oh,' I replied. I sat up, spinning around so that I was

leaning on the edge of the sofa with my legs curled up behind me. I ran my hands through my hair, clumsily attempting to flatten out some of my curls.

'No, don't,' he said, 'I like it.'

There was a brief pause. Our mutual silence was palpable, and I sought for a way to break it.

'Have I been asleep long?' I asked, although I knew from the darkness outside that it must have been several hours.

'Most of the afternoon,' he replied. 'You must have needed it.'

His eyes narrowed and his crooked smile turned into a wide grin. I had the feeling that he was talking about more than the nap.

'Would you like some food?' he asked. 'Or a drink?'

My stomach rumbled, which he took as an assent.

'I don't have much,' he said, putting his pen and half word-covered remaining piece of paper down and pushing up to his feet. His cock and balls dangled invitingly out of my reach.

He returned with an opened bottle of red wine and handed me a glass. As I poured, he walked back to the kitchen and began opening and closing cupboards, shuffling packets of food around and in the end bringing back just a jar of olives and a fork.

We ordered pizza.

By the time it had arrived, we had finished the half bottle

of wine and opened another, and by the time we had finished that, I was feeling relaxed and merry. Arguably, drunk. My dress still lay in a heap in the corner. Neither of us bothered to dress, even when the food arrived. We balanced the pizza box between us on the sofa and ate leaning over it, careful to avoid splashing hot cheese or chilli oil down our bare chests. Antony had ordered extra jalapeños with his already spicy pizza, and he ate every one of the tiny pepper slices without so much as a pause. Sometimes he swallowed his food without chewing, like a man who hadn't eaten for a week. Maybe he hadn't.

'Do you mind if I use your shower?' I asked him, after licking my fingers and noticing that they still carried a lingering coating of grease.

'Of course not,' he said. He produced a clean towel for me, and offered me the use of a spare toothbrush.

I pulled the fluffy navy robe from the hook on his bathroom door and wrapped myself in it as I padded back into the living room where he lay on the couch, finishing the last of the red wine.

He stood as I walked into the room and pulled the robe from my shoulders.

'No,' he said. 'I prefer you naked.'

He took hold of my left breast and squeezed, hard.

'The bedroom, this time,' he whispered, between kisses, pushing me backwards.

His sheets smelled faintly, though not unpleasantly, of his cologne and the scent of his skin. Mingled perhaps with what remained of Alissa's fragrance from the night before. Should it have bothered me that he had so recently spent the night with another woman? Maybe. I knew that some would believe so.

But it didn't bother me. If anything, it spurred me on to ride him even harder, to rid the thought of her from his mind with my own body. There was something else there too. The memory of her long legs, her bare breasts, the faint smell of her perfume. All these things aroused me.

We fucked again.

There was no mention of my catching a taxi home. Not that night, and not the next morning.

We slept entangled and unwashed.

7

This Man

And so it began.

When I had been living with Dominik, our work lives had of their own accord remained strictly segregated. He was a man of words, and I was a creature of the music, and never did the twain meet. We coexisted by allowing each other full liberty to indulge in our respective occupations and stayed at arm's length from the other when the call for inspiration or work called. He was something of an early morning bird when he spent endless hours at his word processor, while I still lounged lazily between the bed sheets. I mostly practised or rehearsed in the afternoons, so he came to occupy that particular time researching or just reading; I could just not bear to work with anyone present, unless it was a piece I was set to play with other musicians, in which case we would normally emigrate to a rehearsal studio or the actual empty stage where we would be performing later, if it proved available.

With Antony, collaborating of necessity meant working together at closer than close quarters, so whenever we weren't fucking we were in the same room. Him expounding, improvising ideas, jotting down notes, attempting rough sketches he would later ask the set designer to perfect and me picking up a thread here and there and attempting to match it in the language of music and navigating through endless melodic tangents which he would dissect with forensic attention to the details, constantly interrupt, query, contradict, sometimes approve and most of the time try to influence in ways I failed to initially understand. It was hard, concentrated work and full of vigorous disagreements and frustrations.

Antony was always careful never to raise his voice, but often I could see him seething, quietly furious, whether at my lack of understanding or the inevitable infelicities of my improvisations when my attention snapped and I lost focus.

He was not a patient man. Likewise in bed where he assumed the dominant role and seemed to find much satisfaction in my own, naturally submissive reactions to his touch and actions.

But our honeymoon as lovers and artistic collaborators barely lasted a few weeks.

I was lounging on the settee in a state of casual undress, both daydreaming and playing tunes in my head, one of my violins set down beside me and untouched for over an hour now, my mind wandering off in all sorts of random directions and my body on edge, casually thinking it would be rather nice if we dropped the task at hand for an hour or two and repaired to the bedroom, or the bath tub or the kitchen floor or anywhere really as I watched his long fingers juggle with his Biro and remembered how earlier that morning they had toyed with me and orchestrated my lust almost to perfection, eliciting sharp cries of welcome pain, sighs and a thorough sentiment of well-being.

He looked deep in thought.

Then turned to me, with a reproachful look in his eyes.

'Summer,' he said, 'I really need a musical reference point of some sort for this middle act, and you're just sitting there with your head in the clouds and your fingers between your legs . . .'

I hurriedly drew my hand back. I hadn't realised I was distractedly touching myself, lost as I had been in the realm of waking dreams. I also happened to be pantiless.

'Oh . . . sorry . . .' I mumbled, switching back to reality.

'I realise that on the day you'll be improvising, but I do need some clue from you at least, a tune or something that would set the mood.'

'I know . . .'

He barely waited for me to respond at all before continuing with his lecture, full throttle. I noticed that his hands remained still, clutching his paper and pen. He did not gesticulate for emphasis, which somehow made the weight of his words even heavier.

'I can't go looking for backers with an unfinished proposal. Without the musical identifiers, it would be like presenting a project with no script and just telling people to trust us on the basis of a verbal pitch.'

'I understand,' I apologised.

I picked up the violin and brought it to my chin and was about to play something and suddenly dried up. I had no ideas remaining.

'Remind me again of the setting and the characters,' I asked Antony.

He stared at me silently, apparently so angry that he was finally lost for words.

'Fuck's sake Summer, you're just pissing me around.'

Antony rarely swore. He was too genteel for cuss words. When he did, it was a sign that he had well and truly lost his temper. He threw his pen down, stood up and began to pace the room in front of me, alternating between balling his palms into fists and running his hands distractedly through his hair, a gesture which only served to make his slight quiff even more unruly.

He looked quite mad, but still managed to enunciate his

words in his usual, bland way. As if he had totally perfected the art of keeping his emotions bottled up.

'You really have to concentrate more ...' He hesitated. 'Or maybe we should just stick to the work and forget about the rest.' He obviously meant the sex. You couldn't say it was a relationship yet, or even the blueprint for one. The sex was great, animalistic, improvised, intense, but we never spoke of anything emotional, or made plans. It just happened. As often as possible. But we both knew that something else was bubbling under the surface.

I must have looked totally nonplussed at his animated reaction. A happy fool.

'Listen,' he said. 'I need to decompress. I'll leave you alone for an hour or two. Go out. Clear my own mind. Maybe on your own, you'll be able to concentrate better and have something for me when I get back. OK?'

I nodded.

'We're falling behind. I need something to present at the end of next week. It's important,' he added. As if I didn't know.

He slipped on a sports sweatshirt that had been hanging on the back of a chair and walked out of the apartment.

The door slammed behind him.

It was pitch dark by the time he returned. I'd in the meantime come up with a rough idea for the act, based on a Prokofiev concerto although I wasn't totally satisfied by it, but knew that when the day came I would inevitably manage to get caught up in it in performance and improve on it. And then I'd waited. And waited.

I wasn't the worrying kind but still felt concerned by the way his absence was dragging on.

I couldn't phone him. In his haste to depart, he had left his cell phone behind and it sat there on the glass table next to his papers.

Finally, close to midnight, Antony arrived back.

I opened my mouth to question him but closed it as soon as I noticed the dark look on his face. He was sullen and withdrawn.

Silent. Did not even greet me or ask how my work had fared in his absence.

He sat down and began shuffling his papers.

I was unsure whether to move next to him, pick up my instrument and play him a rough version of what I had imagined or even hug him in a gesture of closeness.

Finally, I decided to remain silent and wait for him to speak first, but to move alongside him on the sofa nonetheless.

The moment I sat, I knew where he had been.

The strong smell of alcohol was unmistakable. Cigarette smoke soaking his sweatshirt and his hair. And the familiar odour of booze on his breath and skin.

Antony was not a happy drunk. On the rare occasions I

indulged myself, I got tipsy, gently merry and over-talkative, which annoyed me as I felt I was not in full control of my faculties. He, on the other hand, retreated deep into himself, frustrations and past resentments festering away, trying desperately to keep the lid on a volcano of rage and anger.

Until now, I had never seen him drunk and truly angry or upset. Just sensed those dark emotions boiling inside him when we finished too many bottles of wine together over dinner and then fucked afterwards. Me, inhibitions even lower than usual, and him fearsome and tempestuous in a way that I found deeply arousing.

He saw me gazing at him.

'What?' he asked.

His tone of voice was sharp, resentful, as if by implication I was the one who had forced him to walk out and find solace in drink.

Which only served to increase my profound irritation at finding myself in this situation.

He read my thoughts.

'It's not your fault,' he said. 'Sometimes the pressure gets too much and one drink turns into more. I'm quite aware of it.'

There was nothing apologetic about him. Even an ironic sparkle appeared in his eye. 'Why don't you join me? We can explore the depths of our self-loathing together. Only fair, don't you think?'

'I think I've thought of something,' I said, nodding in the direction of my violin.

He stood up and began to move towards the kitchen.

'Oh, it can wait, can't it? Everything can wait,' he added, disappearing past the glass door. I heard a cupboard or drawer being pulled open on its casters and the sound of glass clinking. He arrived back holding a half full bottle of bourbon and two glasses. Turned on his tail again, and then returned once more with a bowl of ice and pair of silver tongs. He raised one eyebrow and smiled, as if he found his attention to detail in such circumstance highly amusing. The smile did not reach his eyes.

'It's good for the inspiration,' he said, setting his bounty down on the table, shuffling the papers to the side.

'I don't think I want to,' I said.

I'd never found any comfort in artificial stimulants, whether soft drugs or booze, and my alcohol intake, though admittedly increased since I had begun dating Antony was normally restricted to at most a couple of glasses of wine at meals. Only twice, once out of a stupid sense of shame following a particularly harsh descent into the sexual depths prior to Dominik and I finally coming together and the other after his sudden death, had I gone binge drinking in search of emotional release and all it had achieved was to make me feel even sicker, and in no way provided any relief to speak of. My only indulgence was for expensive cocktails and only then as a way of celebrating and not in search of escape.

Ignoring me, he filled each tumbler to the brim, adding ice to mine but not to his own.

He looked up at me, silently imploring me to join him.

'No.'

A darkness passed over his face and he brought his glass to his mouth and began drinking, steadily sipping the bourbon as if it were water.

Once he had gulped the drink down, he nodded to the other, still full, glass.

'Come on ...' he said. 'We're collaborators, partners in crime, lovers ... Show me some spirit ...'

'We're not lovers, Antony. Not yet. It's just sex,' I pointed out resentfully.

In my heart of hearts, I didn't believe that to be true. Or at least, I hadn't, until now.

I was beginning to think again.

Previously, I sensed that the sex we shared was becoming more intimate than 'just sex'. Maybe that was all in my head. I was behaving like countless women's magazines told me I would and reading too much into an entirely physical act.

He shrugged his shoulders.

'Same thing, right?'

'No, it isn't. Far from it.' I was becoming increasingly bolshy, provoked by his unfeeling attitude, disappointed in him and I could see a huge row looming unless one of us took steps to defuse it. I also knew that my pride would prevent me from being the one to make the first conciliatory overture.

I was saved by the bell. Literally.

The intercom rang, shaking us out of our uncomfortable status quo.

We both fell silent.

Looked at each other quizzically.

Antony finally stumbled to his feet, walked over to the wall and pressed the button, without even bothering to switch the sound on and query whose presence it might be. Maybe he thought, despite the late hour, it was the post or some salesman, and didn't wish to even waste his breath on the delivery.

He returned to the sofa and for a couple of minutes, we continued to face each other, resentment simmering beneath the surface of our breath.

There was a knock at the door.

'You get it,' he ordered. Beginning to pour himself another bourbon. Four Roses, I noticed from the label.

I was barefoot. His wooden floor was cold, and perfectly smooth. Never an iota of dust in this place, I noticed, even though I'd never heard him mention or seen any hint of a cleaner, or him cleaning. Perhaps he waited until I was well out of sight before attending to such domesticities.

It was Alissa.

'Oh!'

'You?'

She looked me over with an air of connivance.

'You're a fast worker,' she remarked, brushing her way past me. She wore a dark green parka that ended at her knees, and shiny black leather boots with tall, block heels.

'I turn my back for barely a month to embark on a regional tour and here you are making yourself at home.' She glanced at my creased white shirt and likewise crumpled skirt and saw all the signs I had partly moved in.

I was about to retort that Antony and I were just working on a project together, or that the sex had just happened and, particularly now that I had stumbled across his dark side, that I probably had no wish to replace her in his bed on a full-time basis, but she had already reached the main room and saw Antony lazily reclining on the couch with a glass in his hand.

'Ah,' she muttered. 'Back to his old ways, I see. You must be providing some forceful form of inspiration ...'

All I could do, following in her footsteps, was nod. It appeared she might know him better than I thought I did.

She stepped out of her parka. She was wearing a tight little black dress and those shiny boots that made her look a whole foot taller than she was, not a tousled hair out of place and polished to perfection as if on her way to a party.

She noticed the other glass I hadn't picked up, looked back at me and then back at Antony, the low slung table and the glass. Weighed up the situation.

'Not partaking, are you?' she asked me.

And without waiting for an answer, she took the glass intended for me and began to sip from it.

'Cheers, guys,' she said.

Antony had remained silent throughout, not even acknowledging her presence.

'I shouldn't worry, darling,' Alissa remarked, setting her glass down. She hadn't drunk much at all from it. 'He has these moods. But they pass quickly. Makes him interesting, no? But I can assure you I've seen him drink others under the table and he still remains totally functional. As good a fuck drunk as sober, in fact.'

As he listened to her, Antony's face remained expressionless.

Alissa turned to me.

'Tempted?'

I followed her gaze and looked over at him.

He was sitting on the edge of the sofa, elbows balanced on his knees, glass between his hands, staring blankly out of the opposite window. He wasn't wearing anything under his grey sweatshirt and the loose collar revealed the bulk of his shoulders and part of his throat. His dark blond hair was tousled and his jaw line unkempt. He hadn't shaved in days, maybe even weeks, and yet still managed to look as though he sported designer stubble rather than a half-grown beard.

Groomed, Antony was the perfect representative of an attractive dandy, the typical hot man-in-suit with an arty twist. Ungroomed, he was what you might call a hot mess. Even during his worst moments he could not be considered anything besides utterly handsome.

Alissa spoke again and I turned back to her. She had shifted her gaze from him to me.

'I know,' she said, as if she could read my mind. 'Enough to make you sick, right?'

She had moved nearer to me and prodded her elbow into my ribs as she spoke. Alissa was the polar opposite of Antony in that respect. She communicated with her body as much as her voice.

I nodded. Cast him another look, but he still refused to acknowledge our presence. He didn't look lost in thought, or even just lost. He looked bored. As if he was waiting for something to happen. A stone to come smashing through the window. An earthquake. Anything.

So I gave him something.

I turned to Alissa and kissed her.

Her breasts were so large that they pushed against me before I had covered her lips with my own.

She responded in kind immediately, opening her mouth and caressing my bottom lip with her tongue.

Alissa was a good kisser, and once I had made the first move she was all too ready to take the lead. She pulled me closer and ran her hands up the back of my neck under my hair, holding my head in place as she began to really kiss me in earnest.

Finally she pulled away, picked up the glass with what remained of the bourbon and swallowed the lot of it.

'Summer darling,' she said. 'You're so full of sweet surprises.'

She set the glass down and pulled me to her again, this time shifting our positions so that my back was now to Antony and her body likely invisible to him, covered by mine. Our lips met again and I tasted the half sweet, half smoky flavour of the bourbon that lingered in her mouth.

Her hands found the hem of my skirt. She ran her palms up the backs of my legs, lifting the thin material that covered my thighs as she went and not stopping until she had reached my waist, leaving the entirety of my bare arse on display for Antony's perusal.

I knew exactly what she was doing. Playing with us. With him, with me.

Manipulative little cow, I thought, on one hand. And yet on the other . . . her actions triggered all of the buttons that I loved to have pushed. Being (wo)man-handled. Being on display. Not knowing what would happen next. Knowing that Alissa was baiting Antony, trying to get a rise out of him and wondering what he would do, how he would respond. It carried the same kind of dangerous excitement as running down dark roads at night time, cycling without a helmet or passing my hand quickly across an open flame.

'No panties, huh?' she said loudly. 'I take it back. That's no surprise.'

Her nails dug into my buttocks. She was lifting and spreading my cheeks with her hands, displaying my arsehole, still careful to keep the fabric of my skirt hitched up on her wrists so that Antony would have a perfect view.

I was silent. Partly on account of the fact that I couldn't think of anything to say and partly as I was so aroused, my mind couldn't focus enough to articulate a sentence. I might not be drunk, but I wasn't thinking clearly.

Sure, there was a voice inside me that said that an angry threesome wasn't the wisest course of action right now. But that voice was not nearly as strong as the vast current of desire welling up inside me, a massive torrent of lust that required very little provocation and outweighed my sense of reason by a mile.

I moved my body a little so that my right leg was now between hers and pressed the weight of my thigh against her pubis. Her dress was so short that there was very little fabric to lift. I slid my palms up the back of her legs and cupped her buttocks. She wasn't wearing any panties either.

'Amazing how we keep finding things in common, isn't

it?' she said to me, still throwing her voice loud enough to ensure that Antony heard every word.

Finally I heard the chink of his glass coming to rest on the coffee table in front of him, and the rustle of his clothing as he pushed himself to his feet and approached us.

His hand came down on my shoulder, half wrapped around my throat. He pressed his other hand against the space above Alissa's collarbone and pulled us apart. One hand travelled into my hair, the other into hers. He had us both almost by the scruff of our necks, like a dog-owner about to collar his charges.

I stifled a moan, but try as I might, I couldn't hide my obvious arousal. I could feel my nipples straining hard against my blouse. Alissa's were hard too. He stared at my tits, and then at hers.

'Do neither of you girls wear any undergarments?' he asked. 'Got to the stage where you can't afford any, ever?'

'I've never really seen the point of them,' I replied. I knew that my tone was impertinent, almost provocative.

'So the cat hasn't got your tongue after all,' Alissa interjected.

'Not yet, it hasn't,' I immediately jabbed back, my voice purposefully breathy, lewd, full of double entendre.

Antony yanked my hair back and pressed his lips against mine. He didn't start by kissing me gently. He thrust his tongue immediately into my mouth. He tasted of bourbon and pungent tobacco, though thankfully both were fresh. I had always enjoyed the aroma of fresh cigarettes.

'Is this what you want, Summer?' he asked, breaking away. 'To fuck? All of us? Now?'

'Yes,' I replied. Right then, that was exactly what I wanted. Ached for.

'You're not going to ask me?' enquired Alissa, a note of jealousy apparent in her voice.

'I already know what you want,' Antony told her. His presumption sparked an envious note in me, also.

I would show him what she wanted.

We stumbled towards the bedroom. Antony drunken and unsteady on his feet. Me, so aroused that my limbs had seemingly forgotten how to work. And Alissa, struggling to keep up on her high heels with the weight of both of our bodies pushing her sideways and into the wall.

He shoved us towards the bed.

'Undress,' he called, turning and walking back towards the living room.

He returned moments later holding the bottle of bourbon by the neck.

Leaned against the doorway and took a deep swig.

'I thought I told you to undress,' he said. I was lying on the bed with my legs tucked under me and Alissa was sitting on the edge, struggling to remove her long boots.

'Oh, for god's sake,' he muttered, then got down on the

floor on his hands and knees in front of her and unzipped and yanked off one boot, and then the other.

From my vantage point behind her I had a view of Alissa's thighs, now spread apart, and Antony's face looking up at her crotch. I expected him to stay there and bury his tongue into her exposed pussy, but he didn't.

Instead he rose to his feet, picking both of her calves up as he did so and swinging her around so that Alissa now lay next to me, breathless and flat on her back. She promptly turned to face me, pushing herself up onto her elbow.

'Strip,' Antony commanded me. 'I'm not going to help you. I want to watch you undress in front of both of us.'

Alissa giggled. She was genuinely aroused, as I was, but I knew that she was enjoying my humiliation also.

I lifted my blouse over my head and then turned to a sitting position and unbuttoned and slipped off my skirt, lifting my hips and sliding the material over my ankles and kicking it away onto the floor.

'Better,' Antony said. The bland, expressionless mask had left his face. Now his dark eyes reflected a deep hunger. Desire. Something unleashed inside him. I did not look away.

He reached forward and took hold of my left breast, squeezed. Pulled my nipple. Then lifted his arm back and slapped my tit so that it bounced into the other.

Alissa grabbed my right breast and did the same.

I closed my eyes and moaned. The physical sensation, half pain, half pleasure, mixed with the mental impact of Antony's words, his behaviour, sent lust flooding through my veins. My cunt throbbed. I was dripping wet.

'I can see why he likes you,' Alissa breathed.

She was on her knees now with her legs spread apart, her face a picture of curiosity, like a kid who has just discovered a brand new way of misbehaving. She still had her little black dress on, and I could see no obvious way to remove it. Perhaps the fastener was at the back. Certainly it could not be lifted over her head. It may as well have been painted on. The hem had risen even higher, and now just bordered the very tops of her thighs. A hint of pubic hair was visible.

I lifted my fingers and reached for her pussy.

'Ohh,' she said, and began moving her hips back and forward, sliding along my hand. She was at least as wet as I was and her lips had opened, ready for entry. I thrust two fingers inside her. She leaned her head back and pushed against me.

Antony moved behind her and, unlike me, managed to locate the zip on her dress. He pulled it down halfway, and yanked the material up at the bottom so that the fabric bunched at her waist, leaving her breasts and cunt and arse exposed. The length of her dark hair over pale shoulders, her black dress like a belt around her middle and the lustrous thatch of her pubic hair gave her something of a domino effect, black on white. She was undeniably hot, in a terribly fulsome, sexy way.

Antony's hands roamed over her throat and breasts, tweaked her nipples. Not for long, though.

He stepped away. Picked up the bottle of bourbon again and took another swig. Then lifted my chin with his hand, interrupting the smooth rhythm that I was exacting on Alissa's pussy.

'Open your mouth,' he said to me, waving the bottle in front of my face. 'I think you have some catching up to do.'

I did as he said, then choked as he poured quicker than I could swallow and the bourbon burned my throat.

Alissa took my chin from Antony's hand and kissed me. She lifted my fingers – the two that had been inside her moments ago – to her mouth and sucked, licking all of her juices from my skin. She kissed me again, pressing the taste of her cunt into my mouth. She was sweet. Undoubtedly sweeter than the bourbon.

'Like the taste of her, do you?' Antony asked.

Before I could reply he had pushed her onto the bed, and then lifted me up by the hair and directed my face towards her pussy. Alissa was only too happy to oblige, spreading her thighs wide and wriggling her body into a comfortable position.

I bent my head and began to lap. I had little experience

of licking women, and so mimicked the movements that Antony so expertly utilised on me, alternating between fast and slow, gentle and rough and adapting my technique to suit her reactions.

Alissa was a particularly responsive lover, as theatrical in bed as she was in the rest of her life and it did not take her long to begin moaning and grinding her hips against my face. She threaded her fingers through my hair and held me hard against her. Antony placed the palm of his hand on the back of my skull and held me even more firmly in place, so that I was only able to take occasional breaths through my nose.

'Go on,' he said 'Fuck her with your tongue.' He placed his other hand beneath Alissa's hips and lifted her up. 'Lick her arsehole too,' he said.

I did.

Her breathing had turned ragged and I could hear the sound of fingernails scratching fabric as she screwed her hands up into claws and tugged at the bed sheets.

Alissa was visibly close to coming and her desire fuelled mine. I grabbed her thighs and continued to hold her in place so that I could lick her freely from her perineum to her clit as Antony moved away again. I buried my face into her cunt, my tongue shifting between hard, cock-like thrusts and then concentrating on swift, rhythmic licks against her clitoris.

I was so distracted by my task that I didn't register I had moved onto my knees with my arse in the air, or that the slight scraping sound of metal on denim was Antony undoing the button of his jeans, until I felt his rock hard cock plunging straight inside me. The impact of his weight against mine pushed me directly into Alissa's pussy in one final, vigorous stroke and in that moment she grabbed my head and came, thrusting and bucking her hips and grinding against me with all of her strength.

Antony ignored her entirely and continued to plough savagely into me from behind. It was all I could do not to bite Alissa as I was knocked back and forward between them and the force of Antony's cock inside me made me want to scream aloud, it felt so good.

A thin haze of warm liquid sprayed over my face and left a damp patch on the sheets. Alissa had gushed.

'Sorry,' she mouthed, motioning to the wet patch. It was the first time I had seen her blush. She shunted herself out of our way, her limbs loose and relaxed, a look of bliss mixing with embarrassment on her face. Recovering from her orgasm.

'It's fine,' I whispered back, though I'm not sure that she heard me as Antony immediately pushed the side of my face into the wet patch that Alissa had left behind. He wiped his palm on the sheet and then pushed his fingers into my mouth. His cock continued pumping into me and I thrust back against him, both of our bodies now slick with heat and sweat.

For a short while, I forgot that Alissa was even in the room. She was silent, watching us or not, I wasn't sure. I didn't care. The scent of her juices bathed my nostrils and aroused me to the point of explosion. Being fucked with my face pressed into another woman's come. Just the thought of it was enough to send me right to the edge, without any extra stimulation.

Then Antony shifted his body, supporting his weight with one arm, his other searching for my pussy. He found my clitoris and began to rub.

'Oh fuck,' I cried, and came.

My exclamation elicited a groan from Antony. He came inside me. We collapsed together onto the bed and lay motionless until my limbs began to lose feeling and I wriggled beneath him.

He slipped out and off me without a word and walked towards the bathroom.

'Well, that was fun,' Alissa remarked drolly, to no one in particular.

I heard the sound of water running, and the shower door creaking on its rollers.

'I'm getting a snack,' Alissa announced. 'You don't mind if I wear this, do you?' she continued, picking my white blouse up off the floor.

'No, of course not,' I said. Probably I would mind, another

time, but right then I was still too busy basking in the halo of my orgasm and mixed-up emotions to care about what she did.

Though I was taller than her, my blouse covered even less of her body than Antony's shirts did, leaving the flat of her belly and her pussy with its full covering of dark hair totally visible.

She slipped off the bed and walked to the kitchen.

Now alone, I didn't know what else to do with myself. I didn't feel ready to join Antony in the shower and have to begin some conversation about the events of the afternoon, and neither did I want to spark up a conversation with Alissa in the kitchen. Nor did I wish to return on my own to Clapham and leave the two of them together.

I pulled back the covers and slipped into bed, away from the wet patch.

Alissa returned with a plateful of bread and cheese and proceeded to munch the lot under the sheet next to me. Food finished, she rolled over and went straight to sleep.

I was still awake when Antony joined us again, but pretended not to be.

The sex and the shower seemed to have sobered him up. He draped an arm over me tentatively, and I snuggled back against him. A gesture of forgiveness on both parts. If there was anything to forgive. I still wasn't sure if either, or both of us, were in the wrong.

Alissa was snoring softly, seemingly entirely happy to be sleeping alone on the other side of the bed.

Before long, I was dreaming. The usual mixture of strange images, music, the lingering touch of the island's vines on my skin, flashes of lovers future and past, haunted violins, empty stages facing faceless audiences that consisted of just eyes shining in a pool of darkness, and always Antony's face, sometimes loving, sometimes not. I began to twitch in my sleep.

'Shhh . . .' Antony whispered, caressing my arm softly.

He pulled me back against him. Instinctively, I pressed my arse against his groin. He pressed back. I felt his cock growing rigid. I was still wet, partly as I hadn't washed since our earlier fuck or due to those recurring night visions of mine that had an unerring habit of veering towards the erotic, triggering in the process deep-seated and uncontrollable signals at the core of my body.

He reached for his cock and slipped it inside me.

We fucked quietly, barely moving, careful not to wake Alissa. He held me tight in his arms. Pulled back my hair and kissed my ear firmly as he came.

'Sleep, Summer . . .' he whispered. I felt his body relax almost instantly after he orgasmed, but he didn't move away. I drifted off again into slumber in his arms.

Morning arrived even earlier than usual, as we had forgotten to close the blinds, and I was woken by the sun. I glanced at

Antony's bedside clock. It was barely even 7 a.m., and a weekend, at that.

Alissa had a rehearsal to go to and had left. Antony was sleeping peacefully by my side.

Was I kidding myself in thinking that despite the angry words and gestures, the way that he was sometimes dismissive and sometimes affectionate, there was still something between us? That even through the drunken temper he'd displayed last night, there were still moments of tenderness? Plenty of people would have walked straight out and cut the romantic relationship between us off before it could start, but I didn't feel that I had any right to be self-righteous. I had enough flaws of my own.

I felt at sea. Lost without a recognisable star to get my bearings from. Uncertain about the next step. It was like that song I vaguely recalled: 'Should I stay or should I go?'

I had to pee. Slipped out of the bed as quietly as I could manage. Antony stirred, grumbling in his sleep. When I came back, his eyes were wide open and he was lying on his back, watching me tiptoe back towards the bed.

'Maybe I should go home?' I suggested. 'Let all things simmer down?'

'No,' he said. 'Stay.'

I stayed.

'What about . . . ?'

'Alissa?'

'Yes.'

'She's not important,' Antony said. 'Just an ambitious actress who'll do anything to secure a part, really. How do you musicians put it? A divertimento ...'

'And what about me?'

'You on the other hand are a complete partition, Summer.'

I would have preferred a whole symphony. It would have been more eloquent. But beggars can't be choosers, can they?

From what Alissa had alluded to, it appeared that Antony's drinking and his adverse reaction to setbacks was not a new phenomenon. But he seemed to have the matter under control and for the following weeks his anger and blue funk did not manifest themselves again.

Neither of us tacitly brought up the subject and we continued our work on the project. Nor did Alissa come knocking at the door again to suggest a further romp between the bed sheets. Antony let pass that she was on the second leg of a UK regional tour with a small troupe alternating Shakespeare and Chekhov plays. He was unaware what parts she was playing.

I was, however, wary of treading ever so cautiously in his presence and got into the habit most nights of returning to Clapham to sleep rather than stay with him back in his Isle of Dogs penthouse. We still had sex, but it was easy to pretext that I had partitions to consult back home, new clothes to change into and a need for some thinking space. He never objected.

The play was beginning to shape up, and I was now at ease with the half dozen musical reference points, take-off boards for the flight of my improvisations and Antony appeared satisfied with the way they caught the mood of the play he had in mind, and served as an integral part of it rather than an add-on.

So far, he had been financing all the project's expenses himself, preferring to have his concept fine-tuned before launching out in search of backers.

A good friend of his, a lanky Irish guy called Mark Bruen, who had designed the sets for some of Antony's previous productions as well as one of his American movies, came to visit and joined us on several occasions for our work sessions. A week later, he returned with a phantasmagorical construction made out of minuscule slithers of wood, cardboard, paper and glue, a miniature version of the play's set, which spun on itself, and revealed new layers from every perspective you peered into it, a house of dolls of exquisite beauty and precision, hand-painted in places, full of Lilliputian furniture and matchstick characters we began to assign names to. Both Antony and I felt like kids in a sweetshop. All of a sudden, the project was turning so real!

Mark was followed by Wally, a gruff Northerner big on

silences and nods, who agreed to come on board to devise the lighting which would bring the set to life. As Antony, with my occasional prompt, carefully explained the concept and atmosphere we were hoping to summon, Mark would listen with a profound mask of indifference, seemingly uninvolved with the whole process, not even writing down notes.

When I pointed this out to Antony, and questioned the wisdom of Mark's choice, he dismissed my fears with a smile.

'It just looks that way,' he said. 'He's the silent type, but already inside, his gears are moving. Don't worry, he always comes up with the goods. You'll see on the day.'

I had to submit to his experience. The lighting process for my concert and recitals had always been rudimentary by necessity and it was not an area in which I had the slightest expertise.

The words were now all written, bar a few last minute adjustments, and the music was halfway there, partly on the page and more importantly inside my head. I knew I could pull it off, and not get stuck embarrassingly for inspiration in the middle of any of the meticulously planned improvisations. Prokofiev, Vivaldi, Khachaturian, Sibelius, Rimsky-Korsakov, Smetana and entrancing melodic lines appropriated from Counting Crows, Luna and Noir Désir were my roadside markers for the journey.

All we now needed were actors.

And a budget to support the project. For which Antony had invited an experienced accountant to go over all the play's forensic details in order to cost it. When he first remarked that the whole farrago appeared frightfully expensive, I blurted out that I would not be charging any fees to play at every single performance. He barely raised an eyebrow, just giving Antony a sideways look, a sly understanding that the relationship between Antony and me had become more than just professional. If my agent had been in the same room, she would have begged me to reconsider and come up with a hundred valid reasons to do so.

The auditions began.

The first raft of parts filled quickly. A casting director accustomed to working with Antony had narrowed the choices down. Some actors matched the written roles with uncanny accuracy and the moment they began speaking their lines, the character instantly came to life as we sat on the other side of the table watching them as they sort of pulled an invisible switch and moved into the dimension of the words. Other postulants initially seemed quite unlike the characters at any rate in physical appearance but the moment they opened their mouths, they inhabited the part to a tee and you had to abandon every single preconception you harboured. Others were just wrong, and you knew it right away: the face, the posture, the voice didn't click, even though they were clearly talented.

But a vital role was proving increasingly elusive to fill.

Christiansen.

The young woman who would eventually give her name to the Bailly violin, the lost soul whose life would prove the most affected by the instrument's existence. Who would indeed have her soul stolen by the violin.

No one was right.

She had to be neither ingénue or worldly, old or young, a fragile spirit or a survivor. She had to be all those and more.

The actresses paraded in front of us. Some were well-known, even to me, award-winners on the stage or the small screen, while others were beginners. They came in and read for us, voices subtle and hardy, seductive and matter of fact, sexually attractive and ice maidens, some even wanted to demonstrate they could play the violin. In deference to my presence, Antony would indicate to them that, at this stage, it was not necessary to demonstrate their instrument-playing skills, knowing they would inevitably pale in comparison and sparing me the embarrassment to have to sit in judgment.

It was the final piece of the jigsaw and, still, it refused to fall into place.

Even though he never did so in my presence, I knew

Antony had begun drinking again when I wasn't present. I was beginning to know him well enough. He was becoming more short-tempered, bristling at my suggestions and, sometimes, ignorance of the world of the theatre. I tried to ignore this.

Behind his back, I rang Lauralynn and enquired whether she might possibly be aware of any actress with a modicum of musical talent. My thought was that maybe we could manage with a true musician with a smattering of possible acting experience, instead of vice versa. She had no suggestions to offer.

Time was running out.

Alissa returned from her regional tour. Antony must have mentioned to her the difficulty we were having in filling the Christiansen part.

She volunteered herself. Asked him to set up a formal audition the following day.

When I learned about this, I was fuming inside.

No way she could play the part. Absolutely none. She was totally wrong.

Wrong curves, wrong face, wrong temperament (and did I know of her temperament from our erstwhile trio . . .).

I asked Antony to cancel the audition.

She had played minor parts in some of his earlier projects, he revealed, and was surprisingly versatile. Maybe we should give her a chance? Just because she'd fucked him a few times, fucked us, would not influence his decision, he promised me. There was no harm in listening to her, watching her take on the role, was there? She might actually surprise us.

I reluctantly caved in.

8

The Space Between the Notes

I woke up early morning and Antony's top floor apartment was heavy with uncommon silence. With not even a hint of sound winding its way through the bay windows from the outside, neither distant traffic nor the eerie sound of the river sleeping below as it wrapped the Isle of Dogs in its blanket of peace or even faint dawn birdsong stirrings.

I had decided to stay the night.

Antony's arm was slumped against my back, the mere trace of his fingers grazing my skin. The warmth radiating between our bodies was both a comfort and an involuntary provocation. On one hand, I wanted to feel the lightness of his touch and revel in it, relishing the gossamer breath of his casual sensuality while on the other something inside me longed for his touch to become heavier, sexual. A need, a want.

I lay still alongside him and considered the prospect of waking him for sex; nestling into Antony closer, and rousing him into that half asleep, half awake state where he would likely quickly develop a morning erection, and we could spoon-fuck sideways before breakfast.

But he looked so peaceful that I couldn't bring myself to do it.

I shifted slightly onto my side and turned towards him. My hand found its way to the curve where his waist met his hip, just before the onset of his buttocks. He stirred slightly at my touch, but didn't wake. His mouth, half-pressed into the pillow, hung slightly open and his face was relaxed. He had not shaved for nearly two months now, and the groomed stubble that he had previously sported now had a decidedly beard-like appearance. It suited him. The dark border around his mouth made his lips look even redder than they usually did. His facial hair was unexpectedly velvety to the touch and I enjoyed the half soft, half prickly feeling of it beneath my fingers when I took his chin in my hands and kissed him.

We had only just managed to restore a kind of equilibrium between us; an unspoken collaboration of desires expressed and needs met or suffered. Our personal demons were alarmingly alike in many respects, though manifested in different forms. Work quelled whatever beast it was that drove him, for the most part. Sex fed mine. So together we worked, and fucked.

It wasn't always enough though. For him or for me. There were times when he remained awake for strings of days and nights surrounded by a sea of looseleaf papers and jotting notes that I knew he would not be able to decipher when the tide turned and he came back into his normal self again, gaunt and weary, the circles under his eyes like smudges of coal. When I knew just to leave him and hope that in the midst of his fugue he would somewhere get some rest and food or at least leave the drinks cabinet well enough alone.

And there were mornings like this one where I woke with a desperate longing inside that was part irritation and part ache, like an itch that couldn't be scratched, a burr that could not be removed. Moments when all I wanted was to be flipped over and fucked. Filled. The more forcefully, the better.

For both Antony and I, the beast that drove us and brought most of the good into our lives – the sensuality that expressed itself however unwillingly through my music, his playwriting and directing – was the thing that harmed us too. And I knew that we shared a similar risk-loving, adrenaline-seeking nature. That desire to walk straight to the edge of everything and live precariously balanced on a precipice.

Nothing scared me more than feeling as though I was getting comfortable.

But I had learned over the past months that there was nothing really that would ever completely sate the emptiness

I sometimes felt inside of me. I could distract myself, leave it behind for a time, but it would never really go away. I began to think of it as my shadow.

I had now found ways to manage it though, without resorting to roaming the streets at night half naked and half hoping for a pick-up like the man from the Kentish Town sauna. The card that he had given me had long ago been screwed up and tossed in the trash. At least, I presumed it had. I hadn't actually come across it since I had moved out of the house in Hampstead where it had sat for so many weeks on the side table, jolting memories that were probably better left forgotten, each time I strode down the stairs and caught sight of it. Maybe Lauralynn had thrown it away, and done me an involuntary favour by banishing temptation.

Instead, I had developed the habit of turning my mind back to my time on the island, and I did so now. With not a sound or soul stirring in the apartment to bring me back to reality and with Antony's out breath creating a gentle breeze on my cheek it was so wonderfully easy to let my mind wander.

I closed my eyes and imagined that I was caught up in the web of vines again, their smooth lengths like the touch of cool limbs pressing against my skin. The scent of peppermint filled my nostrils and played against my tongue. Was it a scent? Or just the notion of cleansing? I wasn't certain. But in my daydream, it didn't matter.

Music lullabied through the trees. I tried to follow it but could not move, held tightly as I was by the plant's coils that bound me. Unable to go after the source of sound I brought the notes towards me by concentrating every fibre of my being on each layer of the island's symphony, examining each note's place in the choir as if I was panning for gold. It was like unravelling a tapestry, one stitch at a time.

I could no longer feel the cotton sheet beneath me, nor the light duvet cover that was pulled up to my waist. My focus was now so captured by the waking dream that I had created I may as well have been there in the jungle, a captive to my imagination. I ran my hands over my belly and up to my breasts. My skin tingled. Unbidden, my limbs began to twitch and my hips to grind.

Then I felt a hand covering one of my own, still resting on my breast, and give a gentle squeeze. Antony's lips pressed lightly against mine. I opened my eyes. He was still visibly half asleep and had missed most of my mouth with his kiss, which fell half on my mouth and half on my cheek and jaw.

'Summer . . .' he whispered. His eyes were closed. He tugged my wrists, endeavouring to pull my body onto his.

I rolled on top of him. His cock was still half soft, but growing. I shifted my weight so that my groin covered his and began to rub against him, encouraging his hard-on to grow harder. He nuzzled his face into my neck.

'You were twitching in your sleep,' he muttered.

'I had a strange dream,' I replied.

'Grinding your hips,' he continued. 'Sex dreams, I reckon. You should have woken me earlier. I'd have been happy to oblige.'

He sounded amused.

'I didn't wake you,' I protested. I had been very careful not to.

He chuckled. I pressed my mouth against his to shut him up.

His cock hardened, and I took hold of the base of his shaft and guided him inside me.

'Oh,' I moaned, closing my eyes as I slid down onto his dick. I was already wet.

It was like what they said about heroin. The first high was the best. There wasn't another sensation on earth that felt as good as the moment that Antony's cock first breached my entrance.

I pushed down hard, so that I could feel him deeper inside me.

He placed his hands on my hips and rocked me back and forth.

Antony and I rarely fucked like this, me riding him. Usually he was on top of me, or we were side by side, or in a doggy style position. I looked down at him, appreciating this new vantage point. His eyes were closed and the expression on his face was close to pain. He was groaning, trying to hold himself back from coming inside me. The muscles in his shoulders and arms were tensed and highlighted the dips and curves of his upper body. The hollow of his clavicle. The sinews that ran like taut ropes beneath his skin. The vulnerability of his bare throat.

I cupped my hand around the lower part of his neck and squeezed. His eyes snapped open and he smiled. I squeezed harder, and he moved his hand to cover mine and pressed down, encouraging me to squeeze even harder.

The groan that now escaped his lips was a sound that I knew well. One of surrender. Release. He could not hold back any longer and I drove my hips down against him in one final deep thrust and tightened my grip on his throat and he came inside me and then his whole body relaxed, like a wind-up toy that has suddenly come to a halt.

I felt an overwhelming rush of affection for Antony in that moment. With his body now totally limp beneath me, he looked so soft, almost child-like in expression. I leaned down, covering his torso with mine, and buried my face into the gap between his cheek and his shoulder.

We dozed off again like that, sandwiched together in an awkward embrace, the sound and rhythm of our breath moving in and out of our bodies in sync, the morning chorus of couples.

★　　　★　　　★

Autumn

At my specific request, Alissa's audition did not take place at Antony's apartment in the large room I had come to accept as our own work space. His nearby bedroom had proven a natural destination when the mood overwhelmed us or we needed to depressurise. I argued we had to remain detached and fair in assessing Alissa's suitability for the role and that some of our mutual past activities elsewhere in the penthouse would inevitably impair our judgment if we stayed in place. We arranged to meet in Soho, in the basement of a music club Antony had sometimes used in the past. Having picked up the key in the café next door as had been arranged, we arrived a half hour early and walked down the wooden stairs by the light of a single, unprotected electric bulb. The smells of the previous night's gig still lingered in the air, stale beer fumes blending in with the clammy heat of bodies packed in close proximity to each other and the ghosts of abandoned notes and melodies hanging from the low ceiling like high-flying condensation.

We shifted some of the tables and chairs and cleared an area at the centre of the floor, so that Antony and I sat on one side of the table, on which he had placed a small tape recorder and a similarly-sized digital camera. Alissa would read facing us. It took us a while to puzzle out the room's lighting and we directed a discrete spot on her appointed seat. There was no actual stage.

'I'm so excited,' she said, arriving breathless down the

narrow stairs into the club, holding a large canvas bag over-flowing at the brim. My stomach clenched when I noticed a violin case's recognisable shape sticking out from her bag. Surely not? I'd never heard her mentioning she could play the instrument.

She was wearing a spotless cream suede trenchcoat that fell down to her ankles. When she shed it, Alissa revealed herself. She was sporting the shortest black leather skirt I had seen in ages, with only the miracle of its stretch fabric concealing her crotch or, when she turned to hang her coat up, the half moon of her buttocks. The white cotton shirt she had anything but casually slipped on was tapered and clung to her curves with transparent provocation. It was evident she was not wearing a bra. A thin red belt circled her midriff, tight as a corset, emphasising the sharp contrast between the opulence of her top and marbled thighs and the wasp-like delicacy of her waist. A proper miniature sex bomb.

She beamed at us.

'I'm so glad you're giving me a chance,' she said. 'I've researched the part,' she added. 'Even found another book by the guy who wrote this one . . .'

My heart missed a beat.

Dominik's first novel had transparently been based on me and only he and I had known what was real or fiction in the narrative and specific scenes.

'It has this great scene where the violin player plays nude,' she continued. 'Wow, I found that pretty inspiring!'

I was frozen to the spot. Antony's focus had purely been about the violin novel, and I didn't know if he had ever come across Dominik's debut book and realised my involuntary but intimate involvement with it. Although he knew, of course, that I had been close to Dominik. I looked round at him. His features were impassive.

She continued speaking throughout. 'It made me think about the relationship between the violin and the women who played it, how sensual it can be,' she said. 'And . . .'

'Can you actually play the instrument?' I interrupted her, with a barely concealed note of aggression. I would have bet anything she had rehearsed her audition back at her place, standing naked in front of a mirror, holding the violin, her hard and heavy tits bouncing up and down. It was farcical.

'No, but I brought this one along. Just a prop, I know. But it'll keep me grounded.'

I glanced at it as she opened the case and pulled the violin out. It was a cheap Japanese mass-produced instrument, of the sort beginners learned their craft on.

'Enough of this method acting crap,' Antony complained. 'Let's get down to it. Alissa, you know the monologue in Act Two. That's what I want to hear. Then, we'll segue into the scene between Edwina and James from Act Three; I'll read his lines, OK?'

It was just an audition and I would not be involved musically. Just a spectator.

I thought Alissa would sit down and go through her lines, but she chose to remain standing, cleverly using her body language to enhance the words and the emotions in a way I found somewhat manipulative. Antony, watching her, remained stone-faced.

She was good, I had to admit.

She demonstrated a mastery of the technical elements of acting, affecting a faint German accent to evoke the character's origins but without making her a caricature and displaying a fluent ease when moving through a whole range of emotions. Never too quiet or loud, controlling the flow of the words with quiet authority, her body stance veering between elegance and studied disarray as the violin's influence began to weave its curse, spider-like, around Edwina Christiansen's mind. I had initially thought Alissa would use her sexuality, flash us or something outrageous, flaunt her rather considerable assets in an effort to impress, but she quickly managed to make us forget her actual appearance and gradually began to inhabit the repressed but seething thoughts of the character, disappearing behind the words. Her only affectation was to occasionally wrap a silk scarf, a bunch of which she had extracted from her bag, around her head or neck to indicate a switch of emphasis in the text or her interpretation.

She was a natural born performer, I had to concede. Like me, albeit from a different perspective.

There was no transition or pause for breath and she switched into confrontational mode for the scene with James with Antony reading his own lines quite dispassionately, acting as a mere foil.

I could not help but admire her craft, even if I'd been hoping she would be a failure.

'It felt good,' she concluded, as she stuffed her multi-coloured scarves, abundantly annotated script pages and the violin case back into the deep canvas bag. The cheap instrument had remained on the table throughout, just a visual prop for her to focus on and no more.

Antony was unreceptive, detached.

Alissa appeared unconcerned by his lack of immediate response. Holding her trenchcoat in one hand and the bag in the other, she turned and made for the stairs.

'It was fun,' she said. And impertinently, looking me straight in the eyes as if she knew the reality behind Dominik's first novel, deftly raised the tight skirt above the half moon of arse and revealed the fact that she hadn't again been wearing panties throughout the audition, something I had somehow guessed already but was now granted proof of. Her perfect globes swinging gently above her hips, she giggled all the way up the stairs. The whole kink was becoming something of a cliché; I smiled.

As the door to Denmark Street closed behind her, Antony remarked, 'I think she'll be OK.'

Actually, I had thought she was pretty good. And as much as it pained me to admit it, the way that she moved and dressed, tempting and provocative with obviously not a damn given to modesty or convention had caused a pang of arousal to stir inside me, as well as a begrudging respect for her attitude and talent.

Technically, she was right for the part. Hadn't put a foot wrong.

But despite all that, for me, there was something missing. And I was unable to put my finger on it.

The truth.

But that was too intangible to explain. And perhaps impossible for anyone to interpret on the stage. Probably I was the only person in the world who would notice that missing element, as I was the only person who was aware of the reality that lay behind Dominik's story.

I was acutely jealous of Alissa, now, as well as turned on by her. Had it not been for decorum or the agreed parameters of a theatrical audition, I knew she would have performed in the nude, her way of telling me she knew I was the one who had played the violin nude on the bandstand on those occasions, but that her body was more spectacular than mine in so many respects.

Antony interrupted my thoughts.

'I'll ask her to try out with some of the other actors I have in mind next week, and if all goes well, she's in,' he said.

I nodded. Did I have any other choice? It was his project after all and I was just by necessity the musical director.

It was another basement, albeit a much larger and better-lit one, sometimes used as a performance space below a sprawling pub in Maida Vale. What was it about theatre (or Antony?) that held such an attraction to basements?

We'd been encamped there for a whole week now, rehearsing the show.

The casting had finally come to a halt. Following the choice of Alissa for one of the principal parts, Antony had recruited the rest of the troupe. Some actors he had worked with before while a handful of others were new to him, but within a few days around the long rectangular wood table that had been installed down there, they all fitted seamlessly together like a well-drilled ensemble, pieces of a puzzle intricately coming together, playing off each other with grace and instinct. I felt somewhat superfluous: at this stage, all we were doing was systematically going through the lines over and over again as we sat around the table, getting the tone, the rhythm, the words right, with Antony listening to the full text live for the first time and making minor adjustments as we went along, dictated by the dynamics between the actors, the lulls in the flow. It was a slow and somewhat boring process for me, although I could see how necessary breaths of life were being added to the play with every successive reading. I knew I wasn't a good spectator. My music was not required at this early stage, Antony had informed me. Not until the text was smoothed out and ready and I would then be called on to add an ultimate dimension to it.

A hand on my shoulder. Gentle. Solicitous. I opened my eyes.

'Did you fall asleep?' it was Mark, our set designer.

'No. I was just listening.'

I was keeping my eyes closed in a concerted effort to absorb the words, visualise the unfolding play, the words in my head and already conjuring up the music I would super-impose on them, layer upon layer, almost hearing the ghost echo of warring melodies that would bring the whole enter-prise to life, like a match struck in total darkness.

'It's all a bit repetitive at this stage,' he added. 'But neces-sary. You have to build the foundations before you erect the walls . . . The rules of theatre are the same.'

'I know.'

The reading continued. But I had lost my concentration.

I pretexted an errand and left early. Antony wanted to complete another pass over the closing act which still bothering him.

I did not go to his apartment, but returned home to Clapham and my own bed.

I slept fitfully.

My dreams were a maze of entwined limbs, bodies, men, women, forest vines, beds of ochre sand, verdigris vistas that stretched to a distant sky. I felt hot, haunted. Drowning in unknown rivers, buried between cities of indiscribable terror.

Unspeakable premonitions rising from the deep, like a call to arms, to deathly sex. In my mind, I screamed, I groaned like an animal, I came, gushing flows of emotions racing through my crucified limbs. But dreams are just dreams. I awoke breathless to find it was barely midnight.

I was staring mindlessly at the ceiling and conjuring random shadows into actual shapes of countries or faces when my cell phone rang.

'Summer?'

'Hmmm . . .' It was Antony.

'Are you OK?'

'Yes, of course.'

'You don't sound it.'

I lied. 'You woke me up.'

'I'm sorry. There's been a development. Shortly after you left the rehearsal I had a call from Samuel Morris. A change in his plans. He's going to be in London the day after tomorrow and would like for us to have a read-through . . .'

Morris was a well-known theatrical impresario with whom Antony had collaborated on earlier projects. We were planning to present the project to him in a couple of weeks in the hope he would substantially invest in it.

'But we're not ready yet, are we?'

'He has to return to America the following week, so it'll be our only chance,' Antony explained. 'Text-wise, the guys are pretty much there, but it means you'll have to improvise more than you'd hoped, maybe.' I still hadn't had the opportunity to accompany a complete run-through of the play, only isolated sections back at Antony's penthouse, and never with the actual actors present.

I drew a breath.

'I'll do it,' I said. 'It'll be OK.'

'You're sure?'

'Trust me.'

Everyone looked nervous. They all sat around the large rectangular table, uncreasing their pages or toying with their coffee mugs. I'd been given the chair at the top of the table where, until now, Antony had presided. I'd chosen the Bailly for the occasion. It felt like an appropriate choice. I wore one of my black dresses. Antony was all in black and still hadn't shaven.

Samuel Morris arrived. He was a rotund man with a mahogany tan that owed more to a sunbed than anything natural. His eyes retreated singularly into his skull, giving him the appearance of a bird of a prey. His suit was immaculately cut in Prince De Galles material that screamed Burberry at a thousand paces. He was accompanied by two almost identical twins, sleek younger executives with all the bland personality of polished stones.

He greeted Antony effusively with a fierce embrace and a kiss on each cheek before seeking out his chair at the opposite end of the table to mine. His acolytes stationed themselves on each side of him, standing, impassive.

Antony made the introductions. Presenting each of the actors in turn, with an indication of their résumé, then the members of the technical crew who had joined us and, finally, me.

Morris bowed in my direction.

'Ah, the famous Miss Zahova,' he remarked. 'I've heard a lot about you.' He grinned. 'Quite an honour for you to agree to become involved in such an intimate manner with the show ...' I was unable to discern whether he was being ironic.

He paused.

Wally, our electrics and lighting genius, had gerrymandered an improvised set-up which focused the lights in turn on the principal actors, which he controlled from his laptop at the back of the room, and kept a permanent spotlight on my end of the table, where I would be playing.

'Shall we?' Morris suggested.

'Absolutely,' Antony said and nodded to Wally.

The basement was plunged into darkness, leaving just me in the light. I rose from the chair and carefully pushed it aside with my foot.

Even though it was a play and not an opera, Antony had agreed we should open in a state of total darkness with a brief snatch of music derived from Mendelssohn's 'Fingal's Cave'. To set the mood.

I brought the violin to my chin and raised my bow.

I closed my eyes. Blanked out the basement room.

Played.

Although I was in control of the music, it was as if I had also become the instrument, lost myself in its heart, reversed its supposed curse and was now inhabiting it and drawing out sounds whose crystal tones were diamond perfect. I was transported elsewhere, floating like Icarus towards an unseen sun, seeking to be consumed by the melody and the deep, poignant echoes of melancholy rising through Northern waves assaulting the granite walls of the raging seas lapping the legendary caves Mendelssohn had wished to paint in broad musical strokes.

My body temperature dropped.

Antony, Morris, Alissa and all the others present at the reading became ghosts at the feast, perceived through a haze of uncertainty, impersonal spectators, remote filaments of flesh, melting into the sounds and colours of the clouds that sprang from my fingers.

I was the music.

Andante.

The thread of the melody thinned, evolved into a deep-seated sentiment of peace, petered out, disappeared into silence as my improvisation came to its logical conclusion.

I drew my breath.

I still felt miles away, transported by a wave of magic to that secret place where emotions, art and reality were one and the same.

A voice.

One of the male actors. The opening words of the play. His deep, warm tone acting as a Greek chorus of sorts, introducing the enchanted violin. Then another, the faltering voice of the ancient craftsman polishing the wood, shaping the elements that would form the violin, caressing the hardness of its emerging body. Then a young girl's voice, his assistant handing over the materials to him as and when he required them, his tools, passing aimless comments as she did so on the state of the world and the sheer poverty of her love life. He ignores her. His hands move again and again across the wood, embracing it as one would a woman's body. He is a widower, and in his mind, images of the wife he lost a decade ago and the entrancing remembered softness of her flesh. His apprentice passes him a pot of glue, the signal to bring the two halves of the violin's body together, make it whole for the first time.

This is my cue to intervene again, accompany, punctuate, lullaby the birthing of the instrument.

I draw a breath.

Delicately lift my finger from the violin's neck while the bow draws out a sigh.

I play. And play.

I no longer know where the violin ends and my limbs begin. If I were to abandon the instrument and drop it to the ground I feel as if it would not even make a difference and I have the power to touch myself in the right places, my lips, my nipples, my cunt and still draw out similar if not more enchanted sounds. The voices surround me. The actors, Alissa somewhat off-key, no longer in sync with the torrent of music bursting from me, a jarring note. I ignore her, it.

The story unfolds, in turns slow and frantic, tender and anxious.

I play.

I have left Aram Khachaturian's sinuous melodies far behind me and am now improvising in total abandon, my notes mounting a magic carpet that flies from one sky to another, dragging the story and the voices in its wake, a fantastic journey into pathos and exotica.

I feel myself sweating.

I am uneasy on my feet.

I soldier on. Now feverish. But detached. In full control of the world of sounds I have wittingly unleashed.

The vast sea I am skimming over is finally becalmed, a landscape after the battle. The final monologue talks of flowers, of destiny, of the business of living. I take my foot off the pedal, drag my steps through the musical jungle I have created, take my bearings, the melody winds down, *pizzicato, adagio, zero,* and as the final word wings its way across the basement and the reading comes to an end, so does my music, in perfect synchronicity.

The silence is deafening.

My whole body was shaking.

I opened my eyes.

Looked down at the table.

Everyone was staring at me.

The silence continued.

It wasn't a concert or a recital. I had no need to take a bow, I knew.

Finally, Samuel Morris broke the spell, brought his hands together and began clapping. But it was, I felt, a tepid response, more like an obligation he was fulfilling. The actors all kept on glaring at me. What was it? Hadn't they liked the music?

I was still climbing down from my high, slow to react, both mentally and physically exhausted and wondering already whether I was even fit enough to repeat such a per-formance on a daily basis when the play opened.

Morris rose, his assistants moving in unison to flank him, and called out to Antony.

'Can we have a word, Antony? Upstairs?'

Antony followed him, leaving the rest of us sitting at the basement reading table short of words, like uncomfortable morning after a one-night stand protagonists, unable to raise the right words to say, shuffling with copies of the script, fingering the empty coffee cups or biscuit plates. I tucked the Bailly away in its case.

'I thought it all went well,' Alissa finally said. Then, looking at me, 'and you were just spectacular, Summer. Amazing!'

There was something insincere about the compliment.

Antony returned ten minutes later, thanked us all for an excellent job and dismissed the group. He would be in touch in a few days, he said.

Alissa was reluctant to leave us, but Antony's body was ramrod stiff and he had turned his back to her. It was clear that he only wanted just him and me to stay behind.

The door to the street closed and we were left alone.

'So?' I eagerly asked him.

Antony came to the point with no hesitation.

'He won't invest.'

'What the fuck?' I protested.

'And I think I understand why,' he continued.

'Why?'

'You were too good,' Antony said.

'I don't understand.'

'You were spectacular, Summer. Truly. You were like a woman possessed. That music was awesome, it really was.'

'So?'

'So, he felt, and I must agree with him, that it unbalances the whole thing. Either it's a play or it's just you out there creating this incredible music. Somehow, there's a gulf between the two . . .'

I had never been accused of being too good.

'I'm sorry,' I said.

'I'm sorry too,' Antony replied. 'It's back to square one as far as the money goes, then.'

We caught a mini cab back to Antony's apartment, since neither of us was in the mood to face the crowds on the tube. I was surprised that he was even willing to tolerate company at all.

'Do you want me to leave? Return to Clapham?' I asked him softly as a black vehicle with a private car sticker in the window pulled up to the kerb, in answer to his earlier call. 'It's no problem,' I continued, talking quickly to mask my discomfort. 'I have some errands and things to do . . .'

He turned and kissed me, hard, on the mouth, then grabbed my free hand and pulled me after him into the back seat of the taxi.

'No,' he said. 'I want you to stay.'

A mix of expressions flitted across his face, one after the

other. Sadness. Anger. Lust. He looked exactly how I felt right before I picked up my violin and played like a mad woman, or went running or cycling twice as fast as I normally did.

I realised as I slid into the back seat and my shoulders touched the leather covers that I had left my jacket hanging on the back of a chair in the basement where the read-through had taken place. My emotions had been so mixed up and fraught as we left that I hadn't even noticed the cold.

Before I had a chance to ask the driver to stop so that I could run back in and pick it up, Antony had placed his palms on my knees and pulled my legs apart. My black dress was loose and long, and draped all the way to my feet, only prevented from trailing on the ground as I walked by the strappy, six inch heels that I wore. I had stupidly believed that dressing like this would add a touch of glamour that might appeal to the backers. Now I wished I'd worn flats, dressed down, drawn less attention to myself.

He slid one hand beneath the hem and wrapped his fingers around my ankle, then released me and snaked his arm all the way up to the top of my thigh.

Antony's fingers ventured towards the tenuous material of my G-string, a flimsy black thing I'd once picked up at Victoria's Secret on Broadway in Manhattan when I was still living there. He reached the elastic, slipped under it. I had dressed in a hurry and hadn't been able to find a pair of knickers that didn't show beneath the thin velvet of my dress. I could feel the heat emanating from my cunt in response to his movements. He was gripping the inside of my leg as though it were a lifeline, kneading my flesh with the pads of his fingers. Hard enough to leave bruises, I suspected, although such treatment didn't bother me. Quite the reverse. I was aware of my nature. The tighter he held me, the wetter I became.

I could see the back of the cab driver's head twitching as he stole repeated glances in the rear view mirror. Our scuffling in the back seat had not gone unnoticed.

'Feeling shy now?' Antony hissed into my ear. I shook my head, though truthfully I did feel a little awkward. It was the middle of the afternoon, and I was stone cold sober, a far cry from the usual scenario of sharing drunken embraces in the backs of cabs after an evening out.

He slid the palm of his hand up a little higher, stretched out his fingers and brushed against the bare outer lips of my pussy. I stifled a moan.

'Do you think you could do that again?' Antony asked. It took me a moment to realise that he was talking about the music and the way I had played.

He answered his own question before I could respond.

'I do. Of course you could. Look at you. You hum with sex, Summer, it comes out in everything you do. You can't help it. Maybe I should have fucked you in front of Morris instead of having you play.'

'That probably would have made matters worse,' I quipped, though regretted it as soon as the words escaped my lips. Now was not a good time for jokes.

He withdrew his hand from between my legs and pressed it to his brow. I wondered if he could smell me, if the scent of my pussy lingered on his fingers.

'I had a hard-on the whole time you were playing,' he said. 'I swear to God, you're some kind of witch.' He was looking out of the window now, staring aimlessly at the cars moving slowly alongside us as we picked our way through the typically gridlocked central London traffic.

I wasn't sure if he was talking to me, or just talking aloud. The driver glanced in the rear view mirror again. Listening, no doubt, and hoping for a better look, probably.

I reached for Antony's crotch and grabbed his cock through his jeans.

He pressed his hand against mine and squeezed harder.

We travelled like that all the way back to the Isle of Dogs, Antony's hand clamped over mine, covering the erection that strained through his denim.

Antony paid the driver who looked somewhat disappointed that we were getting out of the cab and taking our intimacy elsewhere, took my hand, and half dragged me from the parking bay through the residents' only entry to the lifts.

My high heels clattered on the smooth concrete flooring and as we stopped to wait for the elevator doors to ding open I bent down to undo the straps and remove them. Alissa could stride around everywhere all day in these things if she liked, but I was taking mine off.

I had just released both buckles and was about to hook my thumb over the back straps, slip them off and step out onto my bare feet when I felt Antony's hand caress my forehead. He tangled his fingers into my hair, took hold of a few hanks by the roots and gently pulled me up.

I nearly lost my balance and stumbled against him.

The lift reached our level and the doors swished open. He placed one hand beneath each of my buttocks, lifted me up and half carried, half pushed me in front of him for just a few steps until we reached the metal handrail that ran around the mirrored walls of the elevator at hip height and he balanced me on the edge with my legs half wrapped around his waist.

'My shoes!' I protested. One was still on my foot, dangling by the toe. The other had slipped off and lay discarded on the concrete floor.

He abruptly let me go and stepped out to retrieve it.

I turned to check my make-up and smooth down my hair in the mirror and felt a strange sense of disconnect when I caught sight of my reflection. The same sense I'd had when trying a slightly different hairstyle or the odd occasion that I wore a ponytail or chignon instead of leaving my long locks flowing untamed over my shoulders. Was this person really me?

The dress was an old one. I'd bought it from a market stall in Brick Lane for £10 not long after I had first moved to London. Floor-length black velvet with a modest neckline and a low back cut into a V that seemed as though it might slip at any moment and reveal my buttocks. It hugged my curves in a way that few other garments that hadn't been specially tailored for me did.

The woman staring back at me in the mirror looked elegant, older, worldly, but I certainly didn't feel that way. Inside, I felt like the same gauche, naïve, tempestuous girl I'd been when I found the dress at that market stall, but now the rest of my world had changed and I wore it with sky high heels instead of my old cherry red Doc Martens boots that had long ago been totally worn out and dropped off at a charity store.

'Oh,' I exclaimed, startled, when Antony returned. He'd only disappeared for all of about two seconds but lost in the depths of my own mind time seemed to have slowed down.

He didn't offer a penny for my thoughts.

Instead he grabbed me by the hips and swung me back to face the mirror, pulling me backwards and pushing me down with the flat of his hand so that I was bent over in front of him. He took hold of my wrists and moved my arms to the rail, indicating that he wanted me to hold on to it and then he lifted the fabric of my dress up to my waist. The material billowed down over the front of my legs leaving my calves bare and my arse just with the G-string's narrow elastic and on display to anyone who happened to walk by and press the button to open the lift.

We were at a right angle to the door, and Antony was standing behind me blocking any real view of my parts, but with me bent over in front of him holding the rail with my skirt lifted there was no way that we looked anything besides totally obscene. Being groped like this in a long, formal frock with only the backs of my legs visible seemed even more risqué, in my mind than the same situation in a mini-dress like the one Alissa had worn for her audition, tight and slutty.

Antony's hands moved to my buttocks, kneading and pulling my flesh. He pulled the G-string aside in one swift movement and the material offered no resistance. I felt the sharp point of his belt clasp scrape against my skin. He quickly unbuckled it and pulled his trousers part way down. Maybe he had stood and watched me looking at myself in the mirror for a few moments as his cock, which was now unfettered and banging against my thigh, grew rock hard.

His right palm moved away suddenly and I tensed, sensing

that something was coming although it was not something that he had ever done before, to me, at least. Spanking.

But as if he had changed his mind before carrying through on the motion, he brought his hand back to rest gently on my buttock and then moved lower, and slipped a single finger inside of me. He had evidently noticed what I already knew – I was pretty damn wet, and yet . . . and yet . . . I was faintly disappointed..

'I hate you for having ruined the play's chances, you know, Summer . . . and it makes me want to hurt you. But then I also know you can't avoid being you. It's something you can't control, is it?'

'Hurt me, then.' I nodded my approval.

He grunted.

'Slap me,' I asked him. The words came out in a whisper. I was not in the habit of asking for what I wanted during sex. I shuffled my heels backwards a little and arched my spine, pointing my butt in the air to encourage him.

'No,' he replied, immediately, and another rush of wetness flooded my pussy. As much as I felt foolish, prostrating myself like that, and I desired that sharp sting and the wonderful warmth that always followed a slap just at the right part of my backside, the denial of what I wanted, the control and the humiliation turned me on more than any single sensation could.

Some things never changed.

He pulled my cheeks apart and I moaned, aroused by the thought that he desired that obscene view of both my holes on display, enjoying wondering whether he was considering fucking my arse instead of my cunt. We had not yet tried anal sex.

His hands remained in place, holding me open, and he dropped to his knees and avidly licked me, all over the entrance of my pussy and my anus, making me even wetter than I already was, then slipping his fingers inside me again, first just one, then two.

He pressed his thumb to my rosebud, testing my opening for readiness.

I could hear the soft sound of skin rubbing rapidly on skin; he was masturbating himself as he stimulated me. Then he pushed himself to his feet as if he had either reached the limitations of his patience for holding back or had suddenly decided which opening he wanted and I braced myself, longing for his cock to enter me, as I knew that it would, at any moment.

When he finally gripped my waist to hold me steady and pushed his cock into my cunt he thrust so forcefully that my shoulder banged against the wall of the elevator, but it still wasn't hard enough. I raised my body and pressed my palms onto the mirror, bracing myself so that I could buck back against him.

He wrapped his hands around my throat and squeezed,

restricting my air supply just as I had restricted his when we had fucked in the morning a couple of days ago. We were both pressed up close to the side of the lift now, my hands against the wall holding me steady, my face twisted to the side as he held my neck, my dress still haphazardly bunched around my stomach, his trousers pooled around his ankles.

I caught a split second glimpse of our reflections; brows damp with sweat, expressions scrunched into poses of pleasure so intense they appeared pained, unkempt and messy, faces of fornication. Unable to gasp for breath I was light-headed, giddy, and just as I thought that I might pass out if he kept hold of my throat much longer Antony let go abruptly and slid his hand, hard, over my chin and face, pressing several of his fingers between my lips, simulating forced fellatio. I sucked.

What had begun in the back of the taxi as a gradual build-up of desire had become a tumult. A whirlwind of sensations and thoughts and images appeared in my mind unbidden – the view that I imagined Antony had of me when he held my cheeks apart, a mental film of him holding his own cock and pulling the skin back and forth as he licked me.

The echo of our breathing, panting, moaning, the heat that our bodies had created in that small space, the vision of the cab driver's eyes trying to catch a glimpse of my open thighs in the rear view mirror, the knowledge that at any moment the elevator doors might swish open and offer one of Antony's neighbours a pornographic vision of us rutting like animals in the elevator, the sensation of Antony's cock filling me deep thrust after thrust, his hands around my neck; all of these things blended to create the perfect cocktail of arousal within me until I felt as though every particle of my being might explode at any moment and I would shatter into a million pieces over the cold metal floor.

I heard the sound of muffled voices in the corridor outside, approaching us.

At that same moment I came, all over Antony's cock. My cunt spasmed like crazy and my whole body twitched and shook.

'Oh fuck!' Antony cried into my ear and I felt his body tense like a ramrod as he, in turn, erupted inside me and then immediately flung out an arm and struck the button to the top floor. After a brief moment's pause in which I was certain the doors were about to pull apart and reveal us to whoever was approaching, the lift whirred into life and we glided upwards smoothly, unseen.

He slumped against me, relieved, and we stood pressed together until we arrived at his floor.

Antony stepped back and I sighed as his now soft cock slipped out of me. I loved the moment of entry, but never the moment of exit. No matter how soft his cock was inside me after he had come, its presence made me feel full, at least a little bit.

He pulled up and buttoned his trousers and I straightened out my dress and collected my shoes.

'That was close,' he turned to me and remarked.

It was the first time I'd seen him smile all afternoon.

He hunted for his keys and we shambled into his apartment.

'Damn you, Summer,' Antony said. 'I'm still so angry at the way you took over the read-through and ruined everything. Just by expressing yourself too well. I'd laugh about it if I could.'

My throat was dry.

'Punish me, then,' I said.

Two weeks earlier a delivery van had dropped off a new chest of drawers, dark oakwood-shaded, which Antony had ordered online. The elongated piece of furniture had not fitted into the elevator, so the guys had been forced to pull it up the service stairs all the way to his top floor apartment in an improvised cradle of thick rope. They'd left the rope behind in their hurry to decamp.

I'd stored it away at the back of a cupboard in the guest bedroom.

I handed it to Antony.

★　　　★　　　★

Antony stirred.

'Morning,' I said, spooning against him, seeking out his warmth.

'Hi . . .' He opened his eyes slowly, as if afraid the morning light might dazzle him. It was another grey day outside. A barge tooted its horn on the nearby river.

'Any plans for today?' I asked him.

'I suppose I'll be manning the phones, to see if there are any other impresarios or investment darlings out there who could possibly support the project. But I'm not hopeful. Surely, word that Samuel Morris has turned us down will quickly spread and will discourage others.'

'What about institutions, banks?'

'Not their cup of tea. I know from experience. If I were to bring them another Shakespeare adaptation in modern dress or with a twist of some sort, they'd come running, but they invariably steer clear of anything in the least innovative or experimental.'

'Oh . . .'

The following two days proved awkward. Antony spent most of them on the phone or in town at meetings which never bore fruit and fell into a sullen funk. When we were together, he tried as best he could to conceal his growing disappointment and his natural resentment that I had in a major way been responsible for the project's failure to attract investment.

It was evening and, somehow, we had been together in the same room, both silent, for over an hour if not more. I was treading on eggshells, casually leafing through various coffee table books.

The one I was looking at now was a book of old maps. It was a subject that had always sparked my imagination. The page I had open depicted the Caribbean a few centuries ago, carved slithers of land against the blue of the ocean. It occurred to me that the sea around tropical islands was more green than blue, a delicate shade of emerald that I'd always found soothing and sensual. My mind wandered back to the island. And the conversation I'd briefly had with Aurelia and Andrei.

'I need a drink,' Antony stated, matter of factly.

I knew it was the last thing he needed in his present mood. It had been weeks since he'd gone on his last binge and I was aware that if he went down that perilous slope again, I might lose him. There was only so much the ropes could help him forgive.

'Must you?'

He looked me in the eyes and I knew that he realised that too. He was torn.

On the point of accepting defeat, my gaze returned to the page. An island. THE island. The shadow of a thought frantically swam through my mind. It felt as if it had been on the point of drowning, had reached the bottom of the ocean and was now rushing, out of breath, back towards the surface like a human torpedo.

'I know some people we could talk to about the investment,' I said. 'I think they could be the solution to our problems.'

Antony looked up at me hopefully.

9

Inside the Spiegeltent

During the highs, the lows and the in-betweens of all the seductive madness with Antony (and his alliterative buxom actress) the proposal I had been made by the fascinating Aurelia and her companion, Andrei, at Borough Market had never been far from my mind. Neither had the business card I had secreted away in a corner of my bedside drawer where it had been sitting for several weeks now, like a beacon in darkness whose insistent pulse called to me whenever my thoughts idled during the course of our work on the play, like a reminder of an even more wondrous form of madness. The nagging possibility of another life, attractive but dangerous, compelling but also full of question marks.

The problem was there was no way we could set up a further full-scale table read-through let alone any form of dress rehearsal that could adequately convey to another party what Antony was attempting with the show. If we were not given a go-ahead, and the funds to support it, in the close future, most of the performers and technicians we had lined up and who were up to speed with the text and our intentions would by necessity move on to other jobs. Neither Antony's or my own resources would stretch far enough to subsidise such a large-scale project much longer.

I dialled the number on the card.

It rang three times and the call was then picked up by an automatic recording asking me to just leave my number and assuring me I would be called back.

I felt totally deflated by the impersonal nature of this response. But what had I expected? That Aurelia and Andrei would be hanging on to the phone all day and night in the hope of my eventual contact? I should of course have realised they had other, better things to do with their lives. In all likelihood, they had long given up on me, anyway. I was not indispensable and evidently had a grossly inflated view of my own importance. It's what performing on a stage and the hypocritical convention of obligatory public applause leads you to expect. It spoils you. I should have known that, by now.

But I left my number, trusting it to the buzzing silence on the other end of the line.

I had called from my Clapham flat, in the nervous belief that Antony needed some time on his own following the

Samuel Morris disappointment, although I fervently prayed it would not lead him to drink again. I also needed space to clear my mind.

All I could now do was wait.

And hope.

Rather than mope around, I fixed my gaze on my shelf of precious violins and determinedly grabbed the one I normally used to practise, and played for hours, mindlessly going through all the necessary exercises I knew, up and down the scales through increasing levels of technical difficulty and then impulsively tackled Bach's 'Chaconne', one of the more complex violin solo pieces I had never satisfactorily mastered, until my wrist and chin hurt. Dusk fell.

The call came around midnight.

It was neither Aurelia nor Andrei, but the voice of an older woman, detached, unemotional, with a pleasant accent I thought I recognised but couldn't precisely place in my febrile state.

'They are travelling overseas,' she informed me.

'Oh . . .'

'But I have advised them you had phoned and they are happy to meet.'

'When?'

'Tomorrow afternoon. We will fly you there.'

'Where?'

'Our car can pick you up at 7 a.m.,' she continued.

'You know where I live?'

'Of course ... You'll be back in London by the end of day; there will be no need to pack anything,' she said.

I was speechless. It all sounded unreal. But then everything about Aurelia and her crowd, the island, always did.

'OK,' I mumbled and the line went dead.

What the hell should I wear? Surely they could have given me a clue as to the destination?

The car arrived on the dot. It was a sleek metal grey limo with a uniformed chauffeur in matching colours.

'Miss?' was all he said as he acknowledged me and opened the door, and drove off south.

A small private jet was waiting for us on the tarmac at Croydon Airport, a tiny facility I never knew even existed until today. There was a hostess of sorts standing by the steps waiting to greet me. She was blonde, picture perfect, with a fixed smile and also wore grey. Her skirt barely reached down to her mid-thighs as she ascended the narrow walkway stairs to the aircraft's door, and I had no choice but to contemplate the sway of her firm arse straining against the material of her outfit ahead of me.

She showed me to a seat, handed me a thin-stemmed glass in which a green cocktail fizzed, drew the seat belt across my lap, snapped it closed and retreated to her own seat for take-off, where she sat facing me, her watery blue eyes fixed on me, her thick lips painted into a pout, lost in reverie.

271

Soon, we were in the clouds, leaving England's green landscapes below and behind us. Then we were briefly flying over water and land again unfurled below, geometrical patterns of light brown fields and rivers. Within an hour, we rose to cross mountains capped with snow and the pilot announced that we were about to begin our descent towards the Mediterranean coast.

An identical limousine awaited us by an isolated runway on a private airfield by the emerald ocean. I could have sworn the driver in attendance was the same as had driven me from home in London. Maybe they came off an assembly line.

The villa was in the hills, white-walled and modest, discreetly obscured between nests of old oak trees and abundant shrubbery. The gates closed silently behind the car as we moved slowly up the drive. Aurelia was standing by the door, waiting for me. She was dressed all in white, backlit by the strong midday sun, her long limbs outlined beneath the flimsy material, tantalising hints of a warren of tattoos shimmering across her skin. There was no sign of Andrei.

We were drinking freshly squeezed lemonade on the terrace. Aurelia sat on the bench, her hand idly grazing my knee.

There was a stillness about her that both attracted and fascinated me. On one hand, she was remote, regal and assured while on the other I could feel waves of interest and empathy flowing out towards me. Hers was a simple sort of beauty, one that required no obvious make-up or trickery. And the surprising tendrils of leaves, patterns, flowers, words and mythical creatures partly revealed across the unveiled areas of the porcelain white of her skin hypnotised me, as much as the broad strokes of the images that remained concealed from my view and which I could only guess at. The images painted across her skin almost seemed to have a life of their own. One moment present and the next no longer there or moved along a few inches as if by fluid miracle.

'I knew you'd come,' she said.

'Isn't that somewhat presumptuous?'

'No. Some things are meant to happen.'

I outlined my request.

Emphasising that the read-through we hoped to set up for her and her organisation in order to gain their confidence and funds would by necessity have to be a smaller one than we had been in a position to organise for Samuel Morris. I explained the logistics of the affair and the show we wanted to produce, and the fact that many of the actors we had lined up had now abandoned ship and moved on to other projects, unable as they were to commit to a play whose chances of success were now so arbitrary.

Aurelia quickly interrupted my rushed flow of words,

maybe sensing my desperation and unease at having to beg in such a way.

'Mr Morris has reported back to us,' she indicated. 'The show sounds most interesting, although I gather also something of a challenge from an artistic point of view . . .'

'Morris?'

'It's a small world,' Aurelia said. 'Our organisation has many strands and we pride ourselves for always being on the lookout for performers or spectacles that fit into our vision. We have on occasions actually helped Morris finance shows. It was inevitable that echoes of your reading would filter back to us. I gather he undoubtedly found you the star attraction.'

'That wasn't intended,' I intervened. 'I was only supposed to provide the musical background,' I said.

'Anyway, I think we would be favourably inclined to become involved.'

I felt a weight rise from my chest.

Aurelia's smile remained unreadable.

She rose from her seat.

'Walk with me,' she asked, giving me her hand. Undecipherable words in Latin circled her delicate wrist. We walked to the back of the mansion where a large room opened onto a terrace which overlooked a busy garden full of lush vegetation and flowers. At first sight, it appeared quite unkempt and abandoned. But on closer examination, the garden was actually designed that way to provide the illusion of the wild.

'Isn't it beautiful?' Aurelia said, as the subtle smells of lavender, roses, bougainvillaea, magnolias, mutant-like seemingly carnivorous orchids and a whole rainbow palette of flowers whose names all escaped me, rose towards us, bathing us in a haze of intoxicating scents.

There was a set of steps that led down to the villa's grounds.

As I set foot on the grass, I was briefly reminded of my experience with the vines back on the enchanted island. Aurelia's fleeting gossamer touch guided me through the labyrinth of bushes and flower beds.

Bacchanalian images of sensual excess, feelings on the very verge of madness and celestial music that even my Bailly couldn't summon rushed through my mind as just for a moment I imagined the play being performed in this setting.

'Exactly,' Aurelia said, as if she had read my mind. 'The play could be performed anywhere. There is really no need for an actual theatre, is there?'

'Surely, you have to see it, read it first?'

'We have.'

I dared not ask her how. Had Morris surreptitiously recorded the reading on Aurelia and her cohort's instructions? Might his decision to turn Antony's project down been all along a scheme to throw me into the clutches of Aurelia and Andrei and the powers behind the island? It all felt like a net rapidly closing around me, my own life yet again falling out of my control.

We were navigating a labyrinth of tree stumps and treading through a bed of brown, spongey leaves. At Aurelia's instigation, I had a few minutes ago taken off my shoes, for both convenience and to feel the welcome dampness of the earth and grass under my feet.

'Don't fret, Summer,' Aurelia whispered. 'It'll turn out fine.'

At the back of the garden we came upon a small kidney-shaped pool. A couple of ornately carved metal chairs and a matching table awaited us, installed by the pool's edge. The water shimmered in the midday heat. The grey-suited driver appeared, laid out a checked tablecloth on the table, a jug of iced water and two glasses. He then discreetly moved back towards the house.

'Shall we?' Aurelia pointed towards the drinks and the pool.

We sat.

She explained her proposal. There would be no need for a complete read-through again. Just Antony and Alissa could read all the parts while I performed the music I had created for the show. That would suffice. And if Aurelia and her friends were satisfied and their expectations confirmed, their organisation would willingly finance a limited series of shows in London. Instead of a theatrical setting, they would propose, subject to our agreement, a different venue, as there was a shortage of West End and fringe theatres available at such short notice. They did not wish to work within a fixed set and suggested we use a blank stage, which would be enhanced by use of dancers and extras already contracted to their organisation, which she believed would prove infinitely more colourful and joyous. While I had been travelling here, it seemed, she had taken the opportunity to explain these points to Antony on the phone and he hadn't objected to any of the modifications suggested. Indeed, she revealed, he had proven particularly enthusiastic. By now, he would probably jump at any chance to have the show performed, I figured, and though Aurelia and Andrei's plans were somewhat unorthodox, at least they would not commercialise the whole venture and drain the soul out of it.

So all that was left was for us to meet up again, say the following week in London, for a perfunctory presentation of the text and music, she concluded.

'And . . .'

'And?' I queried.

'And you agree to join our Ball for a period of three months following the final London performance. That's one of our conditions.'

'I see.'

'You must understand that the cost of setting up a limited set of shows will in no way recoup our initial investment. Not that we are especially bothered about this. We are thinking long term . . .'

'I'm not sure my agent will approve. I have other projects planned, you know. Shows, tours . . .'

'We realise that, of course. But I am sure we can make an offer to your agent for use of your services that she will gladly accept.'

Aurelia sounded confident.

She poured water from the jug into our glasses.

'We were thinking we could put the play on for a whole week,' she said. 'We would take responsibility for the logistics: venue, bookings, tickets, etc. . . . It would be discreetly advertised. We've informed Antony that the final night's performance, though, would have to be by invitation only.'

'He's OK with that?'

'It's part of the deal . . .'

I could just see the expression on Antony's face as the conditions had been read out to him. But I knew that beggars couldn't be choosers, and we had both invested so much into the project that its failure would have been a terrible blow after all we'd gone through in its pursuit.

The scents of the garden were becoming stronger as was the Mediterranean heat. I took a deep breath.

'Tired?' Aurelia asked, observing me.

'A little.'

'Why don't we take a swim?' she suggested and, not waiting for my approval or reaction, she rose to her feet and in one swift, practised movement, undid the two knots holding her thin white dress together and let it slide to the ground.

I gasped.

The spread of the tattoos across the surface of her exquisite body was even more extensive than I had guessed. Somehow I hadn't noticed all of them before. A trick of the light, perhaps? Or another of Aurelia's mysteries? They covered her from below her neck all the way to her feet. Complex architectures of ink and white skin, like entwined branches of trees and mythological creatures. And words; calligraphies rising from languages unknown to me. Images: daemons and angels in intimate proximity. Fauna and flora: immemorial beasts and flowers in close entanglement. Only her face, hands and feet were sheltered from the colourful expanses of ink adorning her.

My gaze swam across her body.

She was fully epilated and a dragon's tongue trailed all the way down from her navel to the thin valley of her slit, delving into the painted folds of her labia, teasing, provocative, wonderfully lewd.

I couldn't take my eyes away from her sex.

Aurelia kept on smiling, radiating kindness, accepting the rude persistence of my stare.

I was captivated.

Finally she moved to the edge of the pool and jumped in. Her face emerged.

'Come on, join me ...'

Clumsily I slipped out of my own summer dress and tiptoed to the edge.

She was watching me, her eyes deep wells of fascination.

For an instant, I stood there naked. Poised. Alone. Watching the water rippling around Aurelia's painted body.

'You're beautiful too, you know,' Aurelia said.

I leapt head first into the pool, but it was closer to a belly flop than a dive. Aurelia greeted me with a resounding peal of laughter.

We swam.

Two hours later, I was driven back to the airport.

From then on, Aurelia and her team took over all of the organisational and many of the creative aspects of the play. She possessed such tact and diplomacy that the transition felt minor and seamless, though it was anything but. In fact, she introduced some plans that were radically different from what we had initially intended, particularly in relation to the Spartan nature of the set, lighting, and so on, but rather than cause a furore amongst the play's existing staff, it was as if the path underpinning us all had miraculously shifted and we carried on following it without noticing any particular change.

I felt as though a weight had been lifted from my shoulders as my sole involvement was now to simply play what I wished to play when I wished to play it, with no thought whatsoever to how it might fit in with the script or be received by the audience. Of course, it was expected that what I played on the night *would* fit, but Aurelia emphasised repeatedly that she trusted me to come up with the right material impromptu and she believed the play would be better performed in this way. Aside from the inevitable self-doubt that crept into my mind – could I really do this? Or was I some kind of fraud who had managed to trick Aurelia all this time into believing that I could somehow compose music, rather than just interpret it as I had done throughout my life until this moment? – it was a perfect job.

Even Antony was happy enough to hand over the reins for the project. He had seemed hypnotised by Aurelia, I noticed, when I saw them together one morning having a coffee, poring over some of the final details. He had added milk to his cup although he normally took it black, and had appeared uncharacteristically gauche, dropping his notes on the floor, stumbling over the pitch and fumbling his explanation of what he saw as the play's soul, a peroration that I had heard him deliver a hundred times. It was understandable. She had the same effect on me.

Antony was used to stepping back from his work, by necessity, when investors took control and wanted changes to please the market, he explained to me. It was just part of the business of theatre, or in fact the business of any kind of creative pursuit made public. That was the price you paid for wanting an audience.

I barely saw him for the next few weeks as arrangements were finalised. The script remained the same, but Aurelia had requested that the specifics of the set and details of the dancers and performances that I had not yet viewed would be kept secret from me. It was a mad idea, even madder than my original plan, but on another level it made perfect sense. She wanted the music that I played to be entirely improvised and felt that the newer everything was to me the more my performance would be of the moment, primal, flooding from my core in response to events unfolding around me and not even remotely thought through in advance. I would be playing the music that arose in my heart and soul on each night, circumventing any input that my brain might otherwise have and tapping straight into my soul.

I was not even informed of the location where the performances would take place, until we arrived on the opening night. Antony and Alissa had been involved in dress rehearsals, along with Lauralynn and Viggo who had been brought on board as well, the former to add to the musical score and the latter to assist with stagecraft, but none of them had let on a word to me about how the stage would be set up or even where we would be travelling each night. The lack of creative control felt soothing and familiar to me. In a way, I was submitting to Aurelia, and doing so in such an environment came to me as easily as it did in the bedroom.

A car collected me in late afternoon and whisked me from Clapham to Clapton. When I had previously lived in Hoxton, I had visited other parts of Hackney regularly, but had never been further east than London Fields to visit Broadway Market and swim at the Lido. It certainly was not one of the possible locations that I had expected. But knowing Aurelia as I did, I had no doubt that she and her organisation could transform even the scraggly grass plain of Hackney Downs Park that I walked across with my violin case under my arm to the big tent that the driver had pointed to when he dropped me off by the roadside.

It was still light when I arrived, dressed casually in tight, high-waisted jean style leggings, flat shoes and a loose, long blouse that tied into a bow around my neck. All I carried with me was my instrument, as Aurelia had pointed out that costumes and make-up would all be provided so I would not, on this occasion need to dress myself up as I usually did for even the most prestigious recitals.

From the outside, the tent looked just like a circus big top. The frame was shaped like a hexagon and the walls were made of wood in a warm tan colour, with a draping, vivid red velvet roof overtop. Fairy lights decorated every corner and I imagined that when the sun went down, it would look quite spectacular. A long red carpet led to the pulled back curtains that functioned as a front door and was guarded by security staff – a small woman dressed in a red and gold tasselled outfit, complete with a train-driver style cap that covered her forehead completely. She shifted her stance as I approached and I noticed the taut, beefiness of her muscles rippling beneath her clothes. She apparently possessed a strength that was at odds with her diminutive stature. I showed her my pass and she waved me straight through.

Posters advertising the night decorated the box office area. They were all black and white and stylistic, a bit like a Rorschach ink stain. What appeared to be the curved contours of a musical instrument from some angles looked like the sweep of a narrow waist or the jutting angle of a hip from others. I picked up a programme and flicked through it.

The Violin Diaries

An erotic, immersive theatre experience.

Leave your friends, and your inhibitions, at the door and let the music take you where it will . . .

Punters were encouraged to arrive in cocktail outfits or fancy dress, or risk being forcefully changed by venue staff at the door. Each night featured a different theme. Tonight's was 'marionettes', another 'menagerie'. Masks would be provided, and should be worn at all times.

I put the brochure back down again, somewhat guiltily as I knew that by reading the promotional material I was breaking the rules that Aurelia had set, and stepped out into the main auditorium in search of someone who could tell me where to find the dressing rooms or whatever area had been set aside for that purpose.

A sharp, woody fragrance hit my nostrils, and with it a million memories from my childhood came flooding back. The floor was covered in wood shavings, tightly compacted as if under the weight of a million footsteps so it seemed as though the whole set-up had been sited here forever and not just been erected in the past week. There were no seats. A raised dais – the stage - filled the far end of the room, with a cordoned-off space set out in front for an orchestra. And around that, mirrored pillars reaching from floor to ceiling were stationed at every angle besides any that would impact a view of the main stage. Mirrors covered all of the walls, too. Everywhere I looked, I caught a flash of my own reflection.

I closed my eyes and imagined how it would be when people filled the room, all masked and dressed in costume. Had the showing sold out? I didn't even know. I hoped so. I could see now how incredible the night would be if Aurelia's plans worked. She was making the audience a part of the show, encouraging them to lose their inhibitions. There was no allocated seating, so groups would separate and be left to explore, their faces covered and dress different from the norm to allow them to behave however they wished without fear of social reprisal. Dominik would have approved, I knew, of the way his work was now being adapted, betrayed, enhanced. Besides the mirrors, decorations on set and off were totally stark. The focus was not on the room, or the stage, but rather the people who inhabited both. Signs directing patrons to the toilets and bar seemed deliberately absent to encourage exploration. And my music would be the cord that held all of it together. I would be the Pied Piper, reeling them all in.

If I could pull it off.

A pit of nervous energy bubbled in my stomach. I was beginning to feel nauseous.

I heard familiar footsteps behind me and turned as Lauralynn strode through the main entryway, carrying an oversized duffle bag over one shoulder and wheeling a large suitcase behind her. She was wearing a pair of flat leather combat style boots that I hadn't seen her in before. They looked old and scuffed, but knowing Lauralynn, I guessed they were designer, brand new and artfully dishevelled rather than ancient. Her denim jeans rode low on her hips and her cotton T-shirt was uncharacteristically loose, but cut short so that it didn't quite cover her midriff. Despite the fact that I had never known her to do any exercise at all, besides whatever she did in the bedroom, her stomach was still as flat as a board. For once, she was wearing a bra.

'Come on then,' she said. 'I seem to have been assigned

as your Wardrobe Assistant. May as well get started. You're not supposed to be in here anyway.'

I volunteered to carry the duffle bag, and nearly dropped it straight onto the floor as she slipped it off her shoulder and onto mine.

'Christ, what did you bring in here? Bricks?'

'Make-up,' Lauralynn replied. 'For you.'

In fact, it turned out to be body paint, in an array of colours designed to suit every skin tone on the planet. Four artists armed with a whole briefcase each of different sized brushes and a palette of pale cream tones to match each variation in shade over my entire body painstakingly covered me from head to toe.

'Wait,' Lauralynn cried, as I was about walk over to the full-length mirror that stood at the other end of our makeshift dressing room, a large closed-off area behind the stage. 'Close your eyes.'

I did as she instructed, and she guided me to the mirror, and then placed my violin into my hands. Instinctively I lifted the instrument into position beneath my chin and readied my bow.

'Now open,' she said.

The effect of the make-up was incredible. I had been painted from the base of my neck down to resemble the Bailly, in warm burnished tones of bronze, tan and rich gold. Every striation, every mark that appeared on the instrument's body appeared also on mine, cementing the sensual over-tones of the instrument's relationship with the woman who played her. In fact, it was difficult to tell where I stopped and the Bailly began, or who was playing whom. The V shape that ran between my breasts, and my throat and face remained pale. The rouge on my cheeks and lips was so artfully posi-tioned it seemed natural, but made my cheekbones and lips glow, full and luscious. My hair flowed over my shoulders in a mass of perfectly messy curls, the sort of unkempt look that appeared unfussy but actually took hours to arrange. My eye make-up was plain, dark, and cat-like.

Lauralynn had also been painted but rather than resem-bling her cello, she looked like a human wooden puppet. Her tan skin was now the colour of oak, complete with grain. She had a shine to her, as though she had been lac-quered. Her hair was pulled up into a tight bun on her head and her rouge and eye-powder was somewhat animated, as though she was a cartoon version of herself. She was entirely naked and every inch of her had been covered in paint, with the exception of the large bush that she was sporting.

'Wow,' I said, looking down. 'You stopped waxing?' Lauralynn had been hairless all over for as long as I'd known her.

'Nope,' she grinned. 'It's a merkin. Makes the whole look rather more pornographic, don't you think?'

She was right, it did.

Autumn

The small orchestra that Aurelia and Viggo had recruited to counterpoint my solo violin pieces on the opening night were made-up in a similar way, and all equally nude. Most of the men were totally flaccid, and I could not help but watch the way that their balls hung and guess how hard their cocks might grow when aroused. One, a flautist, looked no older than twenty and was obviously half-erect. If he was embarrassed about his public display of arousal, I couldn't tell, as his face paint covered any signs of blush. Each of the musicians had evidently been chosen for their skill with an instrument rather than the firmness of their nude flesh, as there were as many plump and round limbs on display as there were long and lean, and not all of the bare breasts that caught my gaze were youthful. There was a beauty in it though, something simple and natural about all of the bodies on display, seemingly both covered and uncovered. The perfection of the paint gave even the most ageing flesh a peculiar allure.

A bell rang to signal five minutes to start and the room around us filled. I could not see the audience behind the curtain that surrounded the dais, but I could sense somehow – from the pitch of echoed whispers, breaths, footsteps landing light and fast – there was a different sort of energy to the crowd here than most of the shows that I had played. Classical music tends to draw a particular kind of punter, and these weren't it. Standing raised the feeling of expectation, as if the crowd was waiting for something to happen and longing to be involved, to move with the music, to sway and jump and knock into each other. More like a rock concert than a classical gig or a play.

Another bell chimed and the curtain disappeared, its red velvet folds pulled upwards, folding mechanically into the network of beams and pulleys that spiderwebbed unseen across the tent's ceiling.

The crowd gasped in unison as they caught sight of the naked bodies stationed at the front of the stage, reflected in carefully positioned mirrors so that the small orchestra looked twice as large, and so that every possible angle of their nudity was displayed.

I began to play.

A theme from Stravinsky's 'Firebird'.

Under the influence of the enforced dress code, or was it the constant presence in the audience every single night of Aurelia, Andrei and other now-familiar faces of additional dancers and mute standers-by from the Network, enigmatically stationed around the improvised theatre like a silent Greek chorus from evening to evening, the mood became stranger, more weighted.

Viggo had been engaged, at no doubt a high cost, to record my musical performance on the opening two evenings and I was no longer obligated to play throughout, which both liberated me and gave me leisure to immerse myself deep into the play, the action. Lauralynn had, as agreed taken over some of the sections, adding her own sensual veneer to the melodic tapestry and counterpointed my violin tones with the more masculine echoes of her cello. Viggo's mix of my music enhanced its inherent melancholy and the sometimes unbridled flights of passion and fantasy that took over when I improvised and severed my ties to the reality of the stage. Here and there, he had added electronic beaches of sounds which fitted like a glove, as if he had been reading my mind. Gradually the play was taking on a new dimension, different every night as Antony made profuse notes which he passed on to Alissa and the few other actors (most of whom now played up to two or three of the minor characters) to inflect the angle of their performance. Words began to disappear from the original text as he eliminated dialogue and soon whole sections of the play, and it became ever more visual and musical, no longer as reliant on the power of mere words. I observed these changes with a conflicted mind, admiring the artistry in progress but also nostalgic for the elements in place that inevitably reminded me of Dominik.

No nightly performance was alike as the show constantly evolved, almost as if in reaction to the reactions of the successive audiences.

But the crowds loved it.

The tickets for the remaining shows were like gold dust.

Antony pleaded for the run to be extended, but the actual Spiegeltent was already booked for a circus somewhere in Eastern Europe and would be packed up after our final night. and transported there. He remained hopeful that the splash we had made would attract some West End theatres to offer us a new home and we could transfer there.

The final evening of our ever-evolving show arrived.

The week had gone by like a fever dream.

From opening night to now, the play had metamorphosed radically, turning from theatre to spectacle, from text to emotions, from a blank canvas to some form of unexploded bomb. As soon as we left the stage every night, we were already raring to go again, primed to take things one step further up the scales, eager to see how far we could stretch our limits until something snapped. It was creative madness and quietly encouraged by Aurelia at our debriefs, although she and her friends were always careful not to be specific, just complicit.

Ratcheting up the tension was the fact that, deliberately or not, any sexual interaction between Antony, Alissa and me had been stifled by our exhaustion following each per-formance and cars had been arranged to drive us straight to our respective homes, and we would not meet up until late the following morning to plan the daily evolution of the project and then it would be time to go onstage again.

292

I arrived late, my car having been delayed by traffic crossing the river and I had to rush to the curtained-off area behind the stage where we changed and gathered, hoping that tonight's wardrobe would be simple, quick to slip into and not require any elaborate make-up. Aurelia stood there, waiting.

She handed me a gown. I had become accustomed to the unusual, daily costume changes, so different from the formal black dresses that I always wore, and I was surprised to be assigned a dress for the final night, although as Aurelia held it up I realised that it was no ordinary frock. The fabric was some kind of manufactured satin stretch, but incredibly fine and covered in tiny jewels in shades of black, green and deep blue that shimmered when they caught the light. Feathers were sewn into the back to form a collar around the shoulders. It resembled the costume of something part bird, part fish, and when I pulled the fabric against my flesh I realised that it was so thin it was partly transparent, just a thin layer of decoration beneath which my naked flesh would be visible in the right light.

'I'd like you to wear this,' she said.

Alissa wore something similar, albeit tailored to the lusciousness of her curves. Hers was an olive green tone that suited her skin, and the pattern was decidedly more snake-like. She sat facing a mirror, adjusting her make-up. Antony was in the opposite corner, tightening his belt. He also wasn't dressed in his customary side-stage outfit of jeans and tee. His trousers were a loose fitting leather or hide, with a jacket that covered just his shoulders and flanks and left his torso bare. It was a soft, thin leather so the effect was Pan rather than biker, and as he stood under the bright lights that had been set up in the changing room I was able to admire the smooth hardness of his chest. It was a costume that I had noticed earlier that week, set aside for the main male performer.

'Peter, our male lead, can't make it tonight,' Aurelia said. 'Antony will sit in for him. He knows the play inside out, and anyway the focus will be on you and lovely Alissa, won't it?'

I raised an eyebrow. I doubted any unexpected changes occurred within Aurelia's tightly run ship. And Antony's costume fitted him surprisingly well for something that had been apparently intended for another man to wear. My guess was that she had intended him to play the main male part tonight all along. He had, I knew, previously worked as an actor as well as a writer and knew every word of the script, so appeared unsurprised by the request.

Lauralynn barged in. She wore a shimmering pale gold mesh bodysuit that clung like lycra to her form. Her hair was drawn back and fell against her shoulders like waves of wheat.

I was helped into the dress.

There was curious buzz in the air, a sense of both dread and expectation. A feeling that gnawed at my stomach in unsettling ways.

Lauralynn leaned over and kissed me on the cheek.

'Big night, eh?'

I nodded.

She handed me the Bailly and took my hand. Her instrument was already on stage, next to her seat. There was a countdown from one of the technicians and darkness fell. We walked onstage, took our positions, and then waited for the curtain to rise. Lauralynn and I were responsible for the musical overture of the show, setting its mood. Tonight, we had planned an improvisation on a piece by Kreisler.

I tiptoed to my position on the right hand of the proscenium. Lauralynn sat on the left, directly facing me.

The penumbra around the Spiegeltent's interior began to lighten and my eyes alighted on the audience. Unlike previous nights, tonight's spectators were unmasked.

And each and every one of them was entirely nude, and painted like an animal.

The cats caught my attention first. Both men and women, limbs long and lithe and painted the sleek blue black of panthers or variations of gold, bronze and brown of jaguar, lions and tigers. Some had ornate collars fastened around their necks. One young man had the appearance of a leopard crouched on all fours and was straining against a short black leather leash attached to a thick silver hoop that surrounded his throat. A tall woman covered from head to toe in tones of black and grey held the end of the lead in one hand, her fingers decorated with thick, ornate rings and her bicep bulging with the force required to restrain him, belying the passive expression on her face. Feathered bands were affixed to her wrists and the tops of her arms, ankles and legs. She was an owl, I guessed.

Others were in cages dotted around the room. They behaved as if they were truly dangerous, prowling back and forth, snapping at the gaps in the bars that penned them in and occasionally letting out muffled yelps and roars.

So these, I guessed, were the Network's special guests. For one night only. By invitation only.

It felt like being in a B-movie, part terror and part sex exploitation. I wasn't sure if I should laugh or worry. Or repress the excitement racing through my mind.

I breathed hard as I instinctively brought my violin to my chin, raised my bow and observed Lauralynn lower her arm and her own bow towards the cello's strings.

We began playing.

Following our first cadenza, a dancer was scheduled to pirouette across the front of the stage. Her name was Elena and, although she had been one of Aurelia's additions to the show, she had a classical ballet background. She was delicate and dark-haired, and had a pixie-like presence.

Autumn

As Lauralynn and I struck our notes in unison, Elena sauntered onto the proscenium.

She was totally naked, and in the sea of colour that surrounded us, her bare, unpainted skin seemed even more overtly nude and pornographic than it might have done under other circumstances. Her body was beautiful, and watching her almost caused me to drop my bow to my side, stop playing and just stare.

Her nipples were small and hard and perched in the centre of her firm round breasts like ripe cherries, surrounded by barely a millimetre or two of pale pink areola. As she rose onto her toes and prepared to turn, the muscles in her calves, thighs and arse lifted and the small of her back tilted forward, her core remaining as solid as rock. She lifted her arms over her head with the grace and ease of a flower opening its petals and spun, slowly at first and then increasing her pace with the tempo of the music until she was spinning like a whirligig. Without slowing she lifted one leg so that her calf was level with her ear and continued to turn, flashing her open cunt with each rotation, so swiftly that it was impossible to make out anything besides the barest flash of dark pink flesh.

Lauralynn's face was a mask of concentration and I too was almost out of breath trying to keep up with Elena.

Finally she began to slow and eventually stopped and bowed to a cacophony closer to baying than wild applause but apparently meant in the same way, greeting our overture in effusive manner.

The lights dimmed again and the voiceover began setting the scene, telling the story that I now knew so well it felt as though the voice was speaking inside my own head rather than over a microphone. Then it was Alissa's turn to take the stage. She appeared in spotlight standing completely still and almost reptilian in her ankle-length green gown and as Lauralynn and I launched into a piece inspired by the climactic crescendo of 'The Rite of Spring', she began to move, as sinuous and sensual as a charmed cobra swaying under the hypnotic spell of a snake charmer. The longer I watched her the more I wondered if she was performing under a spell, which extended its reach over all of us here tonight.

Across from me, Lauralynn's lips were opening and closing infinitesimally as though she were mouthing the text to herself. I felt, perhaps for the first time in my life, disengaged from the music that I was playing, as though my arms and hands had temporarily divorced from my mind and spirit, enabling my body to continue playing while my eyes remained fixed on the action on stage.

Alissa was totally uninhibited as ever but she had lost her usual large dose of self-absorption and for the first time, her performance seemed genuine, unrehearsed. Antony had now joined her and was either delivering the most convincing performance of his lifetime or had been so drawn into the spell of the cursed violin that he had lost his hold on reality and was being blindly led along by the musical score, the text and Alissa's cues. He was playing the part to perfection and only someone sitting as near to him as I was could have noticed that his eyes were glazed and he had taken the key romantic scene of the first half far beyond the actual script, and added the flourish of a passionate embrace and smouldering kiss.

His hand then strayed to Alissa's breast and he pulled down one side of her dress, bent his head to her chest and began to suck her nipple. She groaned and leaned into his touch, baring her throat and tipping back her hair so that it fell behind her, grazing her arse.

Waves of heat seemed to rise from the crowd. I knew that it was impossible for me to pick out such fine details in the darkness from my position on the brightly lit stage but I had the sense that across the packed theatre, nipples were hardening, those patrons who were tied were straining against their leashes, those in cages were snapping more furiously than before against the bars, cocks were hardening, cunts becoming wetter, and through it all my bow hand continued to rise and fall against the strings, both provoking and being provoked by the tide of arousal that was rising like a wave and threatening to overwhelm us all.

The audience remained none the wiser but I knew that a

large chunk of dialogue had been entirely dropped and replaced by Antony's continued public fondling of Alissa. Had he gone mad? He did not even seem to be aware that anybody else was in the room. Not even me. He was captivated by every line of her as if he was seeing a naked woman's body for the first time. His fingers trailed over her skin ever so delicately, assuming the role of Adam in the garden of Creation stroking the first rose's petals. Each touch so slow, so deliberate, orchestrating the rise of not just Alissa's desire but the desire of all those present, including me. He moved behind her, unzipped her dress at the back and peeled it just three quarters of the way down her body to reveal her torso, hips, and the top of her pubis, just before the onset of her slit.

She was bare. Alissa had shaved for the occasion. She had been so proud of her bush that I could only imagine that her grooming had been under Aurelia's instruction. The change was evidently a shock to Antony, whose gaze immediately fell to her smooth mound and where his eyes travelled, his fingers followed, trailing down between her nipples to her groin. His hand disappeared behind her back and then reappeared cupped between her legs. An expression of bliss passed across Alissa's face as he found her clitoris and began to rub. His head was nestled into her shoulder and his face was a picture of both relaxation and concentration as his fingertips continued to play between her folds.

Autumn

It was the first time that I had ever seen them together like this, as a voyeur, without being involved. My emotions swam twin streams of jealousy and arousal and through it all I continued to play on until Alissa came. They had continued to instinctively move forward, perhaps by magnetic pull towards the audience, and when she orgasmed and inevitably gushed, her spray of juices showered the lifted faces of those positioned closest to the foot of the stage. The leashed leopard opened his mouth wide and snapped at the droplets that rained down towards him until the curtains closed, signalling the end of the opening half of the show and the beginning of the intermission.

Lauralynn, like the rest of the musicians, was scheduled to break but she continued to play as though welded to her cello. I lowered my violin. My arm ached as though I had been moving my bow over the strings like a madwoman and yet I could not remember a single note that I had played, having left the Stravinsky composition way behind me, trailing in my musical wake.

Aurelia came bursting between the curtains at the back of the stage. Her hair was loose and messy, as though she had just woken up and her cheeks were flushed. Her tattoos flashed and rippled and I immediately glanced at the ink that I always found so captivating, the dragon's tongue that decorated her mons. It was moving maniacally across her slit as though performing cunnilingus.

'Summer, Summer,' she cried breathlessly, looking from one side of the stage to the other as if her eyes had not yet adjusted to the relative darkness and she could not make me out sitting in the corner.

'Yes,' I called. She moved towards me where I was still seated on my chair, placed a hand on each of my shoulders and leaned forwards so that her breasts swung towards my face and then she bent down and kissed my mouth. Her lips were soft and her movements urgent. Our tongues danced together, slick with saliva. She drew away. The sound of Lauralynn's cello continued to cut through the theatre, audible above the increasingly frantic sounds emanating from beyond the curtain. I recognised strains of Schubert.

'That was beautiful,' she said, 'Absolutely beautiful. Perfect.'

'I just don't know what I did,' I replied.

'Look,' she said, lifting up part of the heavy velvet that separated us from the auditorium so that I could see out.

The crowd had converged upon one another. Everywhere I looked there was a tangled pile of painted arms and legs. The leopard had broken free from his leash and was driving his cock into his mistress the owl whose feathers were now in disarray and her face morphed from passive boredom to pleasure. A group of black and white zebra were painted so similarly I could not make out whose limbs belonged to whom as they joined and writhed together. The cages had been opened and whoever or whatever had been restrained behind bars had now been let loose. It was like a scene from a Roman frieze come to life, an orgiastic festival of the senses gone wild.

'You did this,' Aurelia whispered. 'The spell of your music, your own form of magic.'

In truth, I did not really believe her. The audience had seemed on the verge of a riot from the outset. I had little or nothing to do with it. This was the aura of Aurelia, and whatever was behind her organisation, the Network.

I turned away from the curtain and glanced back towards Antony and Alissa. They had stopped their lovemaking and were staring at each other and the space around them as though they had both just woken and were not sure whether they were still experiencing a dream or were now back in reality.

Aurelia followed my gaze, and reached towards me, wrapping her hand around my wrist and giving me a gentle squeeze.

'Go to them,' she said, 'and be kind, they were as caught up in the passion of your playing as the rest.' Then she turned, slipped under the curtain and disappeared into the throng.

'Summer?' It was Antony. He was now nude, his trousers and jacket flung to the corner of the stage. He looked beautiful lying there, his long, lean limbs relaxed against the wooden dais, a picture of repose. He was still sporting a beard, though he had trimmed it neatly for the occasion. I knelt down and kissed him. His mouth was wet and tasted of Alissa's pussy; sweet. I turned to her and lifted her chin with my fingers and we pressed our lips together.

'Summer . . .' she said.

They both sounded dazed.

I nestled into the space between them, resting on my knees, and placed a hand playfully around each of their throats. They groaned in unison.

Hands travelled over my thighs, belly, breasts. My eyes were closed and I wasn't sure which set of fingers belonged to Alissa and which to Antony. They squeezed my nipples gently, delved between the folds of my labia, ran their tongues over my lips, higher and lower.

I opened my eyes in surprise when the bell chimed to signal the end of the interval. I had presumed that we would not be continuing with the second half. But, the curtains raised on cue, indicating that the show would go on. Instead of lighting on Alissa and Antony sharing a passionate kiss as per the script, the spotlight shone on the three of us coupling together on the floor. Alissa and Antony were indeed sharing a passionate kiss, however, she was also grinding her cunt against my face as Antony straddled me and drove his cock into my pussy.

We received a standing ovation, and we were only halfway through the play.

★   ★   ★

As if they knew where I had spent the night, Aurelia's limousine and its blank-faced and grey-suited chauffeur, arrived at the agreed time the next morning at Antony's Isle of Dogs building to pick me up and take me to the airport.

Regardless of the sweet excesses of the previous night and our final performance of the play, I had agreed to work for Aurelia's Network for a period of three months and I took a certain pride in being professional at all times and was determined to fulfil my commitments. In addition they had made an outrageously generous offer to my agent for my fee, and she had enthusiastically recommended the gig to me, despite the unusual circumstances and veil of secrecy surrounding it.

Antony was sleeping soundly as I tiptoed out of the bedroom. I didn't wish to alert him to my departure and forthcoming absence.

We made a detour via my Clapham flat where I picked up the luggage I had prepared a few days earlier. Clothes for a hot climate, I had been warned.

Heathrow's Terminal 4 was a buzz of activity. On arrival, the driver had handed me a buff envelope with my travel details. I pulled the itinerary page out. Las Vegas. I was already checked in and being flown first class.

The destination surprised me. I had never been there before and it was a tawdry city that had never attracted me in the slightest. The only gambles I had ever risked were with my life and emotions and I'd never been desperate or deluded enough to gamble for money.

I wheeled my suitcase to the drop-in area.

10

The Desert Shimmers

Slot machines, one-arm bandits and harsh lighting dominated the arrival concourse as I disembarked from the aircraft. I felt drained. It wasn't just the jet-lag but a deep sense of emptiness following the events of the past few days and the epiphany of the final night's performance of the play and its attendant sweet intoxication.

I was ahead of the queue at immigration and soon found myself in the baggage area, seeking out the right luggage carousel in the cavernous hall. My attention kept on being drawn to the on/off pattern of gaudy colours click clacking in repetitive patterns on the many gambling machines dotted across the walls and pillars. The accompanying mechanical chatter it created was profoundly irritating, random, unmelodic, nagging at my senses as if I was hungover. Fortunately, my suitcase arrived in the first batch of luggage to tumble down the chute, highlighted by its first class colour tag. I was holding my violin case close to my chest, as I had out of habit for most of the flight, and looked around for a trolley.

'You won't be needing one,' a voice said.

I looked round.

In the few years since I had seen her last, she had barely aged. Her long hair still tumbled down halfway to the small of her back, albeit now speckled with grey and the crumpled velvet material of her flowing crimson dress clung to her strong hips as she sashayed towards me with elegance.

It was Madame Denoux, the hostess of the New Orleans club where I had first witnessed the hypnotic spectacle of Luba, the Russian dancer and where Dominik had encouraged me to go on stage and shed so many of my inhibitions and shamelessly exhibit myself.

In truth, it was no surprise to see her waiting for me here.

It seemed as if my whole life was now being lived in the shadow of the Network and not much of a revelation to learn that the shadowy club she had run was, it appeared, part of Aurelia's tentacular organisation. In a way, it proved reassuring. I could think of worse people, entities, to manipulate me like a puppet. And with a tightening in my throat, actually remembered that I had experienced much worse in the way of manipulation along the road to here. Victor. The Kentish Town horror I had so meekly accepted or brought upon myself. And other instances I would now rather forget.

Standing next to her, towering high above her head, stood yet another square-shouldered, uniformed driver, black this time but clad in the customary grey outfit. He took a step towards the carousel and picked up my case as if it was empty or feather light. I knew it wasn't. In my haste to pack and ignorant of what I would be doing during these three months, I had stuffed it with so many clothes that, when weighed at London Heathrow, it had perilously skirted even the first class luggage weight limit.

'Welcome,' Madame Denoux said, with just the faint trace of a French accent in her voice.

'It's nice to see you again, Madame,' I replied.

'Call me Giselle,' she said.

She turned on her heels, and I followed her and the truck-sized driver to the sliding automatic doors that led to the road.

A blanket of dry heat assaulted me as we stepped outside. I stopped. Caught my breath.

Madame Denoux looked at me, with a gentle smile. 'The desert air. Rather dry. But you'll grow accustomed to it,' she said.

The limo was air-conditioned and the immediate contrast made me sneeze.

We drove off.

Dusk was falling over the neon canyons of Las Vegas, an oasis of light shining like an unearthly beacon in the darkness of the surrounding sands. It was my first time here but it felt familiar from countless movies, documentaries, pictures in magazines. Cocooned in the deep silence of the car, everything felt unreal, a travelogue of clichéd images unfolding like a tapestry behind the darkened windows of the sleek limousine we were travelling in.

We glided onto the Strip, glittering hotels, attractions, bizarre and fancy architectures flashing by, crowds of tourists in shades of khaki, chinos, floral dresses, most juggling with plastic cups.

'It's for their coins, their tokens,' Madame Denoux indicated, following the questioning direction of my gaze.

Halfway down the Strip, a wall of solid light facing us ahead, the car took a swift right turn and made its way down narrower avenues and streets, passing parades of smaller, less lavish hotels and buildings, and the artificial daylight began to dim.

I blinked as we crossed a final city block and were swallowed by the darkness of the desert. It had taken just a second to move from the excesses of civilisation and into total night. My eyes adjusted. The rutted skyline of stunted peaks, mesas and hills towered over the inky horizon. The road began to bend.

Madame Denoux noticed how tired I was.

'Sleep, my dear. It's a long journey still. Just relax.'

As I dozed off I reflected with relief that Las Vegas had not been our final destination. For the first time in ages, my sleep was devoid of dreams, a long – or so it felt – waltz into nothingness.

I awoke later to a deep feeling of peace, curled up alone on the leather back seat of the car, the only sound reaching me the purring of the air conditioning. I blinked. Outside the tinted windows, the sun was rising over a nearby hill, white and pale against the predominantly muted red background of our surroundings.

For a brief moment, I felt as if I was in the midst of a western movie, and the cavalry and John Wayne were about to cavalcade past me, hoofs trampling the dirt and stirring up clouds of dust in their wake.

I stirred reluctantly, feeling the deep embrace of sleep holding me back.

'Ah, sleeping beauty wakes,' Madame Denoux said as she opened the car's door and a rush of heat reached me. 'I hope you don't mind we left you there. It felt wrong to disturb you.'

I mumbled something indistinct. My throat was dry.

Beating my words to the draw, she handed over a bottle of water. It was blissfully cold to the touch.

I gulped with undisguised greed.

'Where are we?' I asked her, as I peered out and the

brightness of the rising day began to affirm itself against my waking eyelids.

'We're very close to Monument Valley,' she said.

The name stirred old memories. Movies again.

'We're some distance from Vegas, off the Navajo Tribal Park. This is where the next Ball is being set up,' she said.

She extended her hand to help me step out of the car.

The weight of the outside heat wrapped itself around me as soon as my foot trod the powdery ochre sand of the desert floor.

I turned round, somehow expecting some form of encampment, tents, improvised shacks where we would be staying but my view of the surrounding boulders was blocked by an imposing building, with tall antebellum Greek columns limning its facade. It stood there incongruously, like a giant blot on the landscape, a sign in Spanish designating it as a hotel, 'Gran Mension Del Desierto'. It stood in the middle of nowhere as if dropped from the skies.

'You'll be staying there. We all are,' Madame Denoux said. 'We've already taken your suitcase and your violin to your room.'

The lobby had apparently been taken over by Ball and Network staff. Impromptu circus performances were occurring at the front desk and dotted all around the cavernous terracotta'd space that seemed to me wildly ostentatious and unnecessary considering that its sole purpose was to usher guests and their luggage from the check-in area to their bedrooms.

Right in the centre of the hall, an aerial hoop had been set up and hung down precariously from a fixture in the ceiling. Below it, a large soft mattress was stationed, though in my view it was not nearly large enough considering the heights that the woman on the swing was reaching as she swung, pendulously, sometimes hanging by her hands and then pulling herself up to perform a flip through the hoop or mid-air splits as she dangled, seemingly impervious to the power of gravity. Her ginger hair was cut into a short, gamine crop and she was dressed in a black and white striped body stocking. When she turned the stripes in combination with the form of her long, lean body gave her the appearance of a spinning, zebra-coloured barber's pole.

To the left of the door, two young men clad only from the hips down in soft hemp trousers were performing abdominal crunches with their knees hooked through the top bars of the luggage trolley. Their blond hair hung down and just scraped the floor as they extended their torsos into straight planks, and then their stomach muscles tightened visibly beneath the thin layer of skin without an ounce of fat as they scissored back up again, touching their elbows to the rack when they reached the top. They were identical twins, I realised as they swivelled simultaneously and turned their heads towards the hoopist when she let out a loud triumphant whoop after completing a particularly complex trick.

At the front desk, a group stood with their passports organising rooms and keys with the hotel staff. They were dancers, I guessed, by the light, supple way that they moved, different from ordinary human beings. The women possessed lean calves and girlish narrow hips, and the men sported broad shoulders, slim waists and arses so tight, high and firm I could have cracked the shells of walnuts by throwing them against their buttocks. The sort of physicality that only comes with years of training.

I sighed. It had only been a few days in reality, but it felt like a long time since I'd had any opportunity to go swimming or running, and I missed stretching my limbs, feeling my heart race and my blood pump and the wonderful sense of aliveness that I found in exercise. Antony ran every day, usually ten miles or more, rain or shine, no matter where he was, or what other urgent matters he had to attend to. He didn't talk about it. I had asked him once, about his habits, when I noticed the beaten-up state of his toenails.

'Hey you.'

I jumped about a foot in the air as Antony's voice reached my ears, just as I had been thinking about him.

'Christ!' I said, putting my hand to my heart to still my racing breath. He touched his hand gently to my shoulder.

'Sorry,' he said, laughing, 'did I scare you?'

'I didn't expect to see you here.'

He was wearing sunglasses that were now pushed onto the top of his head, a thin white cotton collared shirt with the two top buttons undone, a pair of sky blue, knee length denim shorts and tan boat shoes. Despite his English heritage he looked unfeasibly tanned. Antony browned easily.

'I meant to call you, but it was all very last minute,' he explained. 'And I figured Aurelia would have let you know. I'm staying on with the show. She's asked me to help direct some of the acts. I don't fully understand myself, to be honest. Someone called just last night and I got on a plane. I don't like to be at a loose end, you know . . .'

He paused and brushed his fingers through his hair, knocking his sunglasses off in the process and catching them in one hand before they fell to the floor. 'And with the play finished, there's nothing to keep me in London for the moment. I didn't have any other work to go on to. So, here I am.'

'Well, it's good to see you.' I clenched my thigh muscles together. Watching the bare-chested twins stomach crunching and gazing at the queuing dancers' arses had made me horny, and Antony's presence would fix that. Besides which, I felt more at home with a familiar face. I'd spent enough of my working life travelling that it had lost its glamour, even with the added theatrical extravagance of the

Ball and its cohorts providing a welcome distraction from the mundanities of yet another hotel room.

'Lauralynn, Viggo and Alissa are on their way as well,' he added. 'They needed more time to pack, so took the later flight.'

'It'll be just like London then,' I said, 'but warmer.'

I was even pleased to hear that Alissa would be joining us. Our initial rivalry had subsided into an easy sort of intimacy, the kind of understanding that develops sometimes between two women who have fucked the same man. I was still acutely jealous of her at times, and wildly jealous of her tits, which she had told me, and I had eventually come to believe, were in fact 100% real and their firmness and unfeasibly high position a result of the genetic lottery, youth, and the vitamin E oil she painstakingly rubbed over her chest each morning after spraying them with an ice cold rinse in the shower to aid her circulation.

Antony took my hand as we approached the desk. The small wheelie bag that contained his few changes of clothes and personal items had already been whisked away. He wasn't usually the type for public displays of affection, but I happily wound my fingers through his without thinking much of it.

We had been booked into separate rooms, it transpired, but neither of us complained as the clerk explained the set-up and programmed our door swipe cards. We both liked to have our own space. Separation made each other's company so much sweeter. We filled in the obligatory paperwork, took the keys and headed for the lifts. Madame Denoux – Giselle – had left us to relax and settle in and would call our rooms later to explain further the working arrangements for our respective projects over dinner.

Though separate, our rooms were right opposite one another and, we discovered once inside, shared a door at one end that separated each of our immense bathrooms.

'Come inside?' Antony asked, as we stood in the hall between our two doorways in a silent standoff, deciding whether to now separate or freshen up together. He did not seem as poised and nonchalant as he usually did. In fact, since Aurelia and the Ball had torpedoed into our lives he had lost that bored, impassive expression that had previously driven me mad at times until I'd learned to just accept it as a part of him.

'Sure,' I said. I couldn't face opening my higgledy-piggledy overpacked and oversized suitcases at that moment anyway. I would make use of the complimentary toiletries and robe in Antony's room and when I could be bothered, pop over for my own things.

He opened the door and we moved inside.

'Wow,' I said, looking around. 'Bit more glamour than what I'm normally used to.' The room was cavernous, occupying nearly one half of the whole floor and containing a kitchen suite, long sofa and two armchairs, a writing desk that was set up by a large window with a view overlooking the desert plain, and a giant super king size bed. The bathroom alone with walk-in shower, hot tub, toilet and bidet was the size of most of the rooms I'd previously stayed in while on tour. It felt so incongruous to come across such lavish use of space, or maybe it was something being in the heart of a desert called for.

I opened a few cabinets and quickly located the tea and coffee facilities. The room only had instant. There was no espresso machine or even a bag of filter and cafetiere in sight. Even Aurelia, and her Network, didn't think of everything, I thought, as I filled the kettle with water, rinsed out a couple of cups and located a plug socket.

Antony was still standing near the doorway, looking lost.

'Are you OK?' I asked him. 'Tired?' I'd had a night's sleep after the flight, I recalled, even if it had been in the back seat of a car parked outside the hotel, and he'd only just arrived.

'Yeah,' he said, 'I'm OK.' He stepped towards me and took the white china mug I was holding out of my hand and set it on the nearby cabinet, then folded me into his arms.

We stood like that for a long while. He held me against him and stroked my hair, and I breathed in his scent, a mixture of cologne and sweat and washing powder and something more, the particular perfume of his skin, masked though it was by the manufactured odours of shower gels and cleansing products.

'Sorry,' he said, stepping away. 'I need a shower.'

'Me too,' I replied.

'Come on then, join me.'

He took my hand and pulled me into the bathroom.

It wasn't like him to be so tactile, or so clingy, I thought, as I slipped out of my clothes and turned the shower tap on. He had gone back to find his toothbrush in his toiletry bag and I had ample time to admire his form when he reappeared. The shower head was in a wet room rather than a cubicle and so there was no foggy screen door to separate us as he stood at the sink by the vanity unit.

I stood, openly voyeuristic, and watched him unfold his neatly arranged bathroom kit and pull out his travel sized tube of toothpaste. His thighs were thick and strong and when he turned his back to me and bent over to reach for the face cloths that were folded and stacked on a shelf below the sink I admired the view of his arse, as pert and firm as any of the dancers that I'd seen at the front desk and complete with a winsome dimple in each cheek. The muscles in his calves were tight and visibly clenched as he leant forward. He turned to face the mirror, and I caught a flash of his cock and balls, hanging down low in the warm humidity of the shower room, firm and thick and half way to a semi hard on.

I silently gave thanks to whatever god or goddess or random act of fate had ensured I had been blessed by a stream of handsome boyfriends. Good looks weren't everything, I knew that, but they sure did help.

Antony finished brushing his teeth, and stepped into the shower.

'No, stay,' he said, as I began to step out from under the shower head and let him get under the water. He squeezed some of the complimentary, rose scented bath gel onto his hands, rubbed his palms together to create a lather and then cupped them onto my breasts. He bent his head down and kissed me, and I shut my eyes to prevent droplets from running into them. I slipped out of his grasp and with a gentle push shifted him into the space that I had been occupying a moment before so that I was out from under the water, and I soaped up my hands and began to run them over his body, paying particular attention to the smooth skin of his penis which was steadily growing under my touch.

I wanted to feel him in my mouth, but didn't much fancy getting down on my knees on the hard ceramic tiles.

'Come to bed,' I said, and stepped away from him to the towel rail, wrapping myself in one large fluffy white towel and holding up another for Antony.

He turned off the water and followed me.

We fucked; the simple, straightforward sort of sex born of desire and affection and tiredness. I crawled onto the bed and turned over onto my back and he slid on top of me. I was already half-wet, and I reached for his cock immediately and positioned him at my entrance as he pressed his lips against my collarbone, each of my breasts, my throat, my mouth, making me wetter still. We lay together partially conjoined, and I kissed him back and caressed the length of his muscled body, marvelling as I always did at the unusual softness of his skin, grabbing the flesh of his firm arse until I became wetter, wet enough for him to slide fully inside me.

'Ohh, fuck,' I moaned. The first stroke always felt so good.

I clung on to his thighs, holding him inside me and pulling him deeper as he thrust until he came and we sank back against the sheets, spent. He lay on top of me for a while, breathing heavily and nuzzling into my neck. I held him tight, my palms pressed against his shoulders in a firm embrace and then moved my hands upwards and stroked the nape of his neck, his hair. He pressed his lips to mine, hard, then his cheek against mine, and then he kissed my ear before carefully disengaging and slowly pulling his cock out of me. He tumbled over onto the bed alongside me and threw out his arm so that I could huddle into the crook in his shoulder.

'Summer,' he said, after we'd lain silently for a few moments.

'Mmm?' I replied, sleepily. I'd known something was coming. He'd seemed more emotive, less distant than usual, and preoccupied, as though words were on the tip of his tongue that he was waiting for the right time to articulate.

'We haven't talked. About Alissa. Or . . . that night in the lift. The rope.'

I knew what he meant. The sex we'd had then had been more violent than any that had gone before. Antony wasn't, in my opinion, a natural dominant, but on that evening he had come closer to dominating me in a truly kinky way than he ever had before and I knew that I had responded so naturally and intuitively I had shown him a side of myself that I had previously kept hidden, a side that might have shocked him. I also knew somehow that it wasn't something that came as a surprise. However I had behaved on that night was no more or less than the hints I'd displayed on other occasions. I hadn't revealed a new side of myself, just maybe uncovered something that he was already aware of but hadn't previously been faced with so starkly.

I lay there silently wondering what to say, but couldn't come up with anything much more than applying further pressure against his chest with the arm that I had draped over him in a squeeze of affection.

He paused, and then when I didn't say anything, carried on.

'I guess what I'm meaning to say is that I know neither of us is perfect, and I know that there are parts of you that maybe I don't fully understand. And that our relationship is unorthodox. But I want to be with you, Summer. I like you, for everything that you are, even the fucked up bits, and if I can ever do anything, or be anything that would help you … then I will.'

I knew that he was talking about sex, about the dark things that I sometimes craved and the high level of my sexual desire, which pop culture, if nothing else, had told me again and again and again was abnormal compared to the rest of the female population.

'I like you too,' I replied, then scooped myself up onto my elbows and haunches and kissed him.

It might not have been everyone's idea of romance, but it worked for us.

We napped together until Giselle called us down for dinner, to meet the rest of the crew, and to hear about what the coming weeks would bring and what we would each be expected to contribute to the Ball.

We'd been working hard for several weeks now, and were just a few days away from our first full dress rehearsal. The main set we would occupy, one of many such being built, would prove unavailable today as the carpenters and rig staff were putting their final touches to it. Andrei suggested all the performers should take a day off, to recharge their batteries and decompress in anticipation of the big night.

I was initially reluctant to do so, absorbed as I was in the flow of my improvisations and unwilling to allow cumbersome external factors to temper my overall mood of melodic detachment. Many of the dancers suggested we go to Vegas to play the tables and let steam off, while others, Viggo and the majority of the dressmakers and set dressers amongst them, suggested we visit the Hoover Dam which was, it appeared, a mighty sight to behold, a minor wonder of the world, Viggo insisted. Antony hesitated between the two alternatives but sensing my lack of enthusiasm said he would defer to my choice. Lauralynn came to the rescue, proposing instead a hike into the desert, to enjoy an old-fashioned picnic. After all, she argued, we were camped amongst some of the greatest beauty of the natural world and all we did was hide away under a variety of canopies and tents, practising and fine-tuning our craft all day long. We agreed to disagree and all go our own ways. Only a few of us opted for the hike. The blonds, as I had come to think of the two twins that I had seen stomach-crunching on the baggage trolley on our first day, and who had subsequently turned out to be two of a group of gymnastic octuplets, initially opted to head for the Strip, much to my disappointment. They were quite something all together and sweating in shorts or swimming topless would have made a wonderful distraction, albeit not necessarily a relaxing one. The two pixie-haired girls, Nina, the ginger-mopped hoopist, and Elena, the brunette with the great tits who had been our opening act for the final night of the play, decided to travel together to the Hoover Dam, and the group of firm-arsed ballerinas who Antony and I had queued behind for so long at the check-in desk just wanted to sit by the hexagonal-shaped hotel pool and sip cocktails.

Then, Alissa got involved. She was evidently unwilling to let Antony and I wander off without tagging along, but more obviously had her eyes set on the blonds. 'Surely I can bag at least one of them, there's eight for god's sake,' she muttered to Lauralynn, as they eventually agreed to neglect the slot machines for another day and follow us. Apart from that first day, when the other six of them had apparently only been standing a few metres away but out of my sight, I had never witnessed them apart. They even shared the same suite, all eight of them housed together though sleeping separately, each in their own bunk bed. None of us girls had a clue what act they would be a part of, though we certainly speculated.

'They're like mini David Beckhams, but younger,' Alissa remarked, staring at them unashamedly over the dinner table. 'Only with no Posh Spice to get in the way.'

I hadn't seen any of them glance in her direction for a moment longer than etiquette allowed, but I didn't doubt for a second that at least one, or possibly all eight, would end up in her bed at some point. What Alissa wanted, she got. And to be fair to her, they hadn't made eyes at anyone else, either. In fact, they lacked any sense of sexuality at all.

Lauralynn took charge of all the arrangements, organising the necessary equipment, food and drink supplies. She was visibly in her element, bossing us around and barking orders, reminding us to wear appropriate clothing and footwear, which Alissa had to be reminded of repeatedly.

And so we set off at dawn before the day's heat had fully extended its sticky fingers in our direction. Lauralynn had a map in hand, although I was puzzled as to how one could navigate through a landscape of just sand, dunes, and occasional arroyos. We would trek for a few hours until we reached the area she had highlighted for the picnic, she announced.

'There are wonderful rock formations in the vicinity,' she informed us. 'A bunch of caves to explore. And enough shade to keep us cool under the midday sun ...' She chuckled.

Unsurprisingly, most of us in the group were quite unfit when it came to desert walking. Running or cycling on London's mostly dead flat roads in cool weather or performing acrobatics on the spot was a completely different matter to treading for hours through the Nevada desert. We moved haltingly on through the hard sands of the desert without ever seeming to make much progress towards any fixed point ahead we focused on. Lauralynn and Viggo led our mini-expedition from the front, a sharp contrast between their advancing silhouettes, Lauralynn square-shouldered and amazon-like, steady, unrelenting, her pace metronomic while Viggo's gait was a touch effeminate, swaying, thin like a matchstick and dwarfed by her determination, but somehow keeping up with her without expending any visible energy.

Antony, Alissa, the eight blonds and I followed some paces back, our gazes mechanically fixed on the steady horizon of their colour-matched backsides as they energetically marched on, hoping against hope their pace would eventually become less relentless, which it never did. I didn't know about my walking companions, but I'd quickly switched off and moved on through a daze, impervious to the savage beauty of the landscapes we were travelling amongst.

I wore a floppy, formless canvas hat that I'd salvaged from one of the Ball's box of props, as did many of the other walkers. Viggo sported a tightly-bound bandanna which barely contained his untamed mop of hair and Antony, who hadn't thought to bring any trekking clothes in his small, minimally packed suitcase had been forced to borrow a baseball cap from the front desk staff which didn't suit him in the slightest, advertising a brand of mountaineering gear he was never likely to wear even in the best of circumstances.

Pummelled by the sun, we all maintained a strained silence

as we progressed, trying to keep up with Lauralynn as we ventured deeper into the desert and maybe unwisely trusted in her innate sense of direction.

Lauralynn finally stopped in the shadow of a group of immense boulders, and promptly stuffed her backpack full of water bottles into a dark fissure in the rocks to shelter it from the midday sun and, as we caught up with her, suggested we do the same. We obediently followed her instructions.

To our left lay an arroyo, a dry creek through which water might have intermittently flowed in other seasons, its stream bed right now just a wash of sand and dust. To our right, behind the boulders, was an enormous wall of rock rising like a wide monolith into the sky.

We paused for breath. Had we been expecting an oasis of sorts?

'Is this it?' Alissa asked. Of all of us, she was the one who appeared to be in the most discomfort, her features red and puffy and cupid lips drier than dry, as she passed her tongue over them over and over in a vain attempt to revive their customary moistness. She had even given up trying to flirt with the blonds, who appeared entirely disinterested in anyone besides themselves and each other, and hadn't spoken a word to the rest of us throughout the entire journey.

We sat in the shadow of the rock, dwarfed by the vastness

of the blue desert sky, like dots in a landscape, performing fleas seeking for a way out of a wide open labyrinth which lacked walls and boundaries and was, as a result, even more devious a prison.

I was fast becoming exasperated by the whole idea of this silly excursion into the wilderness and simmering inside at my own foolishness in accepting its challenge and Lauralynn's foolhardy proposal to embark on this most useless of expeditions. As far as the picnic was concerned, I could as easily have munched on sandwiches and fruit back at the base in total comfort, laid back in the air-conditioned atmosphere of the Grand Desert Inn's dining room or my own top floor bedroom there. Looking around at the faces of my companions, I knew I was far from the only one entertaining such an irritable mood. I badly wanted a shower, the contact of water across my body, my dry skin.

I hunted for the apple I had earlier desultorily packed away in my rucksack and pulled it out and bit avidly into it, enjoying the blissfully sweet juices released in the process, allowing them to filter down my throat and spread a thread of relief. To my left, Alissa had slipped off her checked man's shirt and was down to her sports bra, momentarily seeking relief from the heat and the discomfort of the soaked-through material for the likely brief time we would be sitting in relative shade. Others were eating too, biscuits, chocolate and energy bars, drinking parsimoniously, not knowing how much longer we might remain in the desert, trying to parcel out their water so it lasted.

Lauralynn was climbing one of the squat boulders, her long legs extending in each direction like a spider's limbs. She reached the top and pulled herself up.

'Perfect,' she said, and clambered down.

We all looked at her.

'This is the place,' she confirmed. She had long discarded her map.

I followed the direction of her gaze. Two hundred yards or so beyond the tall set of boulders my eyes were attracted by a shadowy patch of ground, where the uniform red colour of the desert appeared to have made way for a more subtle patchwork of pastel colours, as if the sun above had not been allowed to inflict its baking wounds in full. Apart from a few isolated tree stumps at the periphery of the area, there was no apparent reason for this anomaly.

'What is it?' I asked Lauralynn.

'The magic spot,' she said.

There was a sparkle of excitement in her green eyes. Viggo shuffled up to her and took hold of her hand, as if this place was a secret only he and Lauralynn had previously known about and that they were ready to reveal to us common mortals.

I heard Alissa behind me snort impatiently.

'What sort of crap is this?' she asked Lauralynn.

'Oh fine,' Lauralynn replied. 'Spoilsport. It's not so much magic, as the way in. I was worried that I wasn't going to be able to find it.'

'You brought us all the way out here and you were worried that you wouldn't be able to find the right spot?' Alissa hissed.

'Yes, exactly,' Lauralynn told her. 'But I did find it, so there's no need to get excited.'

Alissa did look as though she was going to explode, either that or throw what remained of her apple core at Lauralynn's head.

'Just in time, too,' Lauralynn added, pointing up. We all lifted our heads skywards. The previously bright blue, cloudless horizon had turned into a blanket of impossible colours, a vivid kaleidoscope of purple, pink, red and orange like a threatening early sunset. The air felt heavy, pregnant with something. Rain? Wind? It was beautiful and terrible at the same time. Sharp gusts coming from several directions at once blew sharp pinpricks of sand onto our bare legs and faces. And I was certain the temperature had become even hotter. We could have baked loaves of bread on the hot rocks.

Lauralynn retrieved her rucksack without saying another word and began to walk towards the blurred area of pastel colours ahead of us. I looked forward, and then up again, and blinked. The strange storm in the sky was like a mirror image of the ground that Lauralynn was now treading on, and I had an urge to run forward and stop her from walking across it. Her form shimmered. It was probably just heat haze but looked uncannily like a science fiction movie portal into another dimension. Alissa was the next to follow after her though obviously reluctantly. She paused with each step, lifted her face and stared at the sky and then hurried after Lauralynn again.

I went next.

None of us spoke, rendered silent by the tension of what was unfolding, of what each of us imagined might happen next if we stayed out in the open. So much about the Ball and the shadowy Network in wait behind it, for the past few weeks, had been characterised by things that shouldn't be, elements that bordered on the supernatural or the impossible. The way they knew us, understood our abilities better than we could, the hieroglyphic tattoos on Aurelia's body that came alive and disappeared seemingly of their own volition. Bizarre weather patterns and unreal landscapes were just another part of the strange series of happenings that somehow I, and no doubt the others, had brushed away to the back of our minds, but the sense of wonder was always present. I'd long suspected that Lauralynn's involvement with the Ball was more than she had ever admitted to and I hoped, some time soon, she would let the cat out of the bag and reveal everything that she knew.

Lauralynn and Alissa ambled through what the tall cellist had described as a magic area, and continued walking to the solid wall of rock that stood behind it, and ran for some way across the sands. As I neared, I noticed that the wall wasn't as flat as it appeared in the distance but rather was decorated with jagged shards and points and crevices, all in the same deep, rust red.

It had begun to rain, just a few gentle spits, and the droplets merged with the dust in the air and coated our skin with streaks of orange. The blonds had all long ago removed their shirts, and the ochre and flame-coloured smears that striped their skin gave them the appearance of tigers, all streaks and muscle.

When we had all finally congregated in the same place, none of us any the wiser as to where we were headed next, Lauralynn beckoned us to follow her again and then apparently disappeared into the wall. Alissa stood stock still for a moment, let out a yelp of surprise and then disappeared after her.

Gingerly, I stepped closer, but was not pulled into a supernatural vortex leading to another realm as I had half expected, but instead discovered that what appeared to be a thin crack from a foot or so away was on closer inspection, in fact a deep fissure, wide enough for a person to step through. The opening led to a short tunnel, and I held my breath for a few short moments of total darkness as I stumbled through, wishing desperately that I had waited for Antony to catch up before entering.

'Ouch!' Alissa cried, as I knocked into her at the exit. 'Watch where you're going.'

'Don't stand right by the end then,' I muttered back.

I looked around, and then understood why she had stopped dead the moment she'd come out into the light.

We had emerged into a large, high-ceilinged cavern, surrounded on all sides and above by the same rust red rock. The floor was totally smooth, apparently ground down by the weight of a million footsteps. In the centre was a huge pool of water, so clear that the bottom was plainly visible and the basin might have appeared empty, if it were not for the liquid sheen of the water's surface.

'Shit,' Antony said, as he stepped through the tunnel behind me. 'This place is amazing.' He removed his baseball cap and flicked his fingers through his fringe. I was tempted to take the cap away from him and lose it amongst the rocks.

Alissa snaked one hand behind her back, popped the hooks on her sports bra and then hung it from a rock. She stared into the water, topless, as though wondering whether some kind of creature might be lurking, invisible, in the crystalline water. Her heavy, gravity-defying breasts glistened with sweat and cut a clean line across her body, the only visible part of her that was not streaked with dust, like two majestic jelly moulds that had been turned out onto a table.

A sharp pop sound echoed through the chamber as all eight of the blonds unbuttoned their shorts in unison and dropped them to their feet. They had surrounded the pool and stood totally nude at equidistance apart, the symmetry of their clock-like circle broken by Alissa who had now removed her khakis and underwear but was still making up her mind whether to jump in or not.

Idly I admired the bodies of the young men. They were beautiful. They lacked the striking curves that Alissa possessed, of course; they were like the low lands in contrast to her collection of hills and valleys in motion, but the fluidity in the movement of their limbs and the juxtaposition between the softness of their skin and the hardness of the muscles that ran beneath it was startlingly attractive. I could not look at them without being aroused. They possessed the confidence of a group of wild cats lounging by a water hole, relaxed in the knowledge that they were too strong, too fast, to even bother to look around and check for predators.

Alissa cleared her throat. She hadn't taken so much as a glance at the boys' cocks dangling between their legs, large and inviting. They were half erect. Their bodies seemed to be in a permanent state of semi-arousal, although their minds never seemed to follow suit, and they were all pierced. A slim bar, about the thickness of a drinking straw ran through the glans. Affixed to either end of the bar was a jewel that I could not quite identify from a distance. It was creamy white, and from afar had the appearance of a just-formed droplet of come. A pearl?

'You can get in,' Lauralynn called. 'It's perfectly safe.' She was smirking, and I suspected had delayed giving us that instruction so she could perve at the naked bodies standing pool-side. It wasn't like the blonds to be nervy. Probably, they hadn't gotten in yet because they were enjoying being looked at.

'What is this place?' Antony asked her. I began undressing, something of a struggle since the heat, sweat and dust accumulated on my clothing made it near impossible to pull off. Antony stepped behind me as he talked and helped me to unhook my bra. As soon as my breasts were free, he caressed my nipples, as though leaving them naked and unmolested was an impossibility. Lauralynn's smirk grew wider and she openly stared at my chest as she responded to him.

'A network of caves, no more than that.' She waved her arm around her. 'It was considered as a possible location for the Ball but the planning group decided against it. Health and Safety and all that.' Her last words were muffled as she used her T-shirt to wipe her face as she spoke.

I chortled.

'Health and Safety? Really? I didn't think the Ball would worry about such mundane details.'

The zipper on my shorts was caught, and Lauralynn

stepped forward to help me with it. She stood closer than she needed to for the purpose and her bare breasts brushed against mine. My nipples hardened instantly.

'Ahh,' she said, changing the subject. 'Summer, you sure have great tits.'

'Thanks,' I replied, drily.

'She does,' Antony agreed. He had moved away from me and was examining the cavern in more detail. 'Great acoustics in here . . .' he said.

'I know,' Viggo nodded. 'It's a shame to let the place waste, without a show.' He was sitting on a rock waiting for Lauralynn, seemingly not discomfited in the slightest by the sharp edges that must be poking into his slim frame.

'Too many unmapped pools,' Lauralynn explained, 'and the ceiling isn't structurally sound enough to rig up the aerial acts. I know it all seems unreal,' she continued, 'but there's a whole bunch of terribly dull stuff going on behind every magical moment. An accountant for every acrobat.'

'Don't ruin it for her,' Viggo interrupted. 'Stagecraft isn't stagecraft when you know where the strings are.'

'You're right,' Lauralynn deferred, in a rare moment of submission. Usually she liked to have the last word.

She squeezed my breasts again and stepped away.

'Why don't you two explore,' she said, pointing towards the far side of the cavern. 'There's more pools through there. So long as you can hear us, you won't get into trouble.'

'And I'll make sure you can hear her, at least,' Viggo quipped.

The others were already in the pool, and the sound of their splashing made me long to dive in and feel the cool water against my skin.

Antony moved towards the passage that Lauralynn had pointed out. He too had stripped off, and was now wearing nothing but his hiking boots, like a caricature from a male strip tease show. I stifled a giggle, and ran forward to slap his buttocks.

'God you have a lovely arse,' I told him. He smiled, and took my hand, and we stepped through a natural arch in the rock wall and arrived together in another, much smaller room, this one peppered with pools with a stream running through them.

'You're filthy,' he said, wiping some of the rusty sand from my side. 'Get in.'

We kissed in the water, warming our bodies again with the heat of each other as soon as we had cooled off.

A sweet madness descended, its sounds echoing from chamber to chamber, cave to cave.

By the time we were released from the magic of the cave and all reunited and gingerly made our way to the exit, dusk was falling on the desert, fantastic clouds circling the outlines of the faraway mountains, the sand cooling under our feet, a gentle breeze taking flight and becalming our ardent skin.

Some of the others were already marching towards the path like a stream of ants in uniform motion. It was time for a slow walk back to the Ball's base.

Yet again it was a night with little sleep as my mind and body seemed unwilling to allow me any rest. But I was serene, almost detached. By my side in the bed, Antony slept heavily, just the steady rise of his chest betraying signs of life, his hair mussed, a mild touch of sunburn colouring the top of his bare shoulders. I watched him endlessly, fearful of waking him and facing the reality that our planned separation in adjoining rooms had failed utterly, we hadn't spent a night apart since arriving in Nevada and what I thought had been silently confirmed as a relatively casual relationship seemed to be growing in affection every day. But I wasn't sure that I was ready for anything more than a lover. I still felt hung up on the past, as though most of me had moved on but a part of my heart still lived in the house that I had shared with Dominik in Hampstead.

Purple streaks coloured the sky outside our window as the desert awakened in profound silence. I grabbed the nearest T-shirt and a pair of flimsy silk panties and tiptoed out of the room, picking up one of my violins from the chest of drawers where I kept them on my way out.

The echoing hotel lobby, its terracotta vases, giant plants, cacti and ornaments standing in the shadows and its lights set on dim, felt like an immense museum. I opened the door to the desert and passed from the air-conditioned coolness of the interior into the muggy, rising heat of the sands. It was still bearable, even pleasant, flimsily attired as I was. I was barefoot, and knew I shouldn't stay outside too long until the earth warmed and made my return painful for the soles of my feet.

I walked for ten minutes in a random direction, beyond the Las Vegas road and the crossroads that led to the nearby lake with its cluster of roadside casinos and the Hoover Dam. In the distance I could hear the sound of an articulated lorry roaring down the road.

Impulsively, I took a turn into the open desert, away from the slowly rising sun.

I reached a small rock formation. I squinted and their shape began to come to life, like a solid Rorschach test, alternately a mineral agglomeration of unlikely bushes and shrubbery morphing formlessly into a group of sitting lions.

With my back to the rocks and facing the immensity of the desert I unlocked my violin case and briefly pondered. Then I gently set it down and stripped. Being naked felt right. It was nothing sexual, just my natural state of being.

I looked down at my body. My small breasts stood firm, nipples still settled into a semi-permanent state of excitement after last night's lovemaking – Antony and I had got into the habit of fucking before we fell asleep, every day without fail, and often in the mornings too. Further down, my cunt lips were puffy from use, almost plump.

I picked up the violin again, brought it up to my chin.

I knew already what I'd be playing at the Ball in a few days, a mixture of existing pieces from my repertoire tempered with a whole load of improvisations I had devised for what was initially going to be the play and which had since flowered into all sorts of unlikely melodic directions, with musical pit-stops along the way from which I could embark on further digressions, switch gears, dependent on my mood, the activities in progress around me, or the reactions of the listeners to my playing. It was mentally engineered to be both structured and loose.

But right now, I wanted to say farewell to my past. Close that solid oak door once and for all before the next chapter began.

So, I chose Vivaldi.

'The Four Seasons'.

The music I had first played for Dominik.

The music I had last played for Dominik.

And decided this would be the final time I would ever play the piece. Enough was enough.

The bow hovered above the taut strings, my fingers at the ready.

I closed my eyes.

I began playing.

In the immense emptiness of the desert the notes emerged with crystal-like purity, the sounds rising through the air like the close heat in which I bathed, in which my naked skin soaked.

The music grabbed me by the throat, every inch of emotion choking its way through my lungs, my heart heavy as a stone, its sublime geometry rushing through my veins reaching every extremity of my body in its liberated flight.

Sweat dripped from my forehead as the sun inexorably rose. I felt the irritation of an ant winding its way up from my ankle to my knee, but resolved not to interrupt my playing and to overcome the growing discomfort caused by its pesky presence. I couldn't move my leg without disrupting the sacred flow of Vivaldi's immortal melodies I was so intimately wedded to. I gritted my teeth.

A wisp of breeze rose and danced across my skin. I opened my eyes again. Never missing a note.

I was alone, a no doubt incongruous vision here in the heart of the Nevada desert, naked, wielding my diminutive violin like a weapon, the sounds of my music disappearing into the air, its invisible notes blending seamlessly into the rising heat haze.

Had I ever been more alone?

The joyous tunes of Vivaldi's 'Summer' bounced along,

my wrist animated by the inner truth of the music. My whole body was now covered, from head to toe, by a glistening sheen of sweat. The ant climbing my leg had now reached the crook of my thigh. Surely it wasn't about to make a beeline for my swollen sex lips?

At the final minute, it diverted and trailed off across my buttock where my sensitivity somehow lost track of it, or maybe it dropped back down to the ground, after its fearless ascent of my human flesh mountain, or I had just tasted wrong to it.

My heart jumped as I segued into yet another season.

The music held me in its embrace, now totally in control, my hands and movements guided by it, a puppet with no other choice but to complete the piece, my offering to the empty skies.

I was dripping.

From everywhere.

My lungs were dry, my throat parched, my lips like old papyrus. I was vaguely aware that I had neglected to bring any water along. Or shoes. Or a hat. But no matter, I had to continue playing.

Until the final note was coaxed into life.

I was swaying.

Unsteady.

Clinging on to consciousness.

My heart heaved, my soul or whatever it was inside that

functioned as my engine for living shuddered on its axis. It even felt like an orgasm, but stronger and totally asexual.

I detached myself from the world.

The music continued.

I flowed along with its slithering, clever, beautiful notes, swam down the river of emotions that flowed in its wake.

The bow attacked the strings one final time.

The world exploded.

My consciousness retreated.

I deliberately held my breath back. Testing how long I could do so without gasping.

The hot desert air stored inside my lungs was screaming to be released.

I let go.

The longest exhale of my life.

It was done.

I would not play Vivaldi's music again.

I had no need to. It was now part of me as never before.

For the first time in ages, I became aware of the light bracelet hanging negligently around my wrist. Ever since I had realised that I had been without it in the Kentish Town sauna I had worn it throughout day and night, as if it had some kind of power that could keep me safe from myself. Dominik's final gift.

I struggled slightly to locate its clasp and undid it.

Scratched around in the red dirt at my feet and dug a small

cavity into which I dropped the bracelet and quickly shoved the dusty earth back above it and buried the memento. The desert winds would do the rest.

My hands unsteady I arranged the violin back into its battered case and closed it, abandoned my T-shirt and panties which I had somehow trampled into the ochre sand and stained forever and began my walk back to the Grand Desert Inn. I didn't care if anyone saw me in my state of nudity. It was me. The way I was born, the way I loved and was made love to. Nude. Exposed. Alive.

I now felt ready for the Ball.

11

The Winged Ballet

I was running late. I grasped my violin case and took a final glance around the bedroom. It looked like a war zone, clothes scattered everywhere, bed sheets tangled in total disarray, a scene of savage devastation.

I rushed outside through the lobby and found the pullman coach waiting, engine purring away. All the other musicians were already onboard and watched me run towards it. In the distance, the sun was falling in slow motion below the mesas and the sky was an organic palette of red, oranges and purples.

The coach wheels crunched the earth of the dirt track, raising small motes of dust as we drove off.

My mind wandered back.

Since the hike, I had seen little of Antony. He had been absorbed in the final preparations for the Ball while I had been engaged in the ultimate rehearsals involving the musicians and dancers and although we continued to share a room, I barely perceived the echo of his warmth between the sheets as we both fell into bed exhausted at different hours and by the time I rose every day he was already gone.

The awkward, affectionate Antony who had wanted to verbally cement our relationship had disappeared, and he was back to his usual, somewhat distant self. Once or twice, I had lain awake desperately horny, and nuzzled into his back, hoping that he would wake up in the same mood but he invariably slept through my subtle demands and I was never disciplined enough to set my alarm earlier so that we could take advantage of an early morning together to fuck before we both set off for the day.

At least, he hadn't begun drinking again. The mini-bar remained untouched, and since we had arrived in America, I hadn't noticed any obvious signs of a hangover, despite the fact that the nature of the Ball's preparations and the fickle personalities of the creative types and performers meant that he spent most of his days figuratively herding cats. I knew that his personal demons would never leave him, and I was even surer that anyone else, including me, could never hold them at bay. But I hoped that he would continue to find solace in his work, as I did, even if that meant that I would lose him to it at times.

Over the past 48 hours, the guests had been arriving, a

non-stop stream of cars, 4 by 4s, coaches, buses, utility vehicles, shiny, sleek Harley-Davidson motorbikes and even a few helicopters landing in an improvised field a stone's throw from the hotel, which had been hastily cleared and over which a latticed artificial surface had been deployed. At first a stream of newcomers dragging heavy cases, trunks and clothes racks trampled through the sands, followed by a ceaseless parade of faceless visitors until I quickly lost interest. There was something anonymous about the crowd, a faceless entity I could not focus on. I had always had the same feeling about audiences, finding it awkward to interact with them. They just 'were'. The car park had rapidly filled out, and the cluster of vehicles and tents and sundry improvised shelters had spread at an exponential rate all around the Grand Desert Inn, like seeds bursting open in a repetitive pattern under the baking sun. Was it like this every year, as they gathered, returned to the Ball, from all points of the globe, in search of hedonism and transcendence, I wondered? What did they do during the rest of the year? Were they normal people, clerks, bank managers, housewives, idle rich or beggars who saved for twelve whole months to afford the travel to the Ball?

We drove away from the setting sun. This would be the first time I was being allowed into the Ball's principal area of activity. The dance and musical preparations had all been restricted to the Inn's echoing basement or varied temporary installations set up in close proximity to it. Only Antony and his construction crew and members of the Ball's inner sanctum had travelled there, leaving daily in early morning, bound to secrecy as to what they had witnessed or been involved in.

I brought my hand up to brush a stray hair away from my face. The simple black onyx ring I was wearing on my middle finger reminded me of its presence.

'This will allow you total access to the Ball's zones and activities after midnight,' Aurelia had said, slipping it onto my finger, forcing it gently past the joint. 'That is if you decide to stay on after your actual performance.'

'I might,' I said to Aurelia.

'I know you will,' she replied.

I had so many questions for her about the nature of the event.

'Tell me more about the Ball,' I asked.

'Such as?'

'How did you first become involved?'

'I had no choice,' Aurelia replied. 'I was born to the Ball.'

My blank face betrayed my lack of comprehension.

'My mother was the Mistress of the Ball, and I had no alternative,' she continued. 'I had to continue in her footsteps.'

I was still puzzled.

'And it takes place every year? Or two?'

'We try to. On occasions, we skip a year. It depends on the amount of preparations involved, the location chosen, the quantity of work required.'

'And you and Andrei run it?'

'No, there is a whole support organisation behind it. So many people are involved in aiding it, bankrolling the project, our activities.'

I remembered the private club in New Orleans and Madame Denoux running it, and the intimation that this was just one of many such establishments.

'How long . . .'

Aurelia interrupted me. 'The Ball goes back centuries. Even those of us who are the most intimately involved with it remain unclear about its origins. Legend has it began in ancient Egypt even . . .'

'Really?'

'But things change,' she added. 'We try and move with the times. Innovate. But certain traditions remain.'

I had a thousand further questions but Aurelia put her fingers to my lips.

'Patience, Summer. The answers will come in their own time.'

The conversation had then moved on to more practical ground and my concepts for the musical overture I had been commissioned to put together for this year's Ball.

I wanted to ask her more. About the hints of magic and

the supernatural that appeared to surround her and the Ball, the impossible events I thought I had witnessed as well as experienced since I had been in contact with her, the force fields of improbability, the seductive atmosphere that trailed in her wake. I was about to open my mouth once more as our dialogue came to a conclusion and I still wished to query matters, but she read my mind.

'It's all illusions, my dear,' Aurelia said and left the room. But there had been a glint in her eye, as if she was toying with me.

I shook myself out of my reverie. The coach slowed. The dirt track we had been following had come to a natural ending. We were in the middle of nowhere.

We had arrived.

Stepping off the coach, the evening's heat slammed into my face as I noted with amazement that the whole desert as far as the eye could see was now dotted with multi-coloured tents and canopies, fragile temporary constructions festooned with banners and streamers, sturdy flag-bearing towers, rigid poles planted into the hard soil joined by a spiderweb jungle of meshes and a scattering of wired, gigantic rigs loaded with generators and pieces of futuristic machinery. It felt as if a giant, multi-tentacular circus had invaded the land and was intent on spreading to all corners.

Madame Denoux awaited us. As usual she wore a long velvet dress but this time it was a deep bronze colour and flowed like a river of glittering gold as she welcomed us and ushered us towards a large tent, out of reach of the sun's fading hammer and we briskly followed her in, stepping in an orderly file through the double flaps in the heavy material into a cooler world. The scores of generators were visibly doing their job well, feeding the air-conditioning units and making all the activities that would take place here possible despite the harshness of the conditions.

'This is where you will change into your costumes and have your make-up applied,' she announced, indicating a row of wall to wall metal stands groaning under the weight of assorted clothing. An untidiness of deep cardboard boxes lay on the ground in front of the multitude of hangers, overflowing with shoes, scarves, and sundry accessories. On the other side of the vast, low-ceilinged tent a line of chairs and small tables with mirrors awaited, by the side of which a half dozen youngsters clad in demure maid's uniforms stood, to help us both dress or assist with the make-up, each with their hair braided all the way down to their waists, all matching each other. Their facial features were each their own, but they moved and spoke in exactly the same way, like a sextuplet of non-identical twins. Instinctively I tried to guess their gender. They were wearing lace-trimmed long shorts rather than skirts, and had a gracefulness to them that suggested femininity yet lacked a sense of obvious girlishness.

'Are they girls, or boys?' I whispered to Giselle.

She looked at me as though the question was totally inane. 'I don't think they've decided yet,' she replied.

For various reasons, we had been unable to have a proper dress rehearsal at the base camp and this would be the first time we would actually see the costumes we were meant to be performing in. Not just us musicians, but also the troupe of lithe if silent dancers we had been demonstrating our music to, whose choreography had been evolving alongside our own improvisations.

Lauralynn brushed by me, heading straight towards the clothes. 'And about time too,' she remarked.

Supervised by a glowering Madame Denoux, our little helpers buzzed around, handing us outfits, shoes, belts, ribbons, perfectly drilled and efficient, intent on assembling the jigsaw of combinations they had evidently prepared for. Each item of clothing on the metal hangers appeared to be numbered, our sizes and roles previously logged so we could be matched up with uncanny precision. The shoes unerringly slid onto our feet like Cinderella's slipper, neither too tight or too loose, every outfit designed for our curves and angles, inch perfect with unerring exactitude.

Soon, we were all dressed, or rather the Ball's version of what performance attire should be. And ready for make-up.

I had been told to trust their judgment and Aurelia had warned me she wanted to see me play in something very special. It was.

I'd never been shy or retiring, to say the least, but what awaited me still came as a shock.

My outfit, or uniform, or whatever you wished to call it, was just a complex combination of belts and metal loops.

'How the hell do I wear this?' I questioned the silent helper who handed me the contraption. 'Isn't there something that goes on underneath? A body stocking at least?'

My helper looked at me blankly and checked the numbered ticket that confirmed that this was indeed my outfit, and nothing went with it besides matching footwear. Majestically high-heeled, totally transparent shoes, that seemed made of glass. Was I to be a modern Cinderella at this ball? In typical Aurelia style, they managed, somehow, to avoid the dire tackiness of Perspex stripper heels, and on my feet looked both tasteful and astonishing by virtue of their architectural properties which combined sleek lines and an odd, geometric shape that was more modern art than bawdy.

Madame Denoux appeared at my side.

'You'll look absolutely stunning,' she said. 'And with those shoes, anyone watching from a distance will have the impression you're floating on air . . .' she added with a smile.

Lauralynn joined us. She was already dressed for our performance. Half-dressed that is. An exquisite pale silk blouse that shimmered with every movement she made, its thin white collar circling her neck like a necklace of milk, highlighting the sunflower yellow of her flowing, shiny hair. I looked down. Below the blouse, she wore nothing. She was totally nude, bottomless. Although of course she also wore high heels, not that her amazonian gait called for them. She towered a full head and a half above me as I stood there still in bare feet.

She had again affixed a neatly trimmed triangle of faux pubic hair to her mons, this time in a deep purple colour that stood in sharp contrast to her pale skin. Her long legs stretched like swans' wings, sculpted, sturdy, in perfect communion with the rest of her body.

'What the . . . ?' I glanced around: all the other musicians were clothed or unclothed in similar manner. Pale silk tops and strictly bottomless. Men as well as women.

Besides Lauralynn, who always had something of a carnal aura around her, no matter what she wore, the effect was surprisingly asexual. All of those bare genitals left nothing to the imagination and therefore left my imagination disinterested. They ought to have seemed pornographic, and yet after a moment's glance, automatically registering and filing away whether they were hairy, trimmed, smooth and large or small of cock or pudenda, I focused straight back to their facial expressions and the instruments they carried.

'Interesting, no?' Lauralynn remarked, her mischievous streak triumphant.

'The Ball's idea?' I asked her.

'Actually mine,' she answered and winked at me.

Well, she was the cello player and the one who would have by necessity to play with her legs splayed open to accommodate the girth of her instrument. None of the other musicians would have to display any such as revealing posture. I noticed Lauralynn and Madame Denoux both had pure black onyx rings on their middle fingers. As I did.

'Come,' Madame Denoux said, nearing me. 'Undress.' I obeyed her instructions.

Once I was fully nude, she pointed at my arms. 'Up,' she ordered. I raised them and she began the meticulous process of assembling the labyrinth of belts, loops and buckles around my limbs and then my body, with Lauralynn and my junior helper in watchful attendance. Lauralynn offered me her hand whenever I had to raise one leg or the other and lacked balance. As she did so, she jokingly nibbled on my ear and blew me a kiss of connivance.

It was like playing a game of twister, contorting my arms, legs and other parts of my body to make the contraption fit, threading myself like a contortionist between the leather webbing.

'There we are,' all three of my attendants watched me admiringly. I dared not look down. They led me to a mirror.

The straps circled my throat, breasts and midriff, tight, emphasising my parts in pornographic detail, squeezing my breasts within their grasp, holding them high, immobilising them albeit without interfering with the circulation of my blood. My nipples had already hardened and jutted wantonly ahead. The assembly of straps around my middle held my cunt in a vice, caging it, exaggerating its plumpness under the conjugated pressure of four belts which fitted me as if I was born to them. The whole outfit just called attention to my tits and genitals, framing them ostentatiously, highlighting them.

I looked like a slave from harem days.

A sacrificial lamb being led to some faraway desert altar.

A buzz of excitement raced through me at the thought of being seen like this by the audience.

The criss-cross pattern of the belts and loops around my body made me look more than naked. Totally on display, on offer. For the entertainment of others.

'Beautiful,' Madame Denoux whispered.

'Stunning,' Lauralynn added.

'Maybe just a little bit tighter,' one of them suggested as I stood there in a daze gazing at the way I had been transformed and fingers flew across me, pulling loops and buckles and squeezing my delicate parts into even more prominence. The young helper retreated into the shadows.

I took a step and realised that the belts were two-sided. On the outside, they were shiny and smooth, polished leather. Internally, rubbing against my naked skin, they were significantly rougher, textured like rope. Already I imagined the marks they would leave imprinted deep into my skin once I was undressed. My throat tightened.

'Antony approved,' Lauralynn said. She led me to a make-up table and I sat down facing the mirror and its circle of bright lights. I notched that bit of information away, once I'd gotten past the slight irritation that anyone had felt he should approve of my outfit. He'd never seen me in anything like this before. I wondered if the contraption would turn him on, or if he would be merely phlegmatic about the whole thing – another wardrobe change to play a part, nothing more.

'I think just a trace of make-up,' Madame Denoux suggested. 'Just the lips. Redder. To match your hair.'

'Yes. Very low-key,' Lauralynn approved.

Another maid-like young helper approached and began vigorously combing my hair. It was mutually agreed I would wear it pulled away from my forehead, bunched at the back. Simple. Vulnerable.

A boiling cauldron of emotions was churning inside of me. I had not felt this way or worn anything like this for a long time. Not since Dominik.

A clasp was put into position to hold my hair in place. I looked away from the make-up mirror. The dancers were already filing out. They looked like thin, nimble gold statues being swallowed by an explosion of light as the setting sun shone warmly upon them as soon as they left the haven of the tent that separated us from the once blazing desert.

Madame Denoux led us out. Lauralynn took my hand, in a gesture of reassurance.

The coach awaited us and we took to our seats, many of us too embarrassed to look at each other now that we were adorned and all strategically unclad to various degrees for what was to come. As I quickly noticed, the golden sheen of the dancers was just body paint, not a costume or a trick of the light and they were as equally exposed as us musicians. A second, smaller coach was parked outside, into which our small band of helpers climbed, each carrying voluminous canvas bags.

Madame Denoux whispered an instruction into the pullman driver's ears and we slowly made our way further into the depths of the desert, away from the encampment of tents and improvised constructions.

We drove in silence, past rock formations and dried-up creeks, in the shadow of squat mountains and plateaus. How much further, I wondered, did the realm of the Ball extend? Most of us were muching on chocolate and energy bars, wraps and sandwiches which had been provided. Trying not to ruin our make-up as we did so. Giselle urged us on as this would be our only food until the Ball's conclusion, she said.

Then, emerging from a narrow pass we reached the plain,

an endless bowl of earth that extended as far as the eye could reach to a blurry, heat-hazed horizon. A gigantic eco-dome occupied its geographical centre, like a futuristic circus tent dropped from a mighty height onto the surface of the planet below. Scores of vehicles were parked close to it. The coach slowed to a halt and, once again, Madame Denoux acted as our leader and we filed towards the edifice in a regimental manner.

Total darkness.

Utter silence, bar a scattered cough or someone hastily clearing their throat in the invisible audience.

A raised platform had been erected on which we stood and sat, instruments at the ready.

As she'd led us to our positions, Madame Denoux had intimated that I would know when to begin playing, that the signal would be unmistakable.

We waited.

The other musicians all watching me to launch the first note.

A sense of trepidation rushed through me, as much as I wanted to keep my calm.

A curious, if arousing scent: spices, flowers, greenery, warm skin all in one floated around the immensity of the dome, caressing my bare skin, soothing and provoking me.

The pitter patter of feet below in the arena. Bodies

shuffling, moving, a faint metallic echo and then a deep well of silence again.

The dancers finding their marks and getting into position.

The sound of a thousand breaths being held back in the audience looming at the opposing end of the dome.

A microscopic pin prick of light appeared, seemingly originating miles away in the depths of the dome's roof. This must be it. I tensed. Raised my violin to my chin and my other hand gripped the bow.

The point of light began to grow in intensity and size and I could not help but notice with an involuntary shudder that its beam was aimed straight at my body, at the precise intersection of the tight combination of belts surrounding my genitals, brightly highlighting the unnatural protuberance of my mons.

At that very moment of realisation, the circle of light began to grow in size until my whole body was caught in its web of blinding brilliance.

'Oh, Antony,' I thought. Only he could have conceived of such a dramatic opening to the concert. In day to day, real life, we made a flawed romantic partnership at best. But at the point where our work collided, my music and his theatrical direction, yet another man who understood instinctively what lay at the very heart of my soul – my sexuality. 'Damn you . . .'

All that the several hundreds or so spectators could now see in the immensity of the eco-dome was my body in full wanton display, captured by the naked light, outlined like fire against a wall of darkness. I had no doubt either that the more distant layers of the audience could also enjoy the sight of my nudity magnified out of all proportion on some screen hanging above me, as happened so often in arena rock concerts.

Bow to string.

Raising the first note. Then another. And yet another.

The sinuous melody that had been haunting my nights for weeks now, expressing my deepest fears, emotions and desires. Sadness, memories, hunger, pain, melancholy, desire, pleasure, hope and despair squeezed into a sound that was now forever part of my inner fabric.

I played alone. Extending the notes until neither my heart nor my instrument could bear it any longer and switched to a minor chord and heard Lauralynn's cello beginning the counterpoint, grounding me, expanding the theme, and then the string section took over and we all soared in unison, like separate streams merging into one as we reached a form of chorus.

The web of light highlighting me had now expanded, no longer focused on my cunt but bathing all of my body, then enlarging until all my fellow musicians were captured in its embrace.

Further streams of light came to life in the dome's roof, streaming down like avalanches across the centre of the arena where the dancers were now waltzing with grace, their steps forming geometric shapes full of rigour and elegance translating in precise patterns the music we were playing.

They formed slim pillars of gold as they glided along, their movements smooth and effortless. A taller pair of dancers, a man and a woman, detached themselves from the main corps de ballet and pirouetted daintily around the massed group. I adjusted my rhythm to theirs and Lauralynn followed suit, reading my intentions perfectly.

The beam of light cleverly following the pair across the dome's floor suddenly changed colour, moving from sharp white to warm gold and their perfect bodies shimmered in its embrace.

They swirled and floated along with consummate ease, with the fluidity of ice skaters, hand in hand and other hand on shoulder. A concentric circle of movement brought them momentarily closer to the orchestra's platform. The female dancer's dark hair flowed freely all the way down her back, her partner's calf muscles taut as he guided her along. As they whizzed past me, they separated briefly and I held my breath; a thin gold chain joined them as they danced, seemingly clipped on in two places to her labia connecting with the cock ring her partner was wearing at the base of his dick. Trying not to miss a single beat, my gaze tried to follow them and see things more clearly, but they quickly merged back into the formless mass of the other dancers and moved into the distance.

There had been no hint of this in our rehearsals, although to be fair, we had all been properly, even conservatively dressed on the occasion and more intent on nailing the melodies and how the dance would dovetail into the music at the time.

The dancers were all bunched together, their bodies a-tremble while, as planned, the front line of the string section unleashed a storm of dramatic pizzicati. I dragged my bow against the violin's neck, ready to launch myself into the middle section of the improvisation which had initially been rooted in a bucolic section of a Mahler symphony, not even a violin piece per se but an orchestral one which resonated strongly for me and allowed me a suitable platform for melodic digressions, like a road opening up to a far horizon with multiple choice exits rushing by, offering themselves in turn and which only instinct could select properly. I was becoming so much more at ease when improvising and even wondered whether I'd ever be capable of faithfully following a set partition again. Or did I even wish to?

In response to my change of musical direction, the pack of dancers burst open, separating, stepping back like a flower opening and I saw they were all connected together by cunt and cock, a daring spider's web of golden bodies pulling at each other's parts, meshes straining, their thin metal chains interlocking in magical patterns, faces contorted with pain or pleasure, bodies animated by waves of sensations I could only guess at, and still they danced, every staccato movement in mathematical harmony with the sounds of my violin, Lauralynn's growling cello and the soothing lullaby of the rest of the orchestra underpinning our irresistible, impassioned flow.

Their timing was impeccable. Like a pulsing heart in motion.

We maintained the beat, spotlights unerringly lingering on our exposed parts as we imperceptibly adjusted our stances to match the gliding, heavenly movements of the yoked dancers.

They expanded and contracted, dripped and ebbed, like a cat's cradle, ever-connected, and vibrating with life and sex.

As I played, I imagined myself on that dance floor, with a golden ring pierced into the most delicate part of my skin, something I'd once seen in an art movie and had left a strong impression on me, into which a thin chain threaded, keeping me spread, open and pulled here and there by a gallery of erect cocks in perpetual motion, forced to keep up, to maintain the rhythm that could either sustain or harm me.

My heart pumped wildly.

My violin was turning into the devil, leading the mad

dance and I was becoming just an instrument in its service. The crescendo reached its inevitable peak.

The lights exploded and the audience roared.

I was bathing in sweat and had reached the end of the melody. The road led no further. I stopped breathing for a brief moment. Behind me, all the other musicians were no doubt watching me, waiting for some signal which I felt too exhausted to provide. On the floor, the dancers had ceased moving, frozen in place like statues, gold peeling from their bodies as the lights began to dim and we were soon again plunged in total darkness.

I could hear the members of the audience shuffling down the stands where they had been sitting, a constant murmur surrounding them as they commented on the events, appreciative, dismissive or indifferent for all I cared.

I waited until silence had re-established its kingdom.

'Come,' Lauralynn said, moving to my side and taking my hand in hers. 'It's over. We can go now.' I hadn't realised we were the only two now left on the platform. All the other musicians had quietly trooped away.

She led me like a guide dog through the obscurity of the eco-dome towards a side exit.

Madame Denoux waited for us there. She looked flushed, gazed at me quizzically and we stumbled our way back to the coach which drove us to the changing tent.

I submitted mindlessly to the touch of my attendants as I

was helped out of the outfit of belts and buckles and loops. Looking at my body in the mirror, I could see how deep the indent of the rope-like underside had bitten into my skin and left it tattooed with a fierce pattern into my flesh.

'That's fucking beautiful, that is,' Lauralynn exclaimed.

'It'll fade fast,' I remarked.

'Not necessarily,' Madame Denoux said, and handed me an unlabelled pot of cream. 'Rub it in,' she suggested. It was refreshingly cool. I massaged it into the criss-cross indentations deforming my skin, now replacing the belts.

'That way the patterns will hold for at least 24 hours,' I was told. She then departed. 'The next part of the Ball commences after midnight,' she said as she walked away. 'You have full access. Enjoy.'

Lauralynn walked over to another table and slipped off her pale silk blouse. She searched through the racks, pulled out an item of clothing and stepped into it, then turned to the mirror.

'That'll do me,' she said. Having revealed her bottom half through the performance she had now reversed the trend, in a pair of navy satin trousers with inbuilt braces that covered her nipples but left the rest of her breasts and her torso bare. She picked up a hat – the sort of style that went with costume-shop issue policewoman outfits, only handmade and no doubt infinitely more expensive – that was balanced precariously on a nearby hat stand, as though someone had thrown it there from across the room and it had landed but not quite settled onto its hook.

I stood there motionless, still overcome by the strength of the sensations that had raced through me towards the end of the performance.

'You?' She held out a garment of some sort towards me.

I didn't even look at whatever she was proposing I should wear for the rest of the Ball.

'No,' I said. I looked down at my body, the deep marks running across my skin and the way they still highlighted my private parts, decorated me. 'I'll just go like this.'

She glanced down, smiled and said, 'Great. The high heels are just right for the outfit . . .'

It occurred to me, as we headed out that I didn't know whether or not I would see Antony tonight. I suspected I would, of course. But I hadn't seen him yet, and I didn't know if Aurelia had also given him a ring. I was acutely aware that the two of us hadn't discussed the confines of our relationship or how we expected the other to behave as part of the Ball, and I wasn't entirely sure what I wanted from tonight, either.

'Antony will be there,' Lauralynn announced, answering the question that I hadn't yet asked and breaking the silence that had fallen between us. 'Though still on duty. Working, till later at least.'

We had first travelled in one of the mini motorised carts that served to carry equipment and people between the multitudinous canopies and trailers that were spread across the desert and had parked near what had appeared from the outside to be just a medium-sized red tent, lacking any remarkable features. Inside though, it seemed to be much larger than it had looked from the outside, and Lauralynn strode ahead as I followed her through a complicated network of passageways and heavy canvas flaps that functioned as doors. We appeared to be travelling downhill, which ought to have been impossible, as I knew the landscape was entirely flat for miles.

'Oh,' I replied. 'Good.' And I realised that I meant it. I was looking forward to seeing him.

'Have you ever given any thought, Summer,' she continued, after another long pause, 'to the undeniable fact that the reason you like to be told what to do is because you don't know what you want? Or you don't have the balls to ask for it?'

I stopped dead, shocked by her out of the blue remark.

'That's a bit harsh,' I replied.

She turned and faced me. Her hat was perched at a jaunty angle covering half of her face, and it was hard to take her seriously when she looked like an expensive dominatrix version of a strippergram.

'Is it? Have you talked to Antony about tonight?'

'Haven't had a chance . . .' I said. 'We've barely seen each other.'

'I didn't mean to be harsh,' she sighed, putting her arm around my neck in a gesture of apology that made me almost lose my balance and stumble against her. After years of nights out and wearing heels to gigs, I still hadn't learned to walk in them. Lauralynn strode along in hers as though her feet had evolved stilettos sometime between adolescence and adulthood and they were now no more an encumbrance to her than fins on a fish. 'It's just that you need to learn to tell people how you're feeling. You can't play it all away. Or fuck it all away, for that matter. Any more than he can drink it all away.'

'You know about that?' I asked her, surprised when she referred to Antony's tendency to hit the bottle when he was depressed.

'Alissa has a big mouth,' she said. I frowned in disapproval. 'But a big heart too,' she added. 'I don't think she was spreading things around. We were just having a girlie chat.'

'I didn't realise you two had got so close.'

'The gal does have her good points,' Lauralynn said, smirking from ear to ear. 'At least two of them,' she chortled.

'Yes, yes, I know . . .' I grumbled. By now Alissa's tits had enough of a reputation they could have had a part of their own in any show.

'All I mean to say is talk to him. Work it out. Tonight will make you feel like a maenad ... Remember the island. Like you've lost control of yourself, but you won't have, really. All the Ball does is give people space where they can behave how they really are. Let themselves go. Some folk are shocked by their own desires, so they blame it on something they can't see. Drugs, booze, magic ... Whatever. But none of that is true. It's an illusion. The notion that participants bear no personal responsibility for what occurs here is what gives them the freedom to do what they like. That's why they keep coming back, Ball after Ball. Humans, huh ... we're such fucked up, predictable creatures.'

I barely absorbed her mini-soliloquy, I was too eager to hear more about how Aurelia, and the Network, created these illusions. Apparently spontaneous orgies I could understand, under the right circumstances. And I'd been involved in enough shows to realise that incredible things could be pulled off with a good set, expert technicians and a pliable audience. But disappearing and reappearing, moving tattoos? Vines that came alive? I thirsted to know more about it, all about it. There was a part of me though, that didn't want to know how it worked, in case that ruined the mystery of it all. I liked believing in magic. And sex *was* magic, in my opinion. The right kind, at least. And the wrong kind, I knew from personal experience, could be just as powerful and traumatic as any form of voodoo curse.

'Illusions? Aurelia said the same thing . . .'

I was about to ask her to tell me how she got involved with it all when the lights went out and a sound like gunfire cracked through the air, sending the fabric on all sides of us billowing outwards as if a huge gust of wind had entered the tent. Then the ground beneath us gave way.

I shrieked, and flailed for something to grab on to with about as much grace as a spider on roller skates. One hand knocked against and instinctively seized one of Lauralynn's breasts, the other clutched at thin air.

We dropped for not even a second before our journey was ever so softly halted by whatever now surrounded us. What had seemed like a natural desert floor of compacted sand had become a tunnel leading directly downward, swirling with something that apparently held back the forces of gravity enabling us to travel safely to our destination at the bottom.

Darkness was replaced by a light that grew steadily brighter and as my eyes adjusted and my body got over the shock of the fall, I began to register what was touching my skin.

Hands.

Dozens of pairs of soft human hands were guiding us downwards, each of them wearing skin tight, ultra thin rubber gloves in a different colour so that when I looked up at those we had already passed by we seemed to be dropping through a field of flowers, the fingers attached to each palm opening and closing like petals waving in the breeze. Their touch was cautious and delicate and at first totally transactional, engaged only in catching our weight and easing us lower. But as we travelled on, the fingers became bolder and I felt firm strokes against my buttocks, my breasts were kneaded, even a gentle exploratory digit navigating the folds of my pussy as other hands wrapped around my ankles and wrists, slowing my progress further and enabling the roamers to traverse the length and breadth of my body at will.

I relaxed. There was nothing else for it. And before long, I drifted into that same heightened sense of arousal that I had experienced on the island. Every gentle breath of wind, every slightest brush of contact on my skin was magnified a thousand times.

'Oh,' I sighed, when we finally reached solid ground again, disappointed that our strange journey was over. The hands were attached to a towering tunnel of acrobats, connected like a long chain, not unlike the barrel of monkeys toy I remembered playing with as a child. When one tired, another acrobat was hoisted into place in a never ending circle of athleticism.

Alissa was waiting for us to arrive, standing nearby and clad in an interesting ensemble of tube-like bits of latex that covered all of the parts of her that would normally be uncovered – her thighs, arms, throat and belly - and left her cunt, arse and breasts bare. I'd seen so much of them lately that her nudity didn't strike me as anything out of the ordinary. It would have been more of a shock to see her fully dressed.

Long lace-up boots encased her calves, but rather than her usual stilettos, they had a high but flat platform and were covered in an alarming array of silver spikes and studs. In one hand she held a thick black leather paddle and her hair had been pulled into a severe knot that balanced on the top of her head like a solitary bun on a baker's tray. Her lipstick was the deep blue red of smashed berries and her eyes ringed with kohl. She looked positively delighted to be playing the part of dominatrix, albeit one with a somewhat backwards approach to allowing the eyes of onlookers to roam unhindered over her body.

'Enjoy the ride, did you?' she asked.

'Didn't you?' I replied.

'I asked to go back up again,' she said. 'But there's plenty more where that came from.'

The expression on her face was like that of a food addict who has just found herself trapped inside a French patisserie.

I followed her gaze, surveying the room.

It wasn't so much a room, as a landscape.

'But . . .' I mouthed.

'I know,' Alissa replied. 'It doesn't seem possible. And yet . . .'

'This is what Antony's been working on.'

She nodded.

The ground that we were standing on was like the surface of the moon, and stretched out so far I could not make out any walls delineating the edge. Up above us, a vast open space loomed, dark and twinkling with stars, like the night sky. A gentle draught of cool air brushed across my face, as though we were outside.

'How did he . . . ?'

'Climate controlled. False ceiling. They've been digging up underneath, that's where they disappear to every day.'

Her mouth was full. She was munching on some kind of confectionery. Custard squeezed between her teeth as she talked and a line of icing sugar powdered her lip.

'You've got to try this,' she said, between mouthfuls, and thrust a cream and pastry covered finger between my lips. It was moist and chewy and tasted of peanut butter, banana and caramel.

Lauralynn opened her mouth, signalling that she would like a bite, or more precisely that she would like Alissa to feed it to her.

To my immense shame, Alissa snapped her fingers in the air to call for a waiter. Within moments, a server stood in front of us holding a flat white platter on which miniature desserts were balanced; skewered fruit coated in chocolate, candied almonds, tiny mounds of jelly and pots of light-as-air mousse equipped with teaspoons smaller than my pinky finger. I picked up what appeared to be a bunch of grapes and popped one of the smooth, emerald green fruits into my mouth where it promptly burst like a bomb on time delay and sprayed my tongue with fizzing, sweet juice that tasted alcoholic.

'Careful with those,' said the server, 'they're full of grenadine. A bunch will leave you punch drunk.' He was dressed to blend into his surroundings in a very thin fabric that stretched tightly over his skin. As he walked away and moved around the room I noticed that his outfit took on the appearance of whatever he stood next to, whether that be another of the unusually clad guests, a piece of furniture or something that appeared to be a rock formation carved out of the earth.

'Where is he?' I asked Alissa. 'Antony. Have you seen him?' I asked her again when she didn't respond. She and Lauralynn had abandoned the pretext of feeding one another cream cakes and were now enthusiastically snogging, each with their hands clamped tight around the other's buttocks. Alissa still had her paddle, dangling by a leather strap wound around her wrist, but I doubted that she would dare use it on Lauralynn.

Finally Alissa disengaged her tongue from my friend's mouth and responded briefly and breathily to my question.

'That way,' she said, pointing into the distance at what looked to me to be just a vast space with no discernible features.

'What way?' I replied, annoyed, as she barely paused for long enough to wave her arm in the right direction.

'Just keep walking, you'll find it,' she hollered, her voice breaking under the arousal elicited by Lauralynn's insistent kisses on her neck.

I began to tread carefully in the direction that she had pointed out, fearful of losing my footing in the low light and uneven ground beneath my impractical shoes but within just a few steps I discovered that I had unwittingly stumbled on a smooth path, and with each step that I took it seemed to grow brighter. Sensors, I wondered, that lit up automatically in response to body weight?

Despite my fantastical surrounds I was finding it difficult to switch off and enjoy the party as my mind kept interrupting with questions, analysing, interpreting my environment, trying to find the key that would reveal the machinations of the Ball and how it all worked. I was like Dorothy seeking out the Wizard of Oz, not content with just listening to the apparent power of his voice but incessantly drawn to discovering whatever lay behind the curtain.

Overhead, the blanket of stars in the faux sky, or whatever it was that we were beneath, were leaping and diving and whizzing across the heavens as though a container load of firecrackers had been trapped and let off in the atmosphere. One dropped suddenly from the sky, landed directly in front of me with a gentle thud and then unfurled and stepped to her feet. It was Nina, the aerialist with the cropped ginger hair who I had seen hanging from a hoop in the Grand Desert Inn lobby when I first arrived. She was dressed from the neck down in a glittering sequined body suit that reflected the light around her so well she sparkled like a disco ball. Her face was bare, without any trace of make-up but her hair was tied into an elaborate array of knots that covered her head, each of them threaded with coloured bulbs that flashed at regular intervals.

She smiled at me and held a finger to her lips.

'Shh, you didn't see me,' she said. 'We're supposed to all be up there for another few hours but I had to come down, I'm dying for a piss.'

To my astonishment, instead of wandering off in search of a bathroom she pulled down the zipper at the front of her suit, peeled it down to her knees and then squatted and peed right next to me on the rough ground alongside the path, aiming her stream carefully so she didn't douse the fabric bunched around her calves and ankles. Then she pulled her costume up again, and tried in vain to kick some dust over the pool that she had left on the rugged floor, before shrugging her shoulders in my direction and jogging away.

It hadn't felt right to address her directly as she urinated, even if by choosing to do so right in front of me she had waived any semblance of privacy. I hadn't walked in on her, after all. Still, I didn't ask the question that hung on my lips as my mouth opened in shock – how on earth did she do that? Instead, I narrowed my eyes and watched carefully as she gathered speed, jumped into the air, and was apparently borne aloft by invisible threads. Bits of her outfit glowed brighter and I heard a faint hum as she powered through the air. A rocket suit of some sort, I decided.

On I travelled, covering ground slowly, in part due to my cautious, small steps, but also as I kept being distracted by other events and sights around me. What had appeared to be a rising dust storm from a few steps away turned out to be a circle of male dancers, all nude besides long ochre-coloured chiffon scarves tied to their wrists, throats, waists and ankles that billowed out as they pirouetted in full flight. My gaze was immediately drawn to their limp dicks. Each of them was utterly bare with not a single pubic hair to distract from the onset of the shafts that bounced, bobbed and swayed between the men's thighs. Their flaccidity was in sharp contrast to the taut shock of the muscles that bulged in their calves and thighs. I imagined the velvety softness of their flesh against my lips if I knelt down in front of them and took each of their cocks into my mouth one by one, like a communion, and sucked until they sprang to life. If they would even stop and allow me to pleasure them. The men danced on around me, unaware of my presence, uncaring.

I paid closer attention from then on to any apparently

natural features in the landscape and noticed that what I had presumed were rock formations or strange desert plants swaying in invisible gusts of wind were in fact groups of people embracing, their limbs and extravagant costumes masquerading as inanimate species. Some were couples, standing and holding on to each other, as still as boulders. Others were triads, or tangles of four, five or more, fucking or pleasuring one another with wandering tongues and fingers.

My ears had suddenly attuned to another frequency, like dialling into a radio station I hadn't previously known existed. The sound of the whispering wind or a coyote howl that I had thought was some kind of desert soundtrack being broadcast through loudspeakers dotted all over was actually the hubbub of bodies sliding against one another, men and women moaning as they were penetrated, the soft shift of skin on skin as people everywhere made love precisely where they happened to be sitting or standing when the mood took them without a care in the world for the roughness of the soil beneath them or who might be watching. There were piles of bedding laid out like nests for the purpose, I noticed, but many were not in use. People were embracing passionately just twenty yards from a bed and then falling on top of one another right then and there with the desperation of lost mountaineers who collapsed just metres from their tents.

My toe stubbed against a metal step.

'Fuck,' I muttered. I'd been too engrossed in the world

around me to notice that I had reached a staircase before I walked straight into it.

I slipped my shoes off and gripped them by the heels with one hand, while steadying myself on the handrail with the other. Whatever lay at the top, it wasn't another one of the Ball's 'activity rooms', I was sure of that. They would have laid out a glass elevator, or a velvet covered escalator, or maybe even a magic carpet. Not this ordinary, cold metal that felt like something out of an industrial warehouse or a mechanical workshop.

The steps led to a short hallway with a doorway at the end of it. I knocked gently and then pushed the door open.

It was a large, brightly lit office packed with video screens and computer equipment, like something from a spy movie depicting the headquarters of the secret service. I recognised Antony by the shape of his shoulders and the back of his head, sitting in a padded leather swivel chair and intently watching several monitors set up in front of him. Occasionally he typed commands into a keypad, pressed buttons or flicked switches that were located on the elaborate control system in front of him.

He turned when he heard the door open.

'Summer,' he said. He waved me over. He was smiling, and seemed pleased to see me, but his eyes were tired.

Wally, one of the technicians who had worked on the *Violin Diaries* play, and Andrei, Aurelia's partner, were also there. We exchanged greetings, but they were too focused on their work to say much, and I didn't want to distract them. They were all wearing a combination of tees and jeans or casual trousers. Andrei was barefoot, Antony in a pair of tan boat shoes.

'You were great,' he said, 'as ever.' He wrapped his arm around the lower part of my waist and bum and pulled me against him. I ruffled my hand through his hair.

'Thank you,' I said. 'What is this place? What are you doing?'

'This,' he said, 'is the control room. Have a look at the monitors.'

I scanned each one. They were like security cameras, set up to relay what was happening in each key area of the Ball, which was far more extensive than I had realised. Numerous other rooms were adjoined to the main area where the Ball's guests danced, ate, drank, and of course, fucked. One area was set up like a dungeon. At its centre, an older man – perhaps in his fifties or sixties; it was hard to tell as his age was evident only in the white of his long flowing hair, and the texture of his skin, while his bearing and the lean, firmness of his body could have belonged to someone two decades younger – was whipping a woman who was cuffed to a St Andrew's Cross in front of him. She was face down so I could not guess her age, but I guessed that she might not be much younger than him. She was not fat, or sagging, by any means, but her skin lacked the obvious plumpness that belongs only to those who don't appreciate it, the under twenty-fives. Her hair was mousey-brown, and tucked into a loose ponytail that had probably been arranged in this manner at the last minute to allow her partner in willing torture access to her flesh. She would have been quite unmemorable if it were not for the large tattoo that covered her upper back, neck and shoulders. It was a stylised bird, pieced together with spirals, cross-hatching patterns and swirls, with open wings that spread over her shoulders, a head that rested against the base of her hairline and a four-feathered tail that ended five inches or so above the onset of her buttocks.

The whip was a single-tail, the sort that delivers an incredible burst of pain, like a localised brand, with each jolt of impact, and requires a great deal of skill to wield. He cracked it at slow, regular intervals and with each hit she barely flinched.

It had been a long time since I had felt the touch of leather against my skin, or the wincing warmth of pain delivered with love. Watching her, I felt two things. Arousal and envy.

I turned to Antony who was absentmindedly trailing his fingertips over the little bumps and indentations that decorated my skin where the buckles of my harness had been pulled tight. Giselle's cream was still working its magic. He hadn't remarked upon, or even seemed to notice, my nudity, but in a situation like this one more naked body was hardly out of place. His eyes were scanning over all of the screens without focusing on any one scene in particular.

'What do you think of that?' I asked him, indicating the TV monitor displaying the pair in the dungeon.

He frowned. 'What do I think?' he asked, making sense of my question. 'Is it too dark? I can raise the lighting.' He reached for a series of knobs above the keyboard.

'No, the lighting's fine, I meant what do you think of them, of what they're doing?'

'Oh,' he said, then shrugged his shoulders. 'Looks painful. But each to their own, I suppose.'

'Would you ever want to do something like that to me?' I asked him, quietly. It wasn't really the place to talk. He was working, and Wally was audible in the background, slurping a mug of instant soup and munching on a bread roll. The air smelled faintly of chicken.

He froze, his fingers hovering over a section of ridges that decorated one side of my hip.

'Honestly? That level of endeavour isn't really for me. Maybe something gentler. Handcuffs and a spanking?'

He stopped his exploration of my marks and instead squeezed me against him in a tight embrace.

'Yeah, I know what you mean,' I replied, as if I felt the same way, although I didn't, really. I could feel the ghost of Lauralynn standing behind me with her arms crossed over her chest, glowering at me for chickening out at the last minute rather than saying what it was that I really felt.

Fuck me, Antony, hurt me, make me yours, tell me to get down on my hands and knees for you like a good little girl . . .

But they weren't words that I could bring myself to say aloud.

'I should go,' I said, pulling away. 'Get back to the party.'

'No,' he said, 'stay.' He glanced at a clock hanging on the wall that read five minutes to three a.m. 'The main event is about to begin. And we've got the best view from here.'

He pulled me onto his lap, and I burrowed into a comfortable position on his knee as he awkwardly reached around me to fiddle with the controls and bring up the large main screen that covered an entire wall behind us.

Wally had finished his snack and leapt into action, activating buttons and computer equipment. Andrei barely looked up from whatever he was doing.

On the monitor, a camera was focused on the centre of the main room. A sound like a thunder clap had echoed through the cavernous space and all those adjoined to it, calling all of the Ball's guests to file into the main space where they formed a giant circle around a dais that had – in response to one of Wally's commands – begun to rise from the earth and formed a high stage.

A gasp rumbled through the crowd as every single light besides those in the office we sat in was extinguished at the same moment, including the electronics that lit up some of the performers' costumes. The darkness felt palpable, thick and viscous like a particularly heavy fog, and seemed to stretch on forever although according to the tick of the wall clock it was just a few seconds.

The light that burst onto the stage was like the sun and moon together, bathing the crowd in alternating rays of white and gold, warmth and coolness. It took me a moment to realise that it was emanating from Aurelia. She was standing with her arms raised over her head and her long hair billowing over her shoulders as if in the face of a mighty wind. Her tattoos danced and leapt across her skin like a painted tapestry brought to life. Watching her was like witnessing the arrival of an archangel come down from heaven to bestow a blessing or a curse onto the earth. I waited to see which it would be.

Andrei turned to watch. His face was relaxed, but his hands were tense. He had picked up an empty coffee cup and was gripping it tightly.

Eight beams appeared across the room from points at equidistance apart converging on Aurelia standing in the centre. They were pinpricks at first, steadily increasing until they formed laser beams bouncing out of the dais. At the far end of each of the points, a winged man appeared, and seemed to glide along the length of the light ray on the current of an invisible wind until all eight reached the stage and gracefully landed, their wings folding up and tucking against their bodies as soon as their feet touched the ground.

'Are they . . . flying?' I asked Antony.

He grinned. He was watching the scene unfold with the same mixture of pride and worry that a father might have overseeing his child's first attempts at riding a bicycle. This was evidently his pièce de résistance.

'No, they're harnessed. The room is full of cables, you just can't see them.'

Aurelia brought her arms down to her side and her tattoos slowed their mad frenzy and subsided to a hypnotic, slow dance.

The camera angle switched to the faces of the winged men. It was the acrobats, I realised. The octuplets who had accompanied us on the desert walk and who Alissa had tried to flirt with but never managed to bag.

Their hair was slicked back against their skulls with gel, making them seem even younger, and highlighting the chiselled perfection of their high cheekbones and smooth jaws. Their lips, though not obviously rouged, were the deep red colour of ripe raspberries and eminently kissable. Their fingernails were painted blue black to match the silky night sky shade of their wings.

Naturally, my eyes dropped to examine their cocks. Unlike the sand storm dancers, they each sported a soft bush of pubic hair. They were flaccid.

Aurelia raised her arms again, this time not over her head but just above her sides, to point at two of the identical young men, one who stood directly in front of her and the other directly behind.

They stepped forward, within reach of her grasp. She inclined her head to each of them in turn, and then laid her hand on their cocks, one after the other, like bestowing a blessing. As soon as she touched them, they sprang erect. Long, thick, and as hard as rock. She returned her arms to her sides and stood with her shoulders held back and her chin up and forward. Majestic. Her hair continued to billow around her face.

I discreetly glanced at Andrei. He was still staring at the screen, apparently hypnotised by the events that were unfolding. His mouth formed a straight line like a cut across his face.

The two appointed men stepped forward and penetrated her, one from in front, and one behind, lifting her leg in order to get themselves into position. Her expression was sublime, like a Madonna in the full throes of ecstasy. The expressions on the faces of her penetrators though, went from joyful release to pain. Their brows furrowed into a grimace. Beads of sweat appeared on their foreheads that they could not brush away for fear of losing their hold on Aurelia's body. On and on they thrust into her, visibly weakening as her power seemed to grow, her locks writhing like Medusa's snakes, her inked portraits again in full flow, her skin becoming ever brighter under the stage light – wait – was it a stage light? Or was Aurelia glowing? I couldn't tell.

They came, and immediately crumpled to the floor.

Dead? Surely not. They were acting.

Two more were appointed to take their place and they pulled the bodies of their fallen brothers aside before sliding their erections into Aurelia's waiting cock and arse.

For the few seconds that she had been untended to, empty, the markings on her skin had wriggled like mad, angry. The dragon that decorated her mons bared its teeth. Aurelia's face was a picture of fury. Filled again, she appeared sated, though undeniably terrifying in her hunger for sex.

I couldn't help but relate to her, and felt faintly embarrassed, in part for the melodrama of the whole scene but also because it seemed like a vice to need or desire anything that much, whether it be a cream cake, a tumbler full of whiskey or a hard dick. I tried to puzzle it through – what I thought, what I felt, who I was, but found no answers, only more questions. I turned my attention back to the screen.

Eventually the men were all used, and lay in puddles of wing and muscle around her feet, jaws slack in defeat.

The stage light narrowed, the point of its beam now focused just on Aurelia.

She smiled.

The audience cheered like a pack of wolves baying at the moon.

Andrei got up and walked out of the room, closing the door behind him with a gentle click.

The lights were turned out.

Darkness spread across the amphitheatre.

12

After the Ball

We were like survivors finally resurfacing to the earth after an apocalypse, when the Ball ended.

Antony and I did try to rejoin the party when Aurelia's grand finale had concluded and his services were no longer required, but neither of us felt able to really get into what remained of the festivities. Alissa and the others were nowhere to be found and the rest of the guests were either too inebriated or overcome by the strange power of the Ball's energy to really connect with. Tucked away in the relative mundanity of the brightly lit control room, we had experienced the events of the past few hours on a different plane to everyone else, as if we were on the outside of a snow globe watching all the action through an invisible pane of glass, voyeurs, unable to participate.

We left slightly early, through a rather anti-climactic,

ordinary looking exit door situated near the back of the main auditorium, after first climbing four flights of stairs. The sun was coming up, and rather than endeavour to trek our way back through the desert without any water, rations, or precise idea where we were going, we opted to settle ourselves onto the relative comfort provided by a pile of flat rocks nearby, watch the sunrise, and wait for one of the coaches that were booked to arrive at regular intervals of the morning and return the partygoers back to the main car park. I didn't have any shoes, besides the glass slippers that I was still clutching in one of my hands by their tall, cool heels.

I was still naked. Instinctively, I pulled my knees in to my chest to cover my body. Antony removed his T-shirt, handed it to me, and I pulled it on over my head, trying in vain to tug the bottom of it down all the way past my buttocks so that I would have some fabric to sit on rather than the gritty surface of the bare rock.

'Wow, that really was something,' Antony said.

'I wonder what the critics would say?' I laughed.

'They'd be speechless,' he replied.

'Oh, I doubt it. They'd think of something. "Ambitious and daring, but ultimately a triumph of style over substance" or "Crude – not creative," or "What about the children!?"' I parroted, putting on a deep voice and squaring my shoulders for effect.

'Yeah, you're right. There's never any way to win. Still,

it was fun, right? A production with a handsome, ridiculously talented cast and a virtually unlimited budget . . . a director's wet dream.'

'Will you do another?' I asked him, thinking about my contract with Aurelia coming to an end. I still had a few weeks left, but I still wasn't sure what I would be needed for.

'A Ball?'

I nodded.

'Yes, for sure, if they ask me.'

He took my hand and we sat in silence watching the sun rise like an enormous round egg yolk cracking over the cloudless blue sky in streaks of orange and yellow.

I swallowed the lump in my throat. So many changes and uncertainties still awaited me. I wondered if my life would ever be any different, or if I was destined to always be chasing the next bright thing that appeared on the horizon.

What was it that I wanted?

The fog was lifting across the waters in Puget Bay as I glanced out of the window, and followed the halting progress of a ferry lazily moving out towards the distant islands.

I still had slightly over a month remaining on the contract I had signed with the Network, although since I'd flown in to Seattle from Las Vegas a few days after the Ball my duties had been vague if non-existent.

'Just relax, decompress,' Madame Denoux had suggested.

The tall, anonymous building in which I was lodging a stone's throw from Pike Place was host to several floors of offices to which I had no access and at least one level which harboured a series of residential apartments. The suite I had been provided with was light, tall-ceilinged and luxurious in a minimalistic manner, all straight lines and modern furniture in shades of oak and metal.

I'd been hoping to see more of Madame Denoux here, but hadn't come across her since arriving. I had so many questions for her. Questions I was nervous asking Aurelia who, I'd been informed, was currently staying in another suite nearby, down the corridor from me. Giselle Denoux had a maternal presence which I found soothing and, I intuited, knew so much about the Ball and the Network, half-hidden secrets I was eager to learn.

Every morning, after coffee and breakfast – the kitchen was always lavishly replenished whenever I happened to be away from the suite – I would check with the reception desk by the central bank of elevators to ascertain if there were any tasks I had to address. There had been a few occasions when my involvement was sought in a studio sited in the bowels of the building to assist audio engineers mix and adjust sound levels on the recordings made at the Ball of the music I, Lauralynn and our musicians had performed, but most days I was left to my own devices and randomly roamed the city, visiting its many hills, Elliott Bay, Capitol Hill or the

University District, pleasantly overdosing on clam chowder and the city's surfeit of coffee bars. I had been assured that Antony would soon be in a position to join me, but was not given any precise date.

The phone rang. The first time it had in days. I picked up the nearest receiver. Aurelia wanted to see me. In her suite. I hadn't set eyes on her since the desert.

I slipped on a pair of jeans and a sweatshirt and made my way down the corridor. I was curious to see Aurelia in a different environment.

The door to her apartment was already open and I ventured in.

To my surprise, there were toys in all colours, shapes and sizes littered across the parquet floor all the way to the living room. What appeared to be Lego pieces, dolls, a legless Wonderwoman figure, furry animals, wooden construction blocks, tiny pink handbags and a miniature plastic cutlery set.

'Come on through,' Aurelia called out to me and I followed the trail of toys.

She was lounging on a deep-cushioned orange angled five-seater sofa by a vast set of bay windows overlooking the Bay. At a nearby desk, Andrei was typing at a computer. On the floor facing Aurelia was a small chubby-faced little girl, with a mass of blonde curls and deep brown eyes. Two years old or thereabouts, I reckoned. The child looked up at me, watched me approach and smiled broadly, then returned to the toys she was playing with.

'This is Alice,' Aurelia said.

I must have looked puzzled.

'Our daughter,' she continued.

It was the last thing I'd have expected. The little girl wore a pair of skinny jeans and a superhero T-shirt and was barefoot. Aurelia's outfit mirrored hers, although her top advertised an oyster bar in New Orleans. Back at his desk, Andrei was similarly casual as he typed away and ignored us.

I was offered a coffee.

I had nothing against children, but felt uncomfortable around them. While we sipped and made small talk, little Alice drank apple juice from a blue plastic cup.

Finally, a Network employee whose face looked vaguely familiar from my sojourn in the desert walked in and took the child away, after Aurelia offered Alice the choice of visiting two nearby playgrounds. Andrei excused himself shortly after, pretexting some errand and we were left alone.

'She is very pretty. Looks a lot like you,' I told Aurelia.

'I know,' she said. 'She's the future, my future.'

I nodded, still coming to terms with the revelation she had a child.

'Will she . . . ?'

'Yes, one day, she will become the Ball's new Mistress. But there is no rush. Lots of time to enjoy her childhood. I owe her that.' Her face darkened as the thought of the heavy burden the child's inheritance carried reminded itself to her and she recalled the roundabout way she had come to assume the position.*

'Anyway,' she composed herself again, 'let's talk about you, shall we? And what your plans for the future might be. It's come to my notice that you haven't played the violin since the night of the Ball. Is everything OK?' she asked.

It was true. Rarely had I spent so much time without practising, rehearsing, playing. Only Dominik's death had caused a longer defection. It all now somehow felt pointless. As if on that night in the desert I had reached a pinnacle, where the music had entered me, become part of me forever and lost its magic in the process. For a brief second I had merged into the music, and it seemed as if there was nowhere else to go now, nothing that could match the experience. Anything would be repetition, imitation, treading unfertile ground.

I tried to explain.

Aurelia listened to me, a thin veil of empathy drawn across her face.

'I think I understand,' she said.

I had thought of telling her that watching her at the Ball's

---

* see the previous volume in the series, *Mistress of Night and Dawn*.

climax had raised a torrent of questions in my mind. That witnessing her in all her glory, so luminous, inhabiting her sexuality so openly had made me realise how minor my own epiphanies were and how insignificant my own adventures among the tides of lust and sex had been. So ordinary. But I knew she already had an inkling of this, a second sense that allowed her to weigh the thoughts of others, as if the tattoos that appeared at will across her pale skin gifted her with extra powers of perception.

Which made the revelation that she was also the mother of a child even more overpowering. Goddess, mother, magician, sorceress, confessor. She felt like all that and more.

She asked me about Antony. And I had no shame telling her about the sex we had, the closeness and attraction, the madness we sometimes achieved, the kinks that made it possible, the despair that we clung on to like a raft which kept it alive and burning against all odds. Our imperfections, our ghosts.

'He arrives later today,' Aurelia told me. 'You'll find his message when you return to your suite. He plans to be here for a week.'

'That's nice,' I said. I was in bad need of a fuck. But the news of his return didn't move me as much as it should have. Because I had come to realise that Antony, men, even Dominik, music were still not enough. I wanted more out of life than just living and fucking and playing and challenging myself by breaking invisible barriers. But what?

'I don't wish to go back to my old life,' I said to Aurelia. 'No more concerts. No more emptiness.'

'Stay with us, then,' she asked.

'Here?'

'Not necessarily in Seattle, although you could base yourself here should you wish. But we own places all over. Remain with the Ball. Full-time. Travel with it. Gift it your soul, Summer, and it will give you so much more in return. You are a creature, a delightful one, of emotions. They're like a vibration skimming across your skin, an aura that floats above you. I can see it. As have others too who've conquered the blindness.'

'I . . .'

'Don't say anything quite yet. Take your time. Spend some time with Antony before you decide . . .'

It would be a different life, I knew. And the moment Aurelia made the offer, I knew she had me hooked and I would agree. Tomorrow. Next week.

And she knew it too.

'Where are the next Balls taking place?' I asked her.

'We have two at advanced stages of preparation,' Aurelia said. 'One in the heart of the rainforest, near the Amazon river. So many wonderful possibilities. And then, to follow, we envisage another in the far north of Iceland, a mostly uninhabited ice plain which we have recently discovered. We're studying the possibilities. Actually, Antony is bringing along some sketches and ideas with him. We've put him on retainer.'

'What would my own role be?'

'You'd create it, make it what you will. Your imagination the limit. There'd be no need for a title. Everything to do with the Ball is fluid, ever-changing. But I know you'd fit in and we'd love you to become one of ours.'

'It's appealing, I must confess,' I admitted.

'Giselle, Madame Denoux, could initially mentor you, if you agreed.'

What would I be leaving behind? London and a lonely flat. A musical career that was already going around in circles. My demons, hopefully?

I left Aurelia, Andrei and Alice's apartment with a lightness in my step at the prospect of this new life I was being offered. Another chance to get it right, maybe.

Antony announced his arrival with just a brief tap on my bedroom door, though he waited for me to call out my approval before he walked in. Even though it had just been a few weeks, I was strangely nervous about the prospect of seeing him and had spent the last hour or so showering, getting dressed into a pyjama set of short cotton pants and matching chemise, white patterned with a deep blue, small floral print, that I hoped was sexy without looking like I was trying too hard and had spent the whole time we'd been apart thinking about him. I left my hair out and dabbed on just enough make-up to cover the dark circles under my eyes, sprayed on a light spritz of perfume and spent at least 20 minutes lying on the bed with a magazine that I didn't look at once and rearranging my position a dozen times to affect an attractive nonchalance.

But when I heard the latch turn, I forgot all of that, and leapt up off the bed to greet him by the door.

'Hi,' he said, dropping his bag on the floor and pulling me into his arms.

We kissed. The softness of his mouth on mine made me greedy to feel his tongue on other parts of me and I moved my hands from their position, slipped down the back of his jeans where I was grabbing his arse, to his belt buckle which I began undoing, all without interrupting the pressure of my lips against his.

He pulled back and held me slightly away from him with his hands wrapped around my bicep muscles, at arm's length.

'I just need a shower,' he said, 'and I'll be right back.'

'Of course,' I agreed. 'Can I get you anything? Tea, coffee, a drink?'

'Glass of water would be great,' he replied, and I pointed out the bathroom. He unzipped his bag, rummaged for his toiletry kit and went off to wash away the journey.

I poured two glasses of sparkling mineral water. Even ventured out of the room to fetch some ice from the machine down the hall.

The water was still running when I returned.

I sat on the bed and sipped from the tumbler, wincing at the cold, and resenting the fact that I now wanted a gin and tonic but it felt mean to pour myself one, since I had guessed, by default, that Antony had given up drinking and to drink without him seemed cruel, but to tempt him into drinking seemed crueller.

His arrival now felt like an anticlimax, and I was frustrated, though also angry at myself for being vexed. In his position, I probably would have wanted a shower too.

No, I wouldn't, I thought. I'd have wanted to fuck right then and there, and the ardours of long distance travel be damned. I wanted him to want me enough that his arousal outweighed his immediate discomfort. And I couldn't have cared less about any slight hint of sweat he might have picked up by wearing the same clothes for the duration of a lengthy flight.

My good mood swiftly returned when he walked out of the bathroom trailing the remnants of a steam cloud, wearing just a towel around his familiar hard-as-washboard stomach and running a hand through his half wet, dark blond hair.

He smelled pleasingly of lightly scented soap, and I chastised myself for being unreasonable.

Then even those thoughts were obliterated as he fell to his knees in front of me, hooked a finger around each side of the waistband of my cotton shorts, pulled them to the floor, parted my legs and began to lick my pussy, without further ado.

'That was incredible,' I told him afterwards, as we lay on our backs alongside one another, getting our breath back. He'd made me come twice with his tongue, and we'd fucked in between. I was utterly relaxed.

'Yes, it was,' he replied, and stretched his arm out into the space that unofficially made up my side of the bed, his silent invitation for me to curl up into the crook of his underarm, my own arm hooked over his chest and one of my thighs folded at a right angle over his legs, our regular post-sex position.

'I missed you,' I told him. It was true. I had missed him. The connection of my past work and his, and the way that being near him, engrossed with his notes and plans for his current or next production, had always encouraged me to pick up my violin and bow when I might otherwise have just lazed a day away. I probably would never have begun creating my own music without Antony's involvement in my life, and that was a skill that now seemed so much a part of me I couldn't imagine a time when riding the free flow of a melody instead of reading a sheet of music and blindly obeying the composer's direction didn't come naturally. Although now I no longer felt the need to actually play the instrument as the music lived inside my head. Constantly.

And I'd missed the feeling of his body against mine. Watching him dress and undress, the taut line of his muscles moving under his skin as he slipped into a pair of shorts, quite unaware of the feast my eyes were making as he covered himself up. The sex was good. It was great. Hard and physical and regular. It was the kind of plain good fucking that I loved. And if we lacked that tiny, extra particle, the D/S connection that I had with Dominik, well, that was easy for me to overlook, almost all of the time.

But not quite all of the time.

I still longed for more. Maybe that was just in my nature.

The rest of the week, predictably, flew by as if it were just a day. When we weren't having sex, and neither I nor Antony was engaged in making plans with Aurelia or Giselle, we spent the time eating in restaurants across Seattle, or sipping cups of coffee on the small balcony attached to my room that overlooked the city, chatting about life in London or ruminating together on what other secrets the Ball might hold that we were not yet privy to.

Alissa, it turned out, was bunking in with Lauralynn and Viggo.

'Dating them?' I asked Antony.

'Well, that might be too strong a term. Fucking them, for

sure. I think your friend Lauralynn is enjoying teaching Alissa to, ah, step into her more precocious self,' he said.

'Poor Viggo,' I remarked, imagining the torture that they were probably subjecting him to.

'Oh, I'm quite sure that he's enjoying himself,' Antony replied.

When I kissed him goodbye at the airport, I didn't want him to leave.

'I'll be back, Summer, I promise,' he said to me, untangling my arms from around his chest as the tannoy announced that the check-in for his flight to London was about to close.

I knew I could still find plenty of things to keep me busy here in Seattle, but that didn't stop my feet feeling like they were made of lead when I turned and walked out of the airport, nor did it hold the feelings of emptiness at bay as I travelled back to the suite.

When I arrived back in my room, I masturbated, and in my fantasies Antony's body loomed over mine. My skin recalled the texture of his touch, my lips the press of his mouth, my cunt the flick of his tongue, until I came.

But the next time that I would try to orchestrate my own pleasure my vision of him was blurred, and he merged in and out of focus along with the faces of a dozen other men who were burned into the fabric of my imagination.

★   ★   ★

Yesterday I had been in New York, seeking out fabrics for a future Ball in the back room of a top floor dim sum emporium that doubled as a warehouse just off Chinatown. I had been led there blindfolded and, initially, only allowed to touch the materials, infusing myself with the silky softness of the folds and heavy rolls of fabric and guessing at the intricate patterns they concealed, practising my second sense, fine-tuning my ability to perceive beauty in new places. Once I had operated an initial sort, I was then finally granted full vision and marvelled at the sheer details and sensuality of the materials I had pre-selected and began to match them to the themes, colours and moods I had been asked to address. This was a new art for me altogether, but I was confident my intuition would serve me well. Beauty was not exclusive to music and could be found, I now knew, in so many avenues of the life sensual.

I'd taken a cab to La Guardia Airport and then a flight to New Orleans, where I would now be based for the foreseeable future. Madame Denoux was returning to her San Francisco retirement and I had been offered to run her establishment there and had jumped at the opportunity. My memories of the night I had spent there would remain with me forever, and this would be a way to establish a bridge between my past and future, in the heady, humid atmosphere of the Crescent City, a city that appeared to be unchanging, unaffected by the arrows of time. Timeless streets, sounds and smells that now marked me inside better than any tattoo or photograph.

It was already dark when I arrived at Louis Armstrong Airport and there was a long line for taxis. I only had carry-on baggage as all my belongings had been forwarded from Seattle some days earlier. It felt odd not to have a car waiting with the Network's traditional grey-uniformed chauffeur in attendance, as if I had been downgraded from star material and was now just another cog in the Network's machine, one of many Ball acolytes scattered across the wide world.

'Are you Summer Zahova?' a strongly Italian-accented voice standing behind me in the queue asked.

I turned round.

A tall urchin-faced young woman with a dazzling smile was staring at me. Her hair was cropped short, dark as ebony, gamine-like. Two heavy cases trailed behind her. 'I saw you playing in Rome a few years ago,' she said. 'You were wonderful.' She pronounced W as a V as in Vonderful. I remembered that concert, the music I played, the dress I wore, the stranger I met at the hotel bar later that night and slept with. But I couldn't recall his name.

'I am,' I said. 'I was.'

'You were my idol,' the young girl said.

'I'm flattered.'

She was from Pescara in Italy, and a dancer, she informed me.

'Your music inspired me,' she said. 'I often dance to the same pieces. What are you doing here?' she asked.

'I've come to live here,' I said. I didn't have the courage to tell her that I had, in all probability, forsaken music.

A cab arrived. Her destination was also the French Quarter, so we agreed to share. She was staying in a small bed and breakfast off Burgundy Street where, she informed me, the old slave quarters had been renovated and turned into small bungalows. She sounded excited by the fact.

The taxi rushed down Veterans Boulevard towards the bright lights of the city ahead. On our right, a vast cemetery and then the taller buildings of Tulane University.

Her name was Marirosa. She had a six weeks engagement as a lounge dancer at the bar of the Monteleone Hotel on Royal Street. It was her first time outside Europe and she was thrilled to bits by the opportunity. I knew the hotel, a highly respectable if fussy establishment with Grande Epoque pretensions. At least the job sounded respectable. I envied her enthusiasm.

As the taxi dropped her off, I gave her my new business card, suggesting we have a coffee together soon. She agreed.

It was already midnight by the time I went to bed in the unfamiliar room that was now going to be mine, in a small recessed building behind the club in the darker reaches of Bourbon Street towards Esplanade Avenue. My new home. A splendid bouquet of flowers awaited me with words of greeting from both Aurelia and Giselle Denoux.

I felt a sense of trepidation, as if this was the first night of the rest of my life. Would it be a life of nights?

Sleep came easily after the extensive travel of the previous days. The heady, characteristic smells of the French Quarter, dragging along with them the scent of flowers, spices and herbs, the echo of faraway music and the lush, rotting vegetation of the nearby Mississippi and neighbouring bayous, streamed around the edges of my consciousness.

Inevitably, the dreams came. An unstoppable procession of images, feelings, a swirl of vivid emotions I was unable to control.

I swam in the sea of dreams.

Like celluloid film racing through a projector. Fast forward in mechanical disarray.

The vines of the island crucifying my extended limbs with agonising tenderness, stretching me, opening me, penetrating me until the pleasure threshold became unbearable and I blacked out.

And then found myself in the desert, embedded within a labyrinth of pale bodies, fucked and fucking, joyous and desperate, lustily reaching for a fire which retreated with every step I clumsily advanced.

I saw myself in the centre of the winged blond boys, being taken from the front and behind, their hard cocks filling me one after the other after the other until each of them was spent and the next forced to take over, to pleasure me, to try to feed the insatiable.

Faces.

All the faces of my past life. Dominik. Simon. Victor. Lauralynn. Viggo. Giselle. Luba. Antony. Alissa. Aurelia. And so many more who flashed by like a stampede of light years.

They all ran across my screen and suddenly were gone, leaving a blank space. A deep feeling of serenity.

In my sleep, I relaxed. Settled back. At peace.

Imagined the Balls to come.

A muddy river, crowded by wildlife on either side, a heavy sun bearing down on my shoulders. The titan-like presence of the jungle, images of lithe dancers and acrobats flying across its immensity like insects made of light and divine music lullabying their soaring movements. The Ball and its invisible tentacles, its magical powers spreading across the land, the river, the immensity of the landscape, orchestrating the rise and rise of an empire of lust.

And I was at its dead centre, guiding, conducting, leading, my body the vessel for its coronation, its apotheosis.

Peace.

New visions.

A vast plain of ice, spreading in all directions like an incandescent stain, human ants in various states of undress tiptoeing across the white architecture of the landscape, connected by delicate chains, streamers, wandering across rainbow-coloured carpets. And every face looked up towards me, with a profound smile of understanding. Acknowledging me. Welcoming me.

I woke up. I was wet with sweat, the bed covers crumpled under and around my naked body.

A New Orleans morning awaited outside. Heavy tropical rain falling noisily. A warm and welcome storm to blow the lingering smells and cobwebs away. I rose from my bed and walked nude down the stairs, opened the door to the garden that separated the small house where I lived from the larger building hosting the club. The garden was full of flowers. Colours washed by the hard slap of water.

I walked into the rain.

The Ball awaited me.

Asking me if I was ready to join the dance.

'Yes, I will,' I said. 'Gladly.'

About the Author

Vina Jackson is the pseudonym for two established writers working together. One is a successful author; the other a published writer who is also a financial professional in London.

THE PLEASURE QUARTET

FROM OPEN ROAD MEDIA

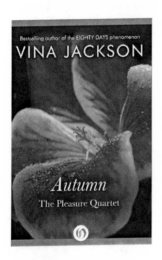 

Available wherever ebooks are sold

OPEN ROAD
INTEGRATED MEDIA

Open Road Integrated Media is a digital publisher and multimedia content company. Open Road creates connections between authors and their audiences by marketing its ebooks through a new proprietary online platform, which uses premium video content and social media.

CPSIA information can be obtained at www.ICGtesting.com
Printed in the USA
BVOW02s0933200715

408866BV00001B/1/P

31192020820724